# MARK TWAIN

## on the Damned Human Race

# MARK TWAIN
## on the Damned Human Race

Edited and with an Introduction by JANET SMITH
Preface by MAXWELL GEISMAR

*American Century Series*
THE NOONDAY PRESS · NEW YORK
*Farrar, Straus and Giroux*

Standard Book Number (paperback edition): 0-374-52151-4
Standard Book Number (clothbound edition): 8090–6765–x
Library of Congress catalog card number 62–15215

FIRST EDITION SEPTEMBER 1962

*Twenty-fifth printing, 1991*

Manufactured in the United States of America

# Preface

The present volume is a collection of Mark Twain's topical writings, most of it in the early years of the twentieth century, and mainly, and most eloquently, concerned with the themes of social justice, of American civilization in its dawning age of imperialism (Europe had showed the way), and of the sinful nature of man in general. Some of these pieces aroused waves of indignant protest when they were published. (They are not innocent, happy, "cheerful" specimens of frontier humor.) Some were never published at the time for the same reason, the fear of further indignation at, or the possible public ostracism of America's most beloved writer.

As a social historian and critic of American literature, I should add that it gives me great pleasure to see these angry, savage, outrageous essays of Mark Twain finally collected in one volume. (It should give you even more pleasure to read them; for Mark Twain somehow contrived to be hilariously funny in the midst of his anger and despair.) Naturally the Russian scholars were quite wrong in their charges of "censorship" about this vein of Mark Twain's writing. They are even ludicrous; except that, as in the case of Mark Twain's own spokesman called Satan, their absolutely specious arguments can leave you with a certain twinge of conscience.

No, it was our prevailing "climate of opinion" during the last forty years, not our official censorship, which had little use for this whole series of social and human indictments written by Mark Twain toward the close of his life. And besides, as certain critics and editors of Mark Twain have claimed, he was innocent and ignorant about historical events. He was childlike; he was still a "boy at heart"; he never developed as an artist beyond his typical hero, Huck Finn—and even the sexual normalcy of this amiable figure has recently been questioned by one of our more lurid Freudian analysts. Perhaps, in a way, all this is true; perhaps it was just what made Mark Twain the great artist that he was, preserving all the innocent illusions of childhood about a human race, and a social system, which were equally corrupt and hypocritical.

But I don't know. Take a look at "To the Person Sitting in Darkness," or "As Regards Patriotism," or "Dr. Loeb's Incredible Discovery," or "The War Prayer," among the other essays in this volume. As to the American scene at the turn of the century, read Mark Twain's "Defence of General Funston," or "The United States of Lyncherdom," or his "Banquet for a Senator," or his "Comments on the Killing of 600 Moros"—and compare these with the "Soliloquies" of the Czar and King Leopold on his Congo Treasurebox. And remember Mark Twain's famous remark about the Jews, that they too were members of the human race, and worse he could say about no man.

You will find all this material in the history books, if you look carefully. But what you have in this volume is a kind of secret history of corruption—social, moral, religious—as it was recorded *while it occurred* by a writer who took it all as a personal affront to what he considered to be man's true honor and dignity. It took great courage for America's favorite popular entertainer to draw up this black indictment of his own country too. And this remarkable moral bravery of Mark Twain's—as is so often the case when a writer speaks from his heart—opened up the floodgates of his eloquence, his wit, his brilliant passages of satire, his devastating anger, his deepest concern for man's fate. I think it is inspired writing—inspired by the Satanic cast of what we call modern civilization.

MAXWELL GEISMAR

Harrison, New York
July 4, 1962

# Acknowledgments

It is impossible to list all the other work on Mark Twain which made it possible to edit this anthology. But the critical materials could not have been assembled without Roger Asselineau's *The Literary Reputation of Mark Twain from 1910 to 1950*. I also used, with gratitude, Arthur L. Scott's *Mark Twain: Selected Criticism* and Caroline Thomas Harnsberger's *Mark Twain At Your Fingertips*.

For various remarks about Mark Twain which appear in "From the Critical Record," I am indebted to the work of the following persons:

Albert Parry who, in "Mark Twain in Russia," *Books Abroad*, April, 1941, quoted the 1930 Soviet preface to *The Stolen White Elephant*.

Arthur L. Vogelback who, in *The Literary Reputation of Mark Twain in America, 1869–1885,* quoted the comment of *The Nation* in 1871.

Philip S. Foner whose *Mark Twain: Social Critic* called my attention to so many matters I should have overlooked—not only the comment on Mark Twain by the late Prime Minister Bandaranaike of Ceylon, but also many of Mark Twain's observations on the war in the Philippines, which were first printed by Dr. Foner.

For background material on the war in the Philippines, I am especially indebted to the fresh materials and insights in Leon Wolff's *Little Brown Brother*.

My further thanks are owed to my publishers; to Edith Mason; to Maxwell Geismar and to Charles Compton of the St. Louis Public Library for their kind encouragement; and to my son, Robert Sherlock Smith, for the best advice an editor ever had.

Lastly, I should like to thank Harper and Brothers for permission to reprint the following material:

From *Europe and Elsewhere* by Mark Twain, Copyright 1923

by The Mark Twain Company: "Corn-Pone Opinions," "As Regards Patriotism," "Bible Teaching and Religious Practice," "Dr. Loeb's Incredible Discovery," "The Dervish and the Offensive Stranger," "The War Prayer," "The United States of Lyncherdom."

From *Mark Twain's Autobiography* edited by Albert Bigelow Paine, Copyright 1924 by Clara Gabrilowitsch, and *Mark Twain in Eruption* by Mark Twain, edited by Bernard DeVoto, Copyright 1922 by Harper and Brothers, Copyright 1940 by The Mark Twain Company: "Reflections on Being the Delight of God," "Banquet for a Senator," "Comments on the Killing of 600 Moros," Archdeacon Wilberforce Discovers the Holy Grail."

# Contents

# Introduction

Make him [the reader] laugh and he will think you a trivial fellow, but
bore him in the right way and your reputation is assured.
                                        —from *The Gentleman in the Parlour*
                                        by W. Somerset Maugham.

The Mark Twain argument began a century ago, when *The
Innocents Abroad* burst upon an unsuspecting world. Overnight
it became an international best seller, and the critical disagreement
commenced. To most European critics, the book was thoroughly
vulgar and even immoral; to most American critics it was good clean
fun.

Before he died, in 1910, Mark Twain had been classed, by
critics both here and in Europe, with Chaucer, Cervantes, Swift,
and some other immortals. Ten or fifteen years later, at the height
of the reaction against the Victorians, he was considered our most
tragic literary failure.

The world has now had a century to mull over Mark Twain. The
time, clearly, has not been long enough. The original disagreement
has become increasingly bitter and complicated. It has also spread
—in 1959, Mark Twain became the center of a sharp American-
Soviet dispute. Thus far, in fact, the world has agreed on only one
point about Mark Twain: *Huckleberry Finn* is a masterpiece.

On Mark Twain's thirty-odd other volumes, the argument, in the
West, is essentially the same old argument: It's entertaining, but
is it art? It's funny, but is it satire? And isn't it all, as Henry James
once believed, "the delight of rudimentary minds"?

There has also been another complaint, first from European
critics, later from American: that Mark Twain's patriotism was
blind and uncritical.

The Soviet contribution to the discussion is that Clemens was a
fearless critic of his own country, but that American censorship

has buried that part of his work. And behind these remarks lies a strange situation: since the late 1940's, Mark Twain has been a best seller in Communist countries on a scale that almost equals his fabulous triumph, last century, in the West. No other foreign literature—and a great deal has been approved by the Communist regimes—has received anything like this reception from Soviet readers.

Soviet critics had long disagreed with ours. But they first made themselves heard, in the Mark Twain controversy, when a third version of Mark Twain's Autobiography was published in this country. Like the first two, this version was composed of excerpts from a huge manuscript which was Clemens' final attempt to speak his mind freely, and which has never been published in full. Unlike the other two, this version contained none of his scathing comments on his own country. Instead, there appeared for the first time his full views on such subjects as baldness, billiards, and phrenology. Such editing, which meant censorship to the Russians, makes no sense except against its proper background.

The purport of Clemens' instructions to his literary executors was that his last testament—the Autobiography—should not be published while it could still give pain or offense to living persons. In addition, he marked his margins with a rich variety of suggestions and orders: one part was not to appear for a century, another not for five.

Parts are still unpublished; nothing like the whole, as Clemens envisioned it, has yet appeared. And the blame has frequently been laid on his absurdly cautious instructions. He had no idea— or so the story has run—how tame his work was, or how soon his ideas would become commonplace.

Perhaps. Yet it is a fact that, almost from the beginning, Mark Twain's heirs and editors have been free to interpret his instructions according to their own best judgment.

To three American editors, this freedom has meant complicated responsibility. Each was of a different generation and none could do more than deal with the enormous manuscript according to the styles and standards of his own day.

The first editor was Clemens' friend, Albert Bigelow Paine. In his edition—*Mark Twain's Autobiography,* published in 1924— both the selections and method of arranging them had been determined before his death, by Mark Twain; Paine simply followed instructions.

The next literary generation felt that this procedure had been "slavish" and also unfair to Mark Twain for two reasons: much of the book, they believed, was so bad that it was hardly worth printing; in any case, Clemens' method—his "methodless method," whereby he talked about whatever came into his head—was so "undisciplined" that it was the first duty of any editor to tidy it up.

Almost twenty years later, in 1940, there appeared *Mark Twain in Eruption*. These selections from the Autobiography, edited by Bernard DeVoto and never printed before, included savagely witty portraits of Clemens' contemporaries—among others, Andrew Carnegie and Teddy Roosevelt. The selections in this volume were not widely admired, for our most influential critics then took a very poor view of all Mark Twain except parts of *Huckleberry Finn* and the first half of *Life on the Mississippi*.[1] Still, it was felt that the editor had done the best possible job with second-rate material.

The latest editor, Charles Neider, was a man of the 1960's. By then Clemens' habit of appearing in his shirtsleeves to discuss whatever was on his mind had long been disapproved of in this country. Neider believed that if the man had lived longer he would have corrected that habit; he also believed that autobiographies should be autobiographical.[2] Thus what he chose from the original were mainly those sections which could be strung together in chronological order to tell some sort of story of Clemens' life.

Secondly, Mr. Neider's selections were determined by his desire to give the world hitherto unpublished Mark Twain.

The result was an American version of Mark Twain's Autobiography which included none of his savage comments on his own country. It was called *The Autobiography of Mark Twain*.

According to the August, 1959, *Moscow Literary Gazette* not only Mr. Neider's editing, but all American treatment of Mark Twain, had been prompted by our desire—in the words of Mr. Yan Bereznitsky—to "shut Twain's trap" with regard to our own shortcomings.

But even the curious notion that we, in this country, now fear Mark Twain's voice, may have its value—for it may help correct a quite different, American notion, also a curious one: that Mark

Twain was not brave enough to criticize his countrymen as they deserved. No doubt we are a strange nation ever to have felt so. For if he did not tell us the tale of our sins—and in a voice that still echoes round the world—no American ever has.

The courage this required has been forgotten—just as it is often forgotten that Mark Twain spoke out loudest when speaking out was most dangerous—that is, in wartime. For we were in the thick of our war with the Filipinos when he published his terrible announcements that the enemy was right, that we were wrong, and that we were dishonoring the flag. He could not have done so, of course, had there been censorship of the press. But even in the freest society, such a position requires considerable courage. It also requires a very deep devotion to some ideals that "dishonored" flag has stood for.

Perhaps, since then, we have never been wrong in our dealings with the rest of the world. If so, it would be for the first time in the history of any nation. But it would not be the first time we have run short, even in peacetime, of men with the courage and devotion to tell us our mistakes. Cowards like Mark Twain, it seems, are not given to every generation.

Mr. Neider answered the Russians—after appealing to Mr. Khrushchev for the chance—in the Moscow *Literary Gazette*. There he said that his editing was an attempt to make "a classic" out of "raw materials"; that it reflected only his own taste and that he did not care for angry or didactic Mark Twain.[3]

Some of this Mark Twain—"Banquet for a Senator" and "Comment on the Killing of 600 Moros"—is reprinted here. Also collected here is that part of Clemens' short satire which, for practical purposes, has long been lost to the world, and which the Russians believe was deliberately "withheld from the general public." [4]

But nothing is here merely because it is long lost Mark Twain. Nothing is here except those items—from familiar sources or obscure—which, all together, may best suggest Clemens' view of the damned race.

If, on the other hand, some of this Mark Twain now seems a strange voice, it is not by coincidence. This voice was familiar once, everywhere. And it was dearly loved, no matter how frenzied, or how painful the latest news on the state of human affairs. But the truth is that what Mark Twain said was never news, to most people. It had long been widely suspected that human nature and human affairs were not what they might be. The joyful surprise was simply that anyone should describe them so perfectly.

Perhaps the world had a stronger stomach once. Or perhaps the damned race will always forget, if it can, whatever it hurts to think of or remember. If this be a fact—and Mark Twain said it was— it might help account for another fact: that so much of this book has long been out of print—some of it for about twenty years, more for about forty, and some for sixty. To this extent, this part of Clemens' work has certainly been "withheld from the general public." But, interestingly, only three such items are un-American. The balance are un-British, un-French, un-Spanish, un-European, un-Belgian, un-Italian or simply—so Mark Twain claimed, although humanity has never agreed with him—antihuman.

It is easy to ridicule the Russian censorship theory; the fact remains that some of Mark Twain's greatest satire has not only been neglected, but belittled; that many earnest words have been written to prove it was not satire at all. He would have written satire if he could, according to various theories, but was prevented by his times, his mother, his wife, his cowardice, his ignorance.

This point of view has deep roots in our cultural traditions. For the very word satire has always been much respected in this country—but so solemnly that we frequently forget that the thing itself is nothing if it is not funny; indeed, no sure test has yet been devised to distinguish it from humor. And yet there has been no generation of Americans which did not sit itself down to ponder whether Mark Twain was "only a humorist."

There can be no doubt about it: humor is very low, satire very high. And yet, in every country, some of the lowest humor— Rabelais, Fielding, and Cervantes—has turned out, after all, to be the highest satire. Unfortunately, this discovery has usually been made on post-mortem examination.

This sort of mistake is certainly not only American. In fact, we have already been luckier with Mark Twain. This is the kind of comment that was appearing at the end of the last century:

It is an anomaly unprecedented in the history of criticism that Mark Twain should live to receive even a doubtful recognition from the schoolmen of his time. . . . His most enthusiastic admirers have been the farthest from suspecting in him the element of greatness. They can

so thoroughly enjoy him without the least sense of intellectual in-
feriority that he seems . . . no better than themselves. . . . The
wonder is that within the last century anyone should have awakened
to the truth.[5]

Mark Twain, however, has run afoul of some traditions about
satire which really are especially American. For, out of the highest
motives, somewhere in our history we established a sort of rule
that making fun of foreigners was not nice; it was rude, philistine,
and even, for some reason, "provincial." Perhaps it all began because we were once considered a nation of belligerent braggarts,
and tried so hard to overcome such habits.

But Mark Twain spent almost a third of his adult life abroad.
He reported from every continent except Antarctica and South
America.[6] And in each one, it appears, he noticed a few sins and
follies. Worse yet, not all of these could be comfortably dismissed
as "human" or "universal." What Clemens saw in France were
French follies; what he saw in Italy were Italian; in England, Eng-
lish—just as, in his United States, the devil acts exactly like an
American.

Even now, except when we are on or over the brink of war, this
observation of other people's faults is considered a little low class.
It is expected from Mark Twain. We also expect that a traveled
GI may report exactly where, and how, they have it worse abroad.
But politer Americans, in print and out, are still apt to keep their
attention exclusively on what is wrong at home.

For practical purposes, of course, there could not be a better
habit; obviously, it is only at home that we are responsible, or that
the wrong can be made right. But art is not always entirely practical—nor is satire, nor humor. These must find their subject matter—human sin and folly—where they can.

Mark Twain found his, not only on five continents but widely
scattered in time. In fact, he admitted that for him history was as
infuriating and as painful to read as the daily papers. In *A Connecticut Yankee in King Arthur's Court,* and elsewhere, he raged
against the habits of the sixth century, and a half dozen others, and
so he ran afoul of another American rule—the time rule—about
what is, and what is not, true and genuine satire.

In England, ridicule of the past is considered almost a sign of
illiteracy. But this has never been so here. Here it is considered a

waste of time and an avoidance of responsibility. For here, always, there has been the urgent pressure of the present, about which something should have been done yesterday. Thus Van Wyck Brooks, a distinguished and a severe critic of Mark Twain's, once wondered aloud how a citizen of the land of Negro lynching could waste his attention on a seventh-century hanging.[7] What Brooks forgot was not only that Clemens was able to attend very adequately both to the lynching and the hanging, but also that, in his hands, they were not so very different, and certainly not unconnected.

In fact, in a century of controversy, some rather simple things may have been forgotten about Mark Twain, and some even simpler rules forgotten. For example, it is not always quite safe to take a man at his own evaluation. Clemens' view of himself was not charitable, for it was exactly the same view he took of the rest of the damned race. No doubt he honestly believed, as he said countless times in public and private, that he was a moral coward. But there are other standards for judging a man than his own ideas on the subject. And the only method, still, of judging a writer is by his work.

If some of Mark Twain's work has been forgotten, it may be because we have been so busy studying his confessions. This is only one of a great many which have been accepted literally:

The human race is a race of cowards: and I am not only marching in that procession but carrying a banner.[8]

This remark is interesting, not because it tells the truth, but because it conveys what, more than anything else, was fundamental in Mark Twain: his total identification with that miserable creature, that coward and hypocrite, that unteachable ass: his fellow man.

This identification is in every line of Mark Twain's work, to the least wisecrack. Usually it is diluted, of course, with everything else that was Mark Twain. Short, savage, and undiluted, it is to be found in "Reflections on Being the Delight of God."

Other writers have rejoiced publicly that they were members of that unexclusive club that Clemens always called the damned human race.[9] Still others have criticized the membership severely. But usually such comments seem to come from members of another race—slightly, or even immeasurably, improved. It is well known that criticism from an insider is always most acceptable to any group. This fact may explain what would otherwise be a curiosity: that any man should spend his life lecturing and raging at humanity and receive adoration in return. But it was so with Mark Twain. The least he deserved for his harsh and witty words was to be ignored. But toward the close of his life there were popular ovations wherever he traveled. In his own country he was still, in 1934, the best read and best loved American writer living or dead.[10] And returns are now in from another branch of the damned race—the Soviet people.

Perhaps, in fact, the race as a whole has understood Mark Twain better than the literary branch of it. For it has accepted the spirit, but not all the details, of his great confession—according to him, the most abject and pitiful any creature could make—that he was a human being.

JANET SMITH

Westport, Connecticut
February, 1962

# From the Critical Record

*It were not best that we should all think alike; it is difference of opinion that makes horse races.*
— Mark Twain, in "Pudd'nhead Wilson's Calendar"

"Mark Twain" . . . has done perhaps more than any other living writer to lower the literary tone of English speaking people.
— John Nichol, in *American Literature, an Historical Sketch, 1620-1880,* 1882

I love to think of the great and godlike Clemens.
— Rudyard Kipling, in a letter to Frank Doubleday, 1903

Its aim [Mark Twain's satire] is to degrade the civilization of Europe, to overthrow the Renaissance Ideal of the complete man, and to substitute the very inferior ideal of the sentimental, broad-bottomed, ranting, dollar-hunting Yankee with all his blather about liberty and progress.
— Richard Aldington, in *The Spectator,* 1924

His deliberate exaggerations were taken for symptoms of mental derangement. . . . All this was a regrettable misunderstanding.
— Eugénie Forgues, in *Revue des Deux Mondes,* 1886

Eduard Engel. . . . rejects the explanation, advanced by Schönbach and supported by Friedmann, that Mark Twain is merely joking.
— Early German discussion of *The Innocents Abroad,* summarized by Edgar Hugo Hemminghaus, in *Mark Twain in Germany*

Twain was a bourgeois writer. . . . but even Twain . . . mercilessly satirized the American police, and therein is his great merit.
— Soviet preface to *The Stolen White Elephant,* Moscow State Publishing House, 1930

I mention this to show you how great is our interest in the work of Mark Twain . . . , how dear to us are all the manifestations of his genius, and what incomprehension and protest is called from us by any attempt to present in an impoverished light his wonderful and many-faceted countenance.

—Yan Bereznitsky, answering Charles Neider in the *Moscow Literary Gazette,* 1959

He . . . gives a good deal of not very refined, perhaps, but, on the whole, harmless amusement to a very large number of people.

—*The Nation,* 1871

Emerson, Longfellow, Lowell, Holmes—I knew them all and the rest of our sages, poets, seers, critics, humorists; they were like one another and like other literary men; but Clemens was sole, incomparable, the Lincoln of our literature.

—William Dean Howells, in *My Mark Twain,* 1910

I lived for ten years with the soul of Robert E. Lee and it really made a little better man of me. Six months of Mark Twain made me a worse. . . . And I am fifty-six years old. . . . What can he not do to boys and girls of sixteen?

—Gamaliel Bradford, in *The Atlantic Monthly,* 1920

Tragic Mark Twain! Irresponsible child that he is, he does not even ask himself whether he is doing right or wrong. . . ."

—Van Wyck Brooks, in *The Ordeal of Mark Twain,* 1920

We are not hostile to the United States. How could I be hostile to a country that produced Mark Twain?

—S. W. R. D. Bandaranaike, late Prime Minister of Ceylon, quoted in *The New York Times,* 1956

# MARK TWAIN
## on the Damned Human Race

# ON THE DAMNED RACE

I am the only man living who understands human nature; God has put me in charge of this branch office; when I retire there will be no one to take my place. I shall keep on doing my duty, for when I get over on the other side, I shall use my influence to have the human race drowned again, and this time drowned good, no omissions, no Ark.—JOHN MACY, *Mark Twain*

I have studied the human race with diligence and strong interest all these years in my own person; in myself I find in big or little proportion every quality and every defect that is findable in the mass of the race.— Mark Twain's Autobiography, published in *Mark Twain in Eruption*

## To the Person Sitting in Darkness

I have always preached. . . . If the humor came of its own accord and uninvited, I have allowed it a place in my sermon, but I was not writing the sermon for the sake of the humor.—Mark Twain's Autobiography, published in *Mark Twain in Eruption*.

"To the Person Sitting in Darkness" is Mark Twain's masterpiece of this kind of preaching. It is also still the most timely of his short satires—strangely, perhaps, for it was certainly not written with an eye to posterity, and many of the events which inspired it are half forgotten. In fact, probably few periods in our history are at present so unfamiliar to the literate reader as the turn-of-the-century wars. Our ten weeks war with Spain, for example, is widely remembered now for the fact that the yellow press—Hearst and Pulitzer—supported it, and, of course, for the sinking of the *Maine* in Havana Harbor by persons still unidentified. More often forgotten is the fact that—according to historians who agree on little else—the basic cause of hostilities was American horror at Spanish colonial methods, and especially at the methods of General Weyler, who, in 1896, exterminated half of the population of Havana Province in *reconcentrado* camps; this was a year after the outbreak of the second Cuban revolution, led by José Martí, and two years before the United States intervened on Cuba's side. Intervention came after Congress guaranteed that the United States would not impose American sovereignty on Cuba. "The people of the island of Cuba," read the resolution, "are, and of right ought to be, free and independent."

The seeds of the Philippine War were sown in the peace treaty with Spain. For President McKinley's peace terms—for which neither this country nor Spain was prepared—were that Spain should not only free Cuba, but cede to us all her West Indian possessions, and sell us the Philippine Islands.

In the Philippines, as in Cuba, native armies were in revolt against Spain; their troops had recently co-operated with ours. The war which the United States fought to establish its sovereignty over the Filipinos, was far more bloody and expensive, and never so popular, as the war with Spain.

The Boer War, which Mark Twain so often likened to the Filipino affair, was also for empire. But a contributing cause was the discovery of gold and diamonds in the farmlands of South Africa. The numerous British settlers attracted by these discoveries were hated by the Boers (settlers of Dutch descent) and were heavily taxed, but denied citizenship. From 1899 to 1902 the British used against the Boers, and later against Boer guerrillas, the methods common to invading armies of the period: burnt countrysides, strings of block-houses, and concentration camps in which masses of the civilian population perished.

When "To the Person Sitting in Darkness" appeared, it produced a cyclone; the sections on the missionaries in China produced savage public warfare between Mark Twain and the American Board of Foreign Missions—a warfare which continued until the Board fell silent.

The reparations extracted by the missionaries, which Mark Twain discusses below, followed upon the victory of an international army, including two thousand Americans, which, in August, 1900, took the city of Peking from Chinese armies led by the Boxers—who were "China's traduced patriots," according to Mark Twain. Supposedly, the international army was to punish antiforeign rioting by the Chinese, but, after China's defeat, the reparations extracted by the Great Powers—except the United States—were at least as rapacious as those

extracted by the missionaries; the great difference was that they were
not the work of professed men of God—and it was this work which
Mark Twain ensured should live in infamy.

The germ of "To the Persons Sitting in Darkness" seems to have
been this New Year's Greeting which Clemens published in the
New York *Herald*, December 30, 1900:

### A GREETING FROM THE NINETEENTH TO THE TWENTIETH CENTURY

I bring you the stately nation named Christendom, returning, bedraggled,
besmirched, and dishonored, from pirate raids in Kiao-Chou, Manchuria,
South Africa, and the Philippines, with her soul full of meanness, her
pocket full of boodle, and her mouth full of hypocrisies. Give her soap and
towel, but hide the looking glass.

In January, 1901, Mark Twain wrote "To the Person Sitting in
Darkness." He then sought advice on publishing it, for, as he said, he
liked advice when it was his way. The wrong advice—from his friend,
the Rev. Joseph Twichell—was received, and is now lost. Clemens'
answer is not:

*I* can't understand it! You are a public guide and teacher, Joe, and are
under a heavy responsibility to men, young and old; if you teach your
people—as you teach me—to hide their opinions when they believe the
flag is being abused and dishonored, lest the utterance do them and a publisher a damage, how do you answer for it to your conscience? You are
sorry for me; in the fair way of give and take, I am willing to be a little
sorry for you.

In the same letter:

. . . I'm not expecting anything but kicks for scoffing, and am expecting
a diminution of my bread and butter by it, but if Livy [Mrs. Clemens] will
let me I will have my say. This nation is like all the others that have been
spewed upon the earth—ready to shout for any cause that will tickle its
vanity or fill its pocket. What a hell of a heaven it will be, when they get
all these hypocrites assembled there!

Livy "let" him. His old friend William Dean Howells also had no
doubt that he should publish, although he did suggest that he hang
himself afterwards.

Thanks partly to those two—the only two whose judgment Mark
Twain entirely respected—"To the Person Sitting in Darkness" appeared in the February issue of the respectable and liberal *North
American Review*. The effect, according to Clemens' biographer,
Albert Bigelow Paine, was "as if he had thrown a great missile into
the human hive. . . . Whatever other effect it may have had, it left
no thinking person unawakened." [1]

Mark Twain's title is from Matthew 4:16: "The people which sat in
the darkness saw a great light. . . ." His article follows:

Christmas will dawn in the United States over a people full of hope and aspiration and good cheer. Such a condition means contentment and happiness. The carping grumbler who may here and there go forth will find few to listen to him. The majority will wonder what is the matter with him and pass on—New York *Tribune,* on Christmas Eve.

FROM the *Sun,* of New York:

The purpose of this article is not to describe the terrible offenses against humanity committed in the name of politics in some of the most notorious East Side districts. *They could not be described, even verbally.* But it is the intention to let the great mass of more or less careless citizens of this beautiful metropolis of the New World get some conception of the havoc and ruin wrought to man, woman, and child in the most densely populated and least-known section of the city. Name, date, and place can be supplied to those of little faith—or to any man who feels himself aggrieved. It is a plain statement of record and observation, written without license and without garnish.

Imagine, if you can a section of the city territory completely dominated by one man,[2] without whose permission neither legitimate nor illegitimate business can be conducted; *where illegitimate business is encouraged and legitimate business discouraged;* where the respectable residents have to fasten their doors and windows summer nights and sit in their rooms with asphyxiating air and 100-degree temperature, rather than try to catch the faint whiff of breeze in their natural breathing places, the stoops of their homes; *where naked women dance by night in the streets, and unsexed men prowl like vultures through the darkness on "business"* not only permitted but encouraged by the police; *where the education of infants begins with the knowledge of prostitution* and the training of little girls is training in the arts of Phryne; where *American* girls brought up with the refinements of *American* homes are imported from small towns upstate, Massachusetts, Connecticut, and New Jersey, and kept as virtually prisoners as if they were locked up behind jail bars until they have lost all semblance of womanhood; *where small boys are taught to solicit for the women of disorderly houses;* where there is an organized society of young men *whose sole business in life is to corrupt young girls and turn them over to bawdy houses;* where men walking with their wives along the street are openly insulted; *where children that have adult diseases are the chief patrons of the hospitals and dispensaries;* where it is the rule, rather than the exception, that *murder, rape, robbery, and theft go unpunished*—in short where the premium of the most awful forms of vice is the profit of the politicians.

The following news from China appeared in the *Sun,* of New York, on Christmas Eve. The italics are mine:

The Rev. Mr. Ament, of the American Board of Foreign Missions, has returned from a trip which he made for the purpose of collecting indemnities for damages done by Boxers. *Everywhere he went he compelled the Chinese to pay.* He says that all his native Christians are now provided for. He had 700 of them under his charge, and 300 were killed. He has *collected* 300 *taels for each* of these murders, and has *compelled full payment for all the property belonging to Christians* that was destroyed. He also assessed *fines* amounting to THIRTEEN TIMES the amount of the indemnity. *This money will be used for the propagation of the Gospel.*

Mr. Ament declares that the compensation he has collected is *moderate* when compared with the amount secured by the Catholics, who demand, in addition to money, *head for head.* They collect 500 taels for each murder of a Catholic. In the Wenchiu country, 680 Catholics were killed, and for this the European Catholics here demand 750,000 strings of cash and 680 *heads.*

In the course of a conversation, Mr. Ament referred to the attitude of the missionaries toward the Chinese. He said:

"I deny emphatically that the missionaries are *vindictive*, that they *generally* looted, or that they have done anything *since* the siege that *the circumstances did not demand.* I criticize the Americans. *The soft hand of the Americans is not as good as the mailed fist of the Germans:*—If you deal with the Chinese with a soft hand they will take advantage of it.

"The statement that the French government will return the loot taken by the French soldiers is the source of the greatest amusement here. The French soldiers were more systematic looters than the Germans, and it is a fact that today *Catholic Christians,* carrying French flags and armed with modern guns, *are looting villages* in the Province of Chili."

By happy luck, we get all these glad tidings on Christmas Eve —just in time [to] enable us to celebrate the day with proper gayety and enthusiasm. Our spirits soar, and we find we can even make jokes: Taels, I win, Heads you lose.

Our Reverend Ament is the right man in the right place. What we want of our missionaries out there is, not that they shall merely represent in their acts and persons the grace and gentleness and charity and loving-kindness of our religion, but that they shall also represent the American spirit. The oldest Americans are the Pawnees. Macallum's History says:

When a white Boxer kills a Pawnee and destroys his property, the other Pawnees do not trouble to seek *him* out, they kill any white person that comes along; also, they make some white village pay deceased's heirs the full cash value of deceased, together with full cash value of the property destroyed; they also make the village pay, in addition, *thirteen times* the value of that property into a fund for the dissemination of the Pawnee religion, which they regard as the best of all religions for the softening and humanizing of the heart of man. It is their idea that it is only fair and right that the innocent should be made to suffer for the guilty, and that it is better that ninety and nine innocent should suffer than that one guilty person should escape.

Our Reverend Ament is justifiably jealous of those enterprising Catholics, who not only get big money for each lost convert, but get "head for head" besides. But he should soothe himself with the reflections that the entirety of their exactions are for their own pockets, whereas he, less selfishly, devotes only 300 taels per head to that service, and gives the whole vast thirteen repetitions of the property-indemnity to the service of propagating the Gospel. His magnanimity has won him the approval of his nation, and will get him a monument. Let him be content with these rewards. We all hold him dear for manfully defending his fellow missionaries from exaggerated charges which were beginning to distress us, but which his testimony has so considerably modified that we can now contemplate them without noticeable pain. For now we know that, even before the siege, the missionaries were not "generally" out looting, and that, "since the siege," they have acted quite handsomely, except when "circumstances" crowded them. I am arranging for the monument. Subscriptions for it can be sent to the American Board; designs for it can be sent to me. Designs must allegorically set forth the thirteen reduplications of the indemnity, and the object for which they were exacted; as ornaments, the designs must exhibit 680 heads, so disposed as to give a pleasing and pretty effect; for the Catholics have done nicely, and are entitled to notice in the monument. Mottoes may be suggested, if any shall be discovered that will satisfactorily cover the ground.

Mr. Ament's financial feat of squeezing a thirteenfold indemnity out of the pauper peasants to square other people's offenses, thus condemning them and their women and innocent little children to inevitable starvation and lingering death, in order that the blood money so acquired might be *"used for the propagation of the Gospel,"* does not flutter my serenity; although the act and the words, taken together, concrete a blasphemy so hideous and so colossal that, without doubt, its mate is not findable in the history of this or of any other age. Yet, if a layman had done that thing and justified it with those words, I should have shuddered, I know. Or, if I had done the thing and said the words myself—However, the thought is unthinkable, irreverent as some imperfectly informed people think me. Sometimes an ordained minister sets out to be blasphemous. When this happens, the layman is out of the running; he stands no chance.

We have Mr. Ament's impassioned assurance that the missionaries are not "vindictive." Let us hope and pray that they will never become so, but will remain in the almost morbidly fair and just and gentle temper which is affording so much satisfaction to their brother and champion today.

The following is from the New York *Tribune* of Christmas Eve. It comes from that journal's Tokyo correspondent. It has a strange and impudent sound, but the Japanese are but partially civilized as yet. When they become wholly civilized they will not talk so:

The missionary question, of course, occupies a foremost place in the discussion. It is now felt as essential that the Western Powers take cognizance of the sentiment here, that religious invasions of Oriental countries by powerful Western organizations are tantamount to filibustering expeditions, and should not only be discountenanced, but that stern measures should be adopted for their suppression. The feeling here is that the missionary organizations constitute a constant menace to peaceful international relations.

*Shall we?* That is, shall we go on conferring our civilization upon the peoples that sit in darkness, or shall we give those poor things a rest? Shall we bang right ahead in our old-time, loud, pious way, and commit the new century to the game; or shall we sober up and sit down and think it over first? Would it not be prudent to get our civilization tools together, and see how much stock is left on hand in the way of glass beads and theology, and maxim guns and hymn books, and trade gin and torches of progress and enlightenment (patent adjustable ones, good to fire villages with, upon occasion), and balance the books, and arrive at the profit and loss, so that we may intelligently decide whether to continue the business or sell out the property and start a new civilization scheme on the proceeds?

Extending the blessings of civilization to our brother who sits in darkness has been a good trade and has paid well, on the whole; and there is money in it yet, if carefully worked—but not enough, in my judgment, to make any considerable risk advisable. The people that sit in darkness are getting to be too scarce—too scarce and too shy. And such darkness as is now left is really of but an indifferent quality, and not dark enough for the game. The most of those people that sit in darkness have been furnished with more light than was good for them or profitable for us. We have been injudicious.

The blessings-of-civilization trust, wisely and cautiously administered, is a daisy. There is more money in it, more territory, more sovereignty, and other kinds of emolument, than there is in any other game that is played. But Christendom has been playing it badly of late years, and must certainly suffer by it, in my opinion. She has been so eager to get every stake that appeared on the green cloth, that the people who sit in darkness have noticed it—they have noticed it, and have begun to show alarm. They have become suspicious of the blessings of civilization. More—they have begun to examine them. This is not well. The blessings of civilization are all right, and a good commercial property; there could not be a better, in a dim light. In the right kind of a light, and at a proper distance, with the goods a little out of focus, they furnish this desirable exhibit to the gentlemen who sit in darkness:

| | |
|---|---|
| LOVE, | LAW AND ORDER, |
| JUSTICE, | LIBERTY, |
| GENTLENESS, | EQUALITY, |
| CHRISTIANITY, | HONORABLE DEAL- |
| PROTECTION TO THE | ING, |
| WEAK, | MERCY, |
| TEMPERANCE, | EDUCATION, |

—and so on.

There. Is it good? Sir, it is pie. It will bring into camp any idiot that sits in darkness anywhere. But not if we adulerate it. It is proper to be emphatic upon that point. This brand is strictly for export—apparently. *Apparently.* Privately and confidentially, it is nothing of the kind. Privately and confidentially, it is merely an outside cover, gay and pretty and attractive, displaying the special patterns of our civilization which we reserve for home consumption, while *inside* the bale is the actual thing that the customer sitting in darkness buys with his blood and tears and land and liberty. That actual thing is, indeed, civilization, but it is only for export. Is there a difference between the two brands? In some of the details, yes.

We all know that the business is being ruined. The reason is not far to seek. It is because our Mr. McKinley, and Mr. Chamberlain,[3] and the Kaiser, and the Czar and the French have been exporting the actual thing *with the outside cover left off*. This is bad for the game. It shows that these new players of it are not sufficiently acquainted with it.

It is a distress to look on and note the mismoves, they are so strange and so awkward. Mr. Chamberlain manufactures a war out of materials so inadequate and so fanciful that they make the boxes grieve and the gallery laugh, and he tries hard to persuade himself that it isn't purely a private raid for cash, but has a sort of dim, vague respectability about it somewhere, if he could only find the spot; and that, by and by, he can scour the flag clean again after he has finished dragging it through the mud, and make it shine and flash in the vault of heaven once more as it had shone and flashed there a thousand years in the world's respect until he laid his unfaithful hand upon it. It is bad play—bad. For it exposes the actual thing to them that sit in darkness, and they say: "What! Christian against Christian? And only for money? Is *this* a case of magnanimity, forbearance, love, gentleness, mercy, protection of the weak—this strange and overshowy onslaught of an elephant upon a nest of field mice, on the pretext that the mice had squeaked an insolence at him—conduct which "no self-respecting government could allow to pass unavenged"? as Mr. Chamberlain said. Was that a good pretext in a small case, when it had not been a good pretext in a large one?—for only recently Russia had affronted the elephant three times and survived alive and unsmitten. Is this civilization and progress? Is it something better than we already possess? These harryings and burnings and desertmakings in the Transvaal—is this an improvement on our darkness? Is it, perhaps, possible that there are two kinds of civilization—one for home consumption and one for the heathen market?"

Then they that sit in darkness are troubled, and shake their heads; and they read this extract from a letter of a British private, recounting his exploits in one of Methuen's victories, some days before the affair of Magersfontein, and they are troubled again:

We tore up the hill and into the intrenchments, and the Boers saw we had them; so they dropped their guns and went down on their knees and put up their hands clasped, and begged for mercy. And we gave it to them—*with the long spoon.*

The long spoon is the bayonet. See *Lloyd's Weekly,* London, of those days. The same number—and the same column—contained some quite unconscious satire in the form of shocked and bitter upbraidings of the Boers for their brutalities and inhumanities!

Next, to our heavy damage, the Kaiser went to playing the game without first mastering it. He lost a couple of missionaries in a riot in Shantung, and in his account he made an overcharge for them. China had to pay a hundred thousand dollars apiece for them, in money; twelve miles of territory, containing several millions of inhabitants and worth twenty million dollars; and to build a monument, and also a Christian church; whereas the people of China could have been depended upon to remember the missionaries without the help of these expensive memorials. This was all bad play. Bad, because it would not, and could not, and will not now or ever, deceive the person sitting in darkness. He knows that it was an overcharge. He knows that a missionary is like any other man: he is worth merely what you can supply his place for, and no more. He is useful, but so is a doctor, so is a sheriff, so is an editor; but a just emperor does not charge war prices for such. A diligent, intelligent, but obscure missionary, and a diligent, intelligent country editor are worth much, and we know it; but they are not worth the earth. We esteem such an editor, and we are sorry to see him go; but when he goes, we should consider twelve miles of territory, and a church, and a fortune, overcompensation for his loss. I mean, if he was a Chinese editor, and we had to settle for him. It is no proper figure for an editor or a missionary; one can get shopworn kings for less. It was bad play on the Kaiser's part. It got this property, true; but it *produced the Chinese revolt,* the indignant uprising of China's traduced patriots, the Boxers. The results have been expensive to Germany, and to the other disseminators of progress and the blessings of civilization.

The Kaiser's claim was paid, yet it was bad play, for it could not fail to have an evil effect upon persons sitting in darkness in China. They would muse upon the event, and be likely to say: "Civilization is gracious and beautiful, for such is its reputation; but can we afford it? There are rich Chinamen, perhaps they can afford it; but this tax is not laid upon them, it is laid upon the peasants of Shantung; it is they that must pay this mighty sum, and their wages are but four cents a day. Is this a better civilization than ours, and holier and higher and nobler? Is not this rapacity? Is not this extortion? Would Germany charge America two hundred thousand dollars for two missionaries, and shake the mailed fist in her face, and send warships, and send soldiers, and say: "Seize twelve miles of territory, worth twenty millions of dollars, as additional pay for the missionaries; and make those peasants build a monument to the missionaries, and a costly Christian church to remember them by?" And later would Germany say to her soldiers: "March through America and slay, *giving no quarter;* make the German face there, as has been our Hun-face here, a terror for a thousand years; march through the great republic and slay, slay, slay, carving a road for our offended religion through its heart and bowels?" Would Germany do like this to America, to England, to France, to Russia? Or only to China, the helpless—imitating the elephant's assault upon the field mice? Had we better invest in this civilization—this civilization which called Napoleon a buccaneer for carrying off Venice's bronze horses, but which steals our ancient astronomical instruments from our walls, and goes looting like common bandits— that is, all the alien soldiers except America's; and (Americans again excepted)[4] storms frightened villages and cables the result to glad journals at home every day: "Chinese losses, 450 killed; ours, *one officer and two men wounded.* Shall proceed against neighboring village tomorrow, where a *massacre* is reported." Can we afford civilization?"

And next Russia must go and play the game injudiciously. She
affronts England once or twice—with the person sitting in darkness observing and noting; by moral assistance of France and Germany, she robs Japan of her hard-earned spoil, all swimming in
Chinese blood—Port Arthur—with the person again observing and
noting; then she seizes Manchuria, raids its villages, and chokes
its great river with the swollen corpses of countless massacred
peasants—that astonished person still observing and noting. And
perhaps he is saying to himself: "It is yet *another* civilized power,
with its banner of the Prince of Peace in one hand and its loot
basket and its butcher knife in the other. Is there no salvation for
us but to adopt civilization and lift ourselves down to its level?"

And by and by comes America, and our master of the game
plays it badly—plays it as Mr. Chamberlain was playing it in
South Africa. It was a mistake to do that; also, it was one which
was quite unlooked for in a master who was playing it so well in
Cuba. In Cuba, he was playing the usual and regular *American*
game, and it was winning, for there is no way to beat it. The
master, contemplating Cuba, said: "Here is an oppressed and
friendless little nation which is willing to fight to be free; we go
partners, and put up the strength of seventy million sympathizers
and the resources of the United States: play!" Nothing but Europe
combined could call the hand: and Europe cannot combine on
anything. There, in Cuba, he was following our great traditions in
a way which made us very proud of him, and proud of the deep
dissatisfaction which his play was provoking in continental Europe.
Moved by a high inspiration, he threw out those stirring words
which proclaimed that forcible annexation would be "criminal
aggression"; and in that utterance fired another "shot heard round
the world." The memory of that fine saying will be outlived by the
remembrance of no act of his but one—that he forgot it within the
twelvemonth, and its honorable gospel along with it.

For, presently, came the Philippine temptation. It was strong;
it was too strong, and he made that bad mistake: he played the
European game, the Chamberlain game. It was a pity; it was a
great pity, that error; that one grievous error, that irrevocable
error. For it was the very place and time to play the American
game again. And at no cost. Rich winnings to be gathered in, too;

rich and permanent; indestructible; a fortune transmissible forever to the children of the flag. Not land, not money, not dominion—no, something worth many times more than that dross: our share, the spectacle of a nation of long harassed and persecuted slaves set free though our influence; our posterity's share, the golden memory of that fair deed. The game was in our hands. If it had been played according to the American rules, Dewey would have sailed away from Manila as soon as he had destroyed the Spanish fleet— after putting up a sign on shore guaranteeing foreign property and life against damage by the Filipinos, and warning the powers that interference with the emancipated patriots would be regarded as an act unfriendly to the United States. The powers cannot combine, in even a bad cause, and the sign would not have been molested.

Dewey could have gone about his affairs elsewhere, and left the competent Filipino army to starve out the little Spanish garrison and send it home, and the Filipino citizens to set up the form of government they might prefer, and deal with the friars and their doubtful acquisitions according to Filipino ideas of fairness and justice—ideas which have since been tested and found to be of as high an order as any that prevail in Europe or America.

But we played the Chamberlain game, and lost the chance to add another Cuba and another honorable deed to our good record.

The more we examine the mistake, the more clearly we perceive that it is going to be bad for the business. The person sitting in darkness is almost sure to say: "There is something curious about this—curious and unaccountable. There must be two Americas: one that sets the captive free, and one that takes a once-captive's new freedom away from him, and picks a quarrel with him with nothing to found it on; then kills him to get his land."

The truth is, the person sitting in darkness *is* saying things like that; and for the sake of the business we must persuade him to look at the Philippine matter in another and healthier way. We must arrange his opinions for him. I believe it can be done; for Mr. Chamberlain has arranged England's opinion of the South African matter, and done it most cleverly and successfully. He presented the facts—some of the facts—and showed those confiding people what the facts meant. He did it statistically, which is a good way.

He used the formula: "Twice 2 are 14, and 2 from 9 leaves 35." Figures are effective; figures will convince the elect.

Now, my plan is a still bolder one than Mr. Chamberlain's though apparently a copy of it. Let us be franker than Mr. Chamberlain; let us audaciously present the whole of the facts, shirking none, then explain them according to Mr. Chamberlain's formula. This daring truthfulness will astonish and dazzle the person sitting in darkness, and he will take the explanation down before his mental vision has had time to get back into focus. Let us say to him:

"Our case is simple. On the first of May, Dewey destroyed the Spanish fleet. This left the archipelago in the hands of its proper and rightful owners, the Filipino nation. Their army numbered 30,000 men, and they were competent to whip out or starve out the little Spanish garrison; then the people could set up a government of their own devising. Our traditions required that Dewey should now set up his warning sign, and go away. But the master of the game happened to think of another plan—the European plan. He acted upon it. This was, to send out an army—ostensibly to help the native patriots put the finishing touch upon their long and plucky struggle for independence, but really to take their land away from them and keep it. That is, in the interest of progress and civilization. The plan developed, stage by stage, and quite satisfactorily. We entered into a military alliance with the trusting Filipinos, and they hemmed in Manila on the land side, and by their valuable help the place, with its garrison of 8,000 or 10,000 Spaniards, was captured—a thing which we could not have accomplished unaided at that time. We got their help by—by ingenuity. We knew they were fighting for their independence, and that they had been at it for two years. We knew they supposed that we also were fighting in their worthy cause—just as we had helped the Cubans fight for Cuban independence—and we allowed them to go on thinking so. *Until Manila was ours and we could get along without them.* Then we showed our hand. Of course, they were surprised—that was natural; surprised and disappointed; disappointed and grieved. To them it looked un-American; uncharacteristic; foreign to our established traditions. And this was natural, too; for we were only playing the American game in public—in private it was the European. It was neatly done, very neatly, and it bewildered them. They could not understand it; for we had been so friendly— so affectionate, even—with those simple-minded patriots! We, our own selves, had brought back out of exile their leader, their hero, their hope, their Washington—Aguinaldo; brought him in a war-ship,[5] in high honor, under the sacred shelter and hospitality of the flag; brought him back and restored him to his people, and got their moving and eloquent gratitude for it. Yes, we had been so friendly to them, and had heartened them up in so many ways! We had lent them guns and ammunition; advised with them; exchanged pleasant courtesies with them; placed our sick and wounded in their kindly care; intrusted our Spanish prisoners to their humane and honest hands; fought shoulder to shoulder with them against "the common enemy" (our own phrase); praised their courage, praised their gallantry, praised their mercifulness, praised their fine and honorable conduct; borrowed their trenches, borrowed strong positions which they had previously captured from the Spaniards; petted them, lied to them—officially proclaiming that our land and naval forces came to give them their freedom and displace the bad Spanish government—fooled them, used them until we needed them no longer; then derided the sucked orange and threw it away. We kept the positions which we had beguiled them of; by and by, we moved a force forward and overlapped patriot ground—a clever thought, for we needed trouble, and this would produce it. A Filipino soldier crossing the ground, where no one had a right to forbid him, was shot by our sentry. The badgered patriots resented this with arms, without waiting to know whether Aguinaldo, who was absent, would approve or not. Aguinaldo did not approve; but that availed nothing. What we wanted, in the interest of progress and civilization, was the archipel-ago, unencumbered by patriots struggling for independence; and war was what we needed. We clinched our opportunity. It is Mr. Chamberlain's case over again—at least in its motive and inten-tion; and we played the game as adroitly as he played it himself."

At this point in our frank statement of fact to the person sitting in darkness, we should throw in a little trade taffy about the blessings of civilization—for a change, and for the refreshment of his spirit—then go on with our tale:

"We and the patriots having captured Manila, Spain's owner-ship of the archipelago and her sovereignty over it were at an end —obliterated—annihilated—not a rag or shred of either remain-ing behind. It was then that we conceived the divinely humorous idea of *buying* both of these specters from Spain! (It is quite safe to confess this to the person sitting in darkness, since neither he nor any other sane person will believe it.) In buying those ghosts for twenty millions, we also contracted to take care of the friars and their accumulations. I think we also agreed to propagate leprosy and smallpox, but as to this there is doubt. But it is not important; persons afflicted with the friars do not mind other diseases.[6]

"With our treaty ratified, Manila subdued, and our ghosts secured, we had no further use for Aguinaldo and the owners of the archipelago. We forced a war, and we have been hunting America's guest and ally through the woods and swamps ever since."

At this point in the tale, it will be well to boast a little of our war work and our heroisms in the field, so as to make our per-formance look as fine as England's in South Africa; but I believe it will not be best to emphasize this too much. We must be cautious. Of course, we must read the war telegrams to the person, in order to keep up our frankness; but we can throw an air of humorous-ness over them, and that will modify their grim eloquence a little, their rather indiscreet exhibitions of gory exultation. Before reading to him the following display heads of the dispatches of November 18, 1900, it will be well to practice on them in private first, so as to get the right tang of lightness and gayety into them:

ADMINISTRATION WEARY OF
PROTRACTED HOSTILITIES!
REAL WAR AHEAD FOR FILIPINO
REBELS *
WILL SHOW NO MERCY!
KITCHENER'S PLAN ADOPTED!

* "Rebels!" Mumble that funny word—don't let the person catch it distinctly. (M.T.)

Kitchener[7] knows how to handle disagreeable people who are fighting for their homes and their liberties, and we must let on that we are merely imitating Kitchener, and have no national interest in the matter, further than to get ourselves admired by the great family of nations, in which august company our master of the game has bought a place for us in the back row.

Of course, we must not venture to ignore our General Mac-Arthur's reports—oh, why do they keep on printing those embarassing things?—we must drop them trippingly from the tongue and take the chances:

During the last ten months our losses have been 268 killed and 750 wounded; Filipino loss, *three thousand two hundred and twenty-seven killed,* and 694 wounded.

We must stand ready to grab the person sitting in darkness, for he will swoon away at this confession saying: "Good God! those 'niggers' spare their wounded, and the Americans massacre theirs!"

We must bring him to, and coax him and coddle him, and assure him that the ways of providence are best, and that it would not become us to find fault with them; and then, to show him that we are only imitators, not originators, we must read the following passage from the letter of an American soldier lad in the Philippines to his mother, published in *Public Opinion,* of Decorah, Iowa, describing the finish of a victorious battle:

"WE NEVER LEFT ONE ALIVE. IF ONE WAS WOUNDED, WE WOULD RUN OUR BAYONETS THROUGH HIM."

Having now laid all the historical facts before the person sitting in darkness, we should bring him to again, and explain them to him. We should say to him:

"They look doubtful, but in reality they are not. There have been lies; yes, but they were told in a good cause. We have been treacherous; but that was only in order that real good might come out of apparent evil. True, we have crushed a deceived and confiding people; we have turned against the weak and the friendless who trusted us; we have stamped out a just and intelligent and well-ordered republic; we have stabbed an ally in the back and slapped the face of a guest; we have bought a shadow from an enemy that hadn't it to sell; we have robbed a trusting friend of his land and his liberty; we have invited our clean young men to shoulder a discredited musket and do bandits' work under a flag which bandits have been accustomed to fear, not to follow; we have debauched America's honor and blackened her face before the world; but each detail was for the best. We know this. The head of every state and sovereignty in Christendom and 90 per cent of every legislative body in Christendom, including our Congress and our fifty state legislatures, are members not only of the church, but also of the blessings-of-civilization trust. This world-girdling accumulation of trained morals, high principles, and justice cannot do an unright thing, an unfair thing, an ungenerous thing, an unclean thing. It knows what it is about. Give yourself no uneasiness; it is all right."

Now then, that will convince the person. You will see. It will restore the business. Also, it will elect the master of the game to the vacant place in the trinity of our national gods; and there on their high thrones the three will sit, age after age, in the people's sight, each bearing the emblem of his service: Washington, the sword of the liberator; Lincoln, the slave's broken chains; the master, the chains repaired.

It will give the business a splendid new start. You will see.

Everything is prosperous, now; everything is just as we should wish it. We have got the archipelago, and we shall never give it up. Also, we have every reason to hope that we shall have an opportunity before very long to slip out of our congressional contract with Cuba and give her something better in the place of it. It is a rich country, and many of us are already beginning to see that the contract was a sentimental mistake.[8] But now—right now— is the best time to do some profitable rehabilitating work—work that will set us up and make us comfortable, and discourage gossip. We cannot conceal from ourselves that, privately, we are a little troubled about our uniform. It is one of our prides; it is acquainted with honor; it is familiar with great deeds and noble; we love it, we revere it; and so this errand it is on makes us uneasy. And our flag—another pride of ours, our chiefest! We have worshiped it so; and when we have seen it in far lands—glimpsing it unexpectedly in that strange sky, waving its welcome and benediction to us—we have caught our breaths, and uncovered our heads, and couldn't speak, for a moment, for the thought of what it was to us and the great ideals it stood for. Indeed, we *must* do something about these things; it is easily managed. We can have a special one—our states do it: we can have just our usual flag, with the white stripes painted black and the stars replaced by the skull and crossbones.

And we do not need the civil commission out there. Having no powers, it has to invent them, and that kind of work cannot be effectively done by just anybody; an expert is required. Mr. Croker can be spared. We do not want the United States represented there, but only the game.

By help of these suggested amendments, progress and civilization in that country can have a boom, and it will take in the persons who are sitting in darkness, and we can resume business at the old stand.

## Corn-Pone Opinions

"Corn-Pone Opinions" was found in Mark Twain's papers after his death. It was first published in 1923 in *Europe and Elsewhere*, edited by Albert Bigelow Paine.

FIFTY YEARS ago, when I was a boy of fifteen and helping to inhabit a Missourian village on the banks of the Mississippi, I had a friend whose society was very dear to me because I was forbidden by my mother to partake of it. He was a gay and impudent and satirical and delightful young black man—a slave—who daily preached sermons from the top of his master's woodpile, with me for sole audience. He imitated the pulpit style of the several clergymen of the village, and did it well, and with fine passion and energy. To me he was a wonder. I believed he was the greatest orator in the United States and would some day be heard from.

But it did not happen; in the distribution of rewards he was over-looked. It is the way, in this world.

He interrupted his preaching, now and then, to saw a stick of wood; but the sawing was a pretense—he did it with his mouth; exactly imitating the sound the bucksaw makes in shrieking its way through the wood. But it served its purpose; it kept his master from coming out to see how the work was getting along. I listened to the sermons from the open window of a lumber room at the back of the house. One of his texts was this:

"You tell me whar a man gits his corn pone, en I'll tell you what his 'pinions is."

I can never forget it. It was deeply impressed upon me. By my mother. Not upon my memory, but elsewhere. She had slipped in upon me while I was absorbed and not watching. The black philosopher's idea was that a man is not independent, and cannot afford views which might interfere with his bread and butter. If he would prosper, he must train with the majority; in matters of large moment, like politics and religion, he must think and feel with the bulk of his neighbors, or suffer damage in his social standing and in his business prosperities. He must restrict himself to corn-pone opinions—at least on the surface. He must get his opinions from other people; he must reason out none for himself; he must have no first-hand views.

I think Jerry was right, in the main, but I think he did not go far enough.

1. It was his idea that a man conforms to the majority view of his locality by calculation and intention.

This happens, but I think it is not the rule.

2. It was his idea that there is such a thing as a first-hand opinion; an original opinion; an opinion which is coldly reasoned out in a man's head, by a searching analysis of the facts involved, with the heart unconsulted, and the jury room closed against out-side influences. It may be that such an opinion has been born some-where, at some time or other, but I suppose it got away before they could catch it and stuff it and put it in the museum.

I am persuaded that a coldly-thought-out and independent verdict upon a fashion in clothes, or manners, or literature, or politics, or religion, or any other matter that is projected into the field of our notice and interest, is a most rare thing—if it has indeed ever existed.

A new thing in costume appears—the flaring hoop skirt, for example—and the passers-by are shocked, and the irreverent laugh. Six months later everybody is reconciled; the fashion has established itself; it is admired, now, and no one laughs. Public opinion resented it before, public opinion accepts it now, and is happy in it. Why? Was the resentment reasoned out? Was the acceptance reasoned out? No. The instinct that moves to conformity did the work. It is our nature to conform; it is a force which not many can successfully resist. What is its seat? The inborn requirement of self-approval. We all have to bow to that; there are no exceptions. Even the woman who refuses from first to last to wear the hoop skirt comes under the law and is its slave; she could not wear the skirt and have her own approval; and that she *must* have, she cannot help herself. But as a rule our self-approval has its source in but one place and not elsewhere—the approval of other people. A person of vast consequences can introduce any kind of novelty in dress and the general world will presently adopt it—moved to do it, in the first place, by the natural instinct to passively yield to that vague something recognized as authority, and in the second place by the human instinct to train with the multitude and have its approval. An empress introduced the hoop skirt, and we know the result. A nobody introduced the bloomer, and we know the result. If Eve should come again, in her ripe renown, and reintroduce her quaint styles—well, we know what would happen. And we should be cruelly embarrassed, along at first.

The hoop skirt runs its course and disappears. Nobody reasons about it. One woman abandons the fashion; her neighbor notices this and follows her lead; this influences the next woman; and so on and so on, and presently the skirt has vanished out of the world, no one knows how nor why; or cares for that matter. It will come again, by and by, and in due course will go again.

Twenty-five years ago, in England, six or eight wine glasses stood grouped by each person's plate at a dinner party, and they were used, not left idle and empty; today there are but three or four in the group, and the average guest sparingly uses about two of them. We have not adopted this new fashion yet, but we shall do it presently. We shall not think it out; we shall merely conform, and let it go at that. We get our notions and habits and opinions from outside influences; we do not have to study them out.

Our table manners, and company manners, and street manners change from time to time, but the changes are not reasoned out; we merely notice and conform. We are creatures of outside influences, as a rule we do not think, we only imitate. We can not invent standards that will stick; what we mistake for standards are only fashions, and perishable. We may continue to admire them, but we drop the use of them. We notice this in literature. Shakespeare is a standard, and fifty years ago we used to write tragedies which we couldn't tell from—from somebody else's; but we don't do it any more, now. Our prose standard, three-quarters of a century ago, was ornate and diffuse; some authority or other changed it in the direction of compactness and simplicity, and conformity followed, without argument. The historical novel starts up suddenly, and sweeps the land. Everybody writes one, and the nation is glad. We had historical novels before; but nobody read them, and the rest of us conformed—without reasoning it out. We are conforming in the other way, now, because it is another case of everybody.

The outside influences are always pouring in upon us, and we are always obeying their orders and accepting their verdicts. The Smiths like the new play; the Joneses go to see it, and they copy the Smith verdict. Morals, religions, politics, get their following from surrounding influences and atmospheres, almost entirely; not from study, not from thinking. A man must and will have his own approval first of all, in each and every moment and circumstance of his life—even if he must repent of a self-approved act the moment after its commission, in order to get his self-approval *again:* but, speaking in general terms, a man's self-approval in the large concerns of life has its source in the approval of the peoples about him, and not in a searching personal examination of the matter. Mohammedans are Mohammedans because they are born and reared among that sect, not because they have thought it out and can furnish sound reasons for being Mohammedans; we know why Catholics are Catholics; why Presbyterians are Presbyterians; why Baptists are Baptists; why Mormons are Mormons; why thieves

are thieves; why monarchists are monarchists; why Republicans
are Republicans and Democrats, Democrats. We know it is a
matter of association and sympathy, not reasoning and examination; that hardly a man in the world has an opinion upon morals,
politics, or religion which he got otherwise than through his associations and sympathies. Broadly speaking, there are none but
corn-pone opinions. And broadly speaking, corn-pone stands for
self-approval. Self-approval is acquired mainly from the approval
of other people. The result is conformity. Sometimes conformity
has a sordid business interest—the bread-and-butter interest—but
not in most cases, I think. I think that in the majority of cases it
is unconscious and not calculated; that it is born of the human
being's natural yearning to stand well with his fellows and have
their inspiring approval and praise—a yearning which is commonly
so strong and so insistent that it cannot be effectually resisted, and
must have its way.

A political emergency brings out the corn-pone opinion in fine
force in its two chief varieties—the pocketbook variety, which has
its origin in self-interest, and the bigger variety, the sentimental
variety—the one which can't bear to be outside the pale; can't
bear to be in disfavor; can't endure the averted face and the cold
shoulder; wants to stand well with his friends, wants to be smiled
upon, wants to be welcome, wants to hear the precious words,
"He's on the right track!" Uttered, perhaps by an ass, but still an
ass of high degree, an ass whose approval is gold and diamonds to
a smaller ass, and confers glory and honor and happiness, and
membership in the herd. For these gauds many a man will dump
his life-long principles into the street, and his conscience along with
them. We have seen it happen. In some millions of instances.

Men think they think upon great political questions, and they
do; but they think with their party, not independently; they read
its literature, but not that of the other side; they arrive at con-
victions, but they are drawn from a partial view of the matter in
hand and are of no particular value. They swarm with their party,
they feel with their party, they are happy in their party's approval;
and where the party leads they will follow, whether for right and
honor, or through blood and dirt and a mush of mutilated morals.

In our late canvass half of the nation passionately believed that

in silver lay salvation, the other half as passionately believed that
that way lay destruction. Do you believe that a tenth part of the
people, on either side, had any rational excuse for having an
opinion about the matter at all? I studied that mighty question to
the bottom—came out empty. Half of our people passionately believe in high tariff, the other half believe otherwise. Does this mean
study and examination, or only feeling? The latter, I think. I
have deeply studied that question, too—and didn't arrive. We all
do no end of feeling, and we mistake it for thinking. And out of
it we get an aggregation which we consider a boon. Its name is
public opinion. It is held in reverence. It settles everything. Some
think it the voice of God.

## My First Lie, and How I Got Out of It

I never could tell a lie that anybody would doubt, nor a truth that anybody would believe.—MARK TWAIN, *Following the Equator*

Mark Twain's accounts of his own lying were—as he said of the
newspaper reports of his death in 1897—"greatly exaggerated." According to William Dean Howells, as quoted by Albert Bigelow Paine in
*Mark Twain's Notebook:*

He was the most truthful man, when it was a question of fact, I have
ever known, particularly when it was a relation of some discreditable oc-
currence in which he had been concerned. I remember once at dinner,
when the conversation turned to the subject of jails . . . he said:
   "I passed a night in jail once."
   Clara, who was present, was shocked.
   "Why, Father," she said, "how in the world did you come to be in
jail?"
   . . . Most of us would have qualified, palliated, let ourselves down
easy. Nothing of the sort; he looked mildly at Clara, and replied:
   "Drunk, I guess."

"My First Lie" appeared in 1899 as the Christmas feature of the
New York Sunday *World*. The first discussions of it came eleven years
later in *Revue du Mois,* where Régis Michaud quoted and commented:

Mark Twain can pardon every lie but one: "The silent colossal national
lie that is the support and confederate of all the tyrannies and shams and

inequalities and unfairnesses that afflict the peoples—that is the one to throw bricks and sermons at." When he is moved on this subject, one feels, under Twain's humor, as under Swift's, black rage.

Ten years later the same passage was quoted by an equally distinguished American critic. But times had changed. Van Wyck Brooks, in *The Ordeal of Mark Twain,* did not share M. Michaud's view that Mark Twain "like Rabelais and Cervantes . . . has more than once given the epic form to satire." Nor did he believe that "His sense of justice is even more alive than his patriotism; he has brought some hard truths home to his compatriots." And he noticed what Michaud had either not noticed or had not taken seriously: that after his advice to throw bricks and sermons at national lies, Mark Twain had added this sentence: "But let us be judicious and let somebody else begin."

Perhaps Brooks did not notice that some pages back Mark Twain himself had begun and was still warming up. At any rate, the chapter on Clemens' failure as a satirist in Brooks' *The Ordeal of Mark Twain,* first published in 1920, still bears a title taken from this selection: "Let Somebody Else Begin."

This selection has another curiosity value: the observation that "Mr. Chamberlain was trying to manufacture a war in South Africa and was willing to pay fancy prices for the materials." This was written—although not published—before October 12, 1899, when the Boer War began and a few months before Mark Twain took a private vow not to take sides on it in public. His position was based on the fact that England's traditional rival, Germany, was backing the Boers. Mark Twain was not alone in his response to this situation; a most important factor in rallying British feeling behind the war was a widely publicized telegram of sympathy which Boer President Paul Kruger received from the Kaiser in 1896. But Mark Twain's special view was most memorably expressed in a letter to Howells, which also contains some prime Mark Twain on the well-known race. From London, January 25, 1900:

Privately speaking, this is a sordid & criminal war, & in every way shameful and excuseless. Every day I write (in my head) bitter magazine articles about it, but I have to stop with that. For England must not fall: it would mean an inundation of Russian & German political degradations which would envelop the globe & steep it in a sort of Middle-Age night and slavery. . . . Even wrong—& she is wrong—England must be upheld. He is an enemy of the human race who shall speak against her now. Why *was* the human race created? Or at least why wasn't something creditable created in place of it. God had His opportunity; He could have made a reputation. But no, He must commit this grotesque folly—a lark which must have cost him a regret or two when He came to think it over & observe effects. For a giddy & unbecoming caprice there has been nothing like it till this war. I talk the war with both sides. . . . I say "My head is with the Briton, but my heart & such rags of morals as I have are with the Boer. . . ." And so we discuss, & have no trouble.*

But of course Clemens had terrible trouble about the Boer War. He broke his vow just once; in "To the Person Sitting in Darkness" he spoke his heart.

Here is "My First Lie, and How I Got Out of It":

As I UNDERSTAND it, what you desire is information about "my first lie, and how I got out of it." I was born in 1835; I am well along, and my memory is not as good as it was. If you had asked about my first truth it would have been easier for me and kinder of you, for I remember that fairly well. I remember it as if it were last week. The family think it was week before, but that is flattery and probably has a selfish project back of it. When a person has become seasoned by experience and has reached the age of sixty-four, which is the age of discretion, he likes a family compliment as well as ever, but he does not lose his head over it as in the old innocent days.

I do not remember my first lie, it is too far back; but I remember my second one very well. I was nine days old at the time, and had noticed that if a pin was sticking in me and I advertised it in the usual fashion, I was lovingly petted and coddled and pitied in a most agreeable way and got a ration between meals besides.

It was human nature to want to get these riches, and I fell. I lied about the pin—advertising one when there wasn't any. You would have done it; George Washington did it, anybody would have done it. During the first half of my life I never knew a child that was able to raise above that temptation and keep from telling that lie. Up to 1867 all the civilized children that were ever born into the world were liars—including George. Then the safety pin came in and blocked the game. But is that reform worth anything? No; for it is reform by force and has no virtue in it; it merely stops that form of lying, it doesn't impair the disposition to lie, by a shade. It is the cradle application of conversion by fire and sword, or of the temperance principle through prohibition.

To return to that early lie. They found no pin and they realized

* *Mark Twain-Howells Letters,* Harry N. Smith and William M. Gibson, editors (Cambridge, Harvard University Press, 1960), Vol. II, pp. 715-716.

that another liar had been added to the world's supply. For by grace
of a rare inspiration a quite commonplace but seldom noticed
fact was borne in upon their understandings—that almost all lies
are acts, and speech has no part in them. Then, if they examined
a little further they recognized that all people are liars from the
cradle onward, without exception, and that they begin to lie as soon
as they wake in the morning, and keep it up without rest or refreshment until they go to sleep at night. If they arrived at that truth
it probably grieved them—*did,* if they had been heedlessly and
ignorantly educated by their books and teachers; for why should
a person grieve over a thing which by the eternal law of his make
he cannot help? He didn't invent the law; it is merely his business
to obey it and keep still; join the universal conspiracy and keep
so still that he shall deceive his fellow-conspirators into imagining
that he doesn't know that the law exists. It is what we all do—we
that know. I am speaking of *the lie of silent assertion;* we can tell
it without saying a word, and we all do it—we that know. In the
magnitude of its territorial spread it is one of the most majestic lies
that the civilizations make it their sacred and anxious care to guard
and watch and propagate.

For instance. It would not be possible for a humane and
intelligent person to invent a rational excuse for slavery; yet you
will remember that in the early days of the emancipation agitation
in the North the agitators got but small help or countenance from
anyone. Argue and plead and pray as they might, they could not
break the universal stillness that reigned, from pulpit and press all
the way down to the bottom of society—the clammy stillness
created and maintained by the lie of silent assertion—the silent
assertion that there wasn't anything going on in which humane
and intelligent people were interested.

From the beginning of the Dreyfus case to the end of it, all
France, except a couple of dozen moral paladins, lay under the
smother of the silent-assertion lie that no wrong was being done to
a persecuted and unoffending man.[9] The like smother was over
England lately, a good half of the population silently letting on
that they were not aware that Mr. Chamberlain was trying to
manufacture a war in South Africa and was willing to pay fancy
prices for the materials.

Now there we have instances of three prominent ostensible civilizations working the silent-assertion lie. Could one find other instances in the three countries? I think so. Not so very many perhaps, but say a billion—just so as to keep within bounds. Are those countries working that kind of lie, day in and day out, in thousands and thousands of varieties, without ever resting? Yes, we know that to be true. The universal conspiracy of the silent-assertion lie is hard at work always and everywhere, and always in the interest of a stupidity or a sham, never in the interest of a thing fine or respectable. Is it the most timid and shabby of all lies? It seems to have the look of it. For ages and ages it has mutely labored in the interest of despotisms and aristocracies and chattel slaveries, and military slaveries, and religious slaveries, and has kept them alive; keeps them alive yet, here and there and yonder, all about the globe; and will go on keeping them alive until the silent-assertion lie retires from business—the silent assertion that nothing is going on which fair and intelligent men are aware of and are engaged by their duty to try to stop.

What I am arriving at is this: When whole races and peoples conspire to propagate gigantic mute lies in the interest of tyrannies and shams, why should we care anything about the trifling lies told by individuals? Why should we try to make it appear that abstention from lying is a virtue? Why should we want to beguile ourselves in that way? Why should we without shame help the nation lie, and then be ashamed to do a little lying on our own account? Why shouldn't we be honest and honorable, and lie every time we get a chance? That is to say, why shouldn't we be consistent, and either lie all the time or not at all? Why should we help the nation lie the whole day long and then object to telling one little individual private lie in our own interest to go to bed on? Just for the refreshment of it, I mean, and to take the rancid taste out of our mouth.

Here in England they have the oddest ways. They won't tell a *spoken* lie—nothing can persuade them. Except in a large moral interest, like politics or religion, I mean. To tell a spoken lie to get even the poorest little personal advantage out of it is a thing which is impossible to them. They make me ashamed of myself sometimes, they are so bigoted. They will not even tell a lie for the fun of it; they will not tell it when it hasn't even a suggestion of damage or advantage in it for anyone. This has a restraining influence upon me in spite of reason, and I am always going out of practice.

Of course, they tell all sorts of little unspoken lies, just like anybody; but they don't notice it until their attention is called to it. They have got me so that sometimes I never tell a verbal lie now except in a modified form; and even in the modified form they don't approve of it. Still, that is as far as I can go in the interest of the growing friendly relations between the two countries; I must keep some of my self-respect—and my health. I can live on a pretty low diet, but I can't get along on no sustenance at all.

Of course, there are times when these people have to come out with a spoken lie, for that is a thing which happens to everybody once in a while, and would happen to the angels if they came down here much. Particularly to the angels, in fact, for the lies I speak of are self-sacrificing ones told for a generous object, not a mean one; but even when these people tell a lie of that sort it seems to scare them and unsettle their minds. It is a wonderful thing to see, and shows that they are all insane. In fact, it is a country which is full of the most interesting superstitions.

I have an English friend of twenty-five years' standing, and yesterday when we were coming downtown on top of the bus I happened to tell him a lie—a modified one, of course; a half-breed, a mulatto; I can't seem to tell any other kind now, the market is so flat. I was explaining to him how I got out of an embarrassment in Austria last year. I do not know what might have become of me if I hadn't happened to remember to tell the police that I belonged to the same family as the Prince of Wales. That made everything pleasant and they let me go; and apologized too, and were ever so kind and obliging and polite, and couldn't do too much for me, and explained how the mistake came to be made, and promised to hang the officer that did it, and hoped I would let bygones be bygones and not say anything about it; and I said they could depend on me. My friend said austerely:

"You call it a modified lie? Where is the modification?"

I explained that it lay in the form of my statement to the police.

"I didn't say I belonged to the royal family; I only said I belonged to the same family as the prince—meaning the human family, of course; and if those people had had any penetration they would have known it. I can't go around furnishing brains to the police; it is not to be expected."

"How did you feel after that performance?"

"Well, of course I was distressed to find that the police had misunderstood me, but as long as I had not told any lie I knew there was no occasion to sit up nights and worry about it."

My friend struggled with the case several minutes turning it over and examining it in his mind, then he said that so far as he could see the modification was itself a lie, it being a misleading reservation of an explanatory fact, and so I had told two lies instead of only one.

"I wouldn't have done it," said he; "I have never told a lie and I should be very sorry to do such a thing."

Just then he lifted his hat and smiled a basketful of surprised and delighted smiles down at a gentleman who was passing in a hansom.

"Who was that, G——?"

"I don't know."

"Then why did you do that?"

"Because I saw he thought he knew me and was expecting it of me. If I hadn't done it he would have been hurt. I didn't want to embarrass him before the whole street."

"Well, your heart was right, G——, and your act was right. What you did was kindly and courteous and beautiful; I would have done it myself; but it was a lie."

"A lie? I didn't say a word. How do you make it out?"

"I know you didn't speak, still you said to him very plainly and enthusiastically in dumb show, 'Hello! *you* in town? Awful glad to see you, old fellow; when did you get back?' Concealed in your actions was what you have called 'a misleading reservation of an explanatory fact'—the fact that you had never seen him before. You expressed joy in encountering him—a lie; and you made that reservation—another lie. It was my pair over again. But don't be troubled—we all do it."

Two hours later, at dinner, when quite other matters were being discussed, he told how he happened along once just in the nick of time to do a great service for a family who were old friends of his.

The head of it had suddenly died in circumstances and surroundings of a ruinously disgraceful character. If known the facts would break the hearts of the innocent family and put upon them a load of unendurable shame. There was no help but in a giant lie, and he girded up his loins and told it.

"The family never found out, G——?"

"Never. In all these years they have never suspected. They were proud of him and had always had reason to be; they are proud of him yet, and to them his memory is sacred and stainless and beautiful."

"They had a narrow escape, G——."

"Indeed they had."

"For the very next man that came along might have been one of these heartless and shameless truth-mongers. You have told the truth a million times in your life, G——, but that one golden lie atones for it all. Persevere."

Some may think me not strict enough in my morals, but that position is hardly tenable. There are many kinds of lying which I do not approve. I do not like an injurious lie, except when it injures somebody else; and I do not like the lie of bravado, nor the lie of virtuous ecstasy; the latter was affected by Byrant, the former by Carlyle.

Mr. Bryant said, "Truth crushed to earth will rise again." [10] I have taken medals at thirteen world's fairs, and may claim to be not without capacity, but I never told as big a one as that. Mr. Bryant was playing to the gallery; we all do it. Carlyle said, in substance, this—I do not remember the exact words: "This gospel is eternal—that a lie shall not live." [11] I have a reverent affection for Carlyle's books, and have read his *Revolution* eight times;[12] and so I prefer to think he was not entirely at himself when he told that one. To me it is plain that he said it in a moment of excitement, when chasing Americans out of his back yard with brickbats. They used to go there and worship. At bottom he was probably fond of them, but he was always able to conceal it. He kept bricks for them, but he was not a good shot, and it is matter of history that when he fired they dodged, and carried off the brick; for as a nation we like relics, and so long as we get them we do not much care what the reliquary thinks about it. I am quite sure that when he told the large one about a lie not being able to live he had just missed an American and was overexcited. He told it about thirty years ago, but it is alive yet; alive, and very healthy and hearty, and likely to outlive any fact in history. Carlyle was truthful when calm, but give him Americans enough and bricks enough and he could have taken medals himself.

As regards that time that George Washington told the truth, a word must be said, of course. It is the principal jewel in the crown of America, and it is but natural that we should work it for all it is worth, as Milton says in his "Lay of the Last Minstrel." It was a timely and judicious truth, and I should have told it myself in the circumstances. But I should have stopped there. It was a stately truth, a lofty truth—a tower; and I think it was a mistake to go on and distract attention from its sublimity by building another tower alongside of it fourteen times as high. I refer to his remark that he "could not lie." I should have fed that to the marines; or left it to Carlyle; it is just in his style. It would have taken a medal at any European fair, and would have got an honorable mention even at Chicago if it had been saved up. But let it pass; the Father of his Country was excited. I have been in those circumstances, and I recollect.

With the truth he told I have no objection to offer, as already indicated. I think it was not premeditated but an inspiration. With his fine military mind, he had probably arranged to let his brother Edward in for the cherry tree results, but by an inspiration he saw his opportunity in time and took advantage of it. By telling the truth he could astonish his father; his father would tell the neighbors; the neighbors would spread it; it would travel to all firesides; in the end it would make him President, and not only that, but First President. He was a far-seeing boy and would be likely to think of these things. Therefore, to my mind, he stands justified for what he did. But not for the other tower; it was a mistake. Still, I don't know about that; upon reflection I think perhaps it wasn't. For indeed it is that tower that makes the other one live. If he hadn't said "I cannot tell a lie" there would have been no convulsion. That was the earthquake that rocked the planet. That is the kind of statement that lives forever, and a fact barnacled to it has a good chance to share its immortality.

To sum up, on the whole I am satisfied with things the way they are. There is a prejudice against the spoken lie, but none against any other, and by examination and mathematical computation I find that the proportion of the spoken lie to the other varieties is as 1 to 22,894. Therefore the spoken lie is of no consequence, and it is not worth while to go around fussing about it and trying to make believe that it is an important matter. The silent colossal national lie that is the support and confederate of all the tyrannies and shams and inequalities and unfairnesses that afflict the peoples— that is the one to throw bricks and sermons at. But let us be judicious and let somebody else begin.

And then—— But I have wandered from my text. How did I get out of my second lie? I think I got out with honor, but I cannot be sure, for it was a long time ago and some of the details have faded out of my memory. I recollect that I reversed and stretched across someone's knee, and that something happened, but I cannot now remember what it was. I think there was music; but it is all dim now and blurred by the lapse of time, and this may be only a senile fancy.

# About Smells

"About Smells" belongs to Mark Twain's brief career as a humor editor—a bleak period for him. He went to work for an ambitious new publication, *The Galaxy*, with misgivings; the first appearance of his department "Memoranda" in May, 1870, carried this announcement:

I would not conduct an exclusively and professedly humorous department for any one. I would always prefer to have the privilege of printing a serious and sensible remark, in case one occurred to me, without the reader's feeling obliged to consider himself outraged. . . .

His resignation appeared in April, 1871:

I have now written for *The Galaxy* a year. For the last eight months, with hardly an interval, I have had for my fellows and comrades, night and day, doctors and watchers of the sick! During these eight months death has taken two members of my home circle and malignantly threatened two others. All this I have experienced, yet all the time have been under contract to furnish "humorous" matter, once a month, for this magazine. . . . Please to put yourself in my place and contemplate the grisly grotesqueness of the situation. I think that some of the "humor" I have written during this period could have been injected into a funeral sermon without disturbing the solemnity of the occasion.

. . . To be a pirate on a low salary, with no share in the profits of the business, used to be my idea of an uncomfortable occupation, but I have other views now. To be a monthly humorist in a cheerless time is drearier.

Just before he resigned—when his department did not appear in an issue—the Chicago *Tribune* said *The Galaxy* had made a mistake in depending so heavily on Mark Twain's reputation: "It is simply impossible for a man to be funny all the time and Mark Twain has no aspirations or abilities in any other direction." [13]

In the eight months Mark Twain mentioned, his father-in-law, Jervis Langdon, had died with the Clemenses as deathbed nurses; a friend, Emma Nye, had died in their home, and Mrs. Clemens, critically ill, had been delivered of a premature child. Some of Mark Twain's humor was as he described; some was not. The May issue included "Disgraceful Persecution of a Boy," and the remarks below on a popular clergyman.

The sins of the fashionable clergy were a favorite theme in "Memoranda." When the Reverend Mr. Sabine declined to bury an actor, that department called attention to "this diseased, this cancerous piety" but gave the pulpit credit:

I am aware that in its honest and well-meaning way it bores the people with uninflammable truisms about doing good; bores them with correct compositions on charity; bores them, chloroforms them, stupefies them with argumentative mercy. . . . And in doing these things the pulpit is doing its duty, and let us believe that it is likewise doing its best . . . but when a pulpit takes to itself authority to pass judgment upon the work and worth of just as legitimate an instrument of God as itself . . . it is fair and just that somebody who believes that actors were made for a high and good purpose . . . should protest.

All sermons on the clergy delivered by *The Galaxy*'s humor editor were heavily illustrated with biblical text and history. Since Bunyan, nobody in English letters has known or loved the Bible better than Mark Twain.

Here is "About Smells":

IN A RECENT issue of the *Independent,* the Rev. T. De Witt Talmage, of Brooklyn, has the following utterance on the subject of "Smells":

I have a good Christian friend who, if he sat in the front pew in church, and a working man should enter the door at the other end, would smell him instantly. My friend is not to blame for the sensitiveness of his nose, any more than you would flog a pointer for being keener on the scent than a stupid watchdog. The fact is, if you had all the churches free, by reason of the mixing up of the common people with the uncommon, you would keep one half of Christendom sick at their stomach. If you are going to kill the church thus with bad smells, I will have nothing to do with this work of evangelization.

We have reason to believe that there will be laboring men in heaven; and also a number of Negroes, and Eskimos, and Terra del Fuegans, and Arabs, and a few Indians, and possibly even some Spaniards and Portuguese. All things are possible with God. We shall have all these sorts of people in heaven; but alas! in getting them we shall lose the society of Dr. Talmage. Which is to say, we shall lose the company of one who could give more real "tone" to celestial society than any other contribution Brooklyn could furnish. And what would eternal happiness be without the Doctor? Blissful, unquestionably—we know that well enough— but would it be *distingué,* would it be *recherché* without him? St. Matthew without stockings or sandals; St. Jerome bareheaded, and with a coarse brown blanket robe dragging the ground; St. Sebastian with scarcely any raiment at all—these we should see, and should enjoy seeing them; but would we not miss a spike-tailed coat and kids, and turn away regretfully, and say to parties from the Orient: "These are well enough, but you ought to see Talmage of Brooklyn." I fear me that in the better world we shall not even have Dr. Talmage's "good Christian friend." For if he were sitting under the glory of the Throne, and the keeper of the keys admitted a Benjamin Franklin or other laboring man, that "friend," with his fine natural powers infinitely augmented by emancipation from hampering flesh, would detect him with a single sniff, and immediately take his hat and ask to be excused.

To all outward seeming, the Rev. T. De Witt Talmage is of the same material as that used in the construction of his early predecessors in the ministry; and yet one feels that there must be a difference somewhere between him and the Saviour's first disciples. It may be because here, in the nineteenth century, Dr. T. has had advantages which Paul and Peter and the others could not and

did not have. There was a lack of polish about them, and a loose-
ness of etiquette, and a want of exclusiveness, which one cannot
help noticing. They healed the very beggars, and held intercourse
with people of a villainous odor every day. If the subject of these
remarks had been among the original Twelve Apostles, he would
not have associated with the rest, because he could not have stood
the fishy smell of some of his comrades who came from around
the Sea of Galilee. He would have resigned his commission with
some such remarks as he makes in the extract quoted above:
"Master, if thou art going to kill the church thus with bad smells,
I will have nothing to do with this work of evangelization." He
is a disciple, and makes that remark to the Master; the only difference is, that he makes it in the nineteenth instead of the first
century.

Is there a choir in Mr. T.'s church? And does it ever occur that
they have no better manners than to sing that hymn which is so
suggestive of laborers and mechanics:

> Son of the Carpenter! receive
> This humble work of mine?

Now, can it be possible that in a handful of centuries the Christian character has fallen away from an imposing heroism that
scorned even the stake, the cross, and the axe, to a poor little
effeminacy that withers and wilts under an unsavory smell? We
are not prepared to believe so, the reverend Doctor and his friend
to the contrary notwithstanding.

## As Regards Patriotism

In the beginning of a change, the patriot is a scarce man, and brave, and
hated and scorned. When his cause succeeds, the timid join him, for then
it costs nothing to be a patriot.—*Mark Twain's Notebook,* 1905

"As Regards Patriotism" was written in the early 1900's; it first
appeared in 1923 in *Europe and Elsewhere.*

IT IS AGREED, in this country, that if a man can arrange his religion so that it perfectly satisfies his conscience, it is not incumbent upon him to care whether the arrangement is satisfactory to anyone else or not.

In Austria and some other countries this is not the case. There the state arranges a man's religion for him, he has no voice in it himself.

Patriotism is merely a religion—love of country, worship of country, devotion to the country's flag and honor and welfare.

In absolute monarchies it is furnished from the throne, cut and dried, to the subject; in England and America it is furnished, cut and dried, to the citizen by the politician and the newspaper.

The newspaper-and-politician-manufactured patriot often gags in private over his dose; but he takes it, and keeps it on his stomach the best he can. Blessed are the meek.

Sometimes, in the beginning of an insane shabby political upheaval, he is strongly moved to revolt, but he doesn't do it—he knows better. He knows that his maker would find out—the maker of his patriotism, the windy and incoherent six-dollar subeditor of his village newspaper—and would bray out in print and call him a traitor. And how dreadful that would be. It makes him tuck his tail between his legs and shiver. We all know—the reader knows it quite well—that two or three years ago[14] nine-tenths of the human tails in England and America performed just that act. Which is to say, nine-tenths of the patriots in England and America turned traitor to keep from being called traitor. Isn't it true? You know it to be true. Isn't it curious?

Yet it was not a thing to be very seriously ashamed of. A man can seldom—very, very seldom—fight a winning fight against his training; the odds are too heavy. For many a year—perhaps always—the training of the two nations had been dead against independence in political thought, persistently inhospitable toward patriotism manufactured on a man's own premises, patriotism reasoned out in the man's own head and fire-assayed and tested and proved in his own conscience. The resulting patriotism was a shopworn product procured at second hand. The patriot did not know just how or when or where he got his opinions, neither did he care, so long as he was with what seemed the majority—which was the main thing, the safe thing, the comfortable thing. Does the reader believe he knows three men who have actual reasons for their pattern of patriotism—and can furnish them? Let him not examine, unless he wants to be disappointed. He will be likely to find that his men got their patriotism at the public trough, and had no hand in its preparation themselves.

Training does wonderful things. It moved the people of this country to oppose the Mexican War; then moved them to fall in with what they supposed was the opinion of the majority—majority patriotism is the customary patriotism—and go down there and fight. Before the Civil War it made the North indifferent to slavery and friendly to the slave interest; in that interest it made Massachusetts hostile to the American flag, and she would not allow it to be hoisted on her State house—in her eyes it was the flag of a faction. Then by and by, training swung Massachusetts the other way, and she went raging South to fight under that very flag and against that aforetime protected interest of hers.

There is nothing that training cannot do. Nothing is above its reach or below it. It can turn bad morals to good, good morals to bad; it can destroy principles, it can recreate them; it can debase angels to men and lift men to angelship. And it can do any one of these miracles in a year—even in six months.

Then men can be trained to manufacture their own patriotism. They can be trained to labor it out in their own heads and hearts and in the privacy and independence of their own premises. It can train them to stop taking it by command, as the Austrian takes his religion.

## Bible Teaching and Religious Practice

"Huck Finn, do you mean to tell me you don't know what a crusade is?"
"No," I says, "I don't. . . ."
"A crusade is a war to recover the Holy Land from the paynim."
"Which Holy Land?"
"Why, *the* Holy Land—there ain't but one."
"What do *we* want of it?"

"Why, can't you understand? It's in the hands of the paynim, and it's our duty to take it away from them."

"How did we come to let them git hold of it?"

"We didn't come to let them git hold of it. They always had it."

"Why, Tom, then it must belong to them, don't it?"

"Why, of course it does. Who said it didn't?"

I studied over it, but couldn't seem to git at the right of it, no way. I says:

"It's too many for me, Tom Sawyer. If I had a farm and it was mine, and another person wanted it, would it be right for him to—"

"Oh shucks! you don't know enough to come in when it rains, Huck Finn. It ain't a farm, it's entirely different. You see, it's like this. They own the land, just the mere land, and that's all they *do* own; but it was our folks, our Jews and Christians, that made it holy, and so they haven't any business to be there defiling it. . . . We ought to march against them and take it away from them."

"Why, it does seem to me it's the most mixed-up thing I ever see! Now, if I had a farm and another person—"

"Didn't I tell you it hasn't got anything to do with farming? Farming is business, just common low-down business; that's all it is, it's all you can say for it; but this is higher, this is religious. . . ."

"Religious to go and take the land away from people that owns it?"

"Certainly; it's always been considered so."

Jim he shook his head, and says:

"Mars Tom, I reckon deys a mistake about it somers—dey mos' sholy is. I's religious myself, en I knows plenty religious people, but I hain't run across none dat acts like dat."—MARK TWAIN, *Tom Sawyer Abroad*

"Bible Teaching and Religious Practice" first appeared in 1923 in *Europe and Elsewhere*.

RELIGION had its share in the changes of civilization and national character, of course. What share? The lion's. In the history of the human race this has always been the case, will always be the case, to the end of time, no doubt; or at least until man by the slow processes of evolution shall develop into something really fine and high—some billions of years hence, say.

The Christian's Bible is a drugstore. Its contents remain the same; but the medical practice changes. For eighteen hundred years these changes were slight—scarcely noticeable. The practice was allopathic—allopathic in its rudest and crudest form. The dull and ignorant physician day and night, and all the days and all the nights, drenched his patient with vast and hideous doses of the most repulsive drugs to be found in the store's stock; he bled him, cupped him, purged him, puked him, salivated him, never gave his system a chance to rally, nor nature a chance to help. He kept him religion-sick for eighteen centuries, and allowed him not a well day during all that time. The stock in the store was made up of about equal portions of baleful and debilitating poisons, and healing and comforting medicines; but the practice of the time confined the physician to the use of the former; by consequence, he could only damage his patient, and that is what he did.

Not until far within our century was any considerable change in the practice introduced; and then mainly, or in effect only, in Great Britain and the United States. In the other countries today, the patient either still takes the ancient treatment or does not call the physician at all. In the English-speaking countries the changes observable in our century were forced by that very thing just referred to—the revolt of the patient against the system; they were not projected by the physician. The patient fell to doctoring himself, and the physician's practice began to fall off. He modified his method to get back his trade. He did it gradually, reluctantly; and never yielded more at a time than the pressure compelled. At first he relinquished the daily dose of hell and damnation, and administered it every other day only; next he allowed another day to pass; then another and presently another; when he had restricted it at last to Sundays, and imagined that now there would surely be a truce, the homeopath arrived on the field and made him abandon hell and damnation altogether, and administered Christ's love, and comfort, and charity and compassion in its stead. These had been in the drugstore all the time, gold labeled and conspicuous among the long shelfloads of repulsive purges and vomits and poisons, and so the practice was to blame that they had remained unused, not the pharmacy. To the ecclesiastical physician of fifty years ago, his predecessor for eighteen centuries was a quack; to the ecclesiastical physician of today, his predecessor of fifty years ago was a quack. To the every-man-his-own-ecclesiastical-doctor of—when?—what will the ecclesiastical physician of today be? Unless evolution, which has been a truth ever since the globes, suns, and planets of the solar system were but wandering films of meteor dust, shall reach a limit and become a lie, there is but one fate in store for him.

The methods of the priest and the parson have been very curious, their history is very entertaining. In all the ages the Roman Church has owned slaves, bought and sold slaves, authorized and encouraged her children to trade in them. Long after some Christian peoples had freed their slaves the Church still held on to hers. If any could know, to absolute certainty, that all this was right, and according to God's will and desire, surely it was she, since she was God's specially appointed representative in the earth and sole authorized and infallible expounder of his Bible. There were the texts; there was no mistaking their meaning; she was right, she was doing in this thing what the Bible had mapped out for her to do. So unassailable was her position that in all the centuries she had no word to say against human slavery. Yet now at last, in our immediate day, we hear a Pope saying slave trading is wrong, and we see him sending an expedition to Africa to stop it. The texts remain: it is the practice that has changed. Why? Because the world has corrected the Bible. The Church never corrects it; and also never fails to drop in at the tail of the procession—and take the credit of the correction. As she will presently do in this instance.

Christian England supported slavery and encouraged it for two hundred and fifty years, and her Church's consecrated ministers looked on, sometimes taking an active hand, the rest of the time indifferent. England's interest in the business may be called a Christian interest, a Christian industry. She had her full share in its revival after a long period of inactivity, and this revival was a Christian monopoly; that is to say, it was in the hands of Christian countries exclusively. English parliaments aided the slave traffic and protected it; two English kings held stock in slave-catching companies. The first regular English slave hunter—John Hawkins, of still revered memory—made such successful havoc on his second voyage, in the matter of surprising and burning villages, and maiming, slaughtering, capturing, and selling their unoffending inhabitants, that his delighted queen conferred the chivalric honor of knighthood on him—a rank which had acquired its chief esteem and distinction in other and earlier fields of Christian effort.

The new knight, with characteristic English frankness and brusque simplicity, chose as his device the figure of a Negro slave, kneeling and in chains. Sir John's work was the invention of Christians, was to remain a bloody and awful monopoly in the hands of Christians for a quarter of a millennium, was to destroy homes, separate families, enslave friendless men and women, and break a myriad of human hearts, to the end that Christian nations might be prosperous and comfortable, Christian churches be built, and the gospel of the meek and merciful Redeemer be spread abroad in the earth; and so in the name of his ship, unsuspected but eloquent and clear, lay hidden prophecy. She was called *The Jesus*.

But at last in England, an illegitimate Christian rose against slavery. It is curious that when a Christian rises against a rooted wrong at all, he is usually an illegitimate Christian, member of some despised and bastard sect. There was a bitter struggle, but in the end the slave trade had to go—and went. The Biblical authorization remained, but the practice changed.

Then—the usual thing happened; the visiting English critic among us began straightway to hold up his pious hands in horror at our slavery. His distress was unappeasable, his words full of bitterness and contempt. It is true we had not so many as fifteen hundred thousand slaves for him to worry about, while his England still owned twelve millions, in her foreign possessions; but that fact did not modify his wail any, or stay his tears, or soften his censure. The fact that every time we had tried to get rid of our slavery in previous generations, but had always been obstructed, balked, and defeated by England, was a matter of no consequence to him; it was ancient history, and not worth the telling.

Our own conversion came at last. We began to stir against slavery. Hearts grew soft, here, there, and yonder. There was no place in the land where the seeker could not find some small budding sign of pity for the slave. No place in all the land but one —the pulpit. It yielded at last; it always does. It fought a strong and stubborn fight, and then did what it always does, joined the procession—at the tail end. Slavery fell. The slavery text remained; the practice changed, that was all.

During many ages there were witches. The Bible said so. The Bible commanded that they should not be allowed to live. Therefore the Church, after doing its duty in but a lazy and indolent way for eight hundred years, gathered up its halters, thumbscrews, and firebrands, and set about its holy work in earnest. She worked hard at it night and day during nine centuries and imprisoned, tortured, hanged, and burned whole hordes and armies of witches, and washed the Christian world clean with their foul blood.

Then it was discovered that there was no such thing as witches, and never had been. One does not know whether to laugh or to cry. Who discovered that there was no such thing as a witch—the priest, the parson? No, these never discover anything. At Salem, the parson clung pathetically to his witch text after the laity had abandoned it in remorse and tears for the crimes and cruelties it had persuaded them to do. The parson wanted more blood, more shame, more brutalities; it was the unconsecrated laity that stayed his hand. In Scotland the parson killed the witch after the magistrate had pronounced her innocent; and when the merciful legislature proposed to sweep the hideous laws against witches from the statute book, it was the parson who came imploring, with tears and imprecations, that they be suffered to stand.

There are no witches. The witch text remains; only the practice has changed. Hell-fire is gone, but the text remains. Infant damnation is gone, but the text remains. More than two hundred death penalties are gone from the law books, but the texts that authorized them remain.

Is it not well worthy of note that of all the multitude of texts through which man has driven his annihilating pen he has never once made the mistake of obliterating a good and useful one? It does certainly seem to suggest that if man continues in the direction of enlightenment, his religious practice may, in the end, attain some semblance of human decency.

## Dr. Loeb's Incredible Discovery

"Dr. Loeb's Incredible Discovery," which follows, first appeared in 1923 in *Europe and Elsewhere*.

Experts in biology will be apt to receive with some skepticism the announcement of Dr. Jacques Loeb of the University of California as to the creation of life by chemical agencies. . . . Doctor Loeb is a very bright and ingenious experimenter, but *a consensus of opinion among biologists* would show that he is voted rather as a man of lively imagination than an inerrant investigator of natural phenomena.—*New York Times,* March 2d, [1905].

I wish I could be as young as that again. Although I seem so old, now, I was once as young as that. I remember, as if it were but thirty or forty years ago, how a paralyzing consensus of opinion accumulated from experts a-setting around, about brother experts who had patiently and laboriously cold-chiseled their way into one or another of nature's safe-deposit vaults and were reporting that they had found something valuable was a plenty for me. It settled it.

But it isn't so now—no. Because, in the drift of the years, I by and by found out that a consensus examines a new thing with its feelings rather oftener than with its mind. You know, yourself, that this is so. Do those people examine with feelings that are friendly to evidence? You know they don't. It is the other way about. They do the examining by the light of their prejudices— now isn't that true?

With curious results, yes. So curious that you wonder the consensuses do not go out of the business. Do you know of a case where a consensus won a game? You can go back as far as you want to and you will find history furnishing you this (until now) unwritten maxim for your guidance and profit: Whatever new thing a consensus coppers (colloquial for "bets against"), bet your money on that very card and do not be afraid.

There was that primitive steam engine—ages back, in Greek times: a consensus made fun of it. There was the Marquis of Worcester's steam engine, 250 years ago: a consensus made fun of it. There was Fulton's steamboat of a century ago: a French consensus, including the Great Napoleon, made fun of it. There was Priestley, with his oxygen: a consensus scoffed at him, mobbed him, burned him out, banished him. While a consensus was proving, by statistics and things, that a steamship could not cross the Atlantic, a steamship did it. A consensus consisting of all the

medical experts in Great Britain made fun of Jenner and inocula-
tion. A consensus consisting of all the medical experts in France
made fun of the stethoscope. A consensus of all the medical experts in Germany made fun of that young doctor (his name?
forgotten by all but doctors, now, revered now by doctors alone) [15]
who discovered and abolished the cause of that awful disease,
puerperal fever; made fun of him, reviled him, hunted him, persecuted him, broke his heart, killed him. Electric telegraph, Atlantic cable, telephone, all "toys," and of no practical value—verdict of the consensuses. Geology, paleontology, evolution—all
brushed into space by a consensus of theological experts, comprising all the teachers in Christendom, assisted by the Duke of
Argyle and (at first) the other scientists. And do look at Pasteur
and his majestic honor roll of prodigious benefactions! Damned—
each and every one of them in its turn—by frenzied and ferocious
consensuses of medical and chemical experts comprising, for years,
every member of the tribe in Europe; damned without even a
casual *look* at what he was doing—and he pathetically imploring them to come and take at least one little look before making
the damnation eternal. They shortened his life by their malignities
and persecutions; and thus robbed the world of the further and
priceless services of a man who—along certain lines and within
certain limits—had done more for the human race than any other
one man in all its long history: a man whom it had taken the expert brotherhood ten thousand years to produce, and whose mate
and match the brotherhood may possibly not be able to bring
forth and assassinate in another ten thousand. The preacher has
an old and tough reputation for bullheaded and unreasoning hostility to new light; why, he is not "in it" with the doctor! Nor,
perhaps, with some of the other breeds of experts that sit around
and get up the consensuses and squelch the new things as fast as
they come from the hands of the plodders, the searchers, the inspired dreamers, the Pasteurs that come bearing pearls to scatter
in the consensus sty.

This is warm work! It puts my temperature up to 106 and
raises my pulse to the limit. It always works just so when the red
rag of a consensus jumps my fence and starts across my pasture.
I have been a consensus more than once myself, and I know the

business—and its vicissitudes. I am a compositor-expert, of old and seasoned experience; nineteen years ago I delivered the final-and-for-good verdict that the linotype would never be able to earn its own living nor anyone else's: it takes fourteen acres of ground, now, to accommodate its factories in England. Thirty-five years ago I was an expert precious-metal quartz-miner. There was an outcrop in my neighborhood that assayed $600 a ton—gold. But every fleck of gold in it was shut up tight and fast in an intractable and impersuadable base-metal shell. Acting as a consensus, I delivered the finality verdict that no human ingenuity would ever be able to set free two dollars' worth of gold out of a ton of that rock. The fact is, I did not foresee the cyanide process. Indeed, I have been a consensus ever so many times since I reached maturity and approached the age of discretion, but I call to mind no instance in which I won out.

These sorrows have made me suspicious of consensuses. Do you know, I tremble and the goose flesh rises on my skin every time I encounter one, now. I sheer warily off and get behind something, saying to myself, "It looks innocent and all right, but no matter, ten to one there's a cyanide process under that thing somewhere."

Now as concerns this "creation of life by chemical agencies." Reader, take my advice: don't you copper it. I don't say bet on it; no, I only say, don't you copper it. As you see, there is a consensus out against it. If you find that you can't control your passions; if you feel that you have *got* to copper something and can't help it, copper the consensus. It is the safest way—all history confirms it. If you are young, you will, of course, have to put up, on one side or the other, for you will not be able to restrain yourself; but as for me, I am old, and I am going to wait for a new deal.[16]

P.S.—In the same number of the *Times* Doctor Funk says: "Man may be as badly fooled by believing too little as by believing too much; the hardheaded skeptic Thomas was the only disciple who was cheated." Is that the right and rational way to look at it? I will not be sure, for my memory is faulty, but it has always been my impression that Thomas was the only one who made an examination and proved a fact, while the others were accepting, or discounting, the fact on trust—like any other consensus. If that is so, Doubting Thomas removed a doubt which must otherwise have confused and troubled the world until now. Including Doctor Funk. It seems to me that we owe that hardheaded—or sound-headed—witness something more than a slur. Why does Doctor Funk *examine* into spiritism, and then throw stones at Thomas. Why doesn't he take it on trust? Has inconsistency become a jewel in Lafayette Place?

OLD-MAN-AFRAID-OF-THE-CONSENSUS

*Extract from Adam's Diary*—Then there was a consensus about it. It was the very first one. It sat six days and nights. It was then delivered of the verdict that a world could not be made out of nothing; that such small things as sun and moon and stars might, maybe, but it would take years and years, if there was considerable many of them. Then the consensus got up and looked out of the window, and there was the whole outfit spinning and sparkling in space! You never saw such a disappointed lot.

his<br>ADAM—i—<br>mark

# The Dervish and the Offensive Stranger

"The Dervish and the Offensive Stranger" first appeared in 1923 in *Europe and Elsewhere*.

THE DERVISH. I will say again, and yet again, and still again, that a good deed——

*The Offensive Stranger*. Peace, and, O man of narrow vision! There is no such thing as a good *deed*——

*The Dervish*. O shameless blasphe——

*The Offensive Stranger.* And no such thing as an evil deed. There are good *impulses,* there are evil impulses, and that is all. Half of the results of a good intention are evil; half the results of an evil intention are good. No man can command the results, nor allot them.

*The Dervish.* And so——

*The Offensive Stranger.* And so you shall praise men for their good intentions, and not blame them for the evils resulting; you shall blame men for their evil intentions, and not praise them for the good resulting.

*The Dervish.* O maniac! will you say——

*The Offensive Stranger.* Listen to the law: From *every* impulse, whether good or evil, flow two streams; the one carries health, the other carries poison. From the beginning of time this law has not changed, to the end of time it will not change.

*The Dervish.* If I should strike thee dead in anger——

*The Offensive Stranger.* Or kill me with a drug which you hoped would give me new life and strength——

*The Dervish.* Very well. Go on.

*The Offensive Stranger.* In either case the results would be the same. Agelong misery of mind for you—an evil result; peace, repose, the end of sorrow for me—a good result. Three hearts that hold me dear would break; three pauper cousins of the third removed would get my riches and rejoice; you would go to prison and your friends would grieve, but your humble apprentice-priest would step into your shoes and your fat sleek life and be happy. And are these all the goods and all the evils that would flow from the well-intended or ill-intended act that cut short my life, O thoughtless one, O purblind creature? The good and evil results that flow from *any* act, even the smallest, breed on and on, century after century, forever and ever and ever, creeping by inches around the globe, affecting all its coming and going populations until the end of time, until the final cataclysm!

*The Dervish.* Then, there being no such thing as a good deed——

*The Offensive Stranger.* Don't I tell you there are good *intentions,* and evil ones, and there an end? The *results* are not foreseeable. They are of both kinds, in all cases. It is the law. Listen: this is far-Western history:

## VOICES OUT OF UTAH

### I

*The White Chief* (*to his people*). This wide plain was a desert. By our heaven-blest industry we have dammed the river and utilized its waters and turned the desert into smiling fields whose fruitage makes prosperous and happy a thousand homes where poverty and hunger dwelt before. How noble, how beneficent, is civilization!

### II

*Indian Chief* (*to his people*). This wide plain, which the Spanish priests taught our fathers to irrigate, was a smiling field, whose fruitage made our homes prosperous and happy. The white American has dammed our river, taken away our water for his own valley, and turned our field into a desert; wherefore we starve.

*The Dervish.* I perceive that the good intention did really bring both good and evil results in equal measure. But a single case cannot prove the rule. Try again.

*The Offensive Stranger.* Pardon me, *all* cases prove it. Columbus discovered a new world and gave to the plodding poor and the landless of Europe farms and breathing space and plenty and happiness——

*The Dervish.* A good result.

*The Offensive Stranger.* And they hunted and harried the original owners of the soil, and robbed them, beggared them, drove them from their homes, and exterminated them, root and branch.

*The Dervish.* An evil result, yes.

*The Offensive Stranger.* The French Revolution brought desolation to the hearts and homes of five million families and drenched the country with blood and turned its wealth to poverty.

*The Dervish.* An evil result.

*The Offensive Stranger.* But every great and precious liberty enjoyed by the nations of continental Europe today are the gift of that revolution.

*The Dervish*. A good result, I concede it.

*The Offensive Stranger*. In our well-meant effort to lift up the Filipino to our own moral altitude with a musket, we have slipped on the ice and fallen down to his.

*The Dervish*. A large evil result.

*The Offensive Stranger*. But as an offset we are a world power.

*The Dervish*. Give me time. I must think this one over. Pass on.

*The Offensive Stranger*. By help of three hundred thousand soldiers and eight hundred million dollars England has succeeded in her good purpose of lifting up the unwilling Boers and making them better and purer and happier than they could ever have become by their own devices.

*The Dervish*. Certainly that is a good result.

*The Offensive Stranger*. But there are only eleven Boers left now.

*The Dervish*. It has the appearance of an evil result. But I will think it over before I decide.

*The Offensive Stranger*. Take yet one more instance. With the best intentions the missionary has been laboring in China for eighty years.

*The Dervish*. The evil result is——

*The Offensive Stranger*. That nearly a hundred thousand Chinamen have acquired our civilization.

*The Dervish*. And the good result is——

*The Offensive Stranger*. That by the compassion of God four hundred millions have escaped it.

# Does the Race of Man Love a Lord?

Unquestionably the person that can get lowest down in cringing before royalty and nobility, and can get most satisfaction out of crawling on his belly before them, is an American. Not all Americans, but when an American does it he makes competition impossible.—*Mark Twain's Notebook*, 1897

Kaiser Wilhelm II's brother, Prince Henry, came to the United States in 1902 on a goodwill mission. His purpose was to improve relations between Germany and America generally, and to strengthen Old World ties with German-Americans.

Prince Henry presented a statue of Frederick the Great to the nation, and a Germanic museum to Harvard University; he ordered a Herreshoff yacht, and asked the President's daughter, Alice Roosevelt, to christen it; he established exchange professorships in the universities; he attracted enormous attention—and he inspired "Does the Race of Man Love a Lord?" It was published in the *North American Review,* April, 1902. Here it is:

Often a quite assified remark becomes sanctified by use and petrified by custom; it is then a permanency, its term of activity a geologic period.

THE DAY after the arrival of Prince Henry I met an English friend, and he rubbed his hands and broke out with a remark that was charged to the brim with joy—joy that was evidently a pleasant salve to an old sore place:

"Many a time I've had to listen without retort to an old saying that is irritatingly true, and until now seemed to offer no chance for a return jibe: 'An Englishman does dearly love a lord'; but after this I shall talk back, and say 'How about the Americans?' "

It is a curious thing, the currency that an idiotic saying can get. The man that first says it thinks he has made a discovery. The man he says it to, thinks the same. It departs on its travels, is received everywhere with admiring acceptance, and not only as a piece of rare and acute observation, but as being exhaustively true and profoundly wise; and so it presently takes its place in the world's list of recognized and established wisdoms, and after that no one thinks of examining it to see whether it is really entitled to its high honors or not. I call to mind instances of this in two well-established proverbs, whose dullness is not surpassed by the one about the Englishman and his love for a lord: one of them records the American's adoration of the almighty dollar, the other the American millionaire-girl's ambition to trade cash for a title, with a husband thrown in.

It isn't merely the American that adores the almighty dollar, it is the human race. The human race has always adored the hatful of shells, or the bale of calico, or the half bushel of brass rings, or the handful of steel fishhooks, or the houseful of black wives, or the zareba full of cattle, or the twoscore camels and asses, or the factory, or the farm, or the block of buildings, or the railroad bonds, or the bank stock, or the hoarded cash, or—anything that stands for wealth and consideration and independence, and can secure to the possessor that most precious of all things, another man's envy. It was a dull person that invented the idea that the American's devotion to the dollar is more strenuous than another's.

Rich American girls do buy titles, but they did not invent that idea; it had been worn threadbare several hundred centuries before America was discovered. European girls still exploit it as briskly as ever; and, when a title is not to be had for the money in hand, they buy the husband without it. They must put up the "dot," or there is no trade. The commercialization of brides is substantially universal, except in America. It exists with us, to some little extent, but in no degree approaching a custom.

"The Englishman dearly loves a lord."

What is the soul and source of his love? I think the thing could be more correctly worded:

"The human race dearly envies a lord."

That is to say, it envies the lord's place. Why? On two accounts, I think: its power and its conspicuousness.

Where conspicuousness carries with it a power which, by the light of our own observation and experience, we are able to measure and comprehend, I think our envy of the possessor is as deep and as passionate as is that of any other nation. No one can care less for a lord than the backwoodsman, who has had no personal contact with lords and has seldom heard them spoken of; but I will not allow that any Englishman has a profounder envy of a lord than has the average American who has lived long years in a European capital and fully learned how immense is the position the lord occupies.

Of any ten thousand Americans who eagerly gather, at vast inconvenience, to get a glimpse of Prince Henry, all but a couple of hundred will be there out of an immense curiosity; they are burning up with desire to see a personage who is so much talked about. They envy him; but it is conspicuousness they envy mainly, not the power that is lodged in his royal quality and position, for they have but a vague and spectral knowledge and appreciation of that; through their environment and associations they have been accustomed to regard such things lightly, and as not being very real; consequently, they are not able to value them enough to consumingly envy them.

But, whenever an American (or other human being) is in the presence, for the first time, of a combination of great power and conspicuousness which he thoroughly understands and appreciates, his eager curiosity and pleasure will be well-sodden with that other passion—envy—whether he suspect it or not. At any time, on any day, in any part of America, you can confer a happiness upon any passing stranger by calling his attention to any other passing stranger and saying:

"Do you see that gentleman going along there? It is Mr. Rockefeller."

Watch his eye. It is a combination of power and conspicuousness which the man understands.

When we understand rank, we always like to rub against it. When a man is conspicuous, we always want to see him. Also, if he will pay us an attention we will manage to remember it. Also, we will mention it now and then, casually; sometimes to a friend, or if a friend is not handy, we will make out with a stranger.

Well, then, what is rank, and what is conspicuousness? At once we think of kings and aristocracies, and of world-wide celebrities in soldierships, the arts, letters, etc., and we stop there. But that is a mistake. Rank holds its court and receives its homage on every round of the ladder, from the emperor down to the rat-catcher; and distinction, also, exists on every round of the ladder, and commands its due of deference and envy.

To worship rank and distinction is the dear and valued privilege of all the human race, and it is freely and joyfully exercised in democracies as well as in monarchies—and even, to some extent, among those creatures whom we impertinently call the lower animals. For even they have some poor little vanities and foibles, though in this matter they are paupers as compared to us.

A Chinese emperor has the worship of his four hundred million of subjects, but the rest of the world is indifferent to him. A Christian emperor has the worship of his subjects and of a large part of the Christian world outside of his dominions; but he is a matter of indifference to all China. A king, class A, has an extensive worship; a king, class B, has a less extensive worship; class C, class D, class E get a steadily diminishing share of worhip; class L (Sultan of Zanzibar), class P (Sultan of Sulu), and class W (half-king of Samoa), get no worship at all outside their own little patch of sovereignty.

Take the distinguished people along down. Each has his group of homage-payers. In the navy, there are many groups; they start with the secretary and the admiral, and go down to the quarter-master—and below; for there will be groups among the sailors, and each of these groups will have a tar who is distinguished for his battles, or his strength, or his daring, or his profanity, and is admired and envied by his group. The same with the army; the same with the literary and journalistic craft, the publishing craft; the cod-fishery craft; Standard Oil; U. S. Steel; the class A hotel—and the rest of the alphabet in that line; the class A prize fighter —and the rest of the alphabet in his line—clear down to the lowest and obscurest six-boy gang of little gamins, with its one boy that can thrash the rest, and to whom he is king of Samoa, bottom of the royal race, but looked up to with a most ardent admiration and envy.

There is something pathetic, and funny, and pretty, about this human race's fondness for contact with power and distinction, and for the reflected glory it gets out of it. The king, class A, is happy in the state banquet and the military show which the emperor provides for him, and he goes home and gathers the queen and the princelings around him in the privacy of the spare room, and tells them all about it, and says:

"His Imperial Majesty put his hand on my shoulder in the most friendly way—just as friendly and familiar, oh, you can't imagine it!—and everybody *seeing* him do it; charming, perfectly charming!"

The king, class G, is happy in the cold collation and the police parade provided for him by the king, class B, and goes home and tells the family all about it, and says:

"And His Majesty took me into his own private cabinet for a smoke and a chat, and there we sat just as sociable, and talking away and laughing and chatting, just the same as if we had been born in the same bunk; and all the servants in the anteroom could see us doing it! Oh, it was too lovely for anything!"

The king, class Q, is happy in the modest entertainment furnished him by the king, class M, and goes home and tells the household about it, and is as grateful and joyful over it as were his predecessors in the gaudier attentions that had fallen to their larger lot.

Emperors, kings, artisans, peasants, big people, little people— at bottom we are all alike and all the same; all just alike on the inside, and when our clothes are off, nobody can tell which of us is which. We are unanimous in the pride we take in good and genuine compliments paid us, in distinctions conferred upon us, in attentions shown us. There is not one of us, from the emperor down, but is made like that. Do I mean attentions shown us by the great? No, I mean simply flattering attentions, let them come whence they may. We despise no source that can pay us a pleasing attention—there is no source that is humble enough for that. You have heard a dear little girl say to a frowzy and disreputable dog: "He came right to me and let me pat him on the head, and he wouldn't let the others touch him!" and you have seen her eyes dance with pride in that high distinction. You have often seen that. If the child were a princess, would that random dog be able to confer the like glory upon her with his pretty compliment? Yes; and even in her mature life and seated upon a throne, she would still remember it, still recall it, still speak of it with frank satisfaction. That charming and lovable German princess and poet, Carmen Sylva, Queen of Rumania, remembers yet that the flowers of the woods and fields "talked to her" when she was a girl, and she sets it down in her latest book; and that the squirrels conferred upon her and her father the valued compliment of not being afraid of them; and "once one of them, holding a nut between its sharp little teeth, ran right up against my father"—it has the very note of "He came right to me and let me pat him on the head"—"and when it saw itself reflected in his boot it was very much surprised, and stopped for a long time to contemplate itself in the polished leather"—then it went its way. And the birds! she still remembers with pride that "they came boldly into my room," when she had neglected her "duty" and put no food on the window sill for them; she knew all the wild birds, and forgets the royal crown on her head to remember with pride that they knew her; also that the wasp and the bee were personal friends of hers, and never forgot that gracious relationship to her injury: "never have I been stung by a wasp or a bee." And here is that proud note again that sings in that little child's elation in being singled out, among all the company of children, for the random dog's honor-conferring attentions. "Even in the very worst summer for wasps, when, in lunching out of doors, our table was covered with them and every one else was stung, they never hurt me."

When a queen whose qualities of mind and heart and character are able to add distinction to so distinguished a place as a throne, remembers with grateful exultation, after thirty years, honors and distinctions conferred upon her by the humble, wild creatures of the forest, we are helped to realize that complimentary attentions, homage, distinctions, are of no caste, but are above all caste—that they are a nobility-conferring power apart.

We all like these things. When the gate-guard at the railway station passes me through unchallenged and examines other people's tickets, I feel as the king, class A, felt when the emperor put the imperial hand on his shoulder, "everybody seeing him do it"; and as the child felt when the random dog allowed her to pat his head and ostracized the others; and as the princess felt when the wasps spared her and stung the rest; and I felt just so, four years ago in Vienna (and remember it yet), when the hel-meted police shut me off, with fifty others, from a street which the emperor was to pass through, and the captain of the squad turned and saw the situation and said indignantly to that guard:

"Can't you see it is the Herr Mark Twain? Let him through!"

It was four years ago; but it will be four hundred before I forget the wind of self-complacency that rose in me, and strained my buttons when I marked the deference for me evoked in the faces of my fellow rabble, and mingled with it, a puzzled and resentful expression which said, as plainly as speech could have worded it: "And who in the nation is the Herr Mark Twain *um Gotteswillen?*"

How many times in your life have you heard this boastful remark:

"I stood as close to him as I am to you; I could have put out my hand and touched him."

We have all heard it many and many a time. It was a proud distinction to be able to say those words. It brought envy to the speaker, a kind of glory; and he basked in it and was happy through all his veins. And who was it he stood so close to? The answer would cover all the grades. Sometimes it was a king; sometimes it was a renowned highwayman; sometimes it was an unknown man killed in an extraordinary way and made suddenly famous by it; always it was a person who was for the moment the subject of public interest—the public interest of a nation, maybe only the public interest of a village.

"I was there, and I saw it myself." That is a common and envy-compelling remark. It can refer to a battle; to a hanging; to a coronation, to the killing of Jumbo by the railway train; to the arrival of Jenny Lind at the Battery; to the meeting of the President and Prince Henry; to the chase of a murderous maniac; to the disaster in the tunnel; to the explosion in the subway; to a remarkable dogfight; to a village church struck by lightning. It will be said, more or less casually, by everybody in America who has seen Prince Henry do anything, or try to. The man who was absent and didn't see him do anything will scoff. It is his privilege; and he can make capital out of it, too; he will seem, even to himself, to be different from other Americans, and better. As his opinion of his superior Americanism grows, and swells, and concentrates and coagulates, he will go further and try to belittle the distinction of those that saw the Prince do things, and will spoil their pleasure in it if he can. My life has been embittered by that kind of persons. If you are able to tell of a special distinction that has fallen to your lot, it gravels them; they cannot bear it; and they try to make believe that the thing you took for a special distinction was nothing of the kind and was meant in quite another way. Once I was received in private audience by an emperor. Last week I was telling a jealous person about it, and I could see him wince under it, see it bite, see him suffer. I revealed the whole episode to him with considerable elaboration and nice attention to detail. When I was through, he asked me what had impressed me most. I said:

"His Majesty's delicacy. They told me to be sure and back out from the presence, and find the doorknob as best I could; it was not allowable to face around. Now the emperor knew it would be a difficult ordeal for me, because of lack of practice; and so, when it was time to part, he turned, with exceeding delicacy, and pretended to fumble with things on his desk, so that I could get out in my own way, without his seeing me."

It went home! It was vitriol! I saw the envy and disgruntlement rise in the man's face; he couldn't keep it  down. I saw him trying to fix up something in his mind to take the bloom off that distinction. I enjoyed that, for I judged that he had his work cut out for him. He struggled along inwardly for quite a while; then he said, with the manner of a person who has to say something and hasn't anything relevant to say:

"You said he had a handful of special-brand cigars lying on the table?"

"Yes; *I* never saw anything to match them." I had him again. He had to fumble around in his mind as much as another minute before he could play; then he said in as mean a way as I ever heard a person say anything:

"He could have been counting the cigars, you know."

I cannot endure a man like that. It is nothing to him how unkind he is, so long as he takes the bloom off. It is all he cares for.

"An Englishman (or other human being) does dearly love a lord," (or other conspicuous person). It includes us all. We love to be noticed by the conspicuous person; we love to be associated with such, or with a conspicuous event, even in a seventh-rate fashion, even in a forty-seventh, if we cannot do better. This accounts for some of our curious tastes in mementos. It accounts for the large private trade in the Prince of Wales's hair, which chambermaids were able to drive in that article of commerce when the Prince made the tour of the world in the long ago—hair which probably did not always come from his brush, since enough of it was marketed to refurnish a bald comet; it accounts for the fact that the rope which lynches a Negro in the presence of ten thousand Christian spectators is salable five minutes later at two dollars an inch; it accounts for the mournful fact that a royal personage does not venture to wear buttons on his coat in public.

We do love a lord—and by that term I mean any person whose situation is higher than our own. The lord of a group, for instance: a group of peers, a group of millionaires, a group of hoodlums, a group of sailors, a group of newsboys, a group of saloon politicians, a group of college girls. No royal person has ever been the object of a more delirious loyalty and slavish adoration than is paid by the vast Tammany herd to its squalid idol of Wantage. There is not a bifucated animal in that menagerie that would not be proud to appear in a newspaper picture in his company. At the same time, there are some in that organization who would scoff at the people who have been daily pictured in company with Prince Henry, and would say vigorously that *they* would not consent to be photographed with him—a statement which would not be true in any instance. There are hundreds of people in America who would frankly say to you that they would not be proud to be photographed in a group with the Prince, if invited; and some of these unthinking people would believe it when they said it; yet in no instance would it be true. We have a large population, but we have not a large enough one, by several millions, to furnish that man. He has not yet been begotten, and in fact he is not begettable.

You may take any of the printed groups, and there isn't a person in it who isn't visibly glad to be there; there isn't a person in the dim background who isn't visibly trying to be vivid; if it is a crowd of ten thousand—ten thousand proud, untamed democrats, horny-handed sons of toil and of politics, and fliers of the eagle— there isn't one who isn't conscious of the camera, there isn't one who is trying to keep out of range, there isn't one who isn't plainly meditating a purchase of the paper in the morning, with the intention of hunting himself out in the picture and of framing and keeping it if he shall find so much of his person in it as his starboard ear.

We all love to get some of the drippings of conspicuousness, and we will put up with a single, humble drip, if we can't get any more. We may pretend otherwise, in conversation; but we can't pretend

it to ourselves privately—and we don't. We do confess in public
that we are the noblest work of God, being moved to it by long
habit, and teaching, and superstition; but deep down in the secret
places of our souls we recognize that, if we *are* the noblest work,
the less said about it the better.

We of the North poke fun at the South for its fondness for titles
—a fondness for titles pure and simple, regardless of whether they
are genuine or pinchbeck. We forget that whatever a Southerner
likes the rest of the human race likes, and that there is no law of
predilection lodged in one people that is absent from another
people. There is no variety in the human race. We are all children,
all children of the one Adam, and we love toys. We can soon
acquire that Southern disease if some one will give it a start. It
already has a start, in fact. I have been personally acquainted
with over eighty-four thousand persons who, at one time or another
in their lives, have served for a year or two on the staffs of our
multitudinous governors, and through that fatality have been generals temporarily, and colonels temporarily, and judge advocates
temporarily; but I have known only nine among them who could
be hired to let the title go when it ceased to be legitimate. I know
thousands and thousands of governors who ceased to be governors
away back in the last century; but I am acquainted with only three
who would answer your letter if you failed to call them "Governor"
in it. I know acres and acres of men who have done time in a
legislature in prehistoric days, but among them is not half an acre
whose resentment you would not raise if you addressed them as
"Mr." instead of "Hon." The first thing a legislature does is to
convene in an impressive legislative attitude, and get itself photographed. Each member frames his copy and takes it to the woods
and hangs it up in the most aggressively conspicuous place in his
house; and if you visit the house and fail to inquire what that accumulation is, the conversation will be brought around to it by
that aforetime legislator, and he will show you a figure in it which
in the course of years he has almost obliterated with the smut of
his finger-marks, and say with a solemn joy, "It's me!"

Have you ever seen a country congressman enter the hotel
breakfast-room in Washington with his letters?—and sit at his
table and let on to read them?—and wrinkle his brows and frown

statesmanlike?—keeping a furtive watchout over his glasses all the while to see if he is being observed and admired?—those same old letters which he fetches in every morning? Have you seen it? Have you seen him show off? It is *the* sight of the national capital. Except one; a pathetic one. That is the ex-Congressman: the poor fellow whose life has been ruined by a two-year taste of glory and of fictitious consequence; who has been superseded, and ought to take his heartbreak home and hide it, but cannot tear himself away from the scene of his lost little grandeur; and so he lingers, and still lingers, year after year, unconsidered, sometimes snubbed, ashamed of his fallen estate, and valiantly trying to look otherwise; dreary and depressed, but counterfeiting breeziness and gaiety, hailing with chummy familiarity, which is not always welcomed, the more-fortunates who are still in place and were once his mates. Have you seen him? He clings piteously to the one little shred that is left of his departed distinction—the "privilege of the floor"; and works it hard and gets what he can out of it. That is the saddest figure I know of.

Yes, we do so love our little distinctions! And then we loftily scoff at a prince for enjoying his larger ones; forgetting that if we only had his chance—ah! "Senator" is not a legitimate title. A Senator has no more right to be addressed by it than have you or I; but, in the several state capitals and in Washington, there are five thousand senators who take very kindly to that fiction, and who purr gratefully when you call them by it—which you may do quite unrebuked. Then those same senators smile at the self-constructed majors and generals and judges of the South!

Indeed, we do love our distinctions, get them how we may. And we work them for all they are worth. In prayer we call ourselves "worms of the dust," but it is only on a sort of tacit understanding that the remark shall not be taken at par. *We*—worms of the dust! Oh, no, we are not that. Except in fact; and we do not deal much in fact when we are contemplating ourselves.

As a race, we do certainly love a lord—let him be Croker, or a duke, or a prize fighter, or whatever other personage shall chance to be the head of our group. Many years ago, I saw a greasy youth in overalls standing by the *Herald* office, with an expectant look in his face. Soon a large man passed out, and gave him a pat on the shoulder. That was what the boy was waiting for—the large man's notice. The pat made him proud and happy, and the exultation inside of him shone out through his eyes; and his mates were there to see the pat and envy it and wish they could have that glory. The boy belonged down cellar in the pressroom, the large man was king of the upper floors, foreman of the composing room. The light in the boy's face was worship, the foreman was his lord, head of his group. The pat was an accolade. It was as precious to the boy as it would have been if he had been an aristocrat's son and the accolade had been delivered by his sovereign with a sword. The quintessence of the honor was all there; there was no difference in values; in truth there was no difference present except an artificial one—clothes.

All the human race loves a lord—that is, it loves to look upon or be noticed by the possessor of power or conspicuousness; and sometimes animals, born to better things and higher ideals, descend to man's level in this matter. In the Jardin des Plantes I have seen a cat that was so vain of being the personal friend of an elephant that I was ashamed of her.

## The War Prayer

Except the selections from the Autobiography, "The War Prayer" is the only posthumously published work in this volume which Mark Twain, to anyone's knowledge, purposely withheld in the belief that it would be too painful or shocking for the world of his day.

It is difficult now to understand why "The War Prayer," out of all Mark Twain's work, should have been withheld or to know to what degree the feeling of his period accounted for his decision. His daughter Jean told him that "The War Prayer" would be regarded as sacrilege. But if Clemens took Jean's advice, or any other, it was because he agreed with it.

"The War Prayer," dictated in 1905, was first published in *Harper's Monthly,* November, 1916.

IT WAS a time of great and exalting excitement. The country was up in arms, the war was on, in every breast burned the holy fire of patriotism; the drums were beating, the bands playing, the toy pistols popping, the bunched firecrackers hissing and spluttering; on every hand and far down the receding and fading spread of roofs and balconies a fluttering wilderness of flags flashed in the sun; daily the young volunteers marched down the wide avenue gay and fine in their new uniforms, the proud fathers and mothers and sisters and sweethearts cheering them with voices choked with happy emotion as they swung by; nightly the packed meetings listened, panting, to patriot oratory which stirred the deepest deeps of their hearts, and which they interrupted at briefest intervals with cyclones of applause, the tears running down their cheeks the while; in the churches the pastors preached devotion to flag and country, and invoked the God of Battles, beseeching His aid in our good cause in outpouring of fervid eloquence which moved every listener. It was indeed a glad and gracious time, and the half dozen rash spirits that ventured to disapprove of the war and cast a doubt upon its righteousness straightway got such a stern and angry warning that for their personal safety's sake they quickly shrank out of sight and offended no more in that way.

Sunday morning came—next day the battalions would leave for the front; the church was filled; the volunteers were there, their young faces alight with martial dreams—visions of the stern advance, the gathering momentum, the rushing charge, the flashing sabers, the flight of the foe, the tumult, the enveloping smoke, the fierce pursuit, the surrender!—then home from the war, bronzed heroes, welcomed, adored, submerged in golden seas of glory! With the volunteers sat their dear ones, proud, happy, and envied by the neighbors and friends who had no sons and brothers to send forth to the field of honor, there to win for the flag, or, failing, die the noblest of noble deaths. The service proceeded; a war chapter from the Old Testament was read; the first prayer was said; it was followed by an organ burst that shook the building, and with one impulse the house rose, with glowing eyes and beating hearts, and poured out that tremendous invocation—

> God the all-terrible! Thou who ordainest,
> Thunder thy clarion and lightning thy sword!

Then came the "long" prayer. None could remember the like of it for passionate pleading and moving and beautiful language. The

burden of its supplication was, that an ever-merciful and benignant
Father of us all would watch over our noble young soldiers, and
aid, comfort, and encourage them in their patriotic work; bless
them, shield them in the day of battle and the hour of peril, bear
them in His mighty hand, make them strong and confident, in-
vincible in the bloody onset; help them to crush the foe, grant to
them and to their flag and country imperishable honor and glory—

An aged stranger entered and moved with slow and noiseless
step up the main aisle, his eyes fixed upon the minister, his long
body clothed in a robe that reached to his feet, his head bare, his
white hair descending in a frothy cataract to his shoulders, his
seamy face unnaturally pale, pale even to ghastliness. With all
eyes following him and wondering, he made his silent way; without
pausing, he ascended to the preacher's side and stood there, waiting. With shut lids the preacher, unconscious of his presence, continued his moving prayer, and at last finished it with the words,
uttered in fervent appeal, "Bless our arms, grant us the victory, O
Lord our God, Father and Protector of our land and flag!"

The stranger touched his arm, motioned him to step aside—
which the startled minister did—and took his place. During some
moments he surveyed the spellbound audience with solemn eyes,
in which burned an uncanny light; then in a deep voice he said:

"I come from the Throne—bearing a message from Almighty
God!" The words smote the house with a shock; if the stranger
perceived it he gave no attention. "He has heard the prayer of His
servant your shepherd, and will grant it if such shall be your
desire after I, His messenger, shall have explained to you its
import—that is to say, its full import. For it is like unto many of
the prayers of men, in that it asks for more than he who utters it
is aware of—except he pause and think.

"God's servant and yours has prayed his prayer. Has he paused
and taken thought? Is it one prayer? No, it is two—one uttered,
the other not. Both have reached the ear of Him who heareth all
supplications, the spoken and the unspoken. Ponder this—keep it
in mind. If you would beseech a blessing upon yourself, beware!
lest without intent you invoke a curse upon a neighbor at the same
time. If you pray for the blessing of rain upon your crop which
needs it, by that act you are possibly praying for a curse upon some

neighbor's crop which may not need rain and can be injured by it.

"You have heard your servant's prayer—the uttered part of it. I am commissioned of God to put into words the other part of it— that part which the pastor—and also you in your hearts—fervently prayed silently. And ignorantly and unthinkingly? God grant that it was so! You heard these words: 'Grant us the victory, O Lord our God!' That is sufficient. The *whole* of the uttered prayer is compact into those pregnant words. Elaborations were not necessary. When you have prayed for victory you have prayed for many unmentioned results which follow victory—*must* follow it, cannot help but follow it. Upon the listening spirit of God the Father fell also the unspoken part of the prayer. He commandeth me to put it into words. Listen!

"O Lord our Father, our young patriots, idols of our hearts, go forth to battle—be Thou near them! With them—in spirit—we also go forth from the sweet peace of our beloved firesides to smite the foe. O Lord our God, help us to tear their soldiers to bloody shreds with our shells; help us to cover their smiling fields with the pale forms of their patriot dead; help us to drown the thunder of the guns with the shrieks of their wounded, writhing in pain; help us to lay waste their humble homes with a hurricane of fire; help us to wring the hearts of their unoffending widows with unavailing grief; help us to turn them out roofless with their little children to wander unfriended the wastes of their desolated land in rags and hunger and thirst, sports of the sun flames of summer and the icy winds of winter, broken in spirit, worn with travail, imploring Thee for the refuge of the grave and denied it—for our sakes who adore Thee, Lord, blast their hopes, blight their lives, protract their bitter pilgrimage, make heavy their steps, water their way with their tears, stain the white snow with the blood of their wounded feet! We ask it, in the spirit of love, of Him who is the Source of Love, and who is the ever-faithful refuge and friend of all that are sore beset and seek His aid with humble and contrite hearts. Amen."

(*After a pause.*) "Ye have prayed it; if ye still desire it, speak! The messenger of the Most High waits."

It was believed afterward that the man was a lunatic, because there was no sense in what he said.

## Reflections on Being the Delight of God

This selection, an undated bit from Mark Twain's Autobiography, was probably dictated in 1906. It first appeared in 1940 in *Mark Twain in Eruption*, a collection of previously unpublished selections from the original manuscript, edited by Bernard DeVoto.

For ourselves we do thoroughly believe that man, as he lives just here on this tiny earth, is in essence and possibilities the most sublime existence in all the range of non-divine being—the chief love and delight of God.—Chicago *Interior* (Presb.)

LAND, it is just for the world the way I feel about it myself, sometimes, even when dry. And when not dry, even those warm words are not nearly warm enough to get up to what I am feeling, when I am holding on to something, and blinking affectionately at myself in the glass, and recollecting that I'm it.

And when I am feeling historical, there is nothing that ecstatifies me like hunting the chief love and delight of God around and around just here on this tiny earth and watching him perform. I watch him progressing and progressing—always progressing—always mounting higher and higher, sometimes by means of the inquisition, sometimes by means of the terror, sometimes by eight hundred years of witch burning, sometimes by help of a St. Bartholomew's, sometimes by spreading hell and civilization in China, sometimes by preserving and elevating the same at home by a million soldiers and a thousand battleships; and when he gets down to today I still look at him spread out over a whole page of the morning paper, grabbing in Congress, grabbing in Albany, grabbing in New York and St. Louis and all around, lynching the innocent, slobbering hypocrisies, reeking, dripping, unsavory, but always recognizable as the same old most sublime existence in all the range of non-divine being, the chief love and delight of God; and then I am more gladder than ever that I am it.

# ON THE UNITED STATES

O beautiful for patriot dream
That sees beyond the years
Thine alabaster cities gleam
Undimmed by human tears!
—KATHERINE LEE BATES,
"America the Beautiful," 1893

In a sordid slime harmonious, Greed was born in yonder ditch;
With a longing in his bosom—for other's goods an itch;
Christ died to make men holy, let men die to make us rich;
Our God is marching on.
—MARK TWAIN, "The Battle Hymn of the
Republic Brought Down to Date," 1901.*

The difference in Mark Twain's work as he aged was less a change than a ripening: his anger at the ways of the world merely grew fiercer as he grew older. Nevertheless, the work of his last years has been called his "pessimism," and millions of words have been written to explain how, apparently, a flippant young wisecracker became a prophet of doom.

The most ingenious explanation has been that his late work is not satire but "pathology"; that Mark Twain "poured vitriol promiscuously over the whole human scene," because he had been a failure as an artist and suffered from frustration.[1]

Simpler explanations have been offered. One is the truism which

* Philip S. Foner, *Mark Twain: Social Critic,* p. 278, © 1958, by International Publishers Co., Inc., printed with permission of The Mark Twain Company.

Clemens, at sixty-seven, put this way in his *Notebook:* "The man who is a pessimist before forty-eight knows too much; if he is an optimist after it, he knows too little."

Another explanation is that his personal tragedies finally embittered him. Certainly he had his share of tragedy. An infant son and two grown daughters died before he did; and in 1904 he lost the wife he adored. From that time—although he was called the "belle of New York"—he was a bitterly lonely old man.

Still another explanation of the "pessimism" is that his late work reflected some horrors in the world around him. This theory is especially borne out by his work on the United States.

In his younger years, when the proposed annexation of the Hawaiian Islands was a lively issue, the New York *Tribune* asked Mark Twain, who had travelled in the islands and lectured and written about them, to express his views. His conclusion, printed in the *Tribune* on January 9, 1873:

> We *must* annex those people. We can afflict them with our wise and beneficent government. We can introduce the novelty of thieves, all the way up from streetcar pickpockets to municipal robbers and Government defaulters and show them how amusing it is to arrest them and try them and then turn them loose—some for cash, and some for "political influence." We can make them ashamed of their simple and primitive justice. . . . We can give them juries composed of the most simple and charming leatherheads. We can give them railway corporations who will buy their Legislatures like old clothes, and run over their best citizens. We can furnish them some Jay Goulds who will do away with their old-time notions that stealing is not respectable. . . . We can give them lecturers! I will go myself. . . .
>
> We can make that little bunch of sleepy islands the hottest corner on earth, and array it in the moral splendor of our high and holy civilization. Annexation is what the poor islanders need. "Shall we to men benighted the lamp of life deny?"

Witty, even devastating, as this may be, it is far from anguished. In fact, he who runs may read—between the lines—that Mark Twain was then happily in love with his own country. It was a love affair that lasted his lifetime. But, as it was happy in the beginning, it was tragic in the end.

A minor theme of Mark Twain's early satire on his own country is the misbehavior and nonsense of Americans abroad. In Italy, there are Americans "who have actually forgotten their mother tongue in three months . . . [and] cannot even write their address in English in a hotel register";[2] In Egypt, there are "reptiles—I mean relic-hunters who, literally, hammer a souvenir from the Sphinx." But the main theme is corruption and graft—the preposterous and monumental corruption and graft of the years after the Civil War. In a remarkable early novel, he gave to this period a name which has stuck: *The Gilded Age.*

*The Gilded Age* contained such an outrageous and uninhibited account of public morals here that critics across the sea shuddered. One English publication disapproved strongly of washing such "dirty linen" in public, and *The Spectator* gave thanks that the book could not be blamed on an Englishman:

Americans, as they read its bitter exposure of American folly and cupidity, will know that their satirists are at least their countrymen. . . .

Characteristically, the book was received with delight by Mark Twain's countrymen. The only trouble was that the novel was the product of a collaboration; half was by Mark Twain and the other half by his staid friend, Charles Dudley Warner. The two halves never fit; Mark Twain's is still uproarious, but Warner's is deadly dull. Perhaps that is why the book, once a best seller, did not live on as a classic.

Oddly, however, at a time when *The Gilded Age* had ceased to be widely read [3]—and at the same time that American critics took the poorest possible view of all other Mark Twain—*The Gilded Age* enjoyed a measure of critical approval here. A typical comment, by Granville Hicks, in 1933, was that it was the only one of Mark Twain's "major fictions" in which he made any "attempt to come to terms with the world in which he lived"—because it was the only one concerned with "movements and events of American life in the latter half of the nineteenth century." [4]

Such standards were, in their way, as American as Mark Twain himself—for these were the standards by which true satire must be rigorously up to date, and rigorously confined to the United States. Thus, it was found that *Huckleberry Finn* was not satire, but nostalgia, because it was based on Mark Twain's childhood and youth, and because, by 1865, slavery was no longer a live issue—or so later generations believed. To the generation involved, the situation was almost reversed. From Howells' remarks, on Clemens' attitude towards the Civil War:

He ridiculed the notion, held by many, that "it was not yet time" to philosophize the events of the great struggle; that we must "wait till its passions had cooled," and "the clouds of strife had cleared away." He maintained that the time would never come when we should see its motives and men and deeds more clearly, and that now, now, was the hour to ascertain them in lasting verity.*

But the American critical standards by which Mark Twain was so widely condemned were seldom applied, in their full severity, to other American literature. For, beginning in the 1920's and continuing for

---

*William Dean Howells, *My Mark Twain* (New York, Harper and Brothers, 1910), p. 37.

more than three decades, the critical reaction against Mark Twain was extremely strong in this country.[5] Granville Hicks was merely speaking for the majority of our responsible literary people when he added, in his comments on Clemens, that "there is, it is at least clear, no one of his books that is wholly satisfactory," and that "he was, and knew he was, merely an entertainer." [6]

In the same period Constance Rourke, a respected authority on American humor, observed: "It is a mistake to look for the social critic—even manqué—in Mark Twain." [7]

The young entertainer who wrote *The Gilded Age* wrote much much more on the same subject, including "The Revised Catechism." This was an attack on New York's Tweed Ring, which, according to Roger Butterfield in *The American Past,* made even grafters in the national government "look like pikers." For:

. . . Tweed and a few Tammany insiders stole $75 million from the city in two years, and their total take from 1865 to 1871 has been estimated as high as $200 million. Tweed bribed the Governor, legislature, Mayor of New York City, and countless small-fry officials. In 1869 he decreed that all contractors doing business with the city must add 100 per cent to their bills and hand back the overcharge in cash to the Ring. Later the fraudulent percentage was raised even higher. Under this scheme New York paid $1,826,278.35 for plastering one city building. . . .[8]

And this is part of "The Revised Catechism," which appeared in the New York *Tribune* on September 27, 1871:

*Q.* What is the chief end of man?
*A.* To get rich.
*Q.* In what way?
*A.* Dishonestly if we can, honestly if we must.
*Q.* Who is God, the only one and true?
*A.* Money is God. Gold and greenbacks and stocks—father, son, and the ghost of the same—three persons in one: these are the true and only God, mighty and supreme; and William Tweed is his prophet.
*Q.* How shall a man attain the chief end of life?
*A.* By furnishing imaginary carpets to the courthouse; apocryphal chairs to the armories, and invisible printing to the city. . . .
*Q.* What works were chiefly prized for the training of the young in former days?
*A. Poor Richard's Almanac,* the *Pilgrim's Progress,* and the Declaration of Independence.
*Q.* What are the best-prized Sunday-school books in this more enlightened age?
*A.* St. Hall's Garbled Reports, St. Fisk's Ingenious Robberies, St. Camochan's Guide to Corruption, St. Gould on the Watering of Stock, St. Barnard's Injunctions, St. Tweed's Handbook of Morals, and the courthouse edition of the Holy Crusade of the Forty Thieves.
*Q.* Do we progress?
*A.* You bet your life.

"The Revised Catechism" is, among other things, a young man's announcement that the country has gone to the dogs. An old man's very different announcements to the same effect may be found in such selections as "A Defence of General Funston" and "Comments on the Killing of 600 Moros."

But the difference between Mark Twain's early and late work on his country reflects much more than the difference in his age. For, to him, political and business corruption, however disgusting and ludicrous, was not a final deadly sin. Nor has it been so to most Americans. As D. W. Brogan has pointed out, Americans are "singularly tolerant" of plundering in high places, so long as the railroads are laid, the cities built and the economic advance continues.[9] Moreover, despite corruption in the Gilded Age, there were for Mark Twain—and no doubt, for many other Americans—special sources of satisfaction in the national life and ideals. For example, our immigration laws were not then what they are now, and Emma Lazarus' words on the Statue of Liberty, placed in New York Harbor by the French nation in 1886, had more meaning:

> Give me your tired, your poor,
> Your huddled masses yearning to breathe free,
> The wretched refuse of your teeming shore,
> Send these, the homeless, tempest-tosst, to me:
> I lift my lamp beside the golden door.

Mark Twain's pride in such national traditions is merely underlined by his disagreeable remarks whenever they were slighted or abridged. For example, in a speech in 1900 at the Waldorf Astoria Hotel in New York:

Behold America, the refuge of the oppressed from everywhere (who can pay fifty dollars' admission)—anyone except a Chinaman. . . .

There are other historical facts which helped make Clemens' early love affair with his own country a happy one. For, in one of his few, and uncharacteristic, national boasts there was a great deal of truth. The following is from "A Defence of General Funston":

We shall . . . be what we were before, a *real* world power . . . by right of the only clean hands in Christendom, the only hands guiltless of the sordid plunder of any helpless people's stolen liberties.

But here Mark Twain was bragging of past glories; the year was 1902, and his long happy honeymoon with his own country was over. We were already deep in our conquest of the Philippines—stealing a helpless people's liberties. And that, for Mark Twain, was the final deadly sin. It moved him to emotion—and to "pessimism" and to literature—which no number of Tweeds or Goulds could have inspired.

## The Caravan and At Galilee

In 1867, a party of American tourists worked its way through a good deal of Europe and all of the Holy Land. One of them was Mark Twain, commissioned by a Western newspaper, the *Alta California*, to report the trip as it went along. He was then almost unknown, except in the American West. His reports, expanded, revised, and published as *The Innocents Abroad* or *The New Pilgrims' Progress*, made him known the world over.

In these selections the pilgrims are in the Holy Land.

### The Caravan

WE LEFT Damascus at noon and rode acros      plain a couple of hours, and then the party stopped awhile in the shade of some fig trees to give me a chance to rest. It was the hottest day we had seen yet—the sun-flames shot down like the shafts of fire that stream out before a blowpipe; the rays seemed to fall in a steady deluge on the head and pass downward like rain from a roof. I imagined I could distinguish between the floods of rays—I thought I could tell when each flood struck my head, when it reached my shoulders, and when the next one came. It was terrible. All the desert glared so fiercely that my eyes were swimming in tears all the time. The boys had white umbrellas heavily lined with dark green. They were a priceless blessing. I thanked fortune that I had one, too, notwithstanding it was packed up with the baggage and was ten miles ahead. It is madness to travel in Syria without an umbrella. They told me in Beirut (these people who always gorge you with advice) that it was madness to travel in Syria without an umbrella. It was on this account that I got one.

But, honestly, I think an umbrella is a nuisance anywhere when its business is to keep the sun off. No Arab wears a brim to his fez, or uses an umbrella or anything to shade his eyes or his face, and he always looks comfortable and proper in the sun. But of all the ridiculous sights I ever have seen, our party of eight is the most so—they do cut such an outlandish figure. They travel single file; they all wear the endless white rag of Constantinople wrapped round and round their hats and dangling down their backs; they all wear thick green spectacles, with side-glasses to them; they all hold white umbrellas, lined with green, over their heads; without exception their stirrups are too short—they are the very worst gang of horsemen on earth; their animals to a horse trot fearfully hard—and when they get strung out one after the other glaring straight ahead and breathless; bouncing high and out of turn, all along the line; knees well up and stiff, elbows flapping like a rooster's that is going to crow, and the long file of umbrellas popping convulsively up and down—when one sees this outrageous picture exposed to the light of day, he is amazed that the gods don't get out their thunderbolts and destroy them off the face of the earth! I do—I wonder at it. I wouldn't let any such caravan go through a country of mine.

## At Galilee

DURING LUNCHEON, the pilgrim enthusiasts of our party, who had been so lighthearted and happy ever since they touched holy ground that they did little but mutter incoherent rhapsodies, could scarcely eat, so anxious were they to "take shipping" and sail in very person upon the waters that had borne the vessels of the Apostles. Their anxiety grew and their excitement augmented with every fleeting moment, until my fears were aroused and I began to have misgivings that in their present condition they might break recklessly loose from all considerations of prudence and buy a whole fleet of ships to sail in instead of hiring a single one for an hour, as quiet folk are wont to do. I trembled to think of the ruined purses this day's performances might result in. I could not help reflecting bodingly upon the intemperate zeal with which middle-aged men are apt to surfeit themselves upon a seductive folly which they have tasted for the first time. And yet I did not feel that I had a right to be surprised at the state of things which was giving me so much concern. These men had been taught from infancy to revere, almost to worship, the holy places whereon their happy eyes were resting now. For many and many a year this very picture had visited their thoughts by day and floated through their dreams by night. To stand before it in the flesh—to see it as they saw it now—to sail upon the hallowed sea, and kiss the holy soil that compassed it about; these were aspirations they had cherished while a generation dragged its lagging seasons by and left its furrows in their faces and its frosts upon their hair. To look upon this picture, and sail upon this sea, they had forsaken home and its idols and journeyed thousands and thousands of miles, in weariness and tribulation. What wonder that the sordid lights of work-day prudence should pale before the glory of a hope like theirs in the full splendor of its fruition? Let them squander millions! I said— who speaks of money at a time like this?

In this frame of mind I followed, as fast as I could, the eager footsteps of the pilgrims, and stood upon the shore of the lake, and swelled, with hat and voice, the frantic hail they sent after the "ship" that was speeding by. It was a success. The toilers of the sea ran in and beached their bark. Joy sat upon every countenance.

"How much?—ask him how much, Ferguson!—how much to take us all—eight of us and you—to Bethsaida, yonder, and to the mouth of Jordan, and to the place where the swine ran down into the sea—quick!—and we want to coast around everywhere— everywhere!—all day long!—*I* could sail a year in these waters!— and tell him we'll stop at Magdala and finish at Tiberias!—ask him how much!—anything—anything whatever!—tell him we don't care what the expense is!" (I said to myself, I knew how it would be.)

*Ferguson* (*interpreting*). "He says two napoleons—eight dollars."

One or two countenances fell. Then a pause.

"Too much!—we'll give him one!"

I never shall know how it was—I shudder yet when I think how the place is given to miracles—but in a single instant of time, as it seemed to me, that ship was twenty paces from the shore, and speeding away like a frightened thing! Eight crestfallen creatures stood upon the shore, and oh, to think of it! this—this—after all that overmastering ecstasy! Oh, shameful, shameful ending, after such unseemly boasting! It was too much like "Ho! let me at him!"

followed by a prudent "Two of you hold him—one can hold me!"

Instantly there was wailing and gnashing of teeth in the camp. The two napoleons were offered—more if necessary—and pilgrims and dragoman shouted themselves hoarse with pleadings to the retreating boatmen to come back. But they sailed serenely away and paid no further heed to pilgrims who had dreamed all their lives of some day skimming over the sacred waters of Galilee and listening to its hallowed story in the whispering of its waves, and had journeyed countless leagues to do it, and—and then concluded that the fare was too high. Impertinent Mohammedan Arabs, to think such things of gentlemen of another faith.

## Disgraceful Persecution of a Boy

The Chinese have for long been a source of difficulty in California. . . .

Now, if all the white folk in California were agreed in thinking the Chinese detestable . . . the Celestials would speedily be bundled out of the State, bag and baggage. But employers of labor, and indeed the well-to-do classes generally, approve of Chinese immigration. John Chinaman is quiet, sober, and obliging, he makes an excellent domestic servant, he is a dexterous cleaner of soiled linen. . . . For these virtues, more than for his alleged immoralities, he is hated by the white working classes, especially by the Irish. "We are ruined by Chinese cheap labor," say they. . . .

San Francisco has been convulsed by these feuds, which practically amount to a veiled civil war between the plug-hats (aristocracy) and the white proletariat (if we may venture to apply such a word to the American working man).—London *Graphic,* May 1, 1880

The London *Graphic* caught the flavor of the American situation, but not the details. The Chinese trouble had nothing to do with the laundry business. Nor were the American employers who once warmly encouraged Chinese immigration looking for domestic help. They were building the great Union Pacific Railroad, which had labor problems. By 1869 these problems were solved; the line had been completed with the aid of coolie labor. The result was that American labor, which was chiefly Irish, became desperately and ferociously anti-Chinese. By the end of the 1880's Chinese immigration was, in effect, excluded by legislation. Until then, and after, the Chinese were more brutally used than any other American minority except the Negro.

The pattern of Clemens' political sophistication was not complete until the late 1860's. In 1867 he wrote, from Honolulu, to the *Sacramento Union:* "You will not always go on paying $80 and $100 a month for labor which you can hire for $5. The sooner California adopts coolie labor the better it will be for her."

It was a note he was never to strike again. The next year he was exulting over the Burlingame treaty with China, which gave Chinese here the same privileges as the nationals of "the most favored nations." Then—in the New York *Tribune* for August 4, 1868—he found the coolie labor trade "infamous."

At the height of the West Coast bitterness, Clemens was working for the San Francisco *Morning Call*. There began a lifetime of devotion to Chinese affairs, both here and in the Orient. Few Americans have been better informed on these matters; very few, at the time, were even interested.

Mark Twain's maiden effort for the Chinese died, in 1865, in the composing room of the *Morning Call,* for commercial reasons explained by his editor. (See Mark Twain's footnote to "Disgraceful Persecution of a Boy.") He was subsequently fired. Fours years later, in New York, as humor editor of *The Galaxy,* he wrote "Disgraceful Persecution of a Boy."

Under the same management, *The Galaxy*'s humor department ran, in installments, "Goldsmith's Friend Abroad Again," purporting to be the letter of one Ah Sing Hi, reporting to a friend in the old country his experiences in California. These must have startled readers looking for something cheerful. They were by the same humorist who, thirty years later, in "To the Person Sitting in Darkness," declared war on the powerful American Board of Foreign Missions, on behalf of his friends the Chinese.


IN SAN FRANCISCO, the other day, "A well-dressed boy, on his way to Sunday school, was arrested and thrown into the city prison for stoning Chinamen." What a commentary is this upon human justice! What sad prominence it gives to our human disposition to tyrannize over the weak! San Francisco has little right to take credit to herself for her treatment of this poor boy. What had the child's education been? How should he suppose it was wrong to stone a Chinaman? Before we side against him, along with outraged San Francisco, let us give him a chance—let us hear the testimony for the defence.

He was a "well-dressed" boy, and a Sunday-school scholar.

and therefore, the chances are that his parents were intelligent, well-to-do people, with just enough natural villainy in their composition to make them yearn after the daily papers, and enjoy them; and so this boy had opportunities to learn all through the week how to do right, as well as on Sunday.

It was in this way that he found out that the great commonwealth of California imposes an unlawful mining-tax upon John the foreigner, and allows Patrick the foreigner to dig gold for nothing—probably because the degraded Mongol is at no expense for whisky, and the refined Celt cannot exist without it.

It was in this way that he found out that a respectable number of the tax-gatherers—it would be unkind to say all of them—collect the taxes twice, instead of once; and that, inasmuch as they do it solely to discourage Chinese immigration into the mines, it is a thing that is much applauded, and likewise regarded as singularly facetious.

It was in this way that he found out that when a white man robs a sluice box (by the term white man is meant Spaniards, Mexicans, Portuguese, Irish, Hondurans, Peruvians, Chileans, etc., etc.) they make him leave the camp; and when a Chinaman does that thing, they hang him.

It was in this way that he found out that in many districts of the vast Pacific coast, so strong is the wild free love of justice in the hearts of the people, that whenever any secret and mysterious crime is committed, they say, "Let justice be done, though the heavens fall," and go straightway and swing a Chinaman.

It was in this way that he found out that by studying one half of each day's "local items," it would appear that the police of San Francisco were either asleep or dead, and by studying the other half it would seem that the reporters were gone mad with admiration of the energy, the virtue, the high effectiveness, and the daredevil intrepidity of that very police—making exultant mention of how "the Argus-eyed officer So-an-so," captured a wretched knave of a Chinaman who was stealing chickens, and brought him gloriously to the city prison; and how "the gallant officer Such-and-such-a-one," quietly kept an eye on the movements of an "unsuspecting, almond-eyed son of Confucius" (your reporter is nothing if not facetious), following him around with that far-off look of vacancy and unconsciousness always so finely affected by that inscrutible being, the forty-dollar policeman, during a walking interval, and captured him at last in the very act of placing his hands in a suspicious manner upon a paper of tacks, left by the owner in an exposed situation; and how one officer performed this prodigious thing, and another officer that, and another the other— and pretty much every one of these performances having for a dazzling central incident a Chinaman guilty of a shilling's worth of crime, an unfortunate, whose misdemeanor must be hurrahed into something enormous in order to keep the public from noticing how many really important rascals went uncaptured in the meantime, and how overrated those glorified policemen actually are.

It was in this way that the boy found out that the legislature, being aware that the Constitution has made America an asylum for the poor and the oppressed of all nations, and that therefore the poor and oppressed who fly to our shelter must not be charged a disabling admission fee, made a law that every Chinaman, upon landing, must be *vaccinated* upon the wharf and pay to the State's appointed officer *ten dollars* for the service, when there are plenty of doctors in San Francisco who would be glad enough to do it for him for fifty cents.

It was in this way that the boy found out that a Chinaman had no rights that any man was bound to respect; that he had no sorrows that any man was bound to pity, that neither his life nor his liberty was worth the purchase of a penny when a white man needed a scapegoat; that nobody loved Chinamen, that nobody befriended them, nobody spared them suffering when it was convenient to inflict it; everybody, individuals, communities, the majesty of the State itself, joined in hating, abusing, and persecuting these humble strangers.

And, therefore, what *could* have been more natural than for this sunny-hearted boy, tripping along to Sunday school, with his mind teeming with freshly-learned incentives to high and virtuous action, to say to himself—

"Ah, there goes a Chinaman! God will not love me if I do not stone him."

And for this he was arrested and put in the city jail.

Everything conspired to teach him that it was a high and holy thing to stone a Chinamen, and yet he no sooner attempts to do his duty than he is punished for it—he, poor chap, who has been aware all his life that one of the principal recreations of the police, out toward the Gold Refinery, is to look on with tranquil enjoyment while the butchers of Brannan Street set their dogs on unoffending Chinamen, and make them flee for their lives.*

Keeping in mind the tuition in the humanities which the entire "Pacific coast" gives its youth, there is a very sublimity of incongruity in the virtuous flourish with which the good city fathers of San Francisco proclaim (as they have lately done) that "The police are positively ordered to arrest all boys of every description and wherever found, who engage in assaulting Chinamen."

Still, let us be truly glad they have made the order, notwithstanding its inconsistency; and let us rest perfectly confident that the police are glad, too. Because there is no personal peril in arresting boys, provided they be of the small kind, and the reporters will have to laud their performances just as loyally as ever, or go without items.

The new form for local items in San Francisco will now be: "The ever vigilant and efficient officer So-and-so succeeded, yesterday afternoon, in arresting Master Tommy Jones, after a determined resistance," etc., etc., followed by the customary statistics and final hurrah, with its unconscious sarcasm: "We are happy in being able to state that this is the forty-seventh boy arrested by this gallant officer since the new ordinance went into effect. The most extraordinary activity prevails in the police department. Nothing like it has been seen since we can remember."

* I have many such memories in my mind, but am thinking just at present of one particular one, where the Brannan Street butchers set their dogs on a Chinaman who was quietly passing with a basket of clothes on his head; and while the dogs mutilated his flesh, a butcher increased the hilarity of the occasion by knocking some of the Chinaman's teeth down his throat with half a brick. This incident sticks in my memory with a more malevolent tenacity perhaps, on account of the fact that I was in the employ of a San Francisco journal at the time, and was not allowed to publish it because it might offend some of the peculiar element that subscribed for the paper. (M.T.)

## A Defence of General Funston

I asked Tom if countries always apologized when they had done wrong, and he says: "Yes; the little ones does."—MARK TWAIN, *Tom Sawyer Abroad*.

Let the faithless sons of freedom crush the patriot with his heel
Lo, greed is marching on.
                                              —MARK TWAIN, "Battle Hymn of the
                                                Republic Brought Down to Date," 1901 *

Modern research has uncovered appalling facts about our war in the Philippines. But even in the thick of the fighting there was widespread uneasiness. Letters from servicemen contained enough reports of burned villages, wholesale massacres of civilians, and torture of prisoners to keep our own civilian population on edge. Our looting of Filipino churches seems also to have been wholesale—perhaps because there was nothing else of value on the islands. The military record of General Funston includes charges that he helped himself to gold altar ornaments and a valuable robe; Funston was, in every way, a typical hero of that war.

However, the press remained free; disquieting war news was printed and discussed. Even in Congress—where, according to Mark Twain, nothing good could be expected, not even respect for George Washington—there were men who felt much as he did, and said so. Of these, the most prominent was Massachusetts Senator George Hoar, whose parting speech to his opponents in the Senate was delivered the year after "A Defence of General Funston" appeared. He remarked:

You, my imperialistic friends, have had your ideals and sentimentalities. One is that the flag shall never be hauled down where it has once floated. Another is that you will not talk or reason with people with arms in their hand. Another is that sovereignty over an unwilling people may be bought with gold. And another is that sovereignty may be got by force of arms. . . .
What has been the practical statesmanship which comes from your ideals and sentimentalities? You have wasted six hundred millions of treasure. You have sacrificed nearly ten thousand American lives, the flower of our youth. You have devastated provinces. You have slain uncounted thousands of the people you desire to benefit. You have established reconcentration camps. Your generals are coming home from their harvest, bringing their sheaves with them, in the shape of other thousands of sick and wounded and insane. . . .

On the other hand were ardent supporters of the war, including President Theodore Roosevelt, who had taken office on the assassination of President McKinley. An extremist was Indiana Senator Albert Beveridge, who told the Senate that God

. . . has marked the American people as His chosen nation to finally lead in the regeneration of the world. This is the divine mission of America. . . . The Philippines are ours forever. We will not repudiate our duty in the archipelago. We will not abandon our opportunity in the Orient. We will not renounce our part in the mission of our race, trustee, under God, of the civilization of the world.

Frederick Funston was thirty-six, and a Brigadier General in the Volunteers, when he captured Filipino General Emilio Aguinaldo by the stunt described below. Since Mark Twain's great declaration the year before, in "To the Person Sitting in Darkness," he had published nothing on the war. Conceivably, he might have remained silent, had not the newly promoted General Funston, describing his own exploits before the fashionable Lotus Club in New York, also described as "traitors" all Americans—and there were many—who had their doubts about the war.

Alongside these remarks, as quoted in the New York *Sun*, Mark Twain pencilled his own:

If I were in the Phil[ippines] I could be imprisoned for a year for publicly expressing the opinion that we ought to withdraw & give those people their independence—an opinion which I desire to express now. What is treason in one part of our States & stealings is doubtless law everywhere under the flag. If so, I am now committing treason . . . & if I were out there I would hire a hall & do it again. On these terms I would rather be a traitor than an archangel. On these terms I am quite willing to be called a traitor—quite willing to wear that honorable badge—& not willing to be affronted with the title of Patriot & classified with the Funstons when so help me God I have not done anything to deserve it.*

"A Defence of General Funston"—in which Clemens claimed the title Traitor—appeared in May 1902, in the *North American Review*. Here it is slightly abridged; in the original Mark Twain develops some truisms at length—the importance of influence and the fact that example breeds imitation. But his alarm lest the influence of Funston should prevail, even over the influence of Washington, was not so groundless as it may sound now. Defenses of Funston—serious and passionate—were appearing in every sort of publication. There was even talk of running him for President.

Moreover, behind Mark Twain's plea that we "let go our obsequious hold on the rear-skirts of the sceptered land-thieves of Europe," there was a good deal of solid and unpleasant fact. Justification of our policy in the Philippines was then most frequently made in terms of what the European nations had done. When General Bell advocated

* Philip S. Foner, *Mark Twain: Social Critic*, pp. 291-292, © 1958, by International Publishers Co., Inc., printed with permission of The Mark Twain Company.

ruthless destruction of the civilian population, General Wheaton agreed with him:

> The nearer we approach the methods found necessary by the other nations through centuries of experience in dealing with Asiatics, the less the national treasury will be expended and the fewer graves will be made.

Mark Twain's careless postscript was probably as confusing to readers a month after it was written as it is now. And yet it is a clue to his greatness. A postscript like this is generally scrawled only on a letter to a close and understanding friend; the American public was such a friend to Mark Twain. It has been said that great literature flourishes only when something like this relationship exists between the artist and society.

I

FEBRUARY 22. Today is the great Birthday; and it was observed so widely in the earth that differences in longitudinal time made curious work with some of the cabled testimonies of respect paid to the sublime name which the date calls up in our minds; for, although they were all being offered at about the same hour, several of them were yesterday to us and several were tomorrow.

There was a reference in the papers to General Funston.

Neither Washington nor Funston was made in a day. It took a long time to accumulate the materials. In each case, the basis or moral skeleton of the man was inborn disposition—a thing which is as permanent as rock, and never undergoes any actual and genuine change between cradle and grave. . . .

Washington did not create the basic skeleton (disposition) that was in him; it was born there, and the merit of its perfection was not his. . . .

Is there a value, then, in having a Washington, since we may not concede to him *personal merit* for what he was and did?

* Philip S. Foner, *Mark Twain: Social Critic,* p. 278, © 1958, by International Publishers Co., Inc., printed with permission of The Mark Twain Company.

Necessarily, there is a value—a value so immense that it defies all estimate. Acceptable outside influence were the materials out of which Washington's native disposition built Washington's character and fitted him for his achievements. Suppose there hadn't *been* any. Suppose he had been born and reared in a pirate's cave; the acceptable materials would have been lacking, the Washingtonian character would not have been built. . . .

Did Washington's great value, then, lie in what he accomplished? No; that was only a minor value. His major value, his vast value, his immeasurable value to us and to the world and to future ages and peoples, lies in his permanent and sky-reaching conspicuousness as an *influence*. . . .

Washington was more and greater than the father of a nation, he was the father of its patriotism—patriotism at its loftiest and best; and so powerful was the influence which he left behind him, that that golden patriotism remained undimmed and unsullied for a hundred years, lacking one; and so fundamentally right-hearted are our people by grace of that long and ennobling teaching, that today, already, they are facing back for home, they are laying aside their foreign-born and foreign-bred imported patriotism and resuming that which Washington gave to their fathers, which is American and the only American—which lasted ninety-nine years and is good for a million more. Doubt—doubt that we did right by the Filipinos—is rising steadily higher and higher in the nation's breast; conviction will follow doubt. The nation will speak; its will is law; there is no other sovereign on this soil; and in that day we shall right such unfairnesses as we have done. We shall let go our obsequious hold on the rear-skirts of the sceptred land-thieves of Europe, and be what we were before, a *real* world power, and the chiefest of them all, by right of the only clean hands in Christendom, the only hands guiltless of the sordid plunder of any helpless people's stolen liberties, hands recleansed in the patriotism of Washington, and once more fit to touch the hem of the revered Shade's garment and stand in its presence unashamed. It was Washington's influence that made Lincoln and all other real patriots the Republic has known; it was Washington's influence that made the soldiers who saved the Union; and that influence will save us always, and bring us back to the fold when we stray.

And so, when a Washington is given us, or a Lincoln, or a Grant, what should we do? Knowing, as we do, that a *conspicuous* influence for good is worth more than a billion obscure ones, without doubt the logic of it is that we should highly value it and make a vestal flame of it, and keep it briskly burning in every way we can—in the nursery, in the school, in the college, in the pulpit, in the newspaper—even in Congress, if such a thing were possible.

The proper inborn disposition was required to start a Washington; the acceptable influences and circumstances and a large field were required to develop and complete him. The same with Funston.

II

"The war was over"—end of 1900. A month later the mountain refuge of the defeated and hunted, and now powerless but not yet hopeless, Filipino chief was discovered. His army was gone, his republic extinguished, his ablest statesman deported, his generals all in their graves or prisoners of war. The memory of his worthy dream had entered upon a historic life, to be an inspiration to less unfortunate patriots in other centuries; the dream itself was dead beyond resurrection, though he could not believe it.

Now came his capture. An admiring author* shall tell us about it. His account can be trusted, for it is correctly synopsized from General Funston's own voluntary confession made by him at the time. The italics are mine.

It was not until February, 1901, that his actual hiding-place was discovered. The clue was in the shape of a letter from Aguinaldo commanding his cousin, Baldormero Aguinaldo, to send him four hundred armed men, the bearer to act as a guide to the same. The order was in cipher, but among other effects captured at various times a copy of the Insurgent cipher was found. The Insurgent courier was convinced of the error of his ways (though by exactly what means, history does not reveal)[10] and offered to lead the way to Aguinaldo's place of hiding. Here . . . was just the kind of a daredevil exploit that appealed to the romantic Funston. . . . He formulated a scheme and asked General MacArthur's permission. It was impossible to refuse the daring adventurer, the hero of the Rio Grande, anything; so Funston set to

* *Aguinaldo.* By Edwin Wildman. Lothrop Publishing Co., Boston. (M.T.)

work, imitating the peculiar handwriting of Lacuna, the Insurgent officer to whom Aguinaldo's communication referred. . . . Having perfected Lacuna's signature, Funston wrote two letters on February 24 and 28, acknowledging Aguinaldo's communication, and informing him that he (Lacuna) was sending him a few of the best soldiers in his command. Added to this neat forgery General Funston dictated a letter which was written by an ex-Insurgent attached to his command, telling Aguinaldo that the relief force had surprised and captured a detachment of Americans, taking five prisoners whom they were bringing to him because of their importance. This ruse was employed to explain the presence of the five Americans: General Funston, Captain Hazzard, Captain Newton, Lieutenant Hazzard, and General Funston's aide, Lieutenant Kitchell, who were to accompany the expedition.

Seventy-eight Macabebes, hereditary enemies of the Tagalogs, were chosen by Funston to form the body of the command. These fearless and hardy natives[11] fell into the scheme with a vengeance. Three Tagalogs and one Spaniard were also invited. The Macabebes were fitted out in castoff Insurgent uniforms, and the Americans donned field-worn uniforms of privates. Three days' rations were provided, and each man was given a rifle. The *Vicksburg* was chosen to take the daring impostors to some spot on the east coast near Palanan, where Aguinaldo was in hiding. Arriving off the coast at Casignan, some distance from the Insurgent-hidden capital, the party was landed. Three Macabebes who spoke Tagalog fluently, were sent into the town to notify the natives that they were bringing additional forces and important American prisoners to Aguinaldo, and request of the local authorities guides and assistance. The Insurgent president readily consented, and the little party, after refreshing themselves and exhibiting their prisoners, started over the ninety-mile trail to Palanan, a mountain retreat on the coast of the Isabella province. Over the stony declivities and through the thick jungle, across bridgeless streams and up narrow passes, the footsore and bone-racked adventurers tramped, until their food was exhausted, and they were *too weak to move*, though but eight miles from Aguinaldo's rendezvous.

A messenger was sent forward to inform Aguinaldo of their position and to *beg for food*. The rebel chieftain promptly replied by despatching rice and a letter to the officer in command, instructing him to treat the American prisoners well, but to leave them outside the town. What better condition could the ingenious Funston have himself dictated? On the 23d of March the party reached Palanan. Aguinaldo sent out eleven men to take charge of the American prisoners, but Funston and his associates succeeded in dodging them and scattering themselves in the jungle until they passed on to meet the Americans whom the Insurgents were notified were left behind.

Immediately joining his command, Funston ordered his little band of daredevils to march boldly into the town and present themselves to Aguinaldo. At the Insurgent headquarters they were received by Aguinaldo's bodyguard, dressed in blue drill uniforms and white hats, drawn up in military form. The spokesman so completely hoodwinked Aguinaldo that he did not suspect the ruse. In the meantime the Macabebes maneuvered around into advantageous positions, directed by the Spaniard until all were in readiness. Then he shouted, "Macabebes, now is your turn!" whereupon they emptied their rifles into Aguinaldo's bodyguard. . . .

The American joined in the skirmish, and two of Aguinaldo's staff were wounded, but escaped, the treasurer of the revolutionary government surrendering. The rest of the Filipino officers got away. Aguinaldo accepted his capture with resignation, though greatly in fear of the vengeance of the Macabebes. But General Funston's assurance of his personal safety set his mind easy on that point, and he calmed down and discussed the situation. He was greatly cast down at his capture, and asserted that *by no other means* would he have been taken alive—an admission which added all the more to Funston's achievement, for Aguinaldo's was a difficult and desperate case, and demanded extraordinary methods.

Some of the customs of war are not pleasant to the civilian; but ages upon ages of training have reconciled us to them as being justifiable, and we accept them and make no demur, even when they give us an extra twinge. Every detail of Funston's scheme—but one—has been employed in war in the past and stands acquitted of blame by history. By the custom of war, it is permissible, in the interest of an enterprise like the one under consideration, for a brigadier general (if he be of the sort that can so choose) to persuade or bribe a courier to betray his trust; to remove the badges of his honorable rank and disguise himself; to lie, to practice treachery, to forge; to associate with himself persons properly fitted by training and instinct for the work; to accept of courteous welcome, and assassinate the welcomers while their hands are still warm from the friendly handshake.

By the custom of war, all these things are innocent, none of them is blameworthy, all of them are justifiable; none of them is new, all of them have been done before, although not by a brigadier general. But there is one detail which is new, absolutely new. It has never been resorted to before in any age of the world, in any country, among any people, savage or civilized. It was the one meant by Aguinaldo when he said that *"by no other means"* would he have been taken alive. When a man is exhausted by hunger to the point where he is "too weak to move," he has a right to make supplication to his enemy to save his failing life; but if he takes so much as one taste of that food—which is holy, by the precept of all ages and all nations—*he is barred from lifting his hand against that enemy for that time.*

It was left to a Brigadier General of Volunteers in the American army to put shame upon a custom which even the degraded Spanish friars had respected. *We promoted him for it.*[12]

Our unsuspecting President[13] was in the act of taking his murderer by the hand when the man shot him down. The amazed world dwelt upon that damning fact, brooded over it, discussed it, blushed for it, said it put a blot and a shame upon our race. Yet, bad as he was, he had not—dying of starvation—begged food of the President to strengthen his failing forces for his treacherous work; he did not proceed against the life of a benefactor who had just saved his own.

*April 14.* I have been absent several weeks in the West Indies; I will now resume this Defence.

It seems to me that General Funston's appreciation of the capture needs editing. It seems to me that, in his after-dinner speeches, he spreads out the heroisms of it—I say it with deference, and subject to correction—with an almost too generous hand. He is a brave man; his dearest enemy will cordially grant him that credit. For his sake it is a pity that somewhat of that quality was not needed in the episode under consideration; that he would have furnished it, no one doubts. But, by his own showing, he ran but one danger—that of starving. He and his party were well disguised, in dishonored uniforms, American and Insurgent; they greatly outnumbered Aguinaldo's guard;* by his forgeries and falsehoods he had lulled suspicion to sleep; his coming was expected, his way was prepared; his course was through a solitude, unfriendly interruption was unlikely; his party were well armed; they would catch their prey with welcoming smiles in their faces, and with hospitable hands extended for the friendly shake—nothing

* Eighty-nine to forty-eight.—*Funston's Lotus Club Confession.* (M.T.)

would be necessary but to shoot these people down. That is what they did. It was hospitality repaid in a brand-new, up-to-date, modern civilization fashion, and would be admired by many.

The spokesman so completely hoodwinked Aguinaldo that he did not suspect the ruse. In the meantime, the Macabebes maneuvered around into advantageous positions, directed by the Spaniard, until all were in readiness; then he shouted, "Macabebes, now is your turn!" whereupon they emptied their rifles into Aguinaldo's bodyguard.—*From Wildman's book, already quoted.*

The utter completeness of the surprise, the total absence of suspicion which had been secured by the forgeries and falsehoods, is best brought out in Funston's humorous account of the episode in one of his rollicking speeches . . . :

The Macabebes fired on those men and two fell dead; the others retreated, firing as they ran, and I might say here that they retreated with such great alacrity and enthusiasm that they dropped eighteen rifles and a thousand rounds of ammunition.
Sigismondo rushed back into the house, pulled his revolver, and told the insurgent officers to surrender. They all threw up their hands except Villia, Aguinaldo's chief of staff; he had on one of those new fangled Mauser revolvers and he wanted to try it. But before he had the Mauser out of its scabbard he was shot twice; Sigismondo was a pretty fair marksman himself.
Alambra was shot in the face. He jumped out of the window; the house, by the way, stood on the bank of the river. He went out of the window and went clear down into the river, the water being twenty-five feet below the bank. He escaped, swam across the river and got away, and surrendered five months afterwards.
Villia, shot in the shoulder, followed him out of the window and into the river, but the Macabebes saw him and ran down to the river bank, and they waded in and fished him out, and kicked him all the way up the bank, and asked him how he liked it. (Laughter.)

While it is true that the daredevils were not in danger upon this occasion, they *were* in awful peril at one time; in peril of a death so awful that swift extinction by bullet, by the axe, by the sword, by the rope, by drowning, by fire, is a kindly mercy contrasted with it; a death so awful that it holds its place unchallenged as the supremest of human agonies—death by starvation.[14] Aguinaldo saved them from that.

These being the facts, we come now to the question, Is Funston to blame? I think not. And for that reason I think too much is being made of this matter. He did not make his own disposition, It was born with him. It chose his ideals for him, he did not choose them. It chose the kind of society It liked, the kind of comrades It preferred, . . . It admired everything that Washington did not admire, and hospitably received and coddled everything that Washington would have turned out of doors—but It, and It only, was to blame, not Funston; . . . It had a native predilection for unsavory conduct, but it would be in the last degree unfair to hold Funston to blame for the outcome of his infirmity; as clearly unfair as it would be to blame him because his conscience leaked out through one of his pores when he was little—a thing which he could not help, and he couldn't have raised it, anyway; It was able to say to an enemy, "Have pity on me, I am starving; I am too weak to move, give me food; I am your friend, I am your fellow patriot, your fellow Filipino, and am fighting for our dear country's liberties, like you—have pity, give me food, save my life, there is no other help!" and It was able to refresh and restore Its marionette with the food, and then shoot down the giver of it while his hand was stretched out in welcome . . . It has the noble gift of humor, and can make a banquet almost die with laughter when it has a funny incident to tell about; this one will bear reading again—and over and over again, in fact:

The Macabebes fired on those men and two fell dead; the others retreated, firing as they ran, and I might say here that they retreated with such alacrity and enthusiasm that they dropped eighteen rifles and a thousand rounds of ammunition.

Sigismondo rushed back into the house, pulled his revolver, and told the insurgent officers to surrender. They all threw up their hands except Villia, Aguinaldo's chief of staff; he had on one of those new-fangled Mauser revolvers and he wanted to try it. But before he had the Mauser out of its scabbard he was shot twice; Sigismondo was a pretty fair marksman himself.

Alambra was shot in the face. He jumped out of the window; the house, by the way, stood on the bank of the river. He went out of the window and went clear down into the river, the water being twenty-five feet below the bank. He escaped, swam across the river and got away, and surrendered five months afterwards.

Villia, shot in the shoulder, followed him out of the window and into the river, but the Macabebes saw him and ran down to the river bank, and they waded in and fished him out, and kicked him all the way up the bank, and asked him how he liked it. (Laughter.)

(This was a wounded man.) But it is only It that is speaking, not Funston. With youthful glee It can see sink down in death the simple creatures who had answered Its fainting prayer for food, and without remorse It can note the reproachful look in their dimming eyes; but in fairness we must remember that this is only It, not Funston; . . . And It—not Funston—comes home now, to teach us children what patriotism is! Surely It ought to know.

It is plain to me, and I think it ought to be plain to all, that Funston is not in any way to blame for the things he has done, does, thinks, and says.

Now, then, we have Funston; he has happened, and is on our hands. The question is, What are we going to do about it? How are we going to meet the emergency? We have seen what happened in Washington's case: he became a colossal example, an example to the whole world, and for all time—because his name and deeds went everywhere, and inspired, as they still inspire, and will always inspire, admiration, and compel emulation. Then the thing for the world to do in the present case is to turn the gilt front of Funston's evil notoriety to the rear, and expose the back aspect of it, the right and black aspect of it, to the youth of the land; otherwise *he* will become an example and a boy-admiration, and will most sorrowfully and grotesquely bring his breed of patriotism into competition with Washington's. This competition has already begun, in fact. Some may not believe it, but it is nevertheless true, that there are now public-school teachers and superintendents who are holding up Funston as a model hero and patriot in the schools.

If this Funstonian boom continues, Funstonism will presently affect the army. In fact, this has already happened. There are weak-headed and weak-principled officers in all armies, and these are always ready to imitate successful notoriety-breeding methods, let them be good or bad. . . . Funston's example has bred many imitators, and many ghastly additions to our history: the torturing of Filipinos by the awful "water cure," [15] for instance, to make them confess—what? Truth? Or lies? How can one know which it is they are telling? For under unendurable pain a man confesses anything that is required of him, true or false, and his evidence is worthless. Yet upon such evidence American officers have actually—but you know about those atrocities which the War Office has been hiding a year or two; and about General Smith's now world-celebrated order of *massacre*—thus summarized by the press from Major Waller's testimony:

> *Kill and burn—this is no time to take prisoners—the more you kill and burn, the better—Kill all above the age of ten—make Samar a howling wilderness!* [16]

You see what Funston's example has produced, just in this little while—even before he produced the example. It has advanced our civilization ever so far—fully as far as Europe advanced it in China. Also, no doubt, it was Funston's example that made us (and England [17]) copy Weyler's *reconcentrado* horror after the pair of us, with our Sunday-school smirk on, and our goody-goody noses upturned toward heaven, had been calling him a "fiend." And the fearful earthquake out there in Krakatoa, that destroyed the island and killed two million people— No, that could not have been Funston's example; I remember now, he was not born then.

However, for all these things I blame only his It, not him. In conclusion, I have defended him as well as I could, and indeed I have found it quite easy, and have removed prejudice from him and rehabilitated him in the public esteem and regard, I think. I was not able to do anything for his It, It being out of my jurisdiction, and out of Funston's and everybody's. As I have shown, Funston is not to blame for his fearful deed; and, if I tried, I might also show that he is not to blame for our still holding in bondage the man he captured by unlawful means, and who is not any more rightfully our prisoner and spoil than he would be if he were stolen money. He is entitled to his freedom. If he were a king of a great power, or an ex-president of our republic, instead of an ex-president of a destroyed and abolished little republic, Civilization (with a large C) would criticize and complain until he got it.

MARK TWAIN

*P. S. April 16.* The President is speaking up, this morning, just as this goes to the printer, and there is no uncertain sound about the note.[18] It is the speech and spirit of a President of a people, not of a party, and we all like it, Traitors and all. I think I may speak for the other Traitors, for I am sure they feel as I do about it. I will explain that we get our title from the Funstonian patriots —free of charge. They are always doing us little compliments like that; they are just born flatterers, those boys.

M.T.

# A Humane Word from Satan

There are still some strange notions current about our grandfathers —among others, that they were gagged not only by prudishness (as they were) but also by many other censorships from which we, at last, are free.

For this nonsense the constant complaining of Mark Twain is at least partly to blame. This is from *Following the Equator:*

It is by the goodness of God that in our country we have those three unspeakably precious things: freedom of speech, freedom of conscience, and the prudence never to practice either of them.

And from *Life on the Mississippi:*

We write frankly and freely but then we "modify" before we print.

Nevertheless, in 1905, "A Humane Word from Satan" did appear in the popular *Harper's Weekly;* nowadays most popular publications would think many times before they published any such article. Among other things its possible effect on organized charity would be carefully considered. But Satan's jeers did not interfere with the philanthropies of John D. Rockefeller, who established the first of the great modern foundations.

The first rich Rockefeller was as great a monopolist as a philanthropist, and Clemens' remarks about perjury were based on the fact that the courts chose to disbelieve Rockefeller's sworn statements about the business methods of the Standard Oil trust. The courts ordered the trust dissolved in 1892, and again in 1911 when it reappeared as the Standard Oil Company of New Jersey.

This is "A Humane Word from Satan" as published in *Harper's Weekly:*

(The following letter, signed by Satan and purporting to come from him, we have reason to believe was not written by him, but by Mark Twain.—EDITOR [of *Harper's Weekly*].)

*To the Editor of Harper's Weekly:*

DEAR SIR AND KINSMAN—Let us have done with this frivolous talk. The American Board accepts contributions from me every year: then why shouldn't it from Mr. Rockefeller? In all the ages, three-fourths of the support of the great charities has been con-science-money, as my books will show: then what becomes of the sting when that term is applied to Mr. Rockefeller's gift? The American Board's trade is financed mainly from the graveyards. Bequests, you understand. Conscience-money. Confession of an old crime and deliberate perpetration of a new one; for deceased's contribution is a robbery of his heirs. Shall the Board decline be-quests because they stand for one of these offenses every time and generally for both?

Allow me to continue. The charge most persistently and resent-fully and remorselessly dwelt upon is that Mr. Rockefeller's con-tribution is incurably tainted by perjury—perjury proved against him in the courts. *It makes us smile*—down in my place! Because there isn't a rich man in your vast city who doesn't perjure himself every year before the tax board. They are all caked with perjury, many layers thick. Ironclad, so to speak. If there is one that isn't, I desire to acquire him for my museum, and will pay Dinosaur rates. Will you say it isn't infraction of law, but only annual evasion of it? Comfort yourselves with that nice distinction if you like—*for the present*. But by and by, when you arrive, I will show you something interesting: a whole hell-full of evaders! Sometimes a frank lawbreaker turns up elsewhere, but I get those others every time.

To return to my muttons. I wish you to remember that my rich perjurers are contributing to the American Board with frequency: it is money filched from the sworn-off personal tax; therefore it is the wages of sin; therefore it is my money; therefore it is *I* that contribute it; and, finally, it is therefore as I have said: since the Board daily accepts contributions from me, why should it decline them from Mr. Rockefeller, who is as good as I am, let the courts say what they may?

SATAN

# The United States of Lyncherdom

The vast majority of the race, whether savage or civilized, are secretly kind-hearted and shrink from inflicting pain, but in the presence of the aggressive and pitiless minority they don't dare to assert themselves. Think of it! One kind-hearted creature spies upon another, and sees to it that he loyally helps in iniquities which revolt both of them.—MARK TWAIN, *The Mysterious Stranger*

During the 1950's, there were eight lynchings in the United States. But at the turn of the century, lynchings were running about a hundred a year, and many Americans apparently felt there was much to be said both for and against them. At any rate, in 1901—the year Mark Twain wrote "The United States of Lyncherdom"—*The Outlook,* a liberal New York weekly, opened its pages to a controversy. In September it ran an editorial condemning lynch law and quoting some Southern publications which also condemned it. In November it presented the other side of the question, by William Hayne Levell, who is introduced this way:

It will add to the reader's interest in this article to know that the writer is pastor of one of the largest Presbyterian churches in Houston, Texas, that he has been pastor of Congregational churches in New Hampshire and Massachusetts, and that he is a Southern Man and of wide influence and the highest character.

It adds to our interest, and to our understanding of the period.

The Rev. Levell begins with an inside report of a triple lynching in Carrolltown, Mississippi. A white couple had been murdered; their Negro tenants—a mother, son, and daughter—were in jail.

A committee of prominent men . . . satisfied itself that those three Negroes did not personally commit the crime, but knew who did, and were as yet not willing to reveal their guilty secret. . . . As the authorities offered practically no resistance, the mob took the Negroes, hanged them just outside the town, and riddled their bodies with bullets. . . .

Realizing that it would be regarded as an impertinent intrusion for me to offer any suggestions, since I was an outsider . . . I rode away home some time before the lynching took place.

After discussing the incident "with some of the best and maturer and more conservative citizens of that part of the State of Mississippi," Rev. Levell found

some . . . who are good citizens in their way, who are yet very nervous over the whole question of the Negro . . . and who assert that for any considerable crime, of whatever nature, committed against a white person by a Negro, they would take the law in their own hands and shoot him down as they would a dog. These are extremists.

The greater part of the educated, conservative, thoughtful . . . citizens approve of lynching for the rape of a white woman, but deplore the seeming necessity for it.

The rest is a defense of lynching—chiefly as a deterrent for rape—"as given me by the . . . most thoughtful and most wise citizens of the South." It appeared in one of the most high-minded and earnest publications of the North.

That is part of the background against which Sam Clemens, of Hannibal, Missouri, wrote "The United States of Lyncherdom." It was inspired by an atrocity in his home state, and intended for immediate publication. But Clemens let some time go by. When he looked again, his polemic was no longer timely, or so he believed, for the Missouri horror on which he had based it had been forgotten.

Even Paine, when he published it some twenty years later, in *Europe and Elsewhere,* had misgivings about its "timeliness."

I

AND SO Missouri has fallen, that great state! Certain of her children have joined the lynchers, and the smirch is upon the rest of us. That handful of her children have given us a character and labeled us with a name, and to the dwellers in the four quarters of the earth we are "lynchers," now, and ever shall be. For the world will not stop and think—it never does, it is not its way; its way is to generalize from a single sample. It will not say, "Those Missourians have been busy eighty years in building an honorable good name for themselves; these hundred lynchers down in the corner of the state are not real Missourians, they are renegades." No, that truth will not enter its mind; it will generalize from the one or two misleading samples and say, "The Missourians are lynchers." It has no reflection, no logic, no sense of proportion. With it, figures go for nothing; to it, figures reveal nothing, it cannot reason upon them rationally; it would say, for instance, that China is being swiftly and surely Christianized, since nine Chinese Christians are being made every day; and it would fail, with him, to notice that the fact that 33,000 pagans are *born* there every day, damages the argument. It would say, "There are a hundred lynchers there, therefore the Missourians are lynchers"; the considerable fact that there are two and a half million Missourians who are *not* lynchers would not affect their verdict.

II

Oh, Missouri!

The tragedy occurred near Pierce City, down in the southwestern corner of the state. On a Sunday afternoon a young white woman who had started alone from church was found murdered. For there are churches there; in my time religion was more general, more pervasive, in the South than it was in the North, and more virile and earnest, too, I think; I have some reason to believe that this is still the case. The young woman was found murdered. Although it was a region of churches and schools the people rose, lynched three Negroes—two of them very aged ones —burned out five Negro households, and drove thirty Negro families into the woods.

I do not dwell upon the provocation which moved the people to these crimes, for that has nothing to do with the matter; the only question is, does the assassin *take the law into his own hands?* It is very simple, and very just. If the assassin be proved to have usurped the law's prerogative in righting his wrongs, that ends the matter; a thousand provocations are no defense. The Pierce City people had bitter provocation—indeed, as revealed by certain of the particulars, the bitterest of all provocations—but no matter, they took the law into their own hands, when by the terms of their statutes their victim would certainly hang if the law had been allowed to take its course, for there are but few Negroes in that region and they are without authority and without influence in overawing juries.

Why has lynching, with various barbaric accompaniments, become a favorite regulator in cases of "the usual crime" [19] in several parts of the country? Is it because men think a lurid and terrible punishment a more forcible object lesson and a more effective deterrent than a sober and colorless hanging done privately in a jail would be? Surely sane men do not think that. Even the average child should know better. It should know that any strange and much-talked-of event is always followed by imitations, the world being so well supplied with excitable people who only need a little stirring up to make them lose what is left of their heads and do mad things which they would not have thought of ordinarily. It should know that if a man jump off Brooklyn Bridge another will imitate him; that if a person venture down Niagara Whirlpool in a barrel another will imitate him; that if a Jack the Ripper make notoriety by slaughtering women in dark alleys he will be imitated; that if a man attempt a king's life and the newspapers carry the noise of it around the globe, regicides will crop up all around. The child should know that one much-talked-of outrage and murder committed by a Negro will upset the disturbed intellects of several other Negroes and produce a series of the very tragedies the community would so strenuously wish to prevent; that each of these crimes will produce another series, and year by year steadily increase the tale of these disasters instead of diminishing it; that, in a word, the lynchers are themselves the worst enemies of their women. The child should also know that by a law of our make, communities, as well as individuals, are imitators; and that a much-talked-of lynching will infallibly produce other lynchings here and there and yonder, and that in time these will breed a mania, a fashion; a fashion which will spread wide and wider, year by year, covering state after state, as with an advancing disease. Lynching has reached Colorado, it has reached California, it has reached Indiana—and now Missouri! I may live to see a Negro burned in Union Square, New York, with fifty thousand people present, and not a sheriff visible, not a governor, not a constable, not a colonel, not a clergyman, not a law-and-order representative of any sort.

*Increase in Lynching.*—In 1900 there were eight more cases than in 1899, and probably this year there will be more than there were last year. The year is little more than half gone, and yet there are eighty-eight cases as compared with one hundred and fifteen for all of last year. The four Southern states, Alabama, Georgia, Louisiana, and Mississippi are the worst offenders. Last year there were eight cases in Alabama, sixteen in Georgia, twenty in Louisiana, and twenty in Mississippi—over one half the total. This year to date there have been nine in Alabama, twelve in Georgia, eleven in Louisiana, and thirteen in Mississippi—again more than one-half the total number in the whole United States.—Chicago *Tribune*.[20]

It must be that the increase comes of the inborn human instinct to imitate—that and man's commonest weakness, his aversion to being unpleasantly conspicuous, pointed at, shunned, as being on the popular side. Its other name is moral cowardice, and is the commanding feature of the make-up of 9,999 men in the 10,000. I am not offering this as a discovery; privately the dullest of us knows it to be true. History will not allow us to forget or ignore this supreme trait of our character. It persistently and sardonically reminds us that from the beginning of the world no revolt against a public infamy or oppression has ever been begun but by the one daring man in the 10,000, the rest timidly waiting, and slowly and reluctantly joining, under the influence of that man and his fellows from the other ten thousands. The abolitionists remember. Privately the public feeling was with them early, but each man was afraid to speak out until he got some hint that his neighbor was privately feeling as he privately felt himself. Then the boom followed. It always does. It will occur in New York, some day; and even in Pennsylvania.

It has been supposed—and said—that the people at a lynching enjoy the spectacle and are glad of a chance to see it. It cannot be true; all experience is against it. The people in the South are made like the people in the North—the vast majority of whom are right-hearted and compassionate, and would be cruelly pained by such a spectacle—and *would attend it,* and let on to be pleased with it, if the public approval seemed to require it. We are made like that, and we cannot help it. The other animals are not so, but we cannot help that, either. They lack the moral sense; we have no way of trading ours off, for a nickel or some other thing above its value. The moral sense teaches us what is right, and how to avoid it—when unpopular.

It is thought, as I have said, that a lynching crowd enjoys a lynching. It certainly is not true; it is impossible of belief. It is

freely asserted—you have seen it in print many times of late—
that the lynching impulse has been misinterpreted; that it is *not*
the outcome of a spirit of revenge, but of a "mere atrocious
hunger *to look upon human suffering.*" If that were so, the crowds
that saw the Windsor Hotel burn down would have enjoyed the
horrors that fell under their eyes. Did they? No one will think that
of them, no one will make that charge. Many risked their lives to
save the men and women who were in peril. Why did they do
that? Because *none would disapprove.* There was no restraint;
they could follow their natural impulse. Why does a crowd of the
same kind of people in Texas, Colorado, Indiana, stand by, smitten to the heart and miserable, and by ostentatious outward signs
pretend to enjoy a lynching? Why does it lift no hand or voice
in protest? Only because it would be unpopular to do it, I think;
each man is afraid of his neighbor's disapproval—a thing which,
to the general run of the race, is more dreaded than wounds and
death. When there is to be a lynching the people hitch up and
come miles to see it, bringing their wives and children. Really to
see it? No—they come only because they are afraid to stay at
home, lest it be noticed and offensively commented upon. We
may believe this, for we all know how *we* feel about such spectacles—also, how we would act under the like pressure. We are not
any better nor any braver than anybody else, and we must not
try to creep out of it.

A Savonarola can quell and scatter a mob of lynchers with a
mere glance of his eye: so can a Merrill * or a Beloat.† For no
mob has any sand in the presence of a man known to be splendidly
brave. Besides, a lynching mob would *like* to be scattered, for
of a certainty there are never ten men in it who would not prefer
to be somewhere else—and would be, if they but had the courage
to go. When I was a boy I saw a brave gentleman deride and insult
a mob and drive it away; and afterward, in Nevada, I saw a noted
desperado make two hundred men sit still, with the house burning
under them, until he gave them permission to retire. A plucky man

* Sheriff of Carroll County, Georgia. (M.T.)
† Sheriff, Princeton, Indiana. By that formidable power which lies in an
established reputation for cold pluck they faced lynching mobs and securely
held the field against them. (M.T.)

can rob a whole passenger train by himself; and the half of a brave man can hold up a stagecoach and strip its occupants.

Then perhaps the remedy for lynchings comes to this: station a brave man in each affected community to encourage, support, and bring to light the deep disapproval of lynching hidden in the secret places of its heart—for it is there, beyond question. Then those communities will find something better to imitate—of course, being human, they must imitate something. Where shall these brave men be found? That is indeed a difficulty; there are not three hundred of them in the earth. If merely *physically* brave men would do, then it were easy; they could be furnished by the cargo. When Hobson called for seven volunteers to go with him to what promised to be certain death, four thousand men responded—the whole fleet, in fact. Because *all the world would approve.* They knew that; but if Hobson's project had been charged with the scoffs and jeers of the friends and associates, whose good opinion and approval the sailors valued, he could not have got his seven.[21]

No, upon reflection, the scheme will not work. There are not enough morally brave men in stock. We are out of moral-courage material; we are in a condition of profound poverty. We have those two sheriffs down South who—but never mind, it is not enough to go around; they have to stay and take care of their own communities.

But if we only *could* have three or four more sheriffs of that great breed! Would it help? I think so.[22] For we are all imitators: other brave sheriffs would follow; to be a dauntless sheriff would come to be recognized as the correct and only thing, and the dreaded disapproval would fall to the share of the other kind; courage in this office would become custom, the absence of it a dishonor, just as courage presently replaces the timidity of the new soldier; then the mobs and the lynchings would disappear, and——

However. It can never be done without some starters, and where are we to get the starters? Advertise? Very well, then, let us advertise.

In the meantime, there is another plan. Let us import American missionaries from China, and send them into the lynching field.

With 1,511 of them out there converting two Chinamen apiece per annum against an uphill birth rate of 33,000 pagans per day,* it will take upward of a million years to make the conversions balance the output and bring the Christianizing of the country in sight to the naked eye; therefore, if we can offer our missionaries as rich a field at home at lighter expense and quite satisfactory in the matter of danger, why shouldn't they find it fair and right to come back and give us a trial? The Chinese are universally conceded to be excellent people, honest, honorable, industrious, trustworthy, kind-hearted, and all that—leave them alone, they are plenty good enough just as they are; and besides, almost every convert runs a risk of catching our civilization. We ought to be careful. We ought to think twice before we encourage a risk like that; for, *once civilized, China can never be uncivilized again.* We have not been thinking of that. Very well, we ought to think of it now. Our missionaries will find that we have a field for them —and not only for the 1,511, but for 15,011. Let them look at the following telegram and see if they have anything in China that is more appetizing. It is from Texas:

The Negro was taken to a tree and swung in the air. Wood and fodder were piled beneath his body and a hot fire was made. *Then it was suggested that the man ought not to die too quickly, and he was let down to the ground while a party went to Dexter, about two miles distant, to procure coal oil.* This was thrown on the flames and the work completed.

We implore them to come back and help us in our need. Patriotism imposes this duty on them. Our country is worse off than China; they are our countrymen, their motherland supplicates their aid in this her hour of deep distress. They are competent; our people are not. They are used to scoffs, sneers, revilings, danger; our people are not. They have the martyr spirit; nothing but the martyr spirit can brave a lynching mob, and cow it and scatter it. They can save their country, we beseech them to come home and do it. We ask them to read that telegram again,

* These figures are not fanciful; all of them are genuine and authentic. They are from official missionary records in China. See Dr. Morrison's book on his pedestrian journey across China; he quotes them and gives his authorities. For several years he has been the London *Times*'s representative in Peking, and was there through the siege. (M.T.)

and yet again, and picture the scene in their minds, and soberly ponder it; then multiply it by 115, add 88; place the 203 in a row, allowing 600 feet of space for each human torch, so that there may be viewing room around it for 5,000 Christian American men, women, and children, youths and maidens; make it night, for grim effect; have the show in a gradually rising plain, and let the course of the stakes be uphill; the eye can then take in the whole line of twenty-four miles of blood-and-flesh bonfires unbroken, whereas if it occupied level ground the ends of the line would bend down and be hidden from view by the curvature of the earth. All being ready, now, and the darkness opaque, the stillness impressive—for there should be no sound but the soft moaning of the night wind and the muffled sobbing of the sacrifices —let all the far stretch of kerosened pyres be touched off simultaneously and the glare and the shrieks and the agonies burst heavenward to the Throne.

There are more than a million persons present; the light from the fires flushes into vague outline against the night the spires of five thousand churches. O kind missionary, O compassionate missionary, leave China! come home and convert these Christians!

I believe that if anything can stop this epidemic of bloody insanities it is martial personalities that can face mobs without flinching; and as such personalities are developed only by familiarity with danger and by the training and seasoning which come of resisting it, the likeliest place to find them must be among the missionaries who have been under tuition in China during the past year or two. We have abundance of work for them, and for hundreds and thousands more, and the field is daily growing and spreading. Shall we find them? We can try. In 75,000,000 there must be other Merrills and Beloats; and it is the law of our make that each example shall wake up drowsing chevaliers of that same great knighthood and bring them to the front.

## Banquet for a Senator

William Penn achieved the deathless gratitude of the savages by merely dealing in a square way with them—well—kind of a square way, anyhow—more rectangular than the savage was used to at any rate. He bought the whole state of Pennsylvania from them and paid for it like a man—paid $40 worth of glass beads and a couple of second-hand blankets. Bought the whole state for that. Why you can't buy its *legislature* for twice the money now.—*Mark Twain's Notebook,* about 1890

Most of Mark Twain's remarks on Congress belong to his younger years. In 1873, he announced in the New York *Tribune*, "To my mind, Judas Iscariot was nothing but a low, mean, premature Congressman."

This is from a discussion of the postal rates, written nine years later: "Reader, suppose you were an idiot. And suppose you were a member of Congress. But I repeat myself."

And this is from *Following the Equator,* written in 1897: "It could probably be shown by facts and figures that there is no distinctly native criminal class except Congress."

But "Banquet for a Senator" belongs to Mark Twain's old age. It was dictated into the Autobiography in 1907, three years before his death; it first appeared in 1940, in *Mark Twain in Eruption.* Of course it is about much more than a Congressman, but the one Mark Twain may have immortalized was William Andrews Clark, the Montana copper king, who began by selling tobacco in Last Chance Gulch, Montana, and ended by spending $5,000,000 on "Clark's Folly," a remarkable Fifth Avenue mansion which housed Titians, Rembrandts, and Van Dycks.

Senator Clark began his national political career in 1889, when he was sent to the Senate by the legislature of the newly admitted State of Montana. After a lively hearing, the Senate Committee on Elections refused to admit him, on the grounds that his seat had cost him $431,000 in bribes, distributed among thirty-five State legislators.

The political shenanigans in connection with pensions to Civil War veterans, which are mentioned here, were long a source of shame and frustration to Mark Twain. A characteristic bit of the Autobiography, written about this time and later published in *Mark Twain in Eruption:*

A year or two ago a veteran of the Civil War asked me if I did not sometimes have a longing to attend the annual great Convention of the Grand Army of the Republic and make a speech. I was obliged to confess that I wouldn't have the necessary moral courage for the venture, for I would want to reproach the old soldiers for not rising up in indignant protest against our government's vote-purchasing additions to the pension list, which is making of the remnant of their brave lives one long blush. I might try to say the words but would lack the guts and would fail. It would be one tottering moral coward trying to rebuke a houseful of like breed— men nearly as timid as himself but not any more so.

Well, there it is—I am a moral coward like the rest; and yet it is amazing to me that out of the hundreds of thousands of physically dauntless men who faced death . . . on a hundred bloody fields, not one solitary individual of them all has had courage enough to rise up and bravely curse the Congresses which have degraded him to the level of the bounty-jumper and the bastards of the same. Everybody laughs at the grotesque additions to the pension fund. . . . Everybody laughs—privately; everybody scoffs— privately; everybody is indignant—privately; everybody is ashamed to look a real soldier in the face—but none of them exposes his feelings publicly.

IN THE MIDDLE of the afternoon day before yesterday, a particular friend of mine whom I will call Jones for this day and train only, telephoned and said he would like to call for me at half past seven and take me to a dinner at the Union League Club. He said he would send me home as early as I pleased, he being aware that I am declining all invitations this year—and for the rest of my life—that make it necessary for me to go out at night, at least to places where speeches are made and the sessions last until past ten o'clock. But Jones is a very particular friend of mine and therefore it cost me no discomfort to transgress my rule and accept his invitation; no, I am in error—it did cost me a pang, a decided pang, for although he said that the dinner was a private one with only ten persons invited, he mentioned Senator Clark of Montana as one of the ten. I am a person of elevated tone and of morals that can bear scrutiny, and am much above associating with animals of Mr. Clark's breed.

I am sorry to be vain—at least I am sorry to expose the fact that I am vain—but I do confess it and expose it; I cannot help being vain of myself for giving such a large proof of my friendship for Jones as is involved in my accepting an invitation to break bread with such a person as Clark of Montana. It is not because he is a United States Senator—it is at least not wholly because he occupies that doubtful position—for there are many Senators whom I hold in a certain respect and would not think of declining to meet socially, if I believed it was the will of God. We have lately sent a United States Senator to the penitentiary, but I am quite well aware that of those who have escaped this promotion there are several who are in some regards guiltless of crime—not guiltless of all crimes, for that cannot be said of any United States Senator, I think, but guiltless of some kinds of crime. They all rob the Treasury by voting for iniquitous pension bills in order to keep on good terms with the Grand Army of the Republic, and with the Grand Army of the Republic Jr., and with the Grand Army of the Republic Jr., Jr., and with other great-grandchildren of the war—and these bills distinctly represent crime and violated senatorial oaths.

However, while I am willing to waive moral rank and associate with the moderately criminal among the Senators—even including Platt and Chauncey Depew[23]—I have to draw the line at Clark of Montana. He is said to have bought legislatures and judges as other men buy food and raiment. By his example he has so excused and so sweetened corruption that in Montana it no longer has an offensive smell. His history is known to everybody; he is as rotten a human being as can be found anywhere under the flag; he is a shame to the American nation, and no one has helped to send him to the Senate who did not know that his proper place was the penitentiary, with a chain and ball on his legs. To my mind he is the most disgusting creature that the Republic has produced since Tweed's time.

I went to the dinner, which was served in a small private room of the club with the usual piano and fiddlers present to make conversation difficult and comfort impossible. I found that the Montana citizen was not merely a guest but that the dinner was given in his honor. While the feeding was going on two of my elbow neighbors supplied me with information concerning the reasons for this tribute of respect to Mr. Clark. Mr. Clark had lately lent to the Union League Club, which is the most powerful political club in America and perhaps the richest, a million dollars' worth of European pictures for exhibition. It was quite plain that my informant regarded this as an act of almost superhuman generosity. One of my informants said, under his breath and with awe and admiration, that if you should put together all of Mr. Clark's several generosities to the club, including this gaudy one, the cost to Mr. Clark first and last would doubtless amount to a hundred thousand dollars. I saw that I was expected to exclaim, applaud, and adore, but I was not tempted to do it, because I had been informed five minutes earlier that Clark's income, as stated under the worshiping informant's breath, was thirty million dollars a year.

Human beings have no sense of proportion. A benefaction of a hundred thousand dollars subtracted from an income of thirty million dollars is not a matter to go into hysterics of admiration and adulation about. If I should contribute ten thousand dollars to a cause, it would be one-ninth of my past year's income, and I could feel it; as matter for admiration and wonder and astonishment and gratitude, it would far and away outrank a contribution of twenty-five million dollars from the Montana jailbird, who would still have a hundred thousand dollars a week left over from his year's income to subsist upon.

It reminded me of the only instance of benevolence exploded upon the world by the late Jay Gould that I had ever heard of. When that first and most infamous corrupter of American commercial morals was wallowing in uncountable stolen millions, he contributed five thousand dollars for the relief of the stricken population of Memphis, Tennessee, at a time when an epidemic of yellow fever was raging in that city. Mr. Gould's contribution cost him no sacrifice; it was only the income of the hour which he daily spent in prayer—for he was a most godly man—yet the storm of worshiping gratitude which welcomed it all over the United States in the newspaper, the pulpit, and in the private circle might have persuaded a stranger that for a millionaire American to give five thousand dollars to the dead and dying poor—when he could have bought a circuit judge with it—was the noblest thing in American history, and the holiest.

In time, the president of the art committee of the club rose and began with that aged and long-ago discredited remark that there were not to be any speeches on this occasion but only friendly and chatty conversation; then he went on, in the ancient and long-ago discredited fashion, and made a speech himself—a speech which was well calculated to make any sober hearer ashamed of the human race. If a stranger had come in at that time he might have supposed that this was a divine service and that the Divinity was present. He would have gathered that Mr. Clark was about the noblest human being the great republic had yet produced and the most magnanimous, the most self-sacrificing, the most limitlessly and squanderingly prodigal benefactor of good causes living in any land today. And it never occurred to this worshiper of money, and money's possessor, that in effect Mr. Clark had merely dropped a dime into the League's hat. Mr. Clark couldn't miss his benefaction any more than he could miss ten cents.

When this wearisome orator had finished his devotions, the president of the Union League got up and continued the service in the same vein, vomiting adulations upon that jailbird which, estimated by any right standard of values, were the coarsest sarcasms, although the speaker was not aware of that. Both of these orators had been applauded all along but the present one ultimately came out with a remark which I judged would fetch a cold silence, a very chilly chill; he revealed the fact that the expenses of the club's loan exhibition of the Senator's pictures had exceeded the income from the tickets of admission; then he paused —as speakers always do when they are going to spring a grand effect—and said that at that crucial time Senator Clark stepped forward of his own motion and put his hand in his pocket and handed out fifteen hundred dollars wherewith to pay half of the insurance on the pictures, and thus the club's pocket was saved whole. I wish I may never die if the worshipers present at this religious service did not break out in grateful applause at that astonishing statement; and I wish I may never permanently die, if the jailbird didn't smile all over his face and look as radiantly happy as he will look some day when Satan gives him a Sunday vacation in the cold storage vault.

Finally, while I was still alive, the president of the club finished his dreary and fatiguing marketing of juvenile commonplaces, and introduced Clark, and sat down. Clark rose to the tune of "The Star-Spangled Banner"—no, it was "God Save the King," frantically sawed and thumped by the fiddlers and the piano, and this was followed by "For he's a jolly good fellow," sung by the whole strength of the happy worshipers. A miracle followed. I have always maintained that no man could make a speech with nothing but a compliment for a text but I know now that a reptile can. Senator Clark twaddled and twaddled and twaddled along for a full half hour with no text but those praises which had been lavished upon his trifling generosities; and he not only accepted at par all these silly phrases but added to them a pile—praising his own so-called generosities and magnanimities with such intensity and color that he took the pigment all out of those other men's compliments and made them look pallid and shadowy. With forty years' experience of human assfulness and vanity at banquets, I have never seen anything of the sort that could remotely approach the assfulness and complacency of this coarse and vulgar and incomparably ignorant peasant's glorification of himself.

I shall always be grateful to Jones for giving me the opportunity to be present at these sacred orgies. I had believed that in my time I had seen at banquets all the different kinds of speech-making animals there are and also all the different kinds of people that go to make our population, but it was a mistake. This was the first time I had ever seen men get down in the gutter and frankly worship dollars and their possessors. Of course I was familiar with such things through our newspapers, but I had never before heard men worship the dollar with their mouths or seen them on their knees in the act.

## Comments on the Killing of 600 Moros

This selection has been out of print since 1924, when it appeared in the first version of Mark Twain's posthumously published Autobiography, edited by Albert Bigelow Paine in accordance with Mark Twain's instructions. The opening sentences illustrate the method which Clemens decided on in Florence, in 1904, and followed thereafter. He had begun his autobiography, in the conventional way, twenty-seven years before, and for twenty-seven years had discarded all his own attempts to tell his life as a narrative. His account of his experiments with technique, and of his objections to the narrative method, are in Paine's version of the Autobiography:

With a pen in the hand, the narrative stream . . . has no blemish except that it is all blemish. It is too literary, too prim, too nice. . . .

Besides:

What a wee little part of a person's life are his acts and his words! His real life is led in his head, and is known to none but himself.

He also found that when he took notes on events and tried to expand them later "Their power to suggest and excite had usually passed away."

Mark Twain was sixty-nine when he developed the method illustrated here, which has since been much criticized:

. . . wander at your free will all over your life; talk only about the thing which interests you for the moment; drop it the moment its interest threatens to pale, and turn your talk upon the new and more interesting thing that has intruded itself. . . .

But Mark Twain's use of what he called "the methodless method of the human mind" "was not confined to his Autobiography. Fourteen years before that appeared, William Dean Howells observed:

So far as I know, Mr. Clemens is the first writer to use in extended writing the fashion we all use in thinking. . . . I, for instance, in putting this paper together, am anxious to observe some sort of logical order. . . . But Mr. Clemens, if he were writing it, would not be anxious to do any such thing. . . . Mr. Clemens uses in work on the larger scale the method of the elder essayists, and you know no more where you are going to bring up in *The Innocents Abroad* or *Following the Equator,* than in an essay of Montaigne. The end you arrive at is the end of the book, and you reach it amused but edified, and sorry for nothing but to be there.[24]

This selection also illustrates Mark Twain's conviction that "news is history in its first and best form, its vivid and fascinating form, and that history is the pale and tranquil reflection of it." In his Autobiography, he was "mixing those two forms together all the time. I am hoping by this method of procedure to secure the values of both."

Also from Mark Twain's account of his method:

I shall scatter through this Autobiography newspaper clippings without end. When I do not copy them into the text it means I do not make them a part of the Autobiography—at least not of the earlier editions. I put them in on the theory that if they are not interesting in the earlier editions, a time will come when it may be well enough to insert them for the reason that age is quite likely to make them interesting. . . .[25]

In this selection, the newspapers are an indispensable part of the story. So too is the candid camera work—including the hour by hour reaction of people to events. For this was the kind of historical detail that Mark Twain himself so dearly loved; for which he read and reread Suetonius, Cellini, and Casanova; which delighted him as much in the *Travels* of Sir John Mandeville as in *The Life of P. T. Barnum, Written by Himself.*

In the selection below the year is 1906—five years after Filipino General Aguinaldo had announced:

> By acknowledging and accepting the sovereignty of the United States throughout the Philippine Archipelago, as I now do, and without any reservation whatsoever, I believe that I am serving thee, my beloved country.

But Mark Twain and some native guerrillas were still fighting, and would continue long after the last Moro had been exterminated.

These are Clemens' "Comments on the Killing of 600 Moros."

WE WILL stop talking about my schoolmates of sixty years ago, for the present, and return to them later. They strongly interest me, and I am not going to leave them alone permanently. Strong as that interest is, it is for the moment pushed out of the way by an incident of today, which is still stronger. This incident burst upon the world last Friday in an official cablegram from the commander of our forces in the Philippines to our government at Washington. The substance of it was as follows:

A tribe of Moros, dark-skinned savages,[26] had fortified themselves in the bowl of an extinct crater not many miles from Jolo; and as they were hostiles, and bitter against us because we have been trying for eight years to take their liberties away from them, their presence in that position was a menace. Our commander, General Leonard Wood, ordered a reconnaissance. It was found that the Moros numbered six hundred, counting women and children; that their crater bowl was in the summit of a peak or mountain twenty-two hundred feet above sea level, and very difficult of access for Christian troops and artillery. Then General Wood ordered a surprise, and went along himself to see the order carried out. Our troops climbed the heights by devious and difficult trails, and even took some artillery with them. The kind of artillery is not specified, but in one place it was hoisted up a sharp acclivity by tackle a distance of some three hundred feet. Arrived at the rim of the crater, the battle began. Our soldiers numbered five hundred and forty. They were assisted by auxiliaries consisting of a detachment of native constabulary in our pay—their numbers not given—and by a naval detachment, whose numbers are not stated. But apparently the contending parties were about equal as to number—six hundred men on our side, on the edge of the bowl; six hundred men, women, and children in the bottom of the bowl. Depth of the bowl, fifty feet.

General Wood's order was, "Kill or capture the six hundred."

The battle began—it is officially called by that name—our forces firing down into the crater with their artillery and their deadly small arms of precision; the savages furiously returning the fire, probably with brickbats—though this is merely a surmise of mine, as the weapons used by the savages are not nominated in the cablegram. Heretofore the Moros have used knives and clubs mainly; also ineffectual trade-muskets when they had any.

The official report stated that the battle was fought with prodigious energy on both sides during a day and a half, and that it ended with a complete victory for the American arms. The completeness of the victory is established by this fact: that of the six hundred Moros not one was left alive. The brilliancy of the victory is established by this other fact, to wit: that of our six hundred heroes only fifteen lost their lives.

General Wood was present and looking on. His order had been, "Kill *or* capture those savages." Apparently our little army considered that the "or" left them authorized to kill *or* capture according to taste, and that their taste had remained what it has been for eight years, in our army out there—the taste of Christian butchers.

The official report quite properly extolled and magnified the "heroism" and "gallantry" of our troops, lamented the loss of the fifteen who perished, and elaborated the wounds of thirty-two of our men who suffered injury, and even minutely and faithfully described the nature of the wounds, in the interest of future historians of the United States. It mentioned that a private had one of his elbows scraped by a missile, and the private's name was mentioned. Another private had the end of his nose scraped by a missile. His name was also mentioned—by cable, at one dollar and fifty cents a word.

Next day's news confirmed the previous day's report and named our fifteen killed and thirty-two wounded *again,* and once more described the wounds and gilded them with the right adjectives.

Let us now consider two or three details of our military history. In one of the great battles of the Civil War ten per cent of the forces engaged on the two sides were killed and wounded. At Waterloo, where four hundred thousand men were present on the two sides, fifty thousand fell, killed and wounded, in five hours, leaving three hundred and fifty thousand sound and all right for further adventures. Eight years ago, when the pathetic comedy called the Cuban War was played, we summoned two hundred and fifty thousand men. We fought a number of showy battles, and when the war was over we had lost two hundred and sixty-eight men out of our two hundred and fifty thousand, in killed and wounded in the field, and just *fourteen times as many* by the gallantry of the army doctors in the hospitals and camps. We did not exterminate the Spaniards—far from it. In each engagement we left an average of *2 per cent* of the enemy killed or crippled on the field.

Contrast these things with the great statistics which have arrived from that Moro crater! There, with six hundred engaged on each side, we lost fifteen men killed outright, and we had thirty-two wounded—counting that nose and that elbow. The enemy numbered six hundred—including women and children—and we abolished them utterly, leaving not even a baby alive to cry for its dead mother. *This is incomparably the greatest victory that was ever achieved by the Christian soldiers of the United States.*

Now then, how has it been received? The splendid news appeared with splendid display heads in every newspaper in this city of four million and thirteen thousand inhabitants, on Friday morning. But there was not a single reference to it in the editorial columns of any one of those newspapers. The news appeared again in all the evening papers of Friday, and again those papers were editorially silent upon our vast achievement. Next day's additional statistics and particulars appeared in all the morning papers, and still without a line of editorial rejoicing or a mention of the matter in any way. These additions appeared in the evening papers of that same day (Saturday) and again without a word of comment. In the columns devoted to correspondence, in the morning and evening papers of Friday and Saturday, nobody said a word about the "battle." Ordinarily those columns are teeming with the passions of the citizen; he lets no incident go by, whether it be large or small, without pouring out his praise or blame, his joy or his indignation, about the matter in the correspondence column. But, as I have said, during those two days he was as silent as the editors themselves. So far as I can find out, there was only one person among our eighty millions who allowed himself the privilege of a public remark on this great occasion—that was the President of the United States. All day Friday he was as studiously silent as the rest. But on Saturday he recognized that his duty required him to say something, and he took his pen and performed that duty. If I know President Roosevelt—and I am sure I do—this utterance cost him more pain and shame than any other that ever issued from his pen or his mouth. I am far from blaming him.[27] If I had been in his place my official duty would have compelled me to say what he said. It was a convention, an old tradition, and he had to be loyal to it. There was no help for it. This is what he said:

WASHINGTON, March 10

WOOD, MANILA:

I congratulate you and the officers and men of your command upon the brilliant feat of arms wherein you and they so well upheld the honor of the American flag.

(Signed) THEODORE ROOSEVELT

His whole utterance is merely a convention. Not a word of what he said came out of his heart. He knew perfectly well that to pen six hundred helpless and weaponless savages in a hole like rats in a trap and massacre them in detail during a stretch of a day and a half, from a safe position on the heights above, was no brilliant feat of arms—and would not have been a brilliant feat of arms even if Christian America, represented by its salaried soldiers, had shot them down with bibles and the Golden Rule instead of bullets. He knew perfectly well that our uniformed assassins had *not* upheld the honor of the American flag, but had done as they have been doing continuously for eight years in the Philippines—that is to say, they had dishonored it.

The next day, Sunday—which was yesterday—the cable brought us additional news—still more splendid news—still more honor for the flag. The first display head shouts this information at us in stentorian capitals:

## WOMEN SLAIN IN MORO SLAUGHTER

"Slaughter" is a good word. Certainly there is not a better one in the Unabridged Dictionary for this occasion.

The next display line says:

*With Children They Mixed in Mob in Crater, and All Died Together.*

They were mere naked savages, and yet there is a sort of pathos about it when that word *children* falls under your eye, for it always brings before us our perfectest symbol of innocence and helplessness; and by help of its deathless eloquence color, creed, and nationality vanish away and we see only that they are children— merely children. And if they are frightened and crying and in trouble, our pity goes out to them by natural impulse. We see a picture. We see the small forms. We see the terrified faces. We see the tears. We see the small hands clinging in supplication to the mother; but we do not see those children that we are speaking about. We see in their places the little creatures whom we know and love.

The next heading blazes with American and Christian glory like to the sun in the zenith:

*Death List Is Now 900.*

I was never so enthusiastically proud of the flag till now!

The next heading explains how safely our daring soldiers were located. It says:

*Impossible to Tell Sexes Apart in Fierce Battle on Top of Mount Dajo.*

The naked savages were so far away, down in the bottom of that trap, that our soldiers could not tell the breasts of a woman from the rudimentary paps of a man—so far away that they couldn't tell a toddling little child from a black six-footer. *This was by all odds the least dangerous battle that Christian soldiers of any nationality were ever engaged in.*

The next heading says:

*Fighting for Four Days.*

So our men were at it four days instead of a day and a half. It was a long and happy picnic with nothing to do but sit in comfort and fire the Golden Rule into those people down there and imagine letters to write home to the admiring families, and pile glory upon glory. Those savages fighting for their liberties had the four days, too, but it must have been a sorrowful time for them. Every day they saw two hundred and twenty-five of their number slain, and this provided them grief and mourning for the night—and doubtless without even the relief and consolation of knowing that in the meantime they had slain four of their enemies and wounded some more on the elbow and the nose.

The closing heading says:

*Lieutenant Johnson Blown from Parapet by Exploding Artillery Gallantly Leading Charge.*

Lieutenant Johnson had pervaded the cablegrams from the first. He and his wound have sparkled around through them like the serpentine thread of fire that goes excursioning through the black crisp fabric of a fragment of burnt paper. It reminds one of Gillette's comedy farce of a few years ago, *Too Much Johnson.* Apparently Johnson was the only wounded man on our side whose wound was worth anything as an advertisement. It has made a great deal more noise in the world than has any similar event since "Humpty Dumpty" fell off the wall and got injured. The official dispatches do not know which to admire most, Johnson's adorable wound or the nine hundred murders. The ecstasies flowing from army headquarters on the other side of the globe to the White House, at one dollar and a half a word, have set fire to similar ecstasies in the President's breast. It appears that the immortally wounded was a Rough Rider under Lieutenant Colonel Theodore Roosevelt at San Juan Hill—that twin of Waterloo—when the colonel of the regiment, the present Major General Dr. Leonard Wood, went to the rear to bring up the pills and missed the fight. The President has a warm place in his heart for anybody who was present at that bloody collision of military solar systems, and so he lost no time in cabling to the wounded hero, "How are you?" And got a cable answer, "Fine, thanks." This is historical. This will go down to posterity.

Johnson was wounded in the shoulder with a slug. The slug was in a shell—for the account says the damage was caused by an exploding shell which blew Johnson off the rim. The people down in the hole had no artillery; therefore it was our artillery that blew Johnson off the rim. And so it is now a matter of historical record that the only officer of ours who acquired a wound of advertising dimensions got it at our hands, and not the enemies'. It seems more than probable that if we had placed our soldiers out of the way of our own weapons, we should have come out of the most extraordinary battle in all history without a scratch.

[*Wednesday, March 14, 1906*]

The ominous paralysis continues. There has been a slight sprinkle—an exceedingly slight sprinkle—in the correspondence columns, of angry rebukes of the President for calling this cowardly massacre a "brilliant feat of arms" and for praising our butchers for "holding up the honor of the flag" in that singular way; but there is hardly a ghost of a whisper about the feat of arms in the editorial columns of the papers.

I hope that this silence will continue. It is about as eloquent and as damaging and effective as the most indignant words could be, I think. When a man is sleeping in a noise, his sleep goes placidly on; but if the noise stops, the stillness wakes him. This silence has continued five days now. Surely it must be waking the drowsy nation. Surely the nation must be wondering what it means. A five-day silence following a world-astonishing event has not happened on this planet since the daily newspaper was invented.

At a luncheon party of men convened yesterday to God-speed George Harvey[28] who is leaving today for a vacation in Europe, all the talk was about the brilliant feat of arms; and no one had anything to say about it that either the President or Major General Dr. Wood or the damaged Johnson would regard as complimentary, or as proper comment to put into our histories. Harvey said he believed that the shock and shame of this episode would eat down deeper and deeper into the hearts of the nation and fester there and produce results. He believed it would destroy the Republican party and President Roosevelt. I cannot believe that the prediction will come true, for the reason that prophecies which promise valuable things, desirable things, good things, worthy things, never come true. Prophecies of this kind are like wars fought in a good cause—they are so rare that they don't count.

Day before yesterday the cable note from the happy General Doctor Wood [29] was still all glorious. There was still proud mention and elaboration of what was called the "desperate hand-to-hand fight," Doctor Wood not seeming to suspect that he was giving himself away, as the phrase goes—since if there was any very desperate hand-to-hand fighting it would necessarily happen that nine hundred hand-to-hand fighters, if really desperate, would surely be able to kill more than fifteen of our men before their last man and woman and child perished.

Very well, there was a new note in the dispatches yesterday afternoon—just a faint suggestion that Doctor Wood was getting ready to lower his tone and begin to apologize and explain. He announces that he assumes full responsibility for the fight. It indicates that he is aware that there is a lurking disposition here amid all this silence to blame somebody. He says there was "no wanton destruction of women and children in the fight, though many of them were killed by force of necessity because the Moros used them as shields in the hand-to-hand fighting."

This explanation is better than none; indeed, it is considerably better than none. Yet if there was so much hand-to-hand fighting there must have arrived a time, toward the end of the four days' butchery, when only one native was left alive. We had six hundred men present: we had lost only fifteen; why did the six hundred kill that remaining man—or woman, or child?

Doctor Wood will find that explaining things is not in his line. He will find that where a man has the proper spirit in him and the proper force at his command, it is easier to massacre nine hundred unarmed animals than it is to explain why he made it so remorselessly complete. Next he furnishes us this sudden burst of unconscious humor, which shows that he ought to edit his reports before he cables them:

"Many of the Moros feigned death and butchered the American hospital men who were relieving the wounded."

We have the curious spectacle of hospital men going around

trying to relieve the wounded savages—for what reason? The savages were all massacred. The plain intention was to massacre them all and leave none alive. Then where was the use in furnishing mere temporary relief to a person who was presently to be exterminated? The dispatches call this battue a "battle." In what way was it a battle? It has no resemblance to a battle. In a battle there are always as many as five wounded men to one killed outright. When this so-called battle was over, there were certainly not fewer than two hundred wounded savages lying on the field. What became of them? Since not one savage was left alive!

The inference seems plain. We cleaned up our four days' work and made it complete by butchering those helpless people.

The President's joy over this achievement brings to mind an earlier presidential ecstasy. When the news came, in 1901, that Colonel Funston had penetrated to the refuge of the patriot, Aguinaldo, in the mountains, and had captured him by the use of these arts, to wit: by forgery, by lies, by disguising his military marauders in the uniform of the enemy, by pretending to be friends of Aguinaldo's and by disarming suspicion by cordially shaking hands with Aguinaldo's officers and in that moment shooting them down—when the cablegram announcing this "brilliant feat of arms" reached the White House, the newspapers said that that meekest and mildest and gentlest of men, President McKinley, could not control his joy and gratitude, but was obliged to express it in motions resembling a dance.

# ON SPAIN

## A Word of Encouragement for Our Blushing Exiles

It is a worthy thing to fight for one's freedom; it is another sight finer to fight for another man's.—MARK TWAIN, on the Spanish-American War, in an 1898 letter to the Reverend Joseph Twichell.

In 1869, Mark Twain published in the *Buffalo Express* some violent ridicule of the Cuban guerrillas. But when the second Cuban revolution broke out he was twenty-six years older, and of a different mind.

"A Word of Encouragement for Our Blushing Exiles" was written from Vienna during the Spanish-American War. At the time, Americans living abroad certainly needed a little encouragement. For Europe, except England, was strongly anti-American and pro-Spanish.

Spain never benefited from this situation. A delegation of the great powers which called on President McKinley to urge peace and "the re-establishment of order in Cuba" merely inflamed feeling here. The Spanish foreign office worked desperately to establish a league of European states which would intervene in its behalf. But English diplomacy prevented that.

English sympathy was also with Cuba. But the English did not share the American dream of helping Cuba establish its independence. What they hoped to see, on that tortured island, was a peaceful American colony. Kipling's famous plea to Americans made that clear:

> Take up the White Man's burden—
> Ye dare not stoop to less—
> Nor call too loud on Freedom
> To cloak your weariness.

121

History books list the reasons that the rest of Europe was with Spain: There was dread that republican institutions would spread; the fear of growing American economic strength; Germany had long dreamed of her own colonies in the Caribbean (she had hopes of ruling Cuba herself). The French had invested heavily in Spanish bonds, many of which were based on Cuban revenues. And finally, according to Carl Russell Fish, writing in 1919:

There was also perhaps some sense of solidarity among the Latin races in Europe and a feeling that the United States was a colossus willfully exerting itself against a weak antagonist. It was not likely that this feeling was strong enough to lead to action, but at least during that summer of 1898 it was somewhat unpleasant for American tourists in Paris. . . .[1]

It must have been especially unpleasant for those exiled Americans who were sensitive—as Americans sometimes are—to opinion around them. Clemens might have written a kindlier word of encouragement. But he could hardly have written a more timely or remarkable history lesson.

"A Word of Encouragement" was found in his papers and published in *Europe and Elsewhere* in 1923. But by then a new American generation had its own doubts about the rights and wrongs of the Spanish-American War; it had become thoroughly mixed, in the national memory, with what immediately followed: our conquest of the Philippines. Many historians regarded it as little more than a prelude to that conquest.

Clemens came home in 1900 and immediately began his heartbroken preachments against the second war. In "To the Person Sitting in Darkness," the Spanish-American War is still the American game, as opposed to the European game which we played with the Filipinos. Mark Twain never failed to make that distinction. But from 1900 on, he was seldom in a frame of mind to encourage Americans anywhere.

Clemens' article follows:

. . . Well, what do you think of our country *now?* And what do you thing of the figure she is cutting before the eyes of the world? For one, I am ashamed.—(Extract from a long and heated letter from a Voluntary Exile, Member of the American Colony, Paris.)

AND SO you are ashamed. I am trying to think out what it can have been that has produced this large attitude of mind and this fine flow of sarcasm. Apparently you are ashamed to look Europe in the face; ashamed of the American name; temporarily ashamed of your nationality. By the light of remarks made to me by an American here in Vienna, I judged that you are ashamed because:

1. We are meddling where we have no business and no right; meddling with the private family matters of a sister nation; intruding upon her sacred right to do as she pleases with her own, unquestioned by anybody.

2. We are doing this under a sham humanitarian pretext.

3. Doing it in order to filch Cuba, the formal and distinct disclaimer in the ultimatum being very, very thin humbug, and easily detectable as such by you and virtuous Europe.

4. And finally you are ashamed of all this because it is new, and base, and brutal, and dishonest; and because Europe, having had no previous experience of such things, is horrified by it and can never respect us nor associate with us any more.

Brutal, base, dishonest? We? Land thieves? Shedders of innocent blood? We? Traitors to our official word? We? Are we going to lose Europe's respect because of this new and dreadful conduct? Russia's, for instance? Is she lying stretched out on her back in Manchuria, with her head among her Siberian prisons and her feet in Port Arthur, trying to read over the fairy tale she told Lord Salisbury, and not able to do it for crying because we are maneuvering to treacherously smouch Cuba from feeble Spain, and because we are ungently shedding innocent Spanish blood?

Is it France's respect that we are going to lose? Is our unchivalric conduct troubling a nation which exists today because a brave young girl saved it when its poltroons had lost it—a nation which deserted her as one man when her day of peril came? Is our treacherous assault upon a weak people distressing a nation which contributed Bartholomew's Day to human history? Is our ruthless spirit offending the sensibilities of the nation which gave us the Reign of Terror to read about? Is our unmanly intrusion into the private affairs of a sister nation shocking the feelings of the people who sent Maximilian to Mexico? [2] Are our shabby and pusillanimous ways outraging the fastidious people who have sent an innocent man (Dreyfus) to a living hell, taken to their embraces the slimy guilty one, and submitted to a thousand indignities Émile Zola—the manliest man in France?

Is it Spain's respect that we are going to lose? Is she sitting sadly conning her great history and contrasting it with our meddling, cruel, perfidious one—our shameful history of foreign rob-

beries, humanitarian shams, and annihilations of weak and unoffending nations? Is she remembering with pride how she sent
Columbus home in chains;[3] how she sent half of the harmless West
Indians into slavery and the rest to the grave, leaving not one alive;
how she robbed and slaughtered the Inca's gentle race, then beguiled the Inca into her power with fair promises and burned
him at the stake; how she drenched the New World in blood, and
earned and got the name of The Nation with the Bloody Foot-
print; how she drove all the Jews out of Spain in a day, allowing
them to sell their property, but forbidding them to carry any
money out of the country; how she roasted heretics by the
thousands and thousands in her public squares, generation after
generation, her kings and her priests looking on as at a holiday
show; how her Holy Inquisition imported hell into the earth; how
she was the first to institute it and the last to give it up—and then
only under compulsion; how, with a spirit unmodified by time,
she still tortures her prisoners today; how, with her ancient passion for pain and blood unchanged, she still crowds the arena with
ladies and gentlemen and priests to see with delight a bull harried
and persecuted and a gored horse dragging his entrails on the
ground; and how, with this incredible character surviving all attempts to civilize it, her Duke of Alva[4] rises again in the person of
General Weyler—today the most idolized personage in Spain—and
we see a hundred thousand women and children shut up in pens
and pitilessly starved to death?

Are we indeed going to lose Spain's respect? Is there no way to
avoid this calamity—or this compliment? Are we going to lose her
respect because we have made a promise in our ultimatum which
she thinks we shall break? And meantime is she trying to recall
some promise of her own which she has kept?

Is the professional official fibber of Europe really troubled with
our morals? Dear Parisian friend, are you taking seriously the daily
remark of the newspaper and the orator about "this noble nation
with an illustrious history"? That is mere kindness, mere charity
for a people in temporary hard luck. The newspaper and the orator
do not mean it. They wink when they say it.

And so you are ashamed. Do not be ashamed; there is no
occasion for it.

# ON FRANCE

## What Paul Bourget Thinks of Us

Though "humor" springs from the mind, whose true homeland is France, it still remains so unfamiliar to us that we have not been able either to define the word or translate it. . . . At heart we feel this carnival of sentiment and ideas to be barbarous . . . it confuses merry tears and heartbroken laughter, reasoning and caricature, until we are thrown into an almost cruel confusion. . . . —Thérèse Bentzon, in a review of *The Innocents Abroad,* in *Revue des Deux-Mondes,* July 15, 1875

"What Paul Bourget Thinks of Us" is, among other things, a most remarkable book review. The book was *Outre-Mer,* an analysis of the United States written in 1894 by a visiting Frenchman. It is just as bad as Mark Twain said it was; the mystery now is how he could have taken it so seriously.

But M. Bourget was once taken seriously everywhere. He was a critic and a member of the French Academy; to his own generation his novels of Parisian high life were psychologically profound and delightfully shocking. And his international reputation was at its height when, at forty-three, he visited the United States.

He stayed six months. His headquarters were Newport—even then a very select community—but he also visited American prisons, slums, and stockyards; and he interviewed countless American women of all kinds. One thing they all had in common, he discovered, was a "chaste depravity." This is from *Outre-Mer* and was inspired by a Sargent portrait of a nameless American woman:

Yes, this woman is an idol, for whose service man labors, whom he has decked with the jewels of a queen, behind each one of whose whims lie days and nights spent in the ardent battle of Wall Street. . . .

She is like a living object of art . . . attesting that the Yankee, who yesterday despairing, vanquished by the Old World, has been able to draw from this savage world upon which fate has cast him a wholly new civilization, incarnated in this woman, her luxury and her pride. Everything is illuminated in this civilization, by the gaze of those fathomless eyes, in the expression of which the painter succeeded in putting all the idealism of this country which has no ideal. . . .

American reviews of *Outre-Mer* ranged from meek to enraged. But a surprising number managed to tread the difficult path between what Frances Stoddard, in *The Outlook*, described as "childish submission and "childish rebellion" toward the "provincial foreigner." *Harper's Weekly*, for example, said that M. Bourget must have "felt us something brutally ugly" but hoped that we had "some compensatory inner loveliness." And added:

We ought even to strive for it, if we find ourselves wanting in it, so that hereafter when some author of our own shall study us as faithfully as M. Bourget has done . . . we shall not be ashamed of the picture, for then it will be a true picture.

But this mixture of dignity and Christian forbearance was not what Mark Twain was striving for. "What Paul Bourget Thinks of Us" was described by a distinguished French critic as "a masterpiece of Anglo-Saxon brutality." Undoubtedly, it is a masterpiece. It would be one even if it did not contain some of Mark Twain's most interesting observations on the writer's relation to society.

These passages were written before the creative writer took himself—and was taken—quite so seriously as now. For Mark Twain, he is not so much a spiritual leader of the community as a professional serving it. "Literature," said Maxim Gorki, "is the way the people find out about each other." Clemens was of the same period, and he takes the same attitude here. But literary standards change. Today, of course, there could be more than one answer to his question: "Does the native novelist try to generalize the nation?"

Mark Twain's feud with the French was once famous, and considered a good joke. It was considered part of the joke when M. Bourget lost his temper at "What Paul Bourget Thinks of Us" and Mark Twain was accused in further exchanges of insulting French womanhood.

But M. Bourget was not France. Most French critics who disliked Mark Twain's work did so, not because of anything he said about France or French womanhood, but because he was the spokesman of a materialistic, democratic, middle-class society. And it would be hard to say which was most distasteful to a literate Frenchman before the twentieth century: the middle classes, democracy, or the sort of materialism associated with the United States.

It is true that these aspects of life had a bad reputation throughout Europe—except among the classes who were emigrating to this country. But, in many ways, France, then, was even farther from America than some other countries, and so the French, especially, tended to paint their own pictures of the remote and primitive civilization that had produced Mark Twain. In an early review, by Thérèse Bentzon,[1] Mark Twain is pictured "roaming the mountains of his native land" with a revolver in one hand and a pick ax in the other. Even in 1910, Régis Michaud, a French critic with a considerable appreciation of Mark Twain's literary quality, described his background thus:

Mark Twain is the Homer of the native Americans who took the country from the Redskins and whose values are completely primitive: physical and moral health, respect for one another, and energy. They scorn the refinements of civilization; the manners, ceremonies and social distinctions of which we are so proud are, for them, the marks either of domination or servitude . . . they practice, on principle, straightforwardness and unceremoniousness. They have respect for only one thing: success. They have only one cult: force.[2]

This appeared six years after M. Bourget had reported on such American refinements as Newport and "chaste depravity." But M. Bourget was one of our few French visitors. The English and the Germans were receiving a flow of first-hand reports from their immigrant populations here; French immigration was a trickle. Few Frenchmen, at the time, had even read much, in English, on the United States. When Mark Twain's *Life on the Mississippi* appeared in France, it was compared unfavorably to Chateaubriand's great work on the new continent, written about a century before. *A Connecticut Yankee in King Arthur's Court* was first translated into French in 1954. Mark Twain's remark in "Paris Notes," was by no means idle abuse: "The Parisian travels but little, he knows no language but his own, reads no literature but his own. . . ." The Parisian, Zola, said the same: "We have no broad views. We concern ourselves only with the fireside, the club, and the asphalt. We rarely acquire other languages, and as a rule read no literature but our own."

On the other hand, Mark Twain's side of the feud was far from the comic affair he sometimes pretended. He dearly loved much that had been France:[3] Joan of Arc, the medieval literature, the French Revolution, Napoleon (if only, he said, Napoleon had won at Waterloo), Victor Hugo, and Zola the man (because of his defence of Dreyfus) although not Zola the novelist.

Mark Twain's distaste for the French, and most French literature of his own day, sprang from the same historic causes as the French distaste for nineteenth-century America. The incompatibility was inevitable. In 1892, he wrote in his *Notebook:*

The Court Gazette of a German paper can be covered with a playing card. In an English paper the movements of titled people take up about three times that room. In the papers of the Republic of France from six to sixteen times as much. There, if a Duke's dog should catch a cold in the head they would stop the press to announce it and cry about it. In Germany they respect titles, in England they revere them, in France they adore them, that is, the French newspapers do.

It is cautious: "that is, the French newspapers do." M. Bourget was not so cautious about drawing conclusions in a strange land. Perhaps it was just as well. Otherwise Mark Twain might never have written "What Paul Bourget Thinks of Us."

It appeared in the *North American Review*, January, 1895.

HE REPORTS the American joke correctly. In Boston they ask, How much does he know? in New York, How much is he worth? in Philadelphia, Who were his parents? And when an alien observer turns his telescope upon us—advertisedly in our own special interest—a natural apprehension moves us to ask, What is the diameter of his reflector?

I take a great interest in M. Bourget's chapters, for I know by the newspapers that there are several Americans who are expecting to get a whole education out of them; several who foresaw, and also foretold, that our long night was over, and a light almost divine about to break upon the land.

*His utterances concerning us are bound to be weighty and well timed.*

*He gives us an object lesson which should be thoughtfully and profitably studied.*

These well-considered and important verdicts were of a nature to restore public confidence, which had been disquieted by questionings as to whether so young a teacher would be qualified to take so large a class as 70,000,000, distributed over so extensive a schoolhouse as America, and pull it through without assistance.

I was even disquieted myself, although I am of a cold, calm temperament, and not easily disturbed. I feared for my country. And I was not wholly tranquilized by the verdicts rendered as above. It seemed to me that there was still room for doubt. In fact, in looking the ground over I became more disturbed than I was before. Many worrying questions came up in my mind. Two were prominent. Where had the teacher gotten his equipment? What was his method?

He had gotten his equipment in France.

Then as to his method! I saw by his own intimations that he was an observer, and had a system—that used by naturalists and other scientists. The naturalist collects many bugs and reptiles and butterflies and studies their ways a long time patiently. By this means he is presently able to group these creatures into families and subdivisions of families by nice shadings of differences observable in their characters. Then he labels all those shaded bugs and things with nicely descriptive group names, and is now happy, for his great work is completed, and as a result he intimately knows every bug and shade of a bug there, inside and out. It may be true, but a person who was not a naturalist would feel safer about it if he had the opinion of the bug. I think it is a pleasant system, but subject to error.

The observer of peoples has to be a classifier, a grouper, a deducer, a generalizer, a psychologizer; and, first and last, a thinker. He has to be all these, and when he is at home, observing his own folk, he is often able to prove competency. But history has shown that when he is abroad observing unfamiliar peoples the chances are heavily against him. He is then a naturalist observing a bug, with no more than a naturalist's chance of being able to tell the bug anything new about itself, and no more than a naturalist's chance of being able to teach it any new ways which it will prefer to its own.

To return to that first question. M. Bourget, as teacher, would simply be France teaching America. It seemed to me that the outlook was dark—almost Egyptian, in fact. What would the new teacher, representing France, teach us? Railroading? No. France knows nothing valuable about railroading. Steamshipping? No. France has no superiorities over us in that matter. Steamboating? No. French steamboating is still of Fulton's date—1809. Postal service? No. France is a back number there. Telegraphy? No, we taught her that ourselves. Journalism? No. Magazining? No, that is our own specialty. Government? No; liberty, equality, fraternity, nobility, democracy, adultery—the system is too variegated for our climate. Religion? No, not variegated enough for our climate. Morals? No, we cannot rob the poor to enrich ourselves. Novel-writing? No. M. Bourget and the others know only one plan, and when that is expurgated there is nothing left of the book.

I wish I could think what he is going to teach us. Can it be deportment? But he experimented in that at Newport and failed to give satisfaction, except to a few. Those few are pleased. They are enjoying their joy as well as they can. They confess their happiness to the interviewer. They feel pretty striped, but they remember with reverent recognition that they had sugar between the cuts. True, sugar with sand in it, but sugar. And true, they had some trouble to tell which was sugar and which was sand, because the sugar itself looked just like the sand, and also had a gravelly taste; still, they knew that the sugar was there, and would have been very good sugar indeed if it had been screened. Yes, they are pleased; not noisily so, but pleased; invaded, or streaked, as one may say, with little recurrent shivers of joy—subdued joy, so to speak, not the overdone kind. And they commune together, these, and massage each other with comforting sayings, in a sweet spirit of resignation and thankfulness, mixing these elements in the same proportions as the sugar and the sand, as a memorial, and saying, the one to the other, and to the interviewer: "It was severe—yes, it was bitterly severe; but oh, how true it was; and it will do us so much good!"

If it isn't deportment, what is left? It was at this point that I seemed to get on the right track at last. M. Bourget would teach us to know ourselves; that was it: he would reveal us to ourselves. That would be an education. He would explain us to ourselves. Then we should understand ourselves; and after that be able to go on more intelligently.

It seemed a doubtful scheme. He could explain *us* to *him*self— that would be easy. That would be the same as the naturalist ex-plaining the bug to himself. But to explain the bug to the bug— that is quite a different matter. The bug may not know himself perfectly, but he knows himself better than the naturalist can know him, at any rate.

A foreigner can photograph the exteriors of a nation, but I think that that is as far as he can get. I think that no foreigner can report its interior—its soul, its life, its speech, its thought. I think that a knowledge of these things is acquirable in only one way; not two or four or six—*absorption;* years and years of unconscious absorption; years and years of intercourse with the life concerned; of living it, indeed; sharing personally in its shames and prides, its joys and griefs, its loves and hates, its prosperities and reverses, its shows and shabbinesses, its deep patriotism, its whirlwinds of political passion, its adorations—of flag, and heroic dead, and the glory of the national name. Observation? Of what real value is it? One learns peoples through the heart, not the eyes or the intellect.

There is only one expert who is qualified to examine the souls and the life of a people and make a valuable report—the native novelist. This expert is so rare that the most populous country can never have fifteen conspicuously and confessedly competent ones in stock at one time. This native specialist is not qualified to begin work until he has been absorbing during twenty-five years. How much of his competency is derived from conscious "observation"? The amount is so slight that it counts for next to nothing in the equipment. Almost the whole capital of the novelist is the slow accumulation of *un*conscious observation—absorption. The native expert's intentional observation of manners, speech, character, and ways of life can have value, for the native knows what they mean without having to cipher out the meaning. But I should be astonished to see a foreigner get at the right meanings, catch the elusive shades of these subtle things. Even the native novelist becomes a foreigner, with a foreigner's limitations, when he steps from the State whose life is familiar to him into a State whose life he has not lived. Bret Harte got his California and his Californians by unconscious absorption, and put both of them into his tales alive. But when he came from the Pacific to the Atlantic and tried to do Newport life from study—conscious observation—his failure was absolutely monumental. Newport is a disastrous place for the unacclimated observer, evidently.

To return to novel-building. Does the native novelist try to generalize the nation? No, he lays plainly before you the ways and speech and life of a few people grouped in a certain place—his own place—and that is one book. In time he and his brethren will report to you the life and the people of the whole nation—the life of a group in a New England village; in a New York village; in a Texan village; in an Oregon village; in villages in fifty States and Territories; then the farm-life in fifty States and Territories; a hundred patches of life and groups of people in a dozen widely separated cities. And the Indians will be attended to; and the cowboys; and the gold and silver miners; and the Negroes; and the idiots and Congressmen; and the Irish, the Germans, the Italians, the Swedes, the French, the Chinamen, the Greasers; and the Catholics, the Methodists, the Presbyterians, the Congregationalists, the Baptists, the Spiritualists, the Mormons, the Shakers, the Quakers, the Jews, the Campbellites, the infidels, the Christian Scientists, the Mind-Curists, the Faith-Curists, the train robbers, the White Caps, the moonshiners. And when a thousand able novels have been written, *there* you have the soul of the people, the life of the people, the speech of the people; and not anywhere else can these be had. And the shadings of character, manners, feelings, ambitions, will be infinite.

*The nature of a people* is always of a similar shade in its vices and its virtues, in its frivolities and in its labor. *It is this physiognomy which it is necessary to discover,* and every document is good, from the hall of a casino to the church, from the foibles of a fashionable woman to the suggestions of a revolutionary leader. I am therefore quite sure that this *American soul*, the principal interest and the great object of my voyage, appears behind the records of Newport for those who choose to see it.—*M. Paul Bourget.*

(The italics are mine.) It is a large contract which he has undertaken. "Records" is a pretty poor word there, but I think the use of it is due to hasty translation. In the original the word is *fastes.* I think M. Bourget meant to suggest that he expected to find the great "American soul" secreted behind the *ostentations* of Newport; and that he was going to get it out and examine it, and generalize it, and psychologize it, and make it reveal to him its hidden vast mystery: "the nature of the people" of the United States of America. We have been accused of being a nation addicted to inventing wild schemes. I trust that we shall be allowed to retire to second place now.

There isn't a single human characteristic that can be safely

labeled "American." There isn't a single human ambition, or
religious trend, or drift of thought, or peculiarity of education, or
code of principles, or breed of folly, or style of conversation, or
preference for a particular subject for discussion, or form of legs
or trunk or head or face or expression or complexion, or gait, or
dress, or manners, or disposition, or any other human detail, inside
or outside, that can rationally be generalized as "American."

Whenever you have found what seems to be an "American"
peculiarity, you have only to cross a frontier or two, or go down
or up in the social scale, and you perceive that it has disappeared.
And you can cross the Atlantic and find it again. There may be a
Newport religious drift, or sporting drift, or conversational style
or complexion, or cut of face, but there are entire empires in
America, north, south, east, and west, where you could not find
your duplicates. It is the same with everything else which one
might propose to call "American." M. Bourget thinks he has
found the American coquette. If he had really found her he would
also have found, I am sure, that she was not new, that she exists
in other lands in the same forms, and with the same frivolous
heart and the same ways and impulses. I think this because I have
seen our coquette; I have seen her in life; better still, I have seen
her in our novels, and seen her twin in foreign novels. I wish M.
Bourget had seen ours. He thought he saw her. And so he applied
his system to her. She was a species. So he gathered a number of
samples of what seemed to be her, and put them under his glass,
and divided them into groups which he calls "types," and labeled
them in his usual scientific way with "formulas"—brief sharp
descriptive flashes that make a person blink, sometimes, they are
so sudden and vivid. As a rule they are pretty farfetched, but
that is not an important matter; they surprise, they compel admiration, and I notice by some of the comments which his efforts have
called forth that they deceive the unwary. Here are a few of the
coquette variants which he has grouped and labeled:

THE COLLECTOR
THE EQUILIBREE
THE PROFESSIONAL BEAUTY
THE BLUFFER
THE GIRL-BOY

If he had stopped with describing these characters we should have been obliged to believe that they exist; that they exist, and that he has seen them and spoken with them. But he did not stop there; he went further and furnished to us light-throwing samples of their behavior, and also light-throwing samples of their speeches. He entered those things in his notebook without suspicion, he takes them out and delivers them to the world with a candor and simplicity which show that he believed them genuine. They throw altogether too much light. They reveal to the native the origin of his find. I suppose he knows how he came to make that novel and captivating discovery, by this time. If he does not, any American can tell him—any American to whom he will show his anecdotes. It was "put up" on him, as we say. It was a jest—to be plain, it was a series of frauds. To my mind it was a poor sort of jest, witless and contemptible. The players of it have their reward, such as it is; they have exhibited the fact that whatever they may be they are not ladies.[4] M. Bourget did not discover a type of coquette; he merely discovered a type of practical joker. One may say *the* type of practical joker, for these people are exactly alike all over the world. Their equipment is always the same: a vulgar mind, a puerile wit, a cruel disposition as a rule, and always the spirit of treachery.

In his Chapter IV M. Bourget has two or three columns gravely devoted to the collating and examining and psychologizing of these sorry little frauds. One is not moved to laugh. There is nothing funny in the situation; it is only pathetic. The stranger gave those people his confidence, and they dishonorably treated him in return.

But one must be allowed to suspect that M. Bourget was a little to blame himself. Even a practical joker has some little judgment. He has to exercise some degree of sagacity in selecting his prey if he would save himself from getting into trouble. In my time I have seldom seen such daring things marketed at any price as these conscienceless folk have worked off at par on this confiding observer. It compels the conviction that there was something about him that bred in those speculators a quite unusual sense of safety, and encouraged them to strain their powers in his behalf. They seem to have satisfied themselves that all he wanted was "significant" facts, and that he was not accustomed to examine the source whence they proceeded. It is plain that there was a sort of conspiracy against him almost from the start—a conspiracy to freight him up with all the strange extravagances those people's decayed brains could invent.

The lengths to which they went are next to incredible. They told him things which surely would have excited anyone else's suspicion, but they did not excite his. Consider this:

*There is not in all the United States an entirely nude statue.*

If an angel should come down and say such a thing about heaven, a reasonably cautious observer would take that angel's number and inquire a little further before he added it to his catch. What does the present observer do? Adds it. Adds it at once. Adds it, and labels it with this innocent comment:

*This small fact is strangely significant.*

It does seem to me that this kind of observing is defective.

Here is another curiosity which some liberal person made him a present of. I should think it ought to have disturbed the deep slumber of his suspicion a little, but it didn't. It was a note from a foghorn for strenuousness, it seems to me, but the doomed voyager did not catch it. If he had but caught it, it would have saved him from several disasters:

If the American knows that you are traveling to take notes, he is interested in it, and at the same time rejoices in it, as in a tribute.

Again, this is defective observation. It is human to like to be praised; one can even notice it in the French. But it is not human to like to be ridiculed, even when it comes in the form of a "tribute." I think a little psychologizing ought to have come in there. Something like this: A dog does not like to be ridiculed, a redskin does not like to be ridiculed, a Negro does not like to be ridiculed, a Chinaman does not like to be ridiculed; let us deduce from these significant facts this formula: the American's grade being higher than these, and the chain of argument stretching unbroken all the way up to him, there is room for suspicion that the person who said the American likes to be ridiculed, and regards it as a tribute, is not a capable observer.

I feel persuaded that in the matter of psychologizing, a professional is too apt to yield to the fascinations of the loftier regions of that great art, to the neglect of its lowlier walks. Every now and then, at half-hour intervals, M. Bourget collects a hatful of airy inaccuracies and dissolves them in a panful of assorted abstractions, and runs the charge into a mould and turns you out a compact principle which will explain an American girl, or an American woman, or why new people yearn for old things, or any other impossible riddle which a person wants answered.

It seems to be conceded that there are a few human peculiarities that can be generalized and located here and there in the world and named by the name of the nation where they are found. I wonder what they are. Perhaps one of them is temperament. One speaks of French vivacity and Germany gravity and English stubbornness. There is no American temperament. The nearest that one can come at it is to say there are two—the composed Northern and the impetuous Southern; and both are found in other countries. Morals? Purity of women may fairly be called universal with us, but that is the case in some other countries. We have no monopoly of it; it cannot be named American. I think that there is but a single specialty with us, only one thing that can be called by the wide name "American." That is the national devotion to ice water. All Germans drink beer, but the British nation drinks beer, too; so neither of those peoples is *the* beer-drinking nation. I suppose we do stand alone in having a drink that nobody likes but ourselves. When we have been a month in Europe we lose our craving for it, and we finally tell the hotel folk that they needn't provide it any more. Yet we hardly touch our native shore again, winter or summer, before we are eager for it. The reasons for this state of things have not been psychologized yet. I drop the hint and say no more.

It is my belief that there are some "national" traits and things scattered about the world that are mere superstitions, frauds that have lived so long that they have the solid look of facts. One of them is the dogma that the French are the only chaste people in the world. Ever since I arrived in France this last time I have been accumulating doubts about that; and before I leave this sunny land again I will gather in a few random statistics and psychologize the plausibilities out of it. If people are to come over to America and find fault with our girls and our women, and psychologize every little thing they do, and try to teach them how to behave, and how to cultivate themselves up to where one cannot tell them from the French model, I intend to find out whether those missionaries are qualified or not. A nation ought always to examine into this detail before engaging the teacher for good. This last one has let fall a remark which renewed those doubts of mine when I read it:

In our high Parisian existence, for instance, we find applied to arts and luxury, and to debauchery, all the powers and all the weaknesses of the French soul.

You see, it amounts to a trade with the French soul; a profession; a science; the serious business of life, so speak, in our high Parisian existence. I do not quite like the look of it. I question if it can be taught with profit in our country, except, of course, to those pathetic, neglected minds that are waiting there so yearningly for the education which M. Bourget is going to furnish them from the serene summits of our high Parisian life.

I spoke a moment ago of the existence of some superstitions that have been parading the world as facts this long time. For instance, consider the dollar. The world seems to think that the love of money is "American"; and that the mad desire to get suddenly rich is "American." I believe that both of these things are merely and broadly human, not American monopolies at all. The love of money is natural to all nations, for money is a good and strong friend. I think that this love has existed everywhere, ever since the Bible called it the root of all evil.

I think that the reason why we Americans seem to be so addicted to trying to get rich suddenly is merely because the *opportunity* to make promising efforts in that direction has offered itself to us with a frequency out of all proportion to the European experience. For eighty years this opportunity has been offering itself in one new town or region after another straight westward, step by step, all the way from the Atlantic coast to the Pacific. When a mechanic could buy ten town lots on tolerably long credit for ten months' savings out of his wages, and reasonably expect to sell them in a couple of years for ten times what he gave for them, it was human for him to try the venture, and he did it no matter what his nationality was. He would have done it in Europe or China if he had had the same chance.

In the flush times in the silver regions a cook or any other humble worker stood a very good chance to get rich out of a trifle of money risked in a stock deal; and that person promptly took that risk, no matter what his or her nationality might be. I was there, and saw it.

But these opportunities have not been plenty in our Southern states; so there you have a prodigious region where the rush for sudden wealth is almost an unknown thing—and has been, from the beginning.

Europe has offered few opportunities for poor Tom, Dick, and Harry; but when she has offered one, there has been no noticeable difference between European eagerness and American. England saw this in the wild days of the Railroad King;[5] France saw it in 1720—time of Law and the Mississippi Bubble. I am sure I have never seen in the gold and silver mines any madness, fury, frenzy to get suddenly rich which was even remotely comparable to that which raged in France in the Bubble day.[6] If I had a cyclopedia here I could turn to that memorable case, and satisfy nearly anybody that the hunger for the sudden dollar is no more "American" than it is French. And if I could furnish an American opportunity to staid Germany, I think I could wake her up like a house afire.

But I must return to the generalizations, psychologizings, deductions. When M. Bourget is exploiting these arts, it is then that he is peculiarly and particularly himself. His ways are wholly original when he encounters a trait or a custom which is new to him. Another person would merely examine the find, verify it, estimate its value, and let it go; but that is not sufficient for M. Bourget: he always wants to know *why* that thing exists, he wants to know how it came to happen; and he will not let go of it until he has found out. And in every instance he will find that reason where no one but himself would have thought of looking for it. He does not seem to care for a reason that is not picturesquely located; one might almost say picturesquely and impossibly located.

He found out that in America men do not try to hunt down young married women. At once, as usual, he wanted to know *why*.

Anyone could have told him. He could have divined it by the lights thrown by the novels of the country. But no, he preferred to find out for himself. He has a trustfulness as regards men and facts which is fine and unusual; he is not particular about the source of a fact, he is not particular about the character and standing of the fact itself; but when it comes to pounding out the reason for the existence of the fact, he will trust no one but himself.

In the present instance here was his fact: American young married women are not pursued by the corruptor; and here was the question: What is it that protects her?

It seems quite unlikely that that problem could have offered difficulties to any but a trained philosopher. Nearly any person would have said to M. Bourget: "Oh, that is very simple. It is very seldom in America that a marriage is made on a commercial basis; our marriages, from the beginning, have been made for love; and where love is there is no room for the corruptor."

Now, it is interesting to see the formidable way in which M. Bourget went at that poor, humble little thing. He moved upon it in column—three columns—and with artillery.

"Two reasons of a very different kind explain"—that fact.

And now that I have got so far, I am almost afraid to say what his two reasons are, lest I be charged with inventing them. But I will not retreat now; I will condense them and print them, giving my word that I am honest and not trying to deceive anyone.

1. Young married women are protected from the approaches of the seducer in New England and vicinity by the diluted remains of a prudence created by a Puritan law of two hundred years ago, which for a while punished adultery with death.

2. And young married women of the other forty or fifty States are protected by laws which afford extraordinary facilities for divorce.

If I have not lost my mind I have accurately conveyed those two Vesuvian irruptions of philosophy. But the reader can consult Chapter IV of *Outre-Mer,* and decide for himself. Let us examine this paralyzing deduction or explanation by the light of a few sane facts.

1. This universality of "protection" has existed in our country *from the beginning;* before the death penalty existed in New

England, and during all the generations that have dragged by
since it was annulled.

2. Extraordinary facilities for divorce are of such recent creation that any middle-aged American can remember a time when
such things had not yet been thought of.

Let us suppose that the first easy divorce law went into effect
forty years ago, and got noised around and fairly started in business thirty-five years ago, when we had, say, 25,000,000 of white
population. Let us suppose that among 5,000,000 of them the
young married women were "protected" by the surviving shudder
of that ancient Puritan scare—what is M. Bourget going to do
about those who lived among the 20,000,000? They were clean
in their morals, they were pure, yet there was no easy divorce law
to protect them.

Awhile ago I said that M. Bourget's method of truth-seeking—
hunting for it in out-of-the-way places—was new; but that was an
error. I remember that when Leverrier discovered the Milky Way,
he and the other astronomers began to theorize about it in substantially the same fashion which M. Bourget employs in his
reasonings about American social facts and their origin. Leverrier
advanced the hypothesis that the Milky Way was caused by
gaseous protoplasmic emanations from the field of Waterloo,
which, ascending to an altitude determinable by their own specific
gravity, became luminous through the development and exposure
—by the natural processes of animal decay—of the phosphorus
contained in them.

This theory was warmly complimented by Ptolemy, who, however, after much thought and research, decided that he could not
accept it as final. His own theory was that the Milky Way was an
emigration of lightning bugs; and he supported and reinforced
this theorem by the well-known fact that the locusts do like that
in Egypt.

Giordano Bruno also was outspoken in his praises of Leverrier's
important contribution to astronomical science, and was at first
inclined to regard it as conclusive; but later, conceiving it to be
erroneous, he pronounced against it, and advanced the hypothesis
that the Milky Way was a detachment or corps of stars which became arrested and held in *suspenso suspensorum* by refraction of

gravitation while on the march to join their several constellations; a proposition for which he was afterwards burned at the stake in Jacksonville, Illinois.

These were all brilliant and picturesque theories, and each was received with enthusiasm by the scientific world; but when a New England farmer, who was not a thinker, but only a plain sort of person who tried to account for large facts in simple ways, came out with the opinion that the Milky Way was just common, ordinary stars, and was put where it was because God "wanted to hev it so," the admirable idea fell perfectly flat.

As a literary artist, M. Bourget is as fresh and striking as he is as a scientific one. He says, "Above all, I do not believe much in anecdotes." Why? "In history they are all false"—a sufficiently broad statement—"in literature all libelous"—also a sufficiently sweeping statement, coming from a critic who notes that we are a people who are peculiarly extravagant in our language—"and when it is a matter of social life, almost all biased." It seems to amount to stultification, almost. He has built two or three breeds of American coquettes out of anecdotes—mainly "biased" ones, I suppose; and, as they occur "in literature," furnished by his pen, they must be "all libelous." Or did he mean not *in* literature or anecdotes *about* literature or literary people? I am not able to answer that. Perhaps the original would be clearer, but I have only the translation of this installment by me. I think the remark had an intention; also that this intention was booked for the trip; but that either in the hurry of the remark's departure it got left, or in the confusion of changing cars at the translator's frontier it got sidetracked.

"But on the other hand I believe in statistics; and those on divorces appear to me to be most conclusive." And he sets himself the task of explaining—in a couple of columns—the process by which easy-divorce conceived, invented, originated, developed, and perfected an empire-embracing condition of sexual purity in the States. *In 40 years.* No, he doesn't state the interval. With all his passion for statistics he forgot to ask how long it took to produce this gigantic miracle.

I have followed his pleasant but devious trail through those columns, but I was not able to get hold of his argument and find out what it was. I was not even able to find out where it left off. It seemed to gradually dissolve and flow off into other matters. I followed it with interest, for I was anxious to learn how easy-divorce eradicated adultery in America, but I was disappointed; I have no idea yet how it did it. I only know it didn't. But that is not valuable; I knew it before.

Well, humor is the great thing, the saving thing, after all. The minute it crops up, all our hardnesses yield, all our irritations and resentments flit away, and a sunny spirit takes their place. And so, when M. Bourget said that bright thing about our grandfathers, I broke all up. I remember exploding its American countermine once, under that grand hero, Napoleon. He was only First Consul then, and I was Consul General—for the United States, of course; but we were very intimate, notwithstanding the difference in rank, for I waived that. One day something offered the opening, and he said:

"Well, General, I suppose life can never get entirely dull to an American, because whenever he can't strike up any other way to put in his time he can always get away with a few years trying to find out who his grandfather was!"

I fairly shouted, for I had never heard it sound better; and then I was back at him as quick as a flash:

"Right, your Excellency! But I reckon a Frenchman's got *his* little stand-by for a dull time, too; because when all other interests fail he can turn in and see if he can't find out who his father was!"

Well, you should have heard him just whoop, and cackle and carry on! He reached up and hit me one on the shoulder, and says:

"Land, but it's good! It's immensely good! I'George, I never heard it said so good in my life before! Say it again."

So I said it again, and he said his again, and I said mine again, and then he did, and then I did, and then he did, and we kept on doing it, and doing it, and I *never* had such a good time, and he said the same. In my opinion there isn't anything that is as killing as one of those dear old ripe pensioners if you know how to snatch it out in a kind of a fresh sort of original way.

But I wish M. Bourget had read more of our novels before he came. It is the only way to thoroughly understand a people. When I found I was coming to Paris, I read *La Terre*.[7]

# ON ITALY

Nothing is so contemptible as poverty in the eyes of an American, especially when it retains the charm of bygone splendor. Thus, Mark Twain despises and detests Italy. . . .—THÉRÈSE BENTZON, in a review of *The Innocents Abroad,* in *Revue des Deux Mondes,* July 15, 1875

Honest poverty is a gem that even a king might feel proud to call his own, but I wish to sell out. I have sported that kind of jewelry long enough. I want some variety. I wish to become rich, so that I can instruct the people and glorify honest poverty a little, like those kind-hearted, fat, benevolent people do. —MARK TWAIN, in the San Francisco *Alta California,* July 21, 1867 [1]

For literary authorities who have disapproved of *The Innocents Abroad,* the worst of it has always been Mark Twain on Italy. Partly, this is because it was in Italy that he made what critics have long considered extremely vulgar remarks on the Old Masters. These are some highlights:

But humble as we are, and unpretending, in the matter of art, our researches among the painted monks and martyrs have not been wholly in vain. We have striven hard to learn. . . . When we see a monk going about with a lion and looking tranquilly up to heaven, we know that that is St. Mark. When we see a monk with a book and pen, looking tranquilly up to heaven, trying to think of a word, we know that that is St. Matthew. When we see a monk sitting on a rock, looking tranquilly up to heaven, with a human skull beside him, and without other baggage, we know that that is St. Jerome. . . . When we see other monks looking tranquilly up to heaven but having no trade-mark, we always ask who those parties are. We do this because we humbly wish to learn. We have seen thirteen thousand St. Jeromes, and twenty-two thousand St. Marks, and sixteen thousand St. Matthews, and sixty thousand St. Sebastians, and four millions of assorted monks, undesignated. . . .

He also got tired of Michelangelo:

I used to worship the mighty genius of Michelangelo. . . . But I do not want Michelangelo for breakfast—for luncheon—for dinner—for tea—for supper—for between meals. I like a change, occasionally. In Genoa, he designed everything; in Milan, he or his pupils designed everything; in Florence, he painted everything, designed everything, nearly, and what he did not design he used to sit on a favorite stone and look at, and they showed us the stone. In Pisa, he designed everything but the old shot-tower, and they would have attributed that to him if it had not been so awfully out of the perpendicular. He designed the piers of Leghorn and the custom-house regulations of Città Vecchia. But here—here it is frightful . . . the eternal bore designed the Eternal City, and unless all men and books do lie, he painted everything in it! Dan said the other day to the guide, "Enough, enough, enough! Say no more! Lump the whole thing! Say that the Creator made Italy from designs by Michelangelo!"

He preferred the copies to the originals:

Maybe the originals were handsome when they were new, but they are not now.

And of "The Last Supper":

"The Last Supper" is painted on the dilapidated wall of what was a little chapel attached to the main church in ancient times, I suppose. It is battered and scarred in every direction, and stained and discolored by time, and Napoleon's horses kicked the legs off most of the disciples when they (the horses, not the disciples) were stabled there more than half a century ago. . . .
What would you think of a man who looked at some decayed, blind, toothless, pock-marked Cleopatra and said: "What matchless beauty! What soul! What expression!" What would you think of a man who stared in ecstasy upon a desert of stumps and said: "Oh, my soul, my beating heart, what a noble forest is here!"
You would think that those men had an astonishing talent for seeing things that had already passed away. It was what I thought when I stood before "The Last Supper" and heard men apostrophizing wonders and beauties and perfections which had faded out of the picture and gone, a hundred years before they were born. . . .
After reading so much about it, I am satisfied that "The Last Supper" was a very miracle of art once. But it was three hundred years ago.

When this was written, most people had hardly even dared to think it. And so most people, the world over, laughed with slightly hysterical relief. But for many decades even critics who otherwise admired Mark Twain refused to listen to his excuse: "It is impossible to travel through Italy without speaking of pictures, and can I see them through other's eyes?"
But there was much more wrong with Mark Twain on Italy than the art criticism. For, even a century ago, Italy was more than a museum.

It was also—except for Spain and Portugal—the poorest and least industrialized country in Western Europe. And to citizens of more prosperous lands, its Old World charm was very precious.

In 1867, the same year that Mark Twain first saw Rome, the brothers Edmund and Jules de Goncourt were there on a holiday. Their reactions are an interesting contrast to his, not merely because the Goncourts, too, were professional writers and, at the moment, tourists, but also because they were representative French intellectuals of the period.

In their joint *Journal*, on that long-ago Italian holiday, they wrote:

Civita Vecchia. Ten in the morning. At last we see torturous streets, lively, swarming, filthy markets, a populace dressed in rags, buildings ready to collapse, things picturesque and artistic, a town without the visible hand of the municipal councillors, and streams of colorful slops. I am overcome by a strange happiness; my eyes are bright at the thought that I have run away from that American France, that Paris towed along in the path of the now.

The ideals of the Goncourts were the ideals of most of educated Europe; that fact may help explain some of the anger and contempt with which *The Innocents Abroad* was once received in Europe.

# They May Be Good People

IN OTHER towns in Italy, the people lie around quietly and wait for you to ask them a question or do some overt act that can be charged for—but in Annunciation [Annunciation was a suburb of Naples] they have lost even that fragment of delicacy; they seize a lady's shawl from a chair and hand it to her and charge a penny; they open a carriage door, and charge for it—shut it when you get out, and charge for it; they help you to take off a duster—two cents; brush your clothes and make them worse than they were before—two cents; smile upon you—two cents; bow, with a lickspittle smirk, hat in hand—two cents; they volunteer all information such as that the mules will arrive presently—two cents—warm day, sir—two cents—take you four hours to make the ascent—two cents. And so they go. They crowd you—infest you—swarm about you, and sweat and smell offensively, and look sneaking and mean, and obsequious. There is no office too degrading for them to perform, for money. I have had no opportunity to find out anything about the upper classes by my own observation, but from what I hear said about them I judge that what they lack in one or two of the bad traits the *canaille* have they make up in one or two others that are worse. How the people beg!—many of them very well dressed, too.

I said I knew nothing against the upper classes by personal observation. I must recall it! I had forgotten. What I saw their bravest and their fairest do last night, the lowest multitude that could be scraped up out of the purlieus of Christendom would blush to do, I think. They assembled by hundreds, and even thousands, in the great theatre of San Carlo, to do—what? Why, simply, to make fun of an old woman—to deride, to hiss, to jeer at an actress they once worshiped, but whose beauty is faded now and whose voice has lost its former richness. Everybody spoke of the rare sport that was to be. They said the theatre would be crammed, because Frezzolini was going to sing. It was said she could not sing well, now, but then the people liked to see her, anyhow. And so we went. And every time the woman sang they hissed and laughed—the whole magnificent house—and as soon as she left the stage they called her on again with applause. Once or twice she was encored five and six times in succession, and received with hisses when she appeared, and discharged with hisses and laughter when she had finished—then instantly encored and insulted again! And how the high-born knaves enjoyed it! White-kidded gentlemen and ladies laughed till the tears came, and clapped their hands in very ecstasy when that unhappy old woman would come meekly out for the sixth time, with uncomplaining patience, to meet a storm of hisses! It was the cruelest exhibition—the most wanton, the most unfeeling. . . . What traits of character must a man have to enable him to help three thousand miscreants to hiss, and jeer, and laugh at one friendless old woman, and shamefully humiliate her? He must have *all* the vile, mean traits there are. My observation persuades me (I do not like to venture beyond my own personal observation) that the upper classes of Naples possess those traits of character. Otherwise they may be very good people; I cannot say.

In this city of Naples, they believe in and support one of the

wretchedest of all the religious impostures one can find in Italy—
the miraculous liquefaction of the blood of St. Januarius. Twice
a year the priests assemble all the people at the Cathedral, and
get out this vial of clotted blood and let them see it slowly dissolve
and become liquid—and every day for eight days this dismal farce
is repeated while the priests go among the crowd and collect
money for the exhibition. The first day, the blood liquefies in
forty-seven minutes—the church is crammed, then, and time must
be allowed the collectors to get around: after that it liquefies a
little quicker and a little quicker, every day, as the houses grow
smaller, till on the eighth day, with only a few dozen present to
see the miracle, it liquefies in four minutes.

And here, also, they used to have a grand procession of priests,
citizens, soldiers, sailors, and the high dignitaries of the city government, once a year, to shave the head of a made-up Madonna—a
stuffed and painted image, like a milliner's dummy—whose hair
miraculously grew and restored itself every twelve months. They
still kept up this shaving procession as late as four or five years
ago. It was a source of great profit to the church that possessed
the remarkable effigy, and the ceremony of the public barbering of
her was always carried out with the greatest possible éclat and
display—the more the better, because the more excitement there
was about it the larger the crowds it drew and the heavier the
revenues it produced—but at last a day came when the Pope and
his servants were unpopular in Naples and the city government
stopped the Madonna's annual show.

# The True Religion

AND NOW— However, another beggar approaches. I will go out
and destroy him, and then come back and write another chapter
of vituperation.

Having eaten the friendless orphan—having driven away his
comrades—having grown calm and reflective at length—I now

feel in a kindlier mood. I feel that after talking so freely about the priests and the churches, justice demands that if I know anything good about either I ought to say it. I *have* heard of many things that redound to the credit of the priesthood, but the most notable matter that occurs to me now is the devotion one of the mendicant orders showed during the prevalence of the cholera last year. I speak of the Dominican friars—men who wear a coarse, heavy brown robe and a cowl, in this hot climate, and go barefoot. They live on alms altogether, I believe. They must unquestionably love their religion, to suffer so much for it. When the cholera was raging in Naples; when the people were dying by hundreds and hundreds every day; when every concern for the public welfare was swallowed up in selfish private interest, and every citizen made the taking care of himself his sole object, these men banded themselves together and went about nursing the sick and burying the dead. Their noble efforts cost many of them their lives. They laid them down cheerfully, and well they might. Creeds mathematically precise, and hair-splitting niceties of doctrine, are absolutely necessary for the salvation of some kinds of souls, but surely the charity, the purity, the unselfishness that are in the hearts of men like these would save their souls though they were bankrupt in the true religion—which is ours.

## The Infernal Machine

. . . I HAD to get my passport *viséd* for Rome in Florence, and then they would not let me come ashore here until a policeman had examined it on the wharf and sent me a permit. They did not even dare to let me take my passport in my hands for twelve hours, I looked so formidable. They judged it best to let me cool down. They thought I wanted to take the town, likely. Little did they know me. I wouldn't have it. They examined my baggage at the depot. They took one of my ablest jokes and read it over carefully twice and then read it backward. But it was too deep for them.

They passed it around, and everybody speculated on it awhile, but it mastered them all.

It was no common joke. At length a veteran officer spelled it over deliberately and shook his head three or four times and said that, in his opinion, it was seditious. That was the first time I felt alarmed. I immediately said I would explain the document, and they crowded around. And so I explained and explained and explained, and they took notes of all I said, but the more I explained the more they could not understand it, and when they desisted at last, I could not even understand it myself. They said they believed it was an incendiary document, leveled at the government. I declared solemnly that it was not, but they only shook their heads and would not be satisfied. Then they consulted a good while; and finally they confiscated it. I was very sorry for this, because I had worked a long time on that joke, and took a good deal of pride in it, and now I suppose I shall never see it any more. I suppose it will be sent up and filed away among the criminal archives of Rome, and will always be regarded as a mysterious infernal machine which would have blown up like a mine and scattered the good Pope all around but for a miraculous providential interference.

## Why Don't They Rob Their Churches

A YEAR ago, when Italy saw utter ruin staring her in the face and her greenbacks hardly worth the paper they were printed on, her parliament ventured upon a *coup de main* that would have appalled the stoutest of her statesmen under less desperate circumstances. They, in a manner, confiscated the domains of the Church! This in priest-ridden Italy! This in a land which has groped in the midnight of priestly superstition for sixteen hundred years! It was a rare good fortune for Italy, the stress of weather that drove her to break from this prison-house.

They do not call it *confiscating* the church property. That would

sound too harshly yet. But it amounts to that. There are thousands
of churches in Italy, each with untold millions of treasures stored
away in its closets, and each with its battalion of priests to be
supported. And then there are the estates of the Church—league
on league of the richest lands and the noblest forests in all Italy—
all yielding immense revenues to the Church, and none paying a
cent in taxes to the state. In some great districts the Church owns
*all* the property—lands, watercourses, woods, mills and factories.
They buy, they sell, they manufacture, and since they pay no taxes,
who can hope to compete with them!

Well, the government has seized all this in effect, and will yet
seize it in rigid and unpoetical reality, no doubt. . . .

Pray glance at some of these churches and their embellishments,
and see whether the government is doing a righteous thing or not.
In Venice, today, a city of a hundred thousand inhabitants, there
are twelve hundred priests. Heaven only knows how many there
were before the parliament reduced their numbers. There was the
great Jesuit Church. Under the old régime it required sixty priests
to engineer it—the government does it with five now, and the
others are discharged from service. All about that church wretched-
ness and poverty abound. At its door a dozen hats and bonnets were
doffed to us, as many heads were humbly bowed, and as many
hands extended, appealing for pennies—appealing with foreign
words we could not understand, but appealing mutely, with sad
eyes, and sunken cheeks, and ragged raiment, that no words were
needed to translate. Then we passed within the great doors, and
it seemed that the riches of the world were before us! Huge
columns carved out of single masses of marble, and inlaid from top
to bottom with a hundred intricate figures wrought in costly verd
antique; pulpits of the same rich materials, whose draperies hung
down in many a pictured fold, the stony fabric counterfeiting the
delicate work of the loom; the grand altar brilliant with polished
facing and balustrades of oriental agate, jasper, verd antique, and
other precious stones, whose names, even, we seldom hear—and
slabs of priceless lapis lazuli lavished everywhere as recklessly as
if the church had owned a quarry of it. In the midst of all this
magnificence, the solid gold and silver furniture of the altar seemed

cheap and trivial. Even the floors and ceilings cost a princely fortune.

Now, where is the use of allowing all those riches to lie idle, while half of that community hardly know, from day to day, how they are going to keep body and soul together? And, where is the wisdom in permitting hundreds upon hundreds of millions of francs to be locked up in the useless trumpery of churches all over Italy, and the people ground to death with taxation to uphold a perishing government?

As far as I can see, Italy, for fifteen hundred years, has turned all her energies, all her finances, and all her industry to the building up of a vast array of wonderful church edifices, and starving half her citizens to accomplish it. She is today one vast museum of magnificence and misery. All the churches in an ordinary American city put together could hardly buy the jeweled frippery in one of her hundred cathedrals. And for every beggar in America, Italy can show a hundred—and rags and vermin to match. It is the wretchedest, princeliest land on earth.

Look at the grand Duomo of Florence—a vast pile that has been sapping the purses of her citizens for five hundred years, and is not nearly finished yet. Like all other men, I fell down and worshiped it, but when the filthy beggars swarmed around me the contrast was too striking, too suggestive, and I said, "Oh, sons of classic Italy, *is* the spirit of enterprise, of self-reliance, of noble endeavor, utterly dead within ye? Curse your indolent worthlessness, why don't you rob your church?"

## If I Were a Roman

WHAT IS there in Rome for me to see that others have not seen before me? What is there for me to touch that others have not touched? What is there for me to feel, to learn, to hear, to know, that shall thrill me before it pass to others? What can I discover? Nothing. Nothing whatsoever. One charm of travel dies here. But if I were only a Roman! If, added to my own, I could be gifted with modern Roman sloth, modern Roman superstition, and modern Roman boundlessness of ignorance, what bewildering worlds of unsuspected wonders I would discover! Ah, if I were only a habitant of the Campagna five and twenty miles from Rome! *Then* I would travel.

*I* would go to America, and see, and learn, and return to the Campagna and stand before my countrymen an illustrious discoverer. I would say:

"I saw there a country which has no overshadowing Mother Church, and yet the people survive. I saw a government which never was protected by foreign soldiers at a cost greater than that required to carry on the government itself. I saw common men and common women who could read; I even saw small children of common country-people reading from books; if I dared think you would believe it, I would say they could write, also. In the cities I saw people drinking a delicious beverage made of chalk and water, but never once saw goats driven through their Broadway or their Pennsylvania Avenue or their Montgomery Street and milked at the doors of the houses. I saw real glass windows in the houses of even the commonest people. Some of the houses are not of stone, nor yet of bricks; I solemnly swear they are made of wood. Houses there will take fire and burn, sometimes—actually burn entirely down, and not leave a single vestige behind. I could state that for a truth, upon my deathbed. And as a proof that the circumstance is not rare, I aver that they have a thing which they call a fire engine, which vomits forth great streams of water, and is kept always in readiness, by night and by day, to rush to houses that are burning. You would think one engine would be sufficient, but some great cities have a hundred; they keep men hired, and pay them by the month to do nothing but put out fires. For a certain sum of money other men will insure that your house shall not burn down; and if it burns they will pay you for it. There are hundreds and thousands of schools, and anybody may go and learn to be wise, like a priest. In that singular country, if a rich man dies a sinner he is damned; he cannot buy salvation with money for masses. There is really not much use in being rich there. Not much use as far as the other world is concerned, but much, very much use, as concerns this; because there, if a man be rich, he is very greatly honored, and can become a legislator, a governor, a general, a senator, no matter how ignorant an ass he is—just as in our beloved Italy the nobles hold all the great places, even though sometimes they are born noble idiots. There, if a man be rich, they give him costly presents, they ask him to feasts, they invite him to drink complicated beverages; but if he be poor and in debt, they require him to do that which they term to "settle." The women put on different dresses almost every day; the dress is usually fine, but absurd in shape; the very shape and fashion of it changes twice in a hundred years; and did I but covet to be called an extravagant falsifier, I would say it changed even oftener. Hair does not grow upon the American women's heads; it is made for them by cunning workmen in the shops, and is curled and frizzled into scandalous and ungodly forms. Some persons wear eyes of glass which they see through with facility perhaps, else they would not use them; and in the mouths of some are teeth made by the sacrilegious hand of man. The dress of the men is laughably grotesque. They carry no musket in ordinary life, nor no long-pointed pole; they wear no wide green-lined cloak; they wear no peaked black felt hat, no leathern gaiters reaching to the knee, no goatskin breeches with the hair side out, no hobnailed shoes, no prodigious spurs. They wear a conical hat termed a "nail kag"; a coat of saddest black; a shirt which shows dirt so easily that it has to be changed every month, and is very troublesome; things called pantaloons, which are held up by shoulder straps, and on their feet they wear boots which are ridiculous in pattern and can stand no wear. Yet dressed in this fantastic garb, these people laughed at *my* costume. In that country, books are so common that it is really no curiosity to see one. Newspapers also. They have a great machine which prints such things by thousands every hour.

"I saw common men there—men who were neither priests nor princes—who yet absolutely owned the land they tilled. It was not rented from the church, nor from the nobles. I am ready to take my oath of this. In that country you might fall from a third-story window three several times, and not mash either a soldier or a priest. The scarcity of such people is astonishing. In the cities you will see a dozen civilians for every soldier, and as many for every priest or preacher. Jews, there, are treated just like human beings, instead of dogs. They can work at any business they please; they can sell brand-new goods if they want to; they can keep drug stores; they can practice medicine among Christians; they can even shake hands with Christians if they choose; they can associate with them, just the same as one human being does with another human being; they don't have to stay shut up in one corner of the towns; they can live in any part of a town they like best; it is said they even have the privilege of buying land and houses, and owning them themselves, though I doubt that myself; they never have had to run races naked through the public streets, against jackasses, to please the people in carnival time; there they never have been driven by soldiers into a church every Sunday for hundreds of years to hear themselves and their relgion especially and particlarly cursed; at this very day, in that curious country, a Jew is allowed to vote, hold office, yea, get up on a rostrum in the public street and express his opinion of the government if the government don't suit him! Ah, it is wonderful. The common people there know a great deal; they even have the effrontery to complain if they are not properly governed, and to take hold and help conduct the government themselves; if they had laws like ours, which give one dollar of every three a crop produces to the government for taxes, they would have that law altered; instead of paying thirty-three dollars in taxes, out of every one hundred they receive, they complain if they have to pay seven. They are curious people. They do not know when they are well off. Mendicant priests do not prowl among them with baskets begging for the church and eating up their substance. One hardly ever sees a minister of the Gospel going around there in his bare feet, with a basket, begging for subsistence. In that country the preachers are not like our mendicant orders of friars—they have two or three suits of clothing, and they wash sometimes. In that land are mountains far higher than the Alban Mountains; the vast Roman Campagna, a hundred miles long and full forty broad, is really small compared to the United States of America; the Tiber, that celebrated river of ours, which stretches its mighty course almost two hundred miles, and which a lad can scarcely throw a stone across at Rome, is not so long, nor yet so wide as the Amercan Mississippi—nor yet the Ohio, nor even the Hudson. In America the people are absolutely wiser and know much more than their grandfathers did. *They* do not plow with a sharpened stick, nor yet with a three-cornered block of wood that merely scratches the top of the ground. We do that because our fathers did, three thousand years ago, I suppose. But those people have no holy reverence for their ancestors. They plow with a plow that is a sharp, curved blade of iron, and it cuts into the earth full five inches. And this is not all. They cut their grain with a horrid machine that mows down whole fields in a day. If I dared, I would say that sometimes they use a blasphemous plow that works by fire and vapor and tears up an acre of ground in a single hour—but—but—I see by your looks that you do not believe the things I am telling you. Alas, my character is ruined, and I am a branded speaker of untruths."

# ON THE JEWS

## Concerning the Jews

They [the Jews] are peculiarly and conspicuously the world's intellectual aristocracy.—*Mark Twain's Notebook,* 1879.

It is difficult to imagine how a modern equivalent of "Concerning the Jews" could be published today. First, there are numerous inaccuracies in it. Second, it could offend members of two sensitive minorities: the Jews and the Irish.

As an intelligent force, and numerically, he [the Irishman] has always been away down, but he has governed the country just the same.

In the light of Mark Twain's other remarks on the Irish, he probably meant not "intelligent," but "educated." If so, there was a basis for part of the remark. Even at the turn of the century, few first generation Americans were educated by American standards—the Germans, English, and Scots were notable exceptions—simply because free public education was not so widespread in Europe as in the United States.

Still, the Irish were not governing the country. Nor were the Jews—despite Mark Twain's remarks on their wealth—a prosperous people. The overwhelming majority of them—"the pivot of the race" according to Anatole Leroy-Beaulieu, an eminent French authority—were in Eastern Europe, chiefly Russia. Mark Twain had no first-hand knowledge of that part of the world. Nor did he make use of information available. This is from "Russia's Treatment of Jewish Subjects," by G. Hubert, Jr., which appeared in the New York *Forum,* March 1893:

156

Jews have always been among the poorest classes of Russians, owing to their large families and heavy taxes, the taxes of a Jew being reckoned at half as much again as that of a Russian Christian Dissenter. But the policy of restricting Jews to the towns has made matters incomparably worse. There are said to be about 25,000 Jewish paupers in Berdicliev, the Russian Jerusalem, and throughout the Pale—the settlement in which the Jews must live—thousands of families have only one meal a day. No wonder that those who find refuge in our country prefer what seems to us to be a miserable existence to such extremity of poverty. . . .

When one realizes that, in the vast area east of the Bowery populated by Russian Jews, the crowding, the filth, the noise and the stenches are beyond description, and that the majority of those people work for 14 to 18 hours a day, often beginning their labor at dawn and continuing it until they fall exhausted on the piles of clothing they make for the cheap shops, he can see that the fate of the Russian Jew who has to stay behind in Russia must be hard indeed.

Those were the economic facts. But by the close of the last century the myth of Jewish wealth was centuries old. The Mark Twain who believed it was—in that respect—a typical uninformed gentile. Moreover, one of his few really naive statements appears in "Concerning the Jews":

The Jew is being legislated out of Russia. The reason is not concealed. The movement was instituted because the Christian peasant and villager stood no chance against his commercial abilities.

Today, students of this part of history are generally agreed that the reason for nineteenth-century Russian anti-Semitic policies was very carefully concealed indeed. For the imperial government, which not only legislated against the Jews, but incited and organized the pogroms, was earnestly engaged in diverting popular unrest to a convenient scapegoat. Nor was commercial competition, either Jewish or gentile, a factor of importance in feudal Russia. The Jews were moneylenders in the Russian villages partly because it was the intent of the government that they should fill this unpopular role, and partly because almost all other occupations were forbidden them. But—as Clemens makes plain below—the barring of the Jews from farming, the professions, and many trades was not confined to Russia, and dated from long before the last century. Wherever such restrictions were relaxed, of course, the Jew became a less specialized, and less special, person. Thus the British and American Jew seemed to Clemens—and to other observers—less gifted intellectually, and in business, than those European Jews whose activities had been sharply restricted for generations.

But Mark Twain had always a delighted admiration for what he regarded as the special intellectual powers of the Jew—as well as a great respect for Jewish generosity. In *Following the Equator* he climaxes his praise of the Indian Parsees: "The Jew himself is not more lavish or catholic in his charities and benevolences."

And this appears in an exuberant 1897 letter about Viennese politics, written to his friend the Rev. Joseph Twitchell (the italics are mine):

It is Christian and Jew by the horns—the advantage with the superior man, as usual—the superior man being the Jew every time and in all countries. Land, Joe, what chance would the Christian have in a country where there were three Jews to ten Christians! . . . The difference between the brain of the average Christian and that of the average Jew—*certainly in Europe*—is about the difference between a tadpole's and an Archbishop's. It's a marvelous race—by long odds the most marvelous that the world has produced, I suppose.

By the Jews themselves, this sort of tribute has been received with mixed feelings.

"Of all such advocates, we can but say 'Heaven save us from our friends,' " said *The Jewish Chronicle,* for October 1899. Other Jewish comment was even stronger. But according to Philip Foner in *Mark Twain: Social Critic*:

In New York's teeming East side, the Jewish immigrants regarded Mark Twain in the most affectionate terms, and nothing that critics of his essay said seems to have influenced their affection for him.[1]

The alarm and indignation of much of the Jewish press was natural; a people which has been feared and envied because it supposedly possesses almost superhuman powers is not apt to rejoice—or even feel easy—when it is credited with anything like such powers. For very similar reasons, Americans of Irish descent have not been wholly gratified by Mark Twain's tributes. For example, after noting that the Jews were nine per cent of the population of Austria-Hungary, he wrote:

The Irish would govern the Kingdom of Heaven if they had a strength there like that.

Now this is not only good-humored wit; it is based on the truth that the Irish, in the United States, have showed a talent for political organization. But again the tribute is too close to an old slander: that the Irish Catholics, by virtue of their political genius, are about to deliver the country to the Vatican.

But historically the slanders against the Jews and the Irish have not been comparable. The slander of the Irish has flourished only in this country, and only for a few generations. It was once expressed in the Ku Klux Klan, in the Know-Nothing party, and in social and job discrimination; it probably kept Al Smith out of the White House.

But the results of the traditional slander of the Jews could not be contained in volumes—certainly not printable volumes.

The fact was that Mark Twain had no more—and no less—against Jews and Catholics than against Hindus and Presbyterians. The fact is remarkable since he was brought up in a community where there was prejudice against Jews and Catholics; but it is no more remarkable than the fact that a writer with his attitude towards the dark races should have come from a slave state. For Mark Twain was not born to tolerance; he achieved it and had it thrust upon him by experience. And perhaps that was why it ran somewhat deeper in him than the lip service which sometimes passes for that quality. In *The Innocents Abroad*, his tribute to the Catholic convents of Palestine—"a priceless blessing to the poor"—is interrupted by this remark:

I have been educated to enmity toward everything that is Catholic, and sometimes, in consequence of this, I find it much easier to discover Catholic faults than Catholic virtues.

In Mark Twain's Notebooks there are references to mild anti-Semitism in Hannibal, and no doubt he once shared this attitude as completely as he shared the community attitude toward Catholics and toward slavery.[2]

Attempts to prove that Clemens was a Jew began, in Germany, in 1910, when the first reference to him as *Salamon* Clemens appeared.[3] Such attempts continued spasmodically, until, under the Nazis, they were widely publicized.

Attempts to prove that Mark Twain was an anti-Semite were delayed until 1939, when a New York publicity man circulated his own anti-Semitic version of parts of "Concerning the Jews." Extensive rewriting was necessary, and was supplied.

"Concerning the Jews" was last reprinted by Mark Twain's publishers, in pamphlet form, in 1934—when rumors of Nazi atrocities were first reaching this country. Now it is, among other things, a reminder of the days when it was still possible to ridicule anti-Semitism —and even to do so gayly. And thus it is dated. Not all Mark Twain's wit can make certain passages gay reading today.

Joseph of Genesis is, of course, a digression in "Concerning the Jews"—and is almost as outrageous as his digression on the French. But Clemens' observations on Joseph have a history. This is from the second volume of *The Innocents Abroad,* much of which is commentary on the Old Testament, which, he once said, was in some ways greater literature than Shakespeare.

Joseph was the real king, the strength, the brain of the monarchy, although Pharaoh held the title. Joseph is one of the truly great men of the Old Testament. And he was the noblest and the manliest, save Esau.

But Mark Twain was young then. His revised view—that Joseph had robbed the poor in the name of religion and had been whitewashed by the clergy ever since—appeared for the first time in this selection. Some eight years afterward, John D. Rockefeller, Jr., moved him to further wrath on this subject. For young Rockefeller's talks on the Bible were then appearing in newspapers throughout the country. And, according to Mark Twain in his Autobiography, if Rockefeller, Jr.,

. . . were travelling upon his mental merit instead of upon his father's money, his explanations of the Bible would . . . not be heard of by the public. But his father ranks as the richest man in the world, and this makes his son's theological gymnastics interesting and important.[4]

The Rockefeller view of Joseph is now lost, but clearly it was conventional:

Eight years ago [Mark Twain wrote in his Autobiography in 1906], I quite painstakingly and exhaustively explained Joseph by the light of the forty-seventh chapter of Genesis.[5] . . . Judge, then, of my surprise and sorrow, when by the newspapers I lately saw that Mr. Rockefeller had taken hold of Joseph . . . and was trying to unsettle him again. . . . He thinks Joseph was Mary's little lamb; this is an error.[6]

In the Autobiography Mark Twain was far too busy with Rockefeller, Joseph, and the clergy to take notice that Joseph was a Jew. And, of course, it was never race or creed which so inflamed him against that particular Patriarch.

But despite digressions—or perhaps because of them—despite factual errors and ill-timed compliments, Mark Twain's pride in the wit and quality of "Concerning the Jew" was entirely justified. It was his "gem of the ocean," he wrote his friend, Henry Rogers. "I have taken a world of pleasure in writing it & doctoring it & fussing at it."

"Concerning the Jews" first appeared in *Harper's Magazine*, September, 1899. The postscript appeared when it was reprinted in 1900 in an English anthology, *The Man That Corrupted Hadleyburg, Etc.* The postscript was published and publicized in this country under the title "The American Jew as a Soldier," but does not appear in any American reprint of "Concerning the Jews." The article follows:

SOME MONTHS ago I published a magazine article descriptive of a remarkable scene in the Imperial Parliament in Vienna. Since then I have received from Jews in America several letters of inquiry. They were difficult letters to answer, for they were not very definite. But at last I have received a definite one. It is from a lawyer, and he really asks the questions which the other writers probably believed they were asking. By help of this text I will do the best I can to publicly answer this correspondent, and also the others—at the same time apologizing for having failed to reply privately. The lawyer's letter reads as follows:

I have read "Stirring Times in Austria." One point in particular is of vital import to not a few thousand people, including myself, being a point about which I have often wanted to address a question to some disinterested person. The show of military force in the Austrian Parliament, which precipitated the riots, was not introduced by any Jew. No Jew was a member of that body. No Jewish question was involved in the Ausgleich[7] or in the language proposition. No Jew was insulting anybody. In short, no Jew was doing any mischief toward anybody whatsoever. In fact, the Jews were the only ones of the nineteen different races in Austria which did not have a party—they are absolutely non-participants. Yet in your article you say that in the rioting which followed, all classes of people were unanimous only on one thing, viz., in being against the Jews. Now, will you kindly tell me why, in your judgment, the Jews have thus ever been, and are even now, in these days of supposed intelligence, the butt of baseless, vicious animosities? I dare say that for centuries there has been no more quiet, undisturbing, and well-behaving citizen, as a class, than that same Jew. It seems to me that ignorance and fanaticism cannot alone account for these horrible and unjust persecutions.

Tell me, therefore, from your vantage point of cold view, what in your mind is the cause. Can American Jews do anything to correct it either in America or abroad? Will it ever come to an end? Will a Jew be permitted to live honestly, decently, and peaceably like the rest of mankind? What has become of the Golden Rule?

I will begin by saying that if I thought myself prejudiced against the Jew, I should hold it fairest to leave this subject to a person not crippled in that way. But I think I have no such prejudice. A few years ago a Jew observed to me that there was no uncourteous reference to his people in my books, and asked how it happened. It happened because the disposition was lacking. I am quite sure that (bar one)[8] I have no race prejudices, and I think I have no color prejudices nor caste prejudices nor creed prejudices. Indeed, I know it. I can stand any society. All that I care to know is that a man is a human being—that is enough for me; he can't be any worse. I have no special regard for Satan; but I can at least claim that I have no prejudice against him. It may even be that I lean a little his way, on account of his not having a fair show. All religions issue Bibles against him, and say the most injurious things about him, but we never hear *his* side. We have none but the evidence for the prosecution, and yet we have rendered the verdict. To my mind, this is irregular. It is un-English; it is un-American; it is French. Without this precedent Dreyfus could not have been condemned. Of course Satan has some kind of a case, it goes without saying. It may be a poor one, but that is nothing; that can be said about any of us. As soon as I can get at the facts I will undertake his rehabilitation myself, if I can find an unpolitic publisher. It is a thing which we ought to be willing to do for any one who is under a cloud. We may not pay Satan reverence, for that would be indiscreet, but we can at least respect his talents. A person who has during all time maintained the imposing position of spiritual head of four-fifths of the human race, and political head of the whole of it, must be granted the possession of executive abilities of the loftiest order. In his large presence the other popes and politicians shrink to midges for the microscope. I would like to see him. I would rather see him and shake him by the tail than any other member of the European Concert. In the present paper I shall allow myself to use the word Jew as if it stood for both religion and race. It is handy; and, besides, that is what the term means to the general world.

In the above letter one notes these points:

1. The Jew is a well-behaved citizen.

2. Can ignorance and fanaticism *alone* account for his unjust treatment?

3. Can Jews do anything to improve the situation?

4. The Jews have no party; they are non-participants.

5. Will the persecution ever come to an end?

6. What has become of the Golden Rule?

*Point No.* 1.—We must grant proposition No. 1, for several sufficient reasons. The Jew is not a disturber of the peace of any country. Even his enemies will concede that. He is not a loafer, he is not a sot, he is not noisy, he is not a brawler nor a rioter, he is not quarrelsome. In the statistics of crime his presence is conspicuously rare—in all countries. With murder and other crimes of violence he has but little to do: he is a stranger to the hangman. In the police court's daily long roll of "assaults" and "drunk and disorderlies" his name seldom appears. That the Jewish home is a home in the truest sense is a fact which no one will dispute. The family is knitted together by the strongest affections; its members show each other every due respect; and reverence for the elders is an inviolate law of the house. The Jew is not a burden on the charities of the state nor of the city; these could cease from their functions without affecting him. When he is well enough, he works; when he is incapacitated, his own people take care of him. And not in a poor and stingy way, but with a fine and large benevolence. His race is entitled to be called the most benevolent of all the races of men. A Jewish beggar is not impossible, perhaps; such a thing may exist, but there are few men that can say they have seen that spectacle. The Jew has been staged in many uncomplimentary forms, but, so far as I know, no dramatist has done him the injustice to stage him as a beggar. Whenever a Jew has real need to beg, his people save him from the necessity of doing it. The charitable institutions of the Jews are supported by Jewish money, and amply. The Jews make no noise about it; it is done quietly; they do not nag and pester and harass us for contributions; they give us peace, and set us an example—an example which we have not found ourselves able to follow; for by nature we are not free givers, and have to be patiently and persistently hunted down in the interest of the unfortunate.

These facts are all on the credit side of the proposition that the Jew is a good and orderly citizen. Summed up, they certify that he is quiet, peaceable, industrious, unaddicted to high crimes and brutal dispositions; that his family life is commendable; that he is not a burden upon public charities; that he is not a beggar; that in benevolence he is above the reach of competition. These are the very quintessentials of good citizenship. If you can add that he is as honest as the average of his neighbors— But I think that question is affirmatively answered by the fact that he is a successful business man. The basis of successful business is honesty; a business cannot thrive where the parties to it cannot trust each other. In the matter of numbers the Jew counts for little in the overwhelming population of New York; but that his honesty counts for much is guaranteed by the fact that the immense wholesale business of Broadway, from the Battery to Union Square, is substantially in his hands.

I suppose that the most picturesque example in history of a trader's trust in his fellow-trader was one where it was not Christian trusting Christian, but Christian trusting Jew. The Hessian Duke who used to sell his subjects to George III to fight George Washington with got rich at it; and by and by, when the wars engendered by the French Revolution made his throne too warm for him, he was obliged to fly the country. He was in a hurry, and had to leave his earnings behind—$9,000,000. He had to risk the money with someone without security. He did not select a Christian, but a Jew—a Jew of only modest means, but of high character; a character so high that it left him lonesome—Rothschild of Frankfort. Thirty years later, when Europe had become quiet and safe again, the Duke came back from overseas, and the Jew returned the loan, with interest added.*

_____

* Here is another piece of picturesque history; and it reminds us that shabbiness and dishonesty are not the monopoly of any race or creed, but are merely human:

"Congress has passed a bill to pay $379.56 to Moses Pendergrass, of Libertyville, Missouri. The story of the reason of this liberality is pathetically interesting, and shows the sort of pickle that an honest man may get into who undertakes to do an honest job of work for Uncle Sam. In 1886 Moses Pendergrass put in a bid for the contract to carry the mail on the route from Knob Lick to Libertyville and Coffman, thirty miles a day, from July 1, 1887, for one year. He got the postmaster at Knob Lick to write the letter for him, and while Moses intended that his bid should be $400, his scribe carelessly made it $4. Moses got the contract, and did not find out about the mistake until the end of the first quarter, when he got his first pay. When he found at what rate he was working he was sorely cast down, and opened communication with the Post Office Department. The department informed him that he must either carry out his contract or throw it up, and that if he threw it up his bondsman would have to pay the Government $1,459.85 damages. So Moses carried out his contract, walked thirty miles every weekday for a year, and carried the mail, and received for his labour $4—or, to be accurate, $6.84; for, the route being extended after his bid was accepted, the pay was proportionately increased. Now, after ten years, a bill was finally passed to pay to Moses the difference between what he earned in that unlucky year and what he received."

The *Sun,* which tells the above story, says that bills were introduced in three or four Congresses for Moses' relief, and that committees repeatedly investigated his claim.

It took six Congresses, containing in their persons the compressed virtues

The Jew has his other side. He has some discreditable ways, though he has not a monopoly of them, because he cannot get entirely rid of vexatious Christian competition. We have seen that he seldom transgresses the laws against crimes of violence. Indeed, his dealings with courts are almost restricted to matters connected with commerce. He has a reputation for various small forms of cheating, and for practicing oppressive usury, and for burning himself out to get the insurance, and for arranging cunning contracts which leave him an exit but lock the other man in, and for smart evasions which find him safe and comfortable just within the strict letter of the law, when court and jury know very well that he has violated the spirit of it. He is a frequent and faithful and capable officer in the civil service, but he is charged with an unpatriotic disinclination to stand by the flag as a soldier—like the Christian Quaker.

Now if you offset these discreditable features by the creditable one summarized in a preceding paragraph beginning with the words. "These facts are all on the credit side," and strike a balance, what must the verdict be? This, I think: that, the merit and demerits being fairly weighed and measured on both sides, the Christian can claim no superiority over the Jew in the matters of good citizenship.

Yet in all countries, from the dawn of history, the Jew has been persistently and implacably hated, and with frequency·persecuted.

*Point No. 2.*—"Can fanaticism *alone* account for this?"

Years ago I used to think that it was responsible for nearly all of it, but latterly I have come to think that this was an error. Indeed, it is now my conviction that it is responsible for hardly any of it.

In this connection I call to mind Genesis, chapter 47.

We have all thoughtfully—or unthoughtfully—read the pathetic story of the years of plenty and the years of famine in Egypt, and

---

of 70,000,000 of people, and cautiously and carefully giving expression to those virtues in the fear of God and the next election, eleven years to find out some way to cheat a fellow Christian out of about $13 on his honestly executed contract, and out of nearly $300 due him on its enlarged terms. And they succeeded. During the same time they paid out $1,000,000,000 in pensions—a third of it unearned and undeserved. This indicates a splendid all-around competency in theft, for it starts with farthings, and works its industries all the way up to shiploads. It may be possible that the Jews can beat this, but the man that bets on it is taking chances. (M.T.)

how Joseph, with that opportunity, made a corner in broken hearts, and the crusts of the poor, and human liberty—a corner whereby he took a nation's money all away, to the last penny; took a nation's livestock all  away, to the last hoof; took a nation's land away, to the last acre; then took the nation itself, buying it for bread, man by man, woman by woman, child by child, till all were slaves; a corner which took everything, left nothing; a corner so stupendous that, by comparison with it, the most gigantic corners in subsequent history are but baby things, for it dealt in hundreds of millions of bushels, and its profits were reckonable by hundreds of millions of dollars, and it was a disaster so crushing that its effects have not wholly disappeared from Egypt today, more than three thousand years after the event.

Is it presumable that the eye of Egypt was upon Joseph the foreign Jew all this time? I think it likely. Was it friendly? We must doubt it. Was Joseph establishing a character for his race which would survive long in Egypt? and in time would his name come to be familiarly used to express the character—like Shylock's? It is hardly to be doubted. Let us remember that this was *centuries before the Crucifixion.*

I wish to come down eighteen hundred years later and refer to a remark made by one of the Latin historians. I read it in a translation many years ago, and it comes back to me now with force. It was alluding to a time when people were still living who could have seen the Saviour in the flesh. Christianity was so new that the people of Rome had hardly heard of it, and had but confused notions of what it was. The substance of the remark was this: Some Christians were persecuted in Rome through error, they being *"mistaken for Jews."*

The meaning seems plain. These pagans had nothing against Christians, but they were quite ready to persecute Jews. For some reason or other they hated a Jew before they ever knew what a Christian was. May I not assume, then, that the persecution of Jews is a thing which *antedates* Christianity and was not born of Christianity? I think so. What was the origin of the feeling?

When I was a boy, in the back settlements of the Mississippi Valley, where a gracious and beautiful Sunday-school simplicity and unpracticality prevailed, the "Yankee" (citizen of the New

England states) was hated with a splendid energy. But religion had nothing to do with it. In a trade, the Yankee was held to be about five times the match of the Westerner. His shrewdness, his insight, his judgment, his knowledge, his enterprise, and his formidable cleverness in applying these forces were frankly confessed, and most competently cursed.

In the cotton states, after the war, the simple and ignorant Negroes made the crops for the white planter on shares. The Jews came down in force, set up shop on the plantation, supplied all the Negro's wants on credit, and at the end of the season was proprietor of the Negro's share of the present crop and of part of his share of the next one. Before long, the whites detested the Jew, and it is doubtful if the Negro loved him.

The Jew is being legislated out of Russia. The reason is not concealed. The movement was instituted because the Christian peasant and villager stood no chance against his commercial abilities. He was always ready to lend money on a crop, and sell vodka and other necessaries of life on credit while the crop was growing. When settlement day came he owned the crop; and next year or year after he owned the farm, like Joseph.

In the dull and ignorant England of John's time everybody got into debt to the Jew. He gathered all lucrative enterprises into his hands; he was the king of commerce; he was ready to be helpful in all profitable ways; he even financed crusades for the rescue of the Sepulchre. To wipe out his account with the nation and restore business to its natural and incompetent channels he had to be banished from the realm.

For the like reasons Spain had to banish him four hundred years ago, and Austria about a couple of centuries later.

In all the ages Christian Europe has been obliged to curtail his activities. If he entered upon a mechanical trade, the Christian had to retire from it. If he set up as a doctor, he was the best one, and he took the business. If he exploited agriculture, the other farmers had to get at something else. Since there was no way to successfully compete with him in any vocation, the law had to step in and save the Christian from the poorhouse. Trade after trade was taken away from the Jew by statute till practically none was left. He was forbidden to engage in agriculture; he was forbidden to practice law; he was forbidden to practice medicine, except among Jews; he was forbidden the handicrafts. Even the seats of learning and the schools of science had to be closed against this tremendous antagonist. Still, almost bereft of employments, he found ways to make money, even ways to get rich. Also ways to invest his takings well, for usury was not denied him. In the hard conditions suggested, the Jew without brains could not survive, and the Jew with brains had to keep them in good training and well sharpened up, or starve. Ages of restriction to the one tool which the law was not able to take from him—his brain—have made that tool singularly competent; ages of compulsory disuse of his hands have atrophied them, and he never uses them now. This history has a very, very commercial look, a most sordid and practical commercial look, the business aspect of a Chinese cheap-labor crusade. Religious prejudices may account for one part of it, but not for the other nine.

Protestants have persecuted Catholics, but they did not take their livelihoods away from them. The Catholics have persecuted the Protestants with bloody and awful bitterness, but they never closed agriculture and the handicrafts against them. Why was that? That has the candid look of genuine religious persecution, not a trade-union boycott in a religious disguise.

The Jews are harried and obstructed in Austria and Germany, and lately in France; but England and America give them an open field and yet survive. Scotland offers them an unembarrassed field too, but there are not many takers. There are a few Jews in Glasgow, and one in Aberdeen; but that is because they can't earn enough to get away. The Scotch pay themselves that compliment, but it is authentic.

I feel convinced that the Crucifixion has not much to do with the world's attitude towards the Jew; that the reasons for it are older than that event, as suggested by Egypt's experience and by Rome's regret for having persecuted an unknown quanity called a Christian, under the mistaken impression that she was merely persecuting a Jew. *Merely* a Jew—a skinned eel who was used to it, presumably. I am persuaded that in Russia, Austria, and Germany nine-tenths of the hostility to the Jew comes from the average Christian's inability to compete successfully with the average Jew in business—in either straight business or the questionable sort.

In Berlin, a few years ago, I read a speech which frankly urged the expulsion of the Jews from Germany; and the agitator's *reason* was as frank as his proposition. It was this: *that 85 per cent* of the successful lawyers of Berlin were Jews, and that about the same percentage of the great and lucrative businesses of all sorts in Germany were in the hands of the Jewish race! Isn't it an amazing confession? It was but another way of saying that in a population of 48,000,000, of whom only 500,000 were registered as Jews, 85 per cent of the brains and honesty of the whole was lodged in the Jews. I must insist upon the honesty—it is an essential of successful business, taken by and large. Of course it does not rule out rascals entirely, even among Christians, but it is a good working rule, nevertheless. The speaker's figures may have been inexact, but *the motive of persecution* stands out as clear as day.

The man claimed that in Berlin the banks, the newspapers, the theatres, the great mercantile, shipping, mining, and manufacturing interests, the big army and city contracts, the tramways, and pretty much all other properties of high value, and *also* the small businesses, were in the hands of the Jews. He said the Jew was pushing the Christian to the wall all along the line; that it was all a Christian could do to scrape together a living; and that the Jew *must* be banished, and soon—there was no other way of saving the Christian. Here in Vienna, last autumn, an agitator said that all these disastrous details were true of Austria-Hungary also; and in fierce language he demanded the expulsion of the Jews. When politicians come out without a blush and read the baby act in this frank way, *unrebuked*, it is a very good indication that they have a market back of them, and know where to fish for votes.

You note the crucial point of the mentioned agitation; the argument is that the Christian cannot *compete* with the Jew, and that hence his very bread is in peril. To human beings this is a much more hate-inspiring thing than is any detail connected with religion. With most people, of a necessity, bread and meat take first rank, religion second. I am convinced that the persecution of the Jew is not due in any large degree to religious prejudice.

No, the Jew is a money-getter; and in getting his money he is a very serious obstruction to less capable neighbors who are on the same quest. I think that that is the trouble. In estimating worldly values the Jew is not shallow, but deep. With precocious wisdom he found out in the morning of time that some men worship rank, some worship heroes, some worship power, some worship God, and that over these ideals they dispute and cannot unite—but that they all worship money; so he made it the end and aim of his life to get it. He was at it in Egypt thirty-six centuries ago; he was at it in Rome when that Christian got persecuted by mistake for him; he has been at it ever since. The cost to him has been heavy; his success has made the whole human race his enemy—but it has paid, for it has brought him envy, and that is the only thing which men will sell both soul and body to get. He long ago observed that a millionaire commands respect, a two-millionaire homage, a multi-millionaire the deepest deeps of adoration. We all know that feeling; we have seen it express itself. We have noticed that when the average man mentions the name of a multimillionaire he does it with that mixture in his voice of awe and reverence and lust which burns in a Frenchman's eye when it falls on another man's centime.

*Point No.* 4.—"The Jews have no party; they are non-participants."

Perhaps you have let the secret out and given yourself away. It seems hardly a credit to the race that it is able to say that; or to you, sir, that you can say it without remorse; more, that you should offer it as a plea against maltreatment, injustice, and oppression. Who gives the Jew the right, who gives any race the right, to sit still in a free country, and let somebody else look after its safety? The oppressed Jew was entitled to all pity in the former times under brutal autocracies, for he was weak and friendless, and had no way to help his case. But he has ways now, and he has had them for a century, but I do not see that he has tried to make serious use of them. When the Revolution set him free in France it was an act of grace—the grace of other people; he does not appear in it as a helper. I do not know that he helped when England set him free. Among the Twelve Sane Men of France who have stepped forward with great Zola at their head to fight (and win, I hope and believe) the battle for the most infamously misused Jew of modern times, do you find a great or rich or illustrious Jew helping? In the United States he was created free in the beginning—he did not need to help, of course. In Austria and Germany and France he has a vote, but of what considerable use is it to him? He doesn't seem to know how to apply it to the best effect. With all his splendid capacities and all his fat wealth he is today not politically important in any country. In America, as early as 1854, the ignorant Irish hod carrier, who had a spirit of his own and a way of exposing it to the weather, made it apparent to all that he must be politically reckoned with; yet fifteen years before that we hardly knew what an Irishman looked like. As an intelligent force and numerically, he has always been away down, but he has governed the country just the same. It was because he was *organized*. It made his vote valuable—in fact, essential.

You will say the Jew is everywhere numerically feeble. That is nothing to the point—with the Irishman's history for an object lesson. But I am coming to your numerical feebleness presently. In all parliamentary countries you could no doubt elect Jews to the legislatures—and even *one* member in such a body is sometimes a force which counts. How deeply have you concerned yourselves about this in Austria, France, and Germany? Or even in America, for that matter? You remark that the Jews were not to blame for the riots in this Reichsrath here, and you add with satisfaction that there wasn't one in that body. That is not strictly correct; if it were, would it not be in order for you to explain it and apologize for it, not try to make a merit of it? But I think that the Jew was by no means in as large force there as he ought to have been, with his chances. Austria opens the suffrage to him on fairly liberal terms, and it must surely be his own fault that he is so much in the background politically.

As to your numerical weakness. I mentioned some figures awhile ago—500,000 as the Jewish population of Germany. I will add some more—6,000,000 in Russia, 5,000,000 in Austria, 250,000 in the United States. I take them from memory; I read them in the Encyclopædia Britannica ten or twelve years ago. Still, I am entirely sure of them. If those statistics are correct, my argument is not as strong as it ought to be as concerns America, but it still has strength. It is plenty strong enough as concerns Austria, for ten years ago 5,000,000 was 9 per cent of the empire's popula-

tion. The Irish would govern the Kingdom of Heaven if they had
a strength there like that.

I have some suspicions; I got them at secondhand, but they
have remained with me these ten or twelve years. When I read in the
"E. B." that the Jewish population of the United States was 250,-
000 I wrote the editor, and explained to him that I was personally
acquainted with more Jews than that in my country, and that his
figures were without a doubt a misprint for 25,000,000. I also
added that I was personally acquainted with *that* many there; but
that was only to raise his confidence in me, for it was not true. His
answer miscarried, and I never got it; but I went around talking
about the matter, and people told me they had reason to suspect
that for business reasons many Jews whose dealings were mainly
with the Christians did not report themselves as Jews in the census.
It looked plausible; it looks plausible yet. Look at the city of New
York; and look at Boston, and Philadelphia, and New Orleans, and
Chicago, and Cincinnati, and San Francisco—how your race
swarms in those places!—and everywhere else in America, down to
the least little village. Read the signs on the marts of commerce
and on the shops: Goldstein (gold stone), Edelstein (precious
stone), Blumenthal (flower-vale), Rosenthal (rose-vale), Veil-
chenduft (violet odor), Sinvogel (song-bird), Rosenzweig (rose
branch), and all the amazing list of beautiful and enviable names
which Prussia and Austria glorified you with so long ago. It is
another instance of Europe's coarse and cruel persecution of your
race; not that it was coarse and cruel to outfit it with pretty and
poetical names like those, but it was coarse and cruel to make it
*pay* for them or else take such hideous and often indecent names
that today their owners never use them; or, if they do, only on
official papers. And it was the many, not the few, who got the
odious names, they being too poor to bribe the officials to grant
them better ones.

Now why was the race renamed? I have been told that in Prussia
it was given to using fictitious names, and often changing them, so
as to beat the tax-gatherers, escape military service, and so on; and
that finally the idea was hit upon of furnishing all the inmates of a
house with *one and the same surname,* and then holding the house

responsible right along for those inmates, and accountable for any disappearances that might occur; it made the Jews keep track of *each other,* for self-interest's sake, and saved the Government the trouble.*

If that explanation of how the Jews of Prussia came to be re-, named is correct, if it is true that they fictitiously registered themselves to gain certain advantages, it may possibly be true that in America they refrain from registering themselves as Jews to fend off the damaging prejudices of the Christian customer. I have no way of knowing whether this notion is well founded or not. There may be other and better ways of explaining why only that poor little 250,000 of our Jews got into the Encyclopædia. I may, of course, be mistaken, but I am strongly of the opinion that we have an immense Jewish population in America.

*Point No. 3.*—"Can Jews do anything to improve the situation?"

I think so. If I may make a suggestion without seeming to be trying to teach my grandmother how to suck eggs, I will offer it. In our days we have learned the value of combination. We apply it everywhere—in railway systems, in trusts, in trade unions, in Salvation Armies, in minor politics, in major politics, in European Concerts. Whatever our strength may be, big or little, we *organize* it. We have found out that that is the only way to get the most out of it that is in it. We know the weakness of individual sticks, and the strength of the concentrated faggot. Suppose you try a scheme like this, for instance. In England and America put every Jew on the census book *as* a Jew (in case you have not been doing that). Get up volunteer regiments composed of Jews solely, and when the drum beats, fall in and go to the front, so as to remove the reproach that you have few Massénas among you, and that you feed on a country but don't like to fight for it. Next, in politics,

---

* In Austria the renaming was merely done because the Jews in some newly-acquired regions had no surnames, but were mostly named Abraham and Moses, and therefore the tax-gatherer could not tell t'other from which, and was likely to lose his reason over the matter. The renaming was put into the hands of the War Department, and a charming mess the graceless young lieutenants made of it. To them a Jew was of no sort of consequence, and they labelled the race in a way to make the angels weep. As an example, take these two: *Abraham Bellyache* and *Schmul Godbedamned.*—Culled from *Namens Studien,* by Karl Emil Franzos. (M.T.)

organize your strength, band together, and deliver the casting vote where you can, and, where you can't, compel as good terms as possible. You huddle to yourselves already in all countries, but you huddle to no sufficient purpose, politically speaking. You do not seem to be organized, except for your charities. There you are omnipotent; there you compel your due of recognition—you do not have to beg for it. It shows what you can do when you band together for a definite purpose.

And then from America and England you can encourage your race in Austria, France, and Germany, and materially help it. It was a pathetic tale that was told by a poor Jew in Galicia a fortnight ago during the riots, after he had been raided by the Christian peasantry and despoiled of everything he had. He said his vote was of no value to him, and he wished he could be excused from casting it, for, indeed, casting it was a sure *damage* to him, since, no matter which party he voted for, the other party would come straight and take its revenge out of him. Nine per cent of the population of the empire, these Jews, and apparently they cannot put a plank into any candidate's platform! If you will send our Irish lads over here I think they will organize your race and change the aspect of the Reichsrath.

You seem to think that the Jews take no hand in politics here, that they are "absolutely non-participants." I am assured by men competent to speak that this is a very large error, that the Jews are exceedingly active in politics all over the empire, but that they scatter their work and their votes among the numerous parties, and thus lose the advantages to be had by concentration. I think that in America they scatter too, but you know more about that than I do.

Speaking of concentration, Dr. Herzl has a clear insight into the value of that. Have you heard of his plan? He wishes to gather the Jews of the world together in Palestine, with a government of their own—under the suzerainty of the Sultan, I suppose. At the Convention of Berne, last year, there were delegates from everywhere, and the proposal was received with decided favor. I am not the Sultan, and I am not objecting; but if that concentration of the cunningest brains in the world were going to be made on a free country (bar Scotland), I think it would be politic to stop it. It will not be well to let that race find out its strength. If the horses knew theirs, we should not ride any more.

*Point No.* 5.—"Will the persecution of the Jews ever come to an end?"

On the score of religion, I think it has already come to an end. On the score of race prejudice and trade, I have the idea that it will continue. That is, here and there in spots about the world, where a barbarous ignorance and a sort of mere animal civilization prevail; but I do not think that elsewhere the Jew need now stand in any fear of being robbed and raided. Among the high civilizations he seems to be very comfortably situated indeed, and to have more than his proportionate share of the prosperities going. It has that look in Vienna. I suppose the race prejudice cannot be removed; but he can stand that; it is no particular matter. By his make and ways he is substantially a foreigner wherever he may be, and even the angels dislike a foreigner. I am using this word foreigner in the German sense—*stranger*. Nearly all of us have an antipathy to a stranger, even of our own nationality. We pile gripsacks in a vacant seat to keep him from getting it; and a dog goes further, and does as a savage would—challenges him on the spot. The German dictionary seems to make no distinction between a stranger and a foreigner; in its view a stranger *is* a foreigner—a sound position, I think. You will always be by ways and habits and predilections substantially strangers—foreigners—wherever you are, and that will probably keep the race prejudice against you alive.

But you were the favorites of Heaven originally, and your manifold and unfair prosperities convince me that you have crowded back into that snug place again. Here is an incident that is significant. Last week in Vienna a hailstorm struck the prodigious Central Cemetery and made wasteful destruction there. In the Christian part of it, according to the official figures, 621 window panes were broken; more than 900 singing birds were killed; five great trees and many small ones were torn to shreds and the shreds scattered far and wide by the wind; the ornamental plants and other decorations of the graves were ruined, and more than a hundred tomb-lanterns shattered; and it took the cemetery's whole force of 300 laborers more than three days to clear away the storm's wreckage. In the report occurs this remark—and in its italics you can hear it grit its Christian teeth: ". . . lediglich die *israelitische* Abtheilung des Friedhofes vom Hagelwetter *gänzlich verschant* worden war." Not a hailstone hit the Jewish reservation! Such nepotism makes me tired.

*Point No. 6.*—"What has become of the Golden Rule?"

It exists, it continues to sparkle, and is well taken care of. It is Exhibit A in the Church's assets, and we pull it out every Sunday and give it an airing. But you are not permitted to try to smuggle it into this discussion, where it is irrelevant and would not feel at home. It is strictly religious furniture, like an acolyte, or a contribution plate, or any of those things. It has never been intruded into business; and Jewish persecution is not a religious passion, it is a business passion.

*To conclude.*—If the statistics are right, the Jews constitute but *one per cent* of the human race. It suggests a nebulous dim puff of star dust lost in the blaze of the Milky Way. Properly the Jew ought hardly to be heard of; but he is heard of, has always been heard of. He is as prominent on the planet as any other people, and his commercial importance is extravagantly out of proportion to the smallness of his bulk. His contributions to the world's list of great names in literature, science, art, music, finance, medicine, and abstruse learning are also away out of proportion to the weakness of his numbers. He has made a marvelous fight in this world, in all the ages; and has done it with his hands tied behind him. He could be vain of himself, and be excused for it. The Egyptian, the Babylonian, and the Persian rose, filled the planet with sound and splendor, then faded to dream-stuff and passed away; the Greek and the Roman followed, and made a vast noise, and they are gone; other peoples have sprung up and held their torch high for a time, but it burned out, and they sit in twilight now, or have vanished. The Jew saw them all, beat them all, and is now what he always was, exhibiting no decadence, no infirmities of age, no weakening of his parts, no slowing of his energies, no dulling of his alert and aggressive mind. All things are mortal but the Jew; all other forces pass, but he remains. What is the secret of his immortality?

### Postscript—THE JEW AS SOLDIER

When I published the above article in *Harper's Monthly,* I was ignorant—like the rest of the Christian world—of the fact that the Jew had a record as a soldier. I have since seen the official statistics, and I find that he furnished soldiers and high officers to the Revolution, the War of 1812, and the Mexican War. In the Civil War he was represented in the armies and navies of both the North and the South by 10 per cent of his numerical strength—the same percentage that was furnished by the Christian population of the two sections. This large fact means more than it seems to mean; for it means that the Jew's patriotism was not merely level with the Christian's, but overpassed it. When the Christian volunteer arrived in camp he got a welcome and applause, but as a rule the Jew got a snub. His company was not desired, and he was made to feel it. That he nevertheless conquered his wounded pride and sacrificed both that and his blood for his flag raises the average and quality of his patriotism above the Christian's. His record for capacity, for fidelity, and for gallant soldiership in the field is as good as any one's. This is true of the Jewish private soldiers and of the Jewish generals alike. Major General O. O. Howard speaks of one of his Jewish staff officers as being "of the bravest and best;" of another—killed at Chancellorsville—as being "a true friend and a brave officer;" he highly praises two of his Jewish brigadier generals; finally, he uses these strong words: "Intrinsically there are no more patriotic men to be found in the country than those who claim to be of Hebrew descent, and who served with me in parallel commands or more directly under my instructions."

Fourteen Jewish Confederate and Union families contributed, between them, fifty-one soldiers to the war. Among these, a father and three sons; and another, a father and four sons.

In the above article I was neither able to endorse nor repel the common reproach that the Jew is willing to feed upon a country but not to fight for it, because I did not know whether it was true or false. I supposed it to be true, but it is not allowable to endorse

wandering maxims upon supposition—except when one is trying
to make out a case. That slur upon the Jew cannot hold up its
head in presence of the figures of the War Department. It has
done its work, and done it long and faithfully, and with high approval: it ought to be pensioned off now, and retired from active
service.


## Stormfield and Goldstein


He [the Jew] has a reputation for various small forms of cheating. . . .
—MARK TWAIN, "Concerning the Jews"

According to Mark Twain in his Autobiography, he made the first
draft of *Captain Stormfield's Visit to Heaven* in 1868; he wrote and
rewrote it the rest of his life. He intended it for posthumous publication, but changed his mind (as he did with many sections of the
Autobiography) and published. "Extract from Captain Stormfield's
Visit to Heaven" appeared in *Harper's Magazine* in December, 1907,
and January, 1908; and it was published as a book in 1909. In 1952,
one of Mark Twain's literary executors, Dixon Wecter, added to it one
of the numerous fragments found in his papers and published the
whole as *Captain Stormfield's Visit to Heaven*. This excerpt is from
that version.

Here Captain Stormfield has been dead eight minutes and is
traveling at the speed of light, bound—he believes—for hell.


I WAS in the dark again, now. In the dark; but I myself wasn't
dark. My body gave out a soft and ghostly glow and I felt like a
lightning bug. I couldn't make out the why of this, but I could read
my watch by it, and that was more to the point.

Presently I noticed a glow like my own a little way off, and was
glad, and made a trumpet of my hands and hailed it—

"Shipmate ahoy!"

"Same to you!"

"Where from?"

"Chatham Street."

"Whither bound?"

"I vish I knew—aind it?"

"I reckon you're going my way. Name?"

"Solomon Goldstein. Yours?"

"Captain Ben Stormfield, late of Fairhaven and Frisco. Come alongside, friend."

He did it. It was a great improvement, having company. I was born sociable, and never could stand solitude. I was trained to a prejudice against Jews—Christians always are, you know—but such of it as I had was in my head, there wasn't any in my heart. But if I had been full of it it would have disappeared then, I was so lonesome and so anxious for company. Dear me, when you are going to—to—where I was going—you are humble-mindeder than you used to be, and thankful for whatever you can get, never mind the quality of it.

We spun along together, and talked, and got acquainted and had a good time. I thought it would be a kindness to Solomon to dissipate his doubts, so that he would have a quiet mind. I could never be comfortable in a state of doubt myself. So I reasoned the thing out, and showed him that his being pointed the same as me was proof of where he was bound for. It cost him a good deal of distress, but in the end he was reconciled and said it was probably best the way it was, he wouldn't be suitable company for angels and they would turn him down if he tried to work in; he had been treated like that in New York, and he judged that the ways of high society were about the same everywhere. He wanted me not to desert him when we got to where we were going, but stay by him, for he would be a stranger and friendless. Poor fellow, I was touched; and promised—"to all eternity."

Then we were quiet a long time, and I let him alone, and let him think. It would do him good. Now and then he sighed, and by and by I found he was crying. You know, I was mad with him in a minute; and says to myself, "Just like a Jew! he has promised some hayseed or other a coat for four dollars, and now he has made up his mind that if he was back he could work off a worse one on him for five. They haven't any heart—that race—nor any principles."

He sobbed along to himself, and I got colder and colder and harder and harder towards him. At last I broke out and said—

"Cheese it! Damn the coat! Drop it out of your mind."

"Goat?"

"Yes. Find something else to cry about."

"Why, I wasn't crying apoud a goat."

"What then?"

"Oh, captain, I loss my little taughter, and now I never, never see her again any more. It break my heart!"

By God, it went through me like a knife! I wouldn't feel so mean again, and so grieved, not for a fleet of ships. And I spoke out and said what I felt; and went on damning myself for a hound till he was so distressed I had to stop; but I wasn't half through. He begged me not to talk so, and said I oughtn't to make so much of what I had done; he said it was only a mistake, and a mistake wasn't a crime.

There now—wasn't it magnanimous? I ask you—wasn't it? I think so. To my mind there was the stuff in him for a Christian; and I came out flat-footed and told him so. And if it hadn't been so late I would have reformed him and made him one, or died in the act.

# ON THE BELGIAN CONGO

## King Leopold's Soliloquy

> Listen to the yell of Leopold's ghost
> Burning in Hell for his hand-maimed host.
> Hear how the demons chuckle and yell,
> Cutting his hands off, down in Hell.
> —VACHEL LINDSAY, *The Congo*

The reports said that a large crowd of Congolese who witnessed the massacre in Kindu [of eleven Italian airmen] dismembered the bodies and tossed the pieces in the Lualaba River. The Congolese were said to have mistaken the Italians for Belgians.—from *The New York Times,* November 19, 1961

The Belgian Congo was the closest thing to Nazidom the nineteenth century produced. Perhaps it was the closest thing any previous century has produced; the Mark Twain who claimed that Leopold's hell had no competition in previous history, was a connoisseur of historical horror stories.

On solid grounds, Mark Twain and the Congo Reform Association claimed that there were ten million murders in the Belgian Congo between 1885, when Leopold took over, and 1905; then Clemens pushed the thing by claiming fifteen million—including the unborn children of the exterminated blacks. The accepted figure for Jewish extermination is six million, but no claim is made for future generations. And if exterminated Gypsies, resistance personnel, and prisoners of war are included, the statistical competition reaches the point to which Mark Twain pushes statistics in "King Leopold's Soliloquy," with that meticulous bookkeeping of skulls, graveyards, and miles of corpses—which, of course, is one way to try to give reality to this kind of situation.

Apart from the grisly statistics, however, Nazidom and the Belgian Congo are not comparable. One of many important differences: the Congo was the property of one man and the operation was conducted solely for profit.

The Congo Reform Association printed "King Leopold's Soliloquy" as a pamphlet, priced at twenty-five cents but widely distributed for nothing. The original paperbacked booklet still has the pasted-in announcement, "Mr. Clemens declines to accept any pecuniary return for this . . . as it is his wish that all proceeds . . . shall be used . . . for relief of the people in the Congo States."

This condensation is about a fourth of the original, which is a compilation of excerpts from reports by missionaries and other persons, loosely tied together by Mark Twain's gallant attempts at humor. It is illustrated by pages of photographs of mutilated blacks. There are also pages of "supplementary material" which have a fascination of their own. From a debate in the Belgian Parliament in 1903:

All the facts we brought forward in this chamber were denied at first most energetically; but later, little by little, they were proved by documents and by official texts.

From *Bilans Congolias,* by Alfred Poskine, in support of Leopold:

Let us repeat after so many others what has become a platitude, the success of the African work is the work of a sole directing will, without being hampered by the hesitation of timorous politicians, carried out under his sole responsibility—intelligent, thoughtful, conscious of the perils and the advantages, discounting with an admirable prescience the great results of a near future.

Finally, there is a precursory hint of the Nuremberg trials—in "Ought King Leopold to Be Hanged?," by W. T. Stead, which also appeared in the enormously influential English *Review of Reviews.* This is Mr. Stead, interviewing the Congo missionary, the Rev. J. H. Harris:

"Unfortunately," I said, "at present the Hague Tribunal is not . . . qualified to place offenders, crowned or otherwise, in the dock. But don't you think that in the evolution of society the constitution of such a criminal court is a necessity?"

"It would be a great convenience at present," said Mr. Harris, "nor would you need one atom of evidence beyond the report of the commission. . . ."

That commission (there were many investigation commissions) was in itself a curiosity. Members had been appointed by Leopold, but they had been "so overwhelmed by the multitudinous horrors" before them, that they corroborated the missionaries. According to Stead, when the Congo's most responsible official (whose name is withheld) read the report, he cut his throat. That was in 1905. But no importance was attached to the suicide in Europe; the report itself was held back eight months and then, says Clemens, "skillfully edited." It was not until three years later that the Belgian Parliament relieved the King of his African responsibilities. Then the atrocities stopped; forced labor continued.

However, for many years, the numerous movements to reform the Congo seemed to accomplish nothing. Mark Twain contributed to them all until, according to Paine, he announced after "Soliloquy":

I have said all I can say on that terrible subject. I am heart and soul in any movement that will rescue the Congo and hang Leopold, but I cannot write any more.

Perhaps it was just as well. The great voice was sometimes almost a croak on this subject. After all, the Mark Twain who compiled these atrocities was the same who paced the floor for hours cursing over only one of the atrocities in the Philippines; the same to whom Paine suggested that he stop reading the papers, since they upset him so. The conversation, according to Paine in his biography:

"No difference," he said, "I read books printed two hundred years ago, and they hurt just the same."
"Those people are all dead and gone," I objected.
"They hurt just the same," he maintained.

This abridgement is from the second, revised edition of the "Soliloquy," published in 1906. Many words have been left out, but none has been changed.


(*Throws down pamphlets which he has been reading. Excitedly combs his flowing spread of whiskers with his fingers; pounds the table with his fists; lets off brisk volleys of unsanctified language at brief intervals, repentantly drooping his head, between volleys, and kissing the Louis XI crucifix hanging from his neck, accompanying the kisses with mumbled apologies; presently rises, flushed and perspiring, and walks the floor, gesticulating.*)

—— ——!! —— ——!! IF I HAD them by the throat! (*Hastily kisses the crucifix, and mumbles.*) In these twenty years I have spent millions to keep the press of the two hemispheres quiet. . . . I have spent other millions on religion and art, and

what do I get for it? . . . In print I get nothing but slanders—
and slanders again. . . .

Miscreants—they are telling *everything!* Oh, everything: how I
went pilgriming among the Powers in tears, with my mouth full of
Bible and my pelt oozing piety at every pore, and implored them
to place the vast and rich and populous Congo Free State in trust
in my hands as their agent, so that I might root out slavery and
stop the slave raids, and lift up those twenty-five millions of gentle
and harmless blacks out of darkness into light, the light of our
blessed Redeemer; . . . how America and thirteen great European states wept in sympathy with me, and were persuaded; how
their representatives met in convention in Berlin and made me
head foreman and superintendent of the Congo State, and drafted
out my powers and limitations, carefully guarding the persons and
liberties and properties of the natives against hurt and harm. . . .
They have told how I planned and prepared my establishment and
selected my horde of officials—"pals" and "pimps" of mine, "un-
speakable Belgians" every one—and hoisted my flag, and "took
in" a President of the United States, and got him to be the first
to recognize it and salute it. . . .

These meddlesome American missionaries! these frank British
consuls! these blabbing Belgian-born traitor officials!—those tire-
some parrots are always talking. . . . They have told how for
twenty years I have ruled the Congo State not as a trustee of the
Powers, . . . but as a sovereign—sovereign over a fruitful domain
four times as large as the German Empire . . . claiming and holding its millions of people as my private property, my serfs, my
slaves. . . .

These pests! . . . May they roast a million eons in—(*Catches
his breath and effusively kisses the crucifix; sorrowfully murmurs,
"I shall get myself damned yet, with these indiscretions of
speech."*)

Yes, they go on telling everything, these chatterers! They tell
how I levy incredibly burdensome taxes upon the natives—taxes
which are a pure theft; taxes which they must satisfy by gathering
rubber under hard and constantly harder conditions, and by raising
and furnishing food supplies gratis—and it all comes out that,
when they fall short of their tasks through hunger, sickness, despair,

and ceaseless and exhausting labor without rest, and forsake their homes and flee to the woods to escape punishment, my black soldiers, drawn from unfriendly tribes, and instigated and directed by my Belgians, hunt them down and butcher them and burn their villages—reserving some of the girls. . . .

(*Contemplating, with an unfriendly eye, a stately pile of pamphlets.*) . . . And nothing is too trivial for them to print. (*Takes up a pamphlet. Reads a passage from report of a "Journey made in July, August and September, 1903 by Rev. A. E. Scrivener, a British missionary."*)

. . . Soon we began talking, and without any encouragement on my part the natives began the tales I had become so accustomed to. They were living in peace and quietness when the white men came in from the lake with all sorts of requests to do this and that, and they thought it meant slavery. So they attempted to keep the white men out of their country but without avail. The rifles were too much for them. So they submitted and made up their minds to do the best they could under the altered circumstances. First came the command to build houses for the soldiers, and this was done without a murmur. Then they had to feed the soldiers and all the men and women—hangers on —who accompanied them. Then they were told to bring in rubber. This was quite a new thing for them to do. There was rubber in the forest several days away from their home, but that it was worth anything was news to them. A small reward was offered and a rush was made for the rubber. "What strange white men, to give us cloth and beads for the sap of a wild vine." They rejoiced in what they thought their good fortune. But soon the reward was reduced until at last they were told to bring in the rubber for nothing. To this they tried to demur; but to their great surprise several were shot by the soldiers, and the rest were told, with many curses and blows, to go at once or more would be killed. Terrified, they began to prepare their food for the fortnight's absence from the village which the collection of rubber entailed. The soldiers discovered them sitting about. "What, not gone yet?" Bang! bang! bang! and down fell one and another, dead, in the midst of wives and companions. There is a terrible wail and an attempt made to prepare the dead for burial, but this is not allowed. All must go at once to the forest. Without food? Yes, without food. And off the poor wretches had to go without even their tinder boxes to make fires. Many died in the forests of hunger and exposure, and still more from the rifles of the ferocious soldiers in charge of the post. In spite of all their efforts the amount fell off and more and more were killed. . . . Lying about on the grass, within a few yards of the house I was occupying, were numbers of human skulls, bones, in some cases complete skeletons. I counted thirty-six skulls, and saw many sets of bones from which skulls were missing. I called one of the men and asked the meaning of it. "When the rubber palaver began," said he, "the soldiers shot so many we grew tired of burying, and very often we were not allowed to bury; and so just dragged the bodies out into the grass and left them. There are hundreds all around if you would like to see them." But I had seen more than enough, and was sickened by the stories that came from men and women alike of the awful time they had passed through. The Bulgarian atrocities might be considered as mildness itself when compared with what was done here. How the people submitted I don't know, and even now I wonder as I think of their patience. That some of them managed to run away is some cause for thankfulness. I stayed there two days and the one thing that impressed itself upon me was the collection of rubber. I saw long files of men come in, as at Bongo, with their little baskets under their arms; saw them paid their milk tin full of salt, and the two yards of calico flung to the headmen; saw their trembling timidity, and in fact a great deal that all went to prove the state of terrorism that exists and the virtual slavery in which the people are held.

That is their way; they spy and spy, and run into print with every foolish trifle. And that British consul, Mr. Casement,[1] is just like them. He gets hold of a *diary which had been kept by one of my government officers,* and, although it is a private diary and intended for no eye but its owner's, Mr. Casement is so lacking in delicacy and refinement as to print passages from it. (*Reads a passage from the diary.*)

Each time the corporal goes out to get rubber, cartridges are given him. He must bring back all not used, and for every one used he must bring back a right hand. M. P. told me that sometimes they shot a cartridge at an animal in hunting; they then cut off a hand from a living man. As to the extent to which this is carried on, he informed me that in six months the State on the Mambogo River had used 6,000 cartridges, which means that 6,000 people are killed or mutilated. It means more than 6,000, for the people have told me repeatedly that the soldiers killed the children with the butt of their guns.

When the subtle consul thinks silence will be more effective than words, he employs it. Here he leaves it to be recognized that a thousand killings and mutilations a month is a large output for so small a region as the Mambogo River concession, silently indicating the dimensions of it by accompanying his report with a map of the prodigious Congo State, in which there is not room for so small an object as that river. . . . (*Reads*.)

Two hundred and forty persons, *men, women and children*, compelled to supply government with *one ton* of carefully prepared foodstuffs *per week*, receiving in remuneration, all told, the princely sum of 15*s*. 10*d!*

Very well, it was liberal. It was not much short of a penny a week for each nigger. It suits this consul to belittle it, yet he knows very well that I could have had both the food and the labor for nothing. I can prove it by a thousand instances. . . . Mm—here is some more of the consul's delicacy! He reports a conversation he had with some natives:

Q. "How do you know it was the *white* men themselves who ordered these cruel things to be done to you? These things must have been done without the white man's knowledge by the black soldiers."
A. "The white men told their soldiers: 'You only kill *women;* you cannot kill men. You must prove that you kill men.' So then the soldiers when they killed us" (here he stopped and hesitated and then pointing to . . . he said:) "then they . . . and took them to the white men, who said: 'It is true, you have killed *men.*'"
Q. "You say this is true? Were many of you so treated after being shot?"
All (*shouting out*.): "*Nkoto! Nkoto!*" ("Very many! Very many!")
There was no doubt that these people were not inventing. Their vehemence, their flashing eyes, their excitement, were not simulated."

Of course the critic had to divulge that; he has no self-respect.

(*Puts down the report, takes up a pamphlet*. . . .) Rev. W. H. Sheppard. Talks with a black raider of mine after a raid; cozens him into giving away some particulars. The raider remarks:

I demanded 30 slaves from this side of the stream and 30 from the other side; 2 points of ivory, 2,500 balls of rubber, 13 goats, 10 fowls and 6 dogs, some corn chumy, etc.
"How did the fight come up?" I asked.
"I sent for all their chiefs, sub-chiefs, men and women to come on a certain day, saying that I was going to finish all the palaver. When they entered these small gates (the walls being made of fences brought from other villages, the high native ones) I demanded all my pay or I would kill them; so they refused to pay me, and I ordered the fence to be closed so they couldn't run away; then we killed them here inside the fence. The panels of the fence fell down and some escaped."

"How many did you kill?" I asked.

"We killed plenty, will you see some of them?"

That was just what I wanted.

He said: "I think we have killed between eighty and ninety, and those in the other villages I don't know, I did not go out but sent my people."

He and I walked out on the plain just near the camp. There were three dead bodies with the flesh carved off from the waist down.

"Why are they carved so, only leaving the bones?" I asked.

"My people ate them," he answered promptly. He then explained, "The men who have young children do not eat people, but all the rest ate them." On the left was a big man, shot in the back and without a head. (All these corpses were nude.)

"Where is the man's head?" I asked.

"Oh, they made a bowl of the forehead to rub up tobacco and diamba in."

We continued to walk and examine until late in the afternoon, and counted forty-one bodies. The rest had been eaten up by the people.

On returning to the camp, we crossed a young woman, shot in the back of the head, one hand was cut away. I asked why, and Mulunba N'Cusa explained that they always cut off the right hand to give to the state on their return.

"Can you not show me some of the hands?" I asked.

So he conducted us to a framework of sticks, under which was burning a slow fire, and there they were, the right hands—I counted them, eighty-one in all.

*Another* detail, as we see!—cannibalism. They report cases of it with a most offensive frequency. My traducers do not forget to remark that, inasmuch as I am absolute and with a word can prevent in the Congo anything I choose to prevent, then whatsoever is done there . . . is my act, my *personal* act; . . . that the hand of my agent is as truly *my* hand as if it were attached to my own arm; and so they picture me in my robes of state, with my crown on my head, munching human flesh, saying grace, mumbling thanks to Him from whom all good things come. Dear, dear, when the soft-hearts get hold of a thing like that missionary's contribution they quite lose their tranquility over it. They speak out profanely and reproach Heaven for allowing such a fiend to live. Meaning me. They think it irregular. They go shuddering around, brooding over the reduction of that Congo population from 25,000,000 to 15,000,000 in the twenty years of my administration; then they burst out and call me "the King with Ten Million Murders on his

Soul." They call me a "record." The most of them do not stop with charging merely the 10,000,000 against me. No, they reflect that but for me the population, by natural increase, would now be 30,000,000, so they charge another 5,00,000 against me and make my total death-harvest 15,000,000. They remark that . . . twice in a generation, in India, the Great Famine destroys 2,000,-000 out of a population of 320,000,000, and the whole world holds up its hands in pity and horror; then they fall to wondering where the world would find room for its emotions if I had a chance to trade places with the Great Famine for twenty years! The idea fires their fancy, and they go on and imagine the Famine coming in state at the end of the twenty years and prostrating itself before me, saying: "Teach me, Lord, I perceive that I am but an apprentice.". . . By this time their diseased minds are under full steam, and they get down their books and expand their labors, with me for text. They hunt through all biography for my match, working Attila, Torquemada, Ghengis Khan, Ivan the Terrible, and the rest of that crowd for all they are worth, and evilly exulting when they cannot find it. Then they examine the historical earthquakes and cyclones and blizzards and cataclysms and volcanic eruptions: verdict, none of them "in it" with me. At last they do really hit it (as they think), and they close their labors with conceding—reluctantly—that I have *one* match in history, but only one—the *Flood*. This is intemperate.

. . . . . . . . . . . . . . . . . . . . . . .

Another madman wants to construct a memorial for the perpetuation of my name, out of my 15,000,000 skulls and skeletons, and is full of vindictive enthusiasm over his strange project. He has it all ciphered out and drawn to scale. Out of the skulls he will build a combined monument and mausoleum to me which shall exactly duplicate the Great Pyramid of Cheops, whose base covers thirteen acres, and whose apex is 451 feet above ground. He desires to stuff me and stand me up in the sky on that apex, robed and crowned, with my "pirate flag" in one hand and a butcher-knife and pendant handcuffs in the other. He will build the pyramid in the center of a depopulated tract, a brooding solitude covered with weeds and the mouldering ruins of burned villages, where the spirits of the starved and murdered dead will voice their laments forever

in the whispers of the wandering winds. Radiating from the pyramid, like the spokes of a wheel, there are to be forty grand avenues
of approach, each thirty-five miles long, and each fenced on both
side by skulless skeletons standing a yard and a half apart and
festooned together in line by short chains stretching from wrist to
wrist and attached to tried and true old handcuffs stamped with
my private trade-mark, a crucifix and butcher-knife crossed, with
motto, "By this sign we prosper"; each osseous fence to consist
of 200,000 skeletons on a side, which is 400,000 to each avenue.
It is remarked with satisfaction that it aggregates three or four
thousand miles (single-ranked) of skeletons—15,000,000 all told—
and would stretch across America from New York to San
Francisco. It is remarked further, in the hopeful tone of a railroad company forecasting showy extensions of its mileage, that
my output is 500,000 corpses a year when my plant is running
full time, and that therefore if I am spared ten years longer there
will be fresh skulls enough to add 175 feet to the pyramid making
it by a long way the loftiest architectural construction on the earth,
and fresh skeletons enough to continue the transcontinental file (on
piles) a thousand miles into the Pacific. The cost of gathering the
materials from my "widely scattered and innumerable private
graveyards," and transporting them, and building the monument
and the radiating grand avenues, is duly ciphered out, running into
an aggregate of millions of guineas, and then, why then (——
————!! —— ————!!) this idiot asks me to *furnish the money!*
(*Sudden and effusive application of the crucifix.*) He reminds me
that my yearly income from the Congo is millions of guineas, and
that *"only"* 5,000,000 would be required for his enterprise. Every
day wild attempts are made upon my purse; . . .

(*Harassed and muttering, walks the floor a while, then takes to
the consul's chapter headings again. Reads.*)

. . . . . . . . . . . . . . . . . . . . . . . . . . .

*The native has been converted into a being without ambition because
without hope.*

They put a knife through a child's stomach.

They cut off the hands and brought them to C. D. (white officer)
and spread them out in a row for him to see. They left them lying

there, because the white man had seen them, so they did not need to take them to P.

Captured children left in the bush to die, by the soldiers.

Friends came to ransom a captured girl; but sentry refused, saying the white man wanted her because she was young.

Extract from a native girl's testimony. "On our way the soldiers saw a little child, and when they went to kill it the child laughed, so the soldier took the butt of his gun and struck the child with it and then cut off its head. One day they killed my half-sister and cut off her head, hands and feet, because she had bangles on. Then they caught another sister, and sold her to the W. W. people, and now she is a slave there."

The child laughed! (*A long pause. . . . Reads.*)

Mutilated children.

Government encouragement of inter-tribal slave-traffic. The monstrous fines levied upon villages tardy in their supplies of foodstuffs compel the natives to sell their fellows—and children—to other tribes in order to meet the fine.

A father and mother forced to sell their little boy.

Widow forced to sell her little girl.

(*Irritated.*) Hang the monotonous grumbler, what would he have me do! Let a widow off merely because she is a widow? . . .

The crucifying of sixty women!

How stupid, how tactless! Christendom's goose flesh will rise with horror at the news. "Profanation of the sacred emblem!" That is what Christendom will shout. . . . It can hear me charged with half a million murders a year for twenty years and keep its composure, but to profane the Symbol is quite another matter. It will regard this as serious. It will wake up and want to look into my record. Buzz? Indeed it will; I seem to hear the distant hum already. . . . It was wrong to crucify the women, clearly wrong, manifestly wrong. I can see it now, myself, and am sorry it happened, sincerely sorry. I believe it would have answered just as well to skin them. . . . (*With a sigh.*) But none of us thought of that; one cannot think of everything; and after all it is but human to err. . . .

(*Rests himself with some more chapter headings. Reads.*)

More mutilation of children. (Hands cut off.)

Testimony of American Missionaries.

Evidence of British Missionaries.

It is all the same old thing—tedious repetitions and duplications of shopworn episodes . . . till one gets drowsy over it. Mr. Morel intrudes at this point. . . .

It is one heartrending story of human misery from beginning to end, and *it is all recent.*

Meaning 1904 and 1905. I do not see how a person can act so. . . . This Morel is a reformer; a Congo reformer. That sizes *him* up. He publishes a sheet in Liverpool called *The West African Mail,* which is supported by the voluntary contributions of the sap-headed and the soft-hearted; and every week it steams and reeks and festers with up-to-date "Congo artrocities" of the sort detailed in this pile of pamphlets here. I will suppress it. I suppressed a Congo atrocity book there, after it was actually in print; it should not be difficult for me to suppress a newspaper.

(*Studies some photographs of mutilated Negroes—throws them down. Sighs.*) The kodak has been a sore calamity to us. . . . In the early years we had no trouble in getting the press to "expose" the tales of the mutilations as slanders, lies, inventions of busybody American missionaries and exasperated foreigners who had found the "open door" of the Berlin-Congo charter closed against them when they innocently went out there to trade; and by the press's help we got the Christian nations everywhere to turn an irritated and unbelieving ear to those tales and say hard things about the tellers of them. Yes, all things went harmoniously and pleasantly in those good days. . . . Then all of a sudden came the crash! That is to say, the incorruptible *kodak*—and all the harmony went to hell! The only witness I have encountered in my long experience that I couldn't bribe. Every Yankee missionary and every inter-rupted trader sent home and got one; and now—oh, well, the pictures get sneaked around everywhere. . . . Ten thousand pulpits and ten thousand presses are saying the good word for me all the time and placidly and convincingly denying the mutilations.

Then that trivial little kodak, that a child can carry in its pocket, gets up, uttering never a word, and knocks them dumb!

. . . What is this fragment? (*Reads.*)

But enough of trying to tally off his crimes! His list is interminable, we should never get to the end of it. His awful shadow lies across his Congo Free State. . . . It is a land of graves; it is *The* Land of Graves; it is the Congo Free Graveyard. It is a majestic thought: that is, this ghastliest episode in all human history is the work of *one man alone;* one solitary man; just a single individual—Leopold, King of the Belgians. . . . He is *sole* master there; he is absolute. He could have prevented the crimes by his mere command; he could stop them today with a word. He withholds the word. For his pocket's sake.

. . . Lust of conquest is royal; kings have always exercised that stately vice; . . . but *lust of money—lust of shillings—lust of nickels—lust of dirty coin,* not for the nation's enrichment but for *the king's alone*—this is new. . . . we shrink from hearing the particulars of how it happened. *We shudder and turn away* when we come upon them in print.

Why, certainly—*that* is my protection. And you will continue to do it. I know the human race.

# ON RUSSIA

## The Czar's Soliloquy

There is a phrase which has grown so common in the world's mouth that it has come to seem to have sense and meaning . . . that is the phrase which refers to this or that or the other nation as possibly being "capable of self-government"; and the implied sense of it is, that there has been a nation somewhere, some time or other, which . . . wasn't as able to govern itself as some self-appointed specialists were or would be to govern it.—MARK TWAIN, *A Connecticut Yankee in King Arthur's Court*

When "The Czar's Soliloquy" was published in March, 1905, not all Americans were quite so thirsty as Mark Twain for the blood of Russia's imperial family. But, on the whole, he expressed the popular sentiment, just as he had a few months before when the newspapers asked him for a Christmas wish:

It is my warm & world-embracing Christmas hope that all of us that deserve it may finally be gathered together in a heaven of rest & peace, & the others permitted to retire into the clutches of Satan, or the Emperor of Russia, according to preference—if they have a preference.

On the other hand, Mark Twain was a most untypical American in the summer of 1905, when President Theodore Roosevelt volunteered to act as mediator in the Russo-Japanese War and arranged for those two countries to sign a peace treaty in Portsmouth, New Hampshire. It now seems that if the treaty had not been signed there, it would have been signed somewhere else. But the President's gesture did win him a Nobel peace prize: it made him a hero to most of the country, and a villain to Mark Twain.

. . . when our windy and flamboyant President [he wrote in his Auto-biography in 1906] conceived the idea, a year ago, of advertising himself to the world as the new Angel of Peace, and set himself the task of bring-ing about the peace between Russia and Japan and had the misfortune to accomplish his misbegotten purpose, no one in all this nation except Doctor Seaman and myself uttered a public protest against this folly of follies.

This, in part, was his protest, published throughout the country by the Associated Press:

Russia was on the highroad to emancipation from an insane and intoler-able slavery. I was hoping that there would be no peace until Russian liberty was safe. I think this was a holy war, in the best and noblest sense of that abused term, and that no war was ever charged with a higher mis-sion.
I think there can be no doubt that that mission is now defeated and Russia's chain riveted; this time to stay. I think the Czar will now with-draw the small humanities that have been forced from him, and resume his medieval barbarisms with a relieved spirit and an immeasurable joy. . . .
I think nothing has been gained by the peace that is remotely comparable to what has been sacrificed by it. . . .[1]

The pessimist was right. The "small humanities"—including a guar-antee of civil liberties—granted by the imperial government as a result of the unpopular war with Japan and the riots and strikes which accompanied it, were withdrawn once peace was established.

"The Czar's Soliloquy" is, among other things, a plea for im-mediate and bloody action. But what Mark Twain had in mind was not revolution, but a program of assassination. This program various Russian groups—mainly Anarchists and Nihilists, and mainly young people—had been enthusiastically pursuing since before 1881, when they assassinated Alexander II, one of the most liberal of the Russian Czars. But Alexander III, who succeeded his father, was of the same stripe as Nicholas II, who came to the throne in 1894, and is the Czar soliloquizing below.

In 1890 Mark Twain wrote his views, by request of the editor, to *Free Russia*, an American publication which he regarded as too moderate. He rebuked the fault in his letter; there he also made plain his ideas for Russia:

Of course I know that the properest way to demolish the Russian throne would be by revolution. But it is not possible to get up a revolution there; so the only thing left to do, apparently, is to keep the throne vacant by dynamite until a day when candidates shall decline with thanks. Then organize the Republic.

The letter remained unmailed; fifteen years later he published these views in the "Soliloquy." The difference is mainly that, in the letter, they were expressed more directly and in more polished prose. For example, his justification of violence, in the letter:

My privilege to write these sanguinary sentences in soft security was bought for me by rivers of blood poured upon many fields, in many lands, but I possess not one single little paltry right or privilege that came to me as a result of petition, persuasion, agitation for reform, or any kindred method of procedure. When we consider that not even the most responsible English monarch ever yielded back a stolen public right until it was wrenched from him by bloody violence, is it rational to suppose that gentler methods can win privileges in Russia?

"The Czar's Soliloquy" is not in Mark Twain's greatest style, but it does contain one of the most basic of all his political ideas. His advice to Russian mothers, on the kind of patriotism to teach their children, is the same advice he had been giving for years to American mothers, fathers, and children. In *A Connecticut Yankee at King Arthur's Court* it appears this way:

You see, my kind of loyalty was loyalty to one's country, not to its institutions or its office-holders. The country is the real thing, the substantial thing, the eternal thing; it is the thing to watch over, and care for, and be loyal to; institutions are extraneous, they are its mere clothing, and clothing can wear out, become ragged, cease to be comfortable, cease to protect the body from winter, disease, and death. To be loyal to rags, to shout for rags, to worship rags, to die for rags—that is a loyalty of unreason, it is pure animal; it belongs to monarchy, was invented by monarchy; let monarchy keep it.

Imperial Russia has been dead over forty years. But one of Mark Twain's comments on the Russians—quoted by Paine in his biography —is as true as when he wrote it, and as useful a lesson for his own countrymen as when he first addressed it to them:

We teach the boys to atrophy their independence. We teach them to take their patriotism at second-hand; to shout with the largest crowd without examining into the right or wrong of the matter. . . . We teach them to regard as traitors, and hold in aversion and contempt, such as do not shout with the crowd, & so here in our democracy we are cheering a thing which of all things is most foreign to it and out of place—the delivery of our political conscience into somebody's else's keeping. This is patriotism on the Russian plan.

"*The Czar's Soliloquy*" is slightly abridged here; in the original Mark Twain's point about clothes is developed at greater length.

After the Czar's morning bath it is his habit to meditate an hour before dressing himself.—*London Times Correspondence.*

(*Viewing himself in the pierglass.*) NAKED, what am I? A lank, skinny, spider-legged libel on the image of God! Look at the wax-work head—the face, with the expression of a melon—the projecting ears—the knotted elbows—the dished breast—the knife-edged shins—and then the feet, all beads and joints and bone-sprays, an imitation X-ray photograph! . . . Is it this that a hundred and forty million Russians kiss the dust before and worship? Manifestly not! . . . Then what is it? . . . Privately, none knows better than I: it is my clothes. . . .

There is no power without clothes. . . . Strip its chiefs to the skin, and no state could be governed; naked officials could exercise no authority; they would look (and be) like everybody else—commonplace, inconsequential. A policeman in plain clothes is one man; in his uniform he is ten. Clothes and title are the most potent thing, the most formidable influence, in the earth. They move the human race to willing and spontaneous respect for the judge, the general, the admiral, the bishop, the ambassador, the frivolous earl, the idiot duke, the sultan, the king, the emperor. . . . The king of the great Fan tribe wears a bit of leopard-skin on his shoulder—it is sacred to royalty; the rest of him is perfectly naked. Without his bit of leopard-skin to awe and impress the people, he would not be able to keep his job.

(*After a silence.*) A curious invention, an unaccountable invention—the human race! The swarming Russian millions have for centuries meekly allowed our family to rob them, insult them, trample them under foot, while they lived and suffered and died with no purpose and no function but to make that family comfortable! These people are horses—just that—horses with clothes and a religion. A horse with the strength of a hundred men will let one man beat him, starve him, drive him; the Russian millions allow a mere handful of soldiers to hold them in slavery—and these very soldiers are their own sons and brothers!

A strange thing, when one considers it: to wit, the world applies to Czar and system the same moral axioms that have vogue and acceptance in civilized countries! Because, in civilized countries, it is wrong to remove oppressors otherwise than by process of law, it is held that the same rule applies in Russia, where there is no such thing as law—except for our family. Laws are merely restraints—they have no other function. In civilized countries they restrain all persons, and restrain them all alike, which is fair and righteous; but in Russia such laws as exist make an exception—our family. We do as we please; we have done as we pleased for centuries. Our common trade has been crime, our common pastime murder, our common beverage blood—the blood of the nation. Upon our heads lie millions of murders. Yet the pious moralist says it is a crime to assassinate us. We and our uncles are a family of cobras set over a hundred and forty million rabbits, whom we torture and murder and feed upon all our days; yet the moralist urges that to kill us is a crime, not a duty.

It is not for me to say it aloud, but to one on the inside—like me—this is naively funny; on its face, illogical. Our family is above all law; there is no law that can reach us, restrain us, protect the people from us. Therefore, we are outlaws. Outlaws are a proper mark for anyone's bullet. Ah! what could our family do without the moralist? He has always been our stay, our support, our friend; today is our *only* friend. Whenever there has been dark talk of assassination, he has come forward and saved us with his impressive maxim, "Forbear: nothing politically valuable was ever yet achieved by violence." He probably believes it. It is because he has by him no child's book of world history to teach him that his maxim lacks the backing of statistics. All thrones have been established by violence; no regal tyranny has ever been overthrown except by violence; by violence my fathers set up our throne; by murder, treachery, perjury, torture, banishment, and the prison they have held it for four centuries, and by these same arts I hold it today. There is no Romanoff of learning and experience but would reverse the maxim and say: "Nothing politically valuable was ever yet achieved *except* by violence." The moralist realizes that today, for the first time in our history, my throne is in real peril and the nation waking up from its immemorial slave-lethargy; but he does not perceive that four deeds of violence are the reason for it: the assassination of the Finland Constitution by my hand; the slaughter, by revolutionary assassins, of Bobrikoff and Plehve;[2] and my massacre of the unoffending innocents the other day. But the blood that flows in my veins—blood informed, trained, educated by its grim heredities, blood alert by its traditions, blood which has been to school four hundred years in the veins of professional assassins, my predecessors—*it* perceives, *it* understands! Those four deeds have set up a commotion in the inert and muddy deeps of the national heart such as no moral suasion could have accomplished; they have aroused hatred and hope in that long-atrophied heart; and, little by little, slowly but surely, that feeling will steal into every breast and possess it. In time, into even the *soldier's* breast—fatal day, day of doom, that! . . . By and by, there will be results! How little the academical moralist knows of the tremendous moral force of massacre and assassination! . . . Indeed there are going to be results! The nation is in labor; and by and by there will be a mighty birth—PATRIOTISM! To put it in rude, plain, unpalatable words—*true* patriotism, real patriotism: loyalty, not to a family and a fiction, but loyalty to the nation itself!

. . . There are twenty-five million families in Russia. There is a man-child at every mother's knee. If these were twenty-five million patriotic mothers, they would teach these man-children daily, saying: "Remember this, take it to heart, live by it, die for it if necessary: that our patriotism is medieval, outworn, obsolete; that the modern patriotism, the true patriotism, the only rational patriotism, is *loyalty to the nation* ALL *the time, loyalty to the government when it deserves it.*" With twenty-five million taught and trained patriots in the land a generation from now, my successor would think twice before he would butcher a thousand helpless poor petitioners humbly begging for his kindness and justice, as I did the other day.

(*Reflective pause.*) Well, perhaps I have been affected by these depressing newspaper-clippings which I found under my pillow. I will read and ponder them again. (*Reads.*)

## POLISH WOMEN KNOUTED.

### Reservists' Wives Treated with Awful Brutality—At Least One Killed.

Special Cable to THE NEW YORK TIMES.

BERLIN, Nov. 27.—Infuriated by the unwillingness of the Polish troops to leave their wives and children, the Russian authorities at Kutno, a town on the Polish frontier, have treated the people in a manner almost incredibly cruel.

It is known that *one woman has been knouted to death* and that a number of others have been injured. Fifty persons have been thrown into jail. Some of the prisoners were *tortured into unconsciousness.*

Details of the brutalities are lacking, but it seems that the Cossacks tore the reservists from the arms of their wives and children and then *knouted the women who followed their husbands into the streets.*

In cases where reservists could not be found *their wives were dragged by their hair into the streets and there beaten. The chief official of the district and the Colonel of a regiment are said to have looked on while this was being done.*

A girl who has assisted in distributing Socialist tracts was *treated in an atrocious manner.*

## CZAR AS LORD'S ANOINTED.

### People Spent Night in Prayer and Fasting Before His Visit to Novgorod.

LONDON TIMES—NEW YORK TIMES.

Special Cablegram.

Copyright, 1904, THE NEW YORK TIMES

LONDON, July 27.—The London *Times's* Russian correspondents say the following extract from the *Petersburger Zeitung,* describing the Czar's recent doings at Novgorod, affords a typical instance of the servile adulation which the subjects of the Czar deem it necessary to adopt:

"The blessing of the troops, *who knelt devoutly before his Majesty,* was a profoundly moving spectacle. His Majesty held the sacred ikon aloft and pronounced aloud a blessing in his own name and that of the Empress.

"Thousands *wept with emotion and spiritual ecstasy.* Pupils of girls' schools scattered roses in the path of the monarch.

"People pressed up to the carriage in order to carry away an indelible memory of the *hallowed features of the Lord's Anointed.* Many old people had spent the night in prayer and fasting *in order to be worthy to gaze at his countenance with pure, undefiled souls.*

"The greatest enthusiasm prevails *at the happiness thus vouchsafed to the people.*"

(*Moved.*) . . . And it was I that got that grovelling and awe-smitten worship! *I*—this thing in the mirror—this carrot! With one hand I flogged unoffending women to death and tortured prisoners to unconsciousness; and with the other I held up the fetish toward my fellow deity in heaven and called down His blessing upon my adoring animals whom, and whose forbears, with His holy approval, I and mine have been instructing in the pains of hell for four lagging centuries. It is a picture! To think that this thing in the mirror

—this vegetable—is an accepted deity to a mighty nation, an innumerable host, and nobody laughs; and at the same time is a
diligent and practical professional devil, and nobody marvels, nobody murmurs about incongruities and inconsistencies! Is the
human race a joke? Was it devised and patched together in a dull
time when there was nothing important to do? Has it no respect for
itself? . . . I think my respect for it is drooping, sinking—and
my respect for myself along with it. . . . There is but one restora-
tive—*Clothes!* I will put them on. . . .

# ON ENGLAND

I perceive now that the English are mentioned in the Bible: "Blessed are the meek, for they shall inherit the earth."—MARK TWAIN, "Queen Victoria's Jubilee"

In England, *A Connecticut Yankee in King Arthur's Court* was regarded as the devil's own work. Until 1889, Mark Twain had been adored there, as at home, by the public, although English critics were slower than ours to approve.[1] But in 1889, when *A Connecticut Yankee* appeared, the English sales of Clemens' books shot down by two-thirds and stayed there for six years. This fact is far more remarkable than the furious reviews the book provoked; Mark Twain received such reviews in every country, and for long after his death. But nowhere else did an outraged nation, in effect, boycott his work.

He had been warned. Not even his English publishers dreamed how violent the reaction would be, but they had been perfectly sure that the book would never go down in England. In response to their pleas that he soften the manuscript, Mark Twain wrote:

GENTLEMEN—Concerning the *Yankee,* I have already revised the story twice . . . and my wife has caused me to strike out several passages . . . and to soften others. . . .

Now, mind you, I have taken all this pain because I wanted to say a Yankee machanic's say against monarchy and its several natural props, and yet make a book which you would be willing to print exactly as it comes to you, without altering a word.

We are spoken of (by Englishmen) as a thin-skinned people. It is you who are thin-skinned. An Englishman may write with the most brutal

202

frankness about any man or institution among us and we re-publish him
without dreaming of altering a line or a word. But England cannot stand
that kind of a book written about herself. . . . It causeth me to smile
when I read the modifications of my language which have been made in my
English editions to fit them for the sensitive English palate.

Now, as I say, I have taken laborious pains to so trim this book of
offense that you might not lack the nerve to print it just as it stands. . . . If
you can publish it without altering a single word, go ahead. Otherwise,
please hand it to J. R. Osgood in time for him to have it published at my
expense.

Whatever sense this attitude made, it was not business sense. Mark
Twain had not been so hard up since his first best seller. For almost
ten years he had poured out his earnings to finance a remarkable
type-setting machine; his own publishing house was moving toward
bankruptcy.

But his later regrets about the *Yankee* were not financial. What he
bitterly regretted were the things left out. "They burn in me . . . but
now they can't ever be said."

What he said was enough for the English. But in the United States,
the reaction was different. Since "monarchy and its several natural
props" did not exist in this country, the American view was that it
did not, really, exist anywhere. Therefore the *Yankee* was regarded
here mainly as riotous entertainment. "Incidentally," said the *Atlantic
Monthly*, "the feudal system gets some hard knocks, but as the feudal
system is dead there is no great harm done, and the moral purpose
shines."

Our critics held to part of this view for many years. Feudalism, for
them, was so thoroughly dead that Mark Twain, in the *Yankee*, was
beating a dead horse. Only later they decided that the moral purpose
did not shine. On the contrary, calling attention to these old, foreign
sins was a means of "flattering the American nation and lulling its
conscience to sleep." [2]

Except for *The Innocents Abroad*, no book of Mark Twain's has
aroused so much resentment as the *Yankee*—or so much bewilderment.
Everyone knew that his countless English friends had wined and dined
and loved him and welcomed him into their most exclusive clubs.
How, then, could Mark Twain really attack the English? The answer
for years—that is, in this country—was that he didn't:

Quite early in his career he planned a book on England and collected
volumes of notes for the purpose, only to give it up because he was afraid
his criticism or his humour would "offend those who had taken him into
their hearts and homes." [3]

That is a critic writing in 1920; the source of his statement is still
older: it first came from Mark Twain's friend and biographer, Albert
Bigelow Paine. [4] But the 1920's were the beginning of Mark Twain's

critical disgrace in his own country; and the more modern authority, Van Wyck Brooks, added that Mark Twain's "fear of public opinion" was "almost incredible," and that he failed to criticize the English because "if he could not write without hurting people's feelings, he would not write at all. . . ." [5]

For many other commentators of this school, as well as for Paine, *A Connecticut Yankee* was not an attack on the England Mark Twain knew, but merely a book about the sixth century.

All his life, Mark Twain complained that whenever he wanted to be especially devastating, his irony became so subtle that people missed the point. Undoubtedly something like this happened with the *Yankee*. Yet, its severest critics would not now say that it is too subtle. Its admirers have said it is the only one of his books that is equal to *Huckleberry Finn*.

The story is of a nineteenth-century factory foreman who is mysteriously transported back to the England of King Arthur and the Knights of the Round Table. There he escapes death at the stake and, thanks to a little ingenuity and thirteen centuries' headstart on the other inhabitants, becomes the king's right-hand man, and is nationally nicknamed The Boss.

The Boss reforms the country—or tries to. He roams through it, disguised, escaping some dreadful fates and seeing some even more dreadful sights. And like Huckleberry Finn, as he tells his own story he says, apparently, whatever comes into his simple head. This was what came into it after a sociable evening with a blacksmith:

> I had the smith's reverence now, because I was apparently immensely prosperous and rich; I could have had his adoration if I had had some little gimcrack title of nobility. And not only his, but any commoner's in the land, though he were the mightiest production of all the ages, in intellect, worth, and character, and I bankrupt in all three. This was to remain so, as long as England should exist in the earth. With the spirit of prophecy upon me, I could look into the future and see her erect statues and monuments to her unspeakable Georges and other royal and noble clothes-horses, and leave unhonored the creators of this world—after God—Gutenberg, Watt, Arkwright, Whitney, Morse, Stephenson, Bell.

And this on another occasion:

> Even down to my birth-century the best of English commoners was still content to see his inferiors impudently continuing to hold a number of positions . . . to which the grotesque laws of his country did not allow him to aspire; in fact, he was not merely contented with this strange condition of things, he was even able to persuade himself he was proud of it. It seems to show that there isn't anything you can't stand, if you are only born and bred to it. [6]

Such passages alone would have accounted for the book's reception in England.

But the *Yankee* is not only about England. It is about feudal traditions everywhere—and these, as we have come to learn, were not only vigorously alive in Mark Twain's day, but are still very much alive in our own. Only, of late, it has been chiefly in the East that kings, emperors, and sultans—"propped" by ancient caste societies—have become so visible on the international scene. According to Mark Twain, the effect of these institutions on the aristocrat was the same as the effect of slavery on the slaveholder. From the *Yankee:*

One needs but to hear an aristocrat speak of the classes below him to recognize—and in but indifferently modified measures—the very air and tone of the actual slaveholder; and behind these are the slaveholder's spirit, the slaveholder's blunted feeling.

Still, undoubtedly in *A Connecticut Yankee*, the race speaks with a strong English accent. And for years the most affectionate English criticism referred sadly to that one misguided book. But, although the English never forgot, they forgave. When Clemens made his last visit to England, three years before his death, to receive a degree from Oxford University, he also received, it was said, "the greatest ovation ever given by the English people to a foreign visitor not a crowned head." [7]

Actually, few crowned heads have received anything like it. From Mark Twain's account, dictated after his return:

Who began it? The very people of all people in the world whom I would have chosen: a hundred men of my own class—grimy sons of labor, the real builders of empires and civilizations, the stevedores! They stood in a body on the dock and charged their masculine lungs and gave me a welcome that went to the marrow of me. [8]

The welcome was continued by the undergraduates of Oxford, who almost mobbed him, by the newspapers, who headlined his least wisecrack, and by King Edward and the Queen.

Despite the *Yankee*, despite his complaint that we copied England whether she was right or wrong, even teaching an unfair, English version of history (unfair to the French Revolution and Napoleon), there can be no doubt that Clemens wholeheartedly returned the affection of the English. Certainly few writers have left a lovelier, or more loving, description of their island. From *Following the Equator:*

It is made up of very simple details—just grass, and trees, and shrubs, and roads, and hedges, and gardens, and houses, and vines, and churches, and castles, and here and there a ruin—and over it all a mellow dream-haze of history. But its beauty is incomparable, and all its own.

Like other apparent contradictions in Mark Twain's work, his attitude toward England has its own consistency. Primarily, of course, it reflects the fact that there has always been more than one England.

In the *Yankee* he expressed himself freely on its aristocratic traditions. But his own family was directly descended from a certain Geoffrey Clement, one of the judges who sentenced Charles I to death. Or so he says in the Autobiography, although he doesn't swear to it:

I have not examined into these traditions myself, partly because I was indolent and partly because I was so busy polishing up this end of the line and trying to make it showy; but the other Clemenses claim that they have made the examination and that it stood the test. . . . My instincts have persuaded me, too. Whenever we have a strong and persistent and ineradicable instinct, we may be sure that it is not original with us, but inherited. . . .

The fact, as he admits later, was that he hastily adopted Geoffrey Clement for an ancestor at a Viennese dinner party when another guest (Count Seckendorff) was a little too eloquent about his illustrious lineage. But his instinct did not mislead him. As an artist, he was descended, probably from a regicide, and certainly from the great English political and religious dissenters. Perhaps that was why he always regarded the English as relatives—although sometimes idiot relatives, and occasionally villainous. But he made this point most memorably in 1900, when Winston Churchill—then twenty-six—came to this country to lecture on his experiences in the Boer War, where he had served with distinction.

Mark Twain had made clear to the world his disapproval of England's part in that war. And so eyebrows were raised when he was asked to introduce Mr. Churchill at a banquet at the Waldorf Astoria. Would he even accept such a task?

He did. And the introduction, delivered in the famous drawl, was quite satisfactory:

Yes, as a missionary I've sung my songs of praise; and yet I think that England sinned when she got herself into a war in South Africa which she could have avoided, just as we have sinned in getting into a similar war in the Philippines. Mr. Churchill by his father is an Englishman; by his mother he is an American; no doubt a blend that makes the perfect man. England and America: yes, we are kin. And now that we are also kin in sin, there is nothing more to be desired. The harmony is complete, the blend is perfect—like Mr. Churchill himself, whom I now have the honor to present to you.

"The Aristocracy" and "The Examination" are from *A Connecticut Yankee in King Arthur's Court.*


## The Aristocracy

Twain has often been compared to Cervantes, whom he loved, and scholars have tried to show that Cervantes influenced his work. The excerpt below does suggest—in a perverse, American way—Don Quixote's fight with the giants whom enchantment has transformed into windmills.

This part of the story begins when the Demoiselle Alisande la Carteloise—The Boss calls her Sandy—arrives at court to explain that "her mistress was a captive in a vast and gloomy castle, along with forty-four other young and beautiful girls, pretty much all of them princesses; they had been languishing in that cruel captivity for twenty-six years; the masters of the castle were three stupendous brothers, each with four arms and one eye. . . ."

The whole Round Table, says The Boss, jumped for a chance to rescue these damsels, "but to their vexation and chagrin the king conferred it upon me, who had not asked for it at all."

Sandy and The Boss travel long. But at last:

"THE CASTLE! The castle! Lo where it looms!"

What a welcome disappointment I experienced! I said:

"Castle? It is nothing but a pigsty; a pigsty with a wattled fence around it."

She looked surprised and distressed. The animation faded out of her face; and during many moments she was lost in thought and silent. Then:

"It was not enchanted aforetime," she said in a musing fashion, as if to herself. "And how strange is this marvel, and how awful—that to the one perception it is enchanted and dight in a base and shameful aspect; yet to the perception of the other it is not enchanted, hath suffered no change, but stands firm and stately still, girt with its moat and waving its banners in the blue air from its towers. And God shield us, how it pricks the heart to see again these gracious captives, and the sorrow deepened in their sweet faces! We have tarried along, and are to blame."

I saw my cue. The castle was enchanted to *me*, not to her. It would be wasted time to try to argue her out of her delusion, it couldn't be done; I must just humor it. So I said:

"This is a common case—the enchanting of a thing in one eye and leaving it in its proper form to another. You have heard of it before, Sandy, though you haven't happened to experience it. But no harm is done. In fact, it is lucky the way it is. If these ladies were hogs to everybody and to themselves, it would be necessary to break the enchantment, and that might be impossible if one failed to find out the particular process of the enchantment. And hazardous, too; for in attempting a disenchantment without the true key, you are liable to err, and turn your hogs into dogs, and the dogs into cats, the cats into rats, and so on, and end by reducing your materials to nothing finally, or to an odorless gas which you can't follow—which, of course, amounts to the same thing. But here, by good luck, no one's eyes but mine are under the enchantment, and so it is of no consequence to dissolve it. These ladies remain ladies to you, and to themselves, and to everybody else; and at the same time they will suffer in no way from my delusion, for when I know that an ostensible hog is a lady, that is enough for me, I know how to treat her."

"Thanks, oh, sweet my lord, thou talkest like an angel. And I know that thou wilt deliver them, for that thou art minded to great deeds and art as strong a knight of your hands and as brave to will and to do, as any that is on live."

"I will not leave a princess in the sty, Sandy. Are those three yonder that to my disordered eyes are starveling swineherds—"

"The ogres? Are *they* changed also? It is most wonderful. Now am I fearful; for how canst thou strike with sure aim when five of their nine cubits of stature are to thee invisible? Ah, go warily, fair sir; this is a mightier emprise than I wend."

"You be easy, Sandy. All I need to know is, how *much* of an ogre is invisible; then I know how to locate his vitals. Don't you be afraid, I will make short work of these bunco-steerers. Stay where you are."

I left Sandy kneeling there, corpse-faced but plucky and hopeful, and rode down to the pigsty, and struck up a trade with the swineherds. I won their gratitude by buying out all the hogs at the lump sum of sixteen pennies, which was rather above latest quotations. I was just in time; for the Church, the lord of the manor, and the rest of the tax-gatherers would have been along next day and swept off pretty much all the stock, leaving the swineherds very short of hogs and Sandy out of princesses. But now the tax people could be paid in cash, and there would be a stake left besides. One of the men had ten children; and he said that last year when a priest came and of his ten pigs took the fattest one for tithes, the wife burst out upon him, and offered him a child and said:

"Thou beast without bowels of mercy, why leave me my child, yet rob me of the wherewithal to feed it?"

How curious. The same thing had happened in the Wales of my day, under this same old Established Church, which was supposed by many to have changed its nature when it changed its disguise.[9]

I sent the three men away, and then opened the sty gate and beckoned Sandy to come—which she did; and not leisurely, but with the rush of a prairie fire. And when I saw her fling herself upon those hogs, with tears of joy running down her cheeks, and strain them to her heart, and kiss them, and caress them, and call them reverently by grand princely names, I was ashamed of her, ashamed of the human race.

We had to drive those hogs home—ten miles; and no ladies were ever more fickle-minded or contrary. They would stay in no road, no path; they broke out through the brush on all sides, and flowed away in all directions, over rocks, and hills, and the roughest places they could find. And they must not be struck, or roughly accosted; Sandy could not bear to see them treated in ways unbecoming their rank. The troublesomest old sow of the lot had to be called my Lady, and your Highness, like the rest. It is annoying and difficult to scour around after hogs, in armor. There was one small countess, with an iron ring in her snout and hardly any hair on her back, that was the devil for perversity. She gave me a race of an hour, over all sorts of country, and then we were right where we had started from, having made not a rod of real progress. I seized her at last by the tail, and brought her along squealling. When I overtook Sandy she was horrified, and said it was in the last degree indelicate to drag a countess by her train.

We got the hogs home just at dark—most of them. The princess Nerovens de Morganore was missing, and two of her ladies in waiting: namely, Miss Angela Bohun, and the Demoiselle Elaine Courtemains, the former of these two being a young black sow with a white star in her forehead, and the latter a brown one with thin legs and a slight limp in the forward shank on the starboard side—a couple of the tryingest blisters to drive that I ever saw. Also among the missing were several mere baronesses—and I wanted them to stay missing; but no, all that sausage-meat had to be found; so servants were sent out with torches to scour the woods and hills to that end.

Of course, the whole drove was housed in the house, and great guns!—well, I never saw anything like it. Nor ever heard anything like it. And never smelt anything like it. It was like an insurrection in a gasometer. . . .

The next morning Sandy assembled the swine in the dining room and gave them their breakfast, waiting upon them personally and manifesting in every way the deep reverence which the natives of her island, ancient and modern, have always felt for rank, let its outward casket and the mental and moral content be what they may. I could have eaten with the hogs if I had had birth approaching my lofty official rank; but I hadn't, and so accepted the unavoidable slight and made no complaint. Sandy and I had our breakfast at the second table. The family were not at home. I said:

"Well, then, whose house is this?"

"Ah, wit you well I would tell you an I knew myself."

"Come—you don't even know these people? Then who invited us here?"

"None invited us. We but came; that is all."

"Why, woman, this is a most extraordinary performance. The effrontery of it is beyond admiration. We blandly march into a man's house, and cram it full of the only really valuable nobility the sun has yet discovered in the earth, and then it turns out that we don't even know the man's name. How did you ever venture to take this extravagant liberty? I supposed, of course, it was your home. What will the man say?"

"What will he say? Forsooth what can he say but give thanks?"

"Thanks for what?"

Her face was filled with a puzzled surprise:

"Verily, thou troublest mine understanding with strange words. Do ye dream that one of his estate is like to have the honor twice in his life to entertain company such as we have brought to grace his house withal?"

"Well, no—when you come to that. No, it's an even bet that this is the first time he had had a treat like this."

"Then let him be thankful, and manifest the same by grateful speech and due humility, he were a dog, else, and the heir and ancestor of dogs."

To my mind, the situation was uncomfortable. It might become more so. It might be a good idea to muster the hogs and move on. So I said:

"The day is wasting, Sandy. It is time to get the nobility together and be moving."

"Wherefore, fair sir and Boss?"

"We want to take them to their home, don't we?"

"La, but list to him! They be of all the regions of the earth! Each must hie to her own home. . . ."

While she was gone to cry her farewells over the pork, I gave that whole peerage away to the servants. And I asked them to take a duster and dust around a little where the nobilities had mainly lodged and promenaded; but they considered that that would be hardly worth while, and would moreover be a rather grave departure from custom, and therefore likely to make talk. A departure from custom—that settled it; it was a nation capable of committing any crime but that. The servants said they would follow the fashion, a fashion grown sacred through immemorial observance; they would scatter fresh rushes in all the rooms and halls, and then the evidence of the aristocratic visitation would be no longer visible.


The Examination

One of the least of The Boss's projects was a little West Point. But he did expect that his graduates would do well before the Board which was selecting officers by competitive examination.


My candidate was called first, out of courtesy to me, and the head of the Board opened on him with official solemnity:

"Name?"

"Mal-ease."

"Son of?"

"Webster."

"Webster—Webster. H'm—I—my memory faileth to recall the name. Condition?"

"Weaver."

"Weaver!—God keep us!"

The king was staggered, from his summit to his foundations; one clerk fainted, and the others came near it. The chairman pulled himself together, and said indignantly:

"It is sufficient. Get you hence."

But I appealed to the king. I begged that my candidate might be examined. The king was willing, but the Board, who were all well-born folk, implored the king to spare them the indignity of examining the weaver's son. I know they didn't know enough to examine him anyway, so I joined my prayers to theirs and the king turned the duty over to my professors. I had had a blackboard prepared, and it was put up now, and the circus began. It was beautiful to hear the lad lay out the science of war, and wallow in details of battle and siege, of supply, transportation, mining and countermining, grand tactics, big strategy and little strategy, signal service, infantry, cavalry, artillery, and all about siege guns, field guns. Gatling guns, rifled guns, smooth bores, musket practice, revolver practice—and not a solitary word of it all could these catfish make head or tail of, you understand—and it was handsome to see him chalk off mathematical nightmares on the blackboard that would stump the angels themselves, and do it like nothing, too—all about eclipses, and comets, and solstices, and constellations, and mean time, and sidereal time, and dinnertime, and bedtime, and every other imaginable thing above the clouds or under them that you could harry or bullyrag an enemy with and make him wish he hadn't come—and when the boy made his military salute and stood aside at last, I was proud enough to hug him, and all those other people were so dazed they looked partly petrified, partly drunk, and wholly caught out and snowed under. I judged that the cake was ours, and by a large majority.

Education is a great thing. This was the same youth who had come to West Point so ignorant that when I asked him, "If a general officer should have a horse shot under him on the field of battle, what ought he to do?" answered up naively and said:

"Get up and brush himself."

One of the young nobles was called up now. I thought I would question him a little myself. I said:

"Can your lordship read?"

His face flushed indignantly, and he fired this at me:

"Takest me for a clerk? I trow I am not of a blood that—"

"Answer the question!"

He crowded his wrath down and made out to answer "No."

"Can you write?"

He wanted to resent this, too, but I said:

"You will confine yourself to the questions, and make no comments. You are not here to air your blood or your graces, and nothing of the sort will be permitted. Can you write?"

"No."

"Do you know the multiplication table?"

"I wit not what ye refer to."

"How much is nine times six?"

"It is a mystery that is hidden from me by reason that the emergency requiring the fathoming of it hath not in my life-days occurred, and so, not having no need to know this thing, I abide barren of the knowledge."

"If A trade a barrel of onions to B, worth twopence the bushel, in exchange for sheep worth fourpence and a dog worth a penny, and C kill the dog before delivery, because bitten by the same, who mistook him for D, what sum is still due to A from B, and which party pays for the dog, C or D, and who gets the money? If A, is the penny sufficient, or may he claim consequential damages in the form of additional money to represent the possible profit which might have inured from the dog, and classifiable as earned increment, that is to say, usufruct?"

"Verily, in the all-wise and unknowable providence of God, who moveth in mysterious ways His wonders to perform, have I never heard the fellow to this question for confusion of the mind and congestion of the ducts of thought. Wherefore I beseech you let the dog and the onions and these people of the strange and godless names work out their several salvations from their piteous and wonderful difficulties without help of mine, for indeed their trouble

is sufficient as it is, whereas an I tried to help I should but damage
their cause the more and yet mayhap not live myself to see the
desolation wrought."

"What do you know of the laws of attraction and gravitation?"

"If there be such, mayhap his grace the king did promulgate
them whilst that I lay sick about the beginning of the year and
thereby failed to hear his proclamation."

"What do you know of the science of optics?"

"I know of governors of places, and seneschals of castles, and
sheriffs of counties, and many like small offices and titles of honor,
but him you call the Science of Optics I have not heard of before;
peradventure it is a new dignity."

"Yes, in this country."

. . . After nagging him a little more, I let the professors
loose on him and they turned him inside out, on the line of
scientific war, and found him empty, of course. He knew somewhat about the warfare of the time—bushwhacking around for
ogres, and bullfights in the tournament ring, and such things—but
otherwise he was empty and useless. Then we took the other
young noble in hand, and he was the first one's twin, for ignorance
and incapacity. I delivered them into the hands of the chairman of
the Board with the comfortable consciousness that their cake was
dough. They were examined in the previous order of precedence.

"Name, so please you?"

"Pertipole, son of Sir Pertipole, Baron of Barley Mash."

"Grandfather?"

"Also Sir Pertipole, Baron of Barley Mash."

"Great-grandfather?"

"The same name and title."

"Great-great-grandfather?"

"We had none, worshipful sir, the line failing before it had
reached so far back."

"It mattereth not. It is a good four generations, and fulfilleth
the requirements of the rule."

"Fulfils what rule?" I asked.

"The rule requiring four generations of nobility or else the
candidate is not eligible."

"A man not eligible for a lieutenancy in the army unless he can prove four generations of noble descent?"

"Even so; neither lieutenant nor any other officer may be commissioned without that qualification."

"Oh, come, this is an astonishing thing. What good is such a qualification as that?"

"What good? It is a hardy question, fair sir and Boss, since it doth go far to impugn the wisdom of even our holy Mother Church herself."

"As how?"

"For that she hath established the selfsame rule regarding saints. By her law none may be canonized until he hath lain dead four generations."

"I see, I see—it is the same thing. It is wonderful. In the one case a man lies dead-alive four generations—mummified in ignorance and sloth—and that qualifies him to command live people, and take their weal and woe into his impotent hands; and in the other case, a man lies bedded with death and worms four generations, and that qualifies him for office in the celestial camp. Does the king's grace approve of this strange law?"

The king said:

"Why, truly I see naught about it that is strange. All places of honor and of profit do belong, by natural right, to them that be of noble blood, and so these dignities in the army are their property and would be so without this or any rule. The rule is but to mark a limit. Its purpose is to keep out too recent blood, which would bring into contempt these offices, and men of lofty lineage would turn their backs and scorn to take them. I were to blame an I permitted this calamity. *You* can permit it and you are minded so to do, for you have the delegated authority, but that the king should do it were a most strange madness and not comprehensible to any."

"I yield. Proceed, sir Chief of the Herald's College."

The chairman resumed as follows:

"By what illustrious achievement for the honor of the Throne and state did the founder of your great line lift himself to the sacred dignity of the British nobility?"

"He built a brewery."

"Sire, the Board finds this candidate perfect in all the requirements and qualifications for military command, and doth hold his
case open for decision after due examination of his competitor."

The competitor came forward and proved exactly four generations of nobility himself. So there was a tie in military qualifications that far.

He stood aside a moment, and Sir Pertipole was questioned
further:

"Of what condition was the wife of the founder of your line?"

"She came of the highest landed gentry, yet she was not noble;
she was gracious and pure and charitable, of a blameless life and
character, insomuch that in these regards was she peer of the
best lady in the land."

"That will do. Stand down." He called up the competing lord-
ling again, and asked: "What was the rank and condition of the
great-grandmother who conferred British nobility upon your great
house?"

"She was a king's leman and did climb to that splendid eminence
by her own upholpen merit from the sewer where she was born."[10]

"Ah, this, indeed, is true nobility, this is the right and perfect
intermixture. The lieutenancy is yours, fair lord. Hold it not in
contempt; it is the humble step which will lead to grandeurs more
worthy of the splendor of an origin like to thine."


## Archdeacon Wilberforce Discovers the Holy Grail


Mark Twain's remarks, at the end of this selection, on the American
and English press, are the faint echo of a battle fought some twenty
years before, when the English critic, Matthew Arnold, scolded the
American press for irreverence. Mark Twain himself had scolded it
far more savagely than Mr. Arnold—but never for irreverence. His
reply to the English critic, who also missed in our newspapers what
Goethe had called "the thrill of awe," appeared in *The American
Claimant*. Paradoxically, this is a novel in which Mark Twain ridiculed
American pretensions to genuine democracy. Nevertheless, he worked

into it a debate at a Mechanics Club, where an "essayist" reads a paper:

> The essayist thought that Mr. Arnold . . . ought to have perceived that the very quality which he so regretfully missed from our press—respectfulness, reverence—was exactly the thing that would make our press useless to us if it had it . . . its frank and cheerful irreverence being by all odds the most valuable of all its qualities. "For its mission—overlooked by Mr. Arnold—is to stand guard over a nation's liberties, not its humbugs and shams."

Moreover:

> In the sense of the poet Goethe—that meek idolatater of provincial three-caret royalty and nobility[11]—our press is certainly bankrupt in the "thrill of awe"—otherwise reverence; reverence for nickel plate and brummagem. Let us sincerely hope that this fact will remain a fact forever.

But all that belonged to Mark Twain's younger years. The events described here happened during his last visit to England, three years before his death. He dictated this account on his return to the United States—for posthumous publication in his Autobiography, of course, for Basil Wilberforce was an old and valued friend.

The account was first published in 1940, in *Mark Twain in Eruption*. It begins as Mark Twain is paying a call on his old friend, Lady Stanley, the widow of the explorer.

SHE [Lady Stanley] is an intense spiritualist and has long lived in the atmosphere of that cult. Mrs. Myers, her widowed sister, was the wife of the late president of the British Psychical Society, who was a chief among spiritualists. To me, who take no interest in otherworldly things and am convinced that we know nothing whatever about them and have been wrongly and uncourteously and contemptuously left in total ignorance of them, it is a pleasure and a refreshment to have converse with a person like Lady Stanley, who uncompromisingly believes in them; and not only believes in them but considers them important. She was as exactly and as comprehensively happy and content in her beliefs as I am in my destitution of them, and I perceived that we could exchange places and both of us be precisely as well off as we were before; for when all is said and done, the one sole condition that makes spiritual happiness and preserves it is the absence of doubt. . . .

Lady Stanley wanted to convert me to her beliefs and her faith, and there has been a time when I would have been eager to convert her to my position, but that time has gone by; I would not now try to unsettle any person's religious faith, where it was untroubled by doubt—not even the savage African's. I have found it pretty hard to give up missionarying—that least excusable of all human trades—but I was obliged to do it because I could not continue to exercise it without private shame while publicly and privately deriding and blaspheming the other missionaries.

. . . .

I will mix my dates again—this in order to bring into immediate juxtaposition a couple of curiosities in the way of human intellectual gymnastics. Lady Stanley believes that Stanley's spirit is with her all the time and talks with her about her ordinary daily concerns—a thing which is to me unthinkable. I wonder if it would be unthinkable to Archdeacon Wilberforce, also? I do not know, but I imagine that that would be the case. I imagine that the Immaculate Conception and the rest of the impossibilities recorded in the Bible would have no difficulties for him, because in those cases he has been trained from the cradle to believe the unbelievable and is so used to it that it comes natural and handy to him— but that kind of teaching is no preparation for acceptance of other unbelievable things, to whose examination one comes with an untwisted and unprejudiced mind. Wilberforce is educated, cultured, and has a fine and acute mind, and he comes of an ancestry similarly equipped; therefore he is competent to examine new marvels with an open mind, and I think the chances are that he rejects the claims of spiritualism with fully as much confidence as he accepts Immaculate Conception. Is it possible that Mr. Wilberforce has been trained from the cradle up to believe in the Holy Grail? It does not seem likely; yet he does believe in it and not only believes in it but believes he has it in his possession.

. . . .

The text for what I am talking about now I find in this note of Ashcroft's: "*Sunday, June 23*. In the afternoon Mr. Clemens visited Archdeacon Wilberforce, 20 Dean's Yard, Westminster. Sir William Crookes, Sir James Knowles, Mr. Myers (widow of the author of *Human Personality and Its Survival of Bodily Death*) and perhaps seventy-five or a hundred others were there." [12]

. As soon as I entered I was told by the Archdeacon that a most remarkable event had occurred—that the long-lost Holy Grail had at last been found and that there could be no mistake whatever about its identity! I could not have been more startled if a gun had gone off at my ear. For a moment, or at least half a moment, I supposed that he was not in earnest; then that supposition vanished; manifestly he was in earnest—indeed he was eagerly and excitedly in earnest. He leading, we plowed through the crowd to the center of the drawing-room, where Sir William Crookes, the renowned scientist, was standing. Sir William is a spiritualist. We closed in upon Sir William, Mrs. Myers accosting me and joining us. Mr. Wilberforce then told me the rest of the story of the Holy Grail, and it was apparent that Sir William already knew all about it and was, moreover, a believer in the marvel. In brief, the story was that a young grain merchant, a Mr. Pole, had recently been visited in a vision by an angel who commanded him to go to a certain place outside the ancient Glastonbury Abbey, and said that upon digging in that place he would find the Holy Grail. Mr. Pole obeyed. He sought out the indicated spot and dug there, and under four feet of packed and solid earth he found the relic. All this had happened a week or ten days before this present conversation of June 23.

The Holy Grail was in the house. A proper spirit of reverence forbade its exhibition to a crowd but Mr. Wilberforce offered to grant me a private view of it, therefore I followed him and Sir William; Mrs. Myers joined us. When we arrived at the room where the relic was, we found there the finder of it and one man— a guardian of the place, this latter seemed to be. Mr. Pole brought a wooden box of a quite humble and ordinary sort, and took from it a loose bundle of white linen cloth, handling it carefully, and gave it into Mr. Wilberforce's hands, who proceeded to unwind its envelope—not hastily but with cautious pains and impressively; the pervading silence was itself impressive and I was affected by it. Stillness and solemnity have a subduing power of their own, let the occasion be what it may. This power had time and opportunity to deepen and gather force, degree by degree, for the linen bandage was of considerable length. At last the sacred vessel, which tradition asserts received the precious blood of the crucified Christ, lay exposed to view.

In the belief of two persons present, this was the very vessel which was brought by night and secretly delivered to Nicodemus nearly nineteen centuries ago, after the creator of the universe had delivered up His life on the cross for the redemption of the human race; the very cup which the stainless Sir Galahad had sought with knightly devotion in far fields of peril and adventure, in Arthur's time, fourteen hundred years ago; the same cup which princely knights of other bygone ages had laid down their lives in long and patient efforts to find, and had passed from life disappointed—and here it was at last, dug up by a Liverpool grain broker at no cost of blood or travel and apparently no purity required of him above the average purity of the twentieth-century dealer in cereal futures; not even a stately name required—no Sir Galahad, no Sir Bors de Ganis, no Sir Lancelot of the the Lake—nothing but a mere Mr. Pole; given name not known, probably Peterson. No armor or shining steel required; no plumed helmet, no emblazoned shield, no death-dealing spear, no formidable sword endowed with fabulous powers: in fact no armor at all, and no weapons, but just a plebeian pick and shovel. Here, right under our very eyes, was the Holy Grail, renowned for nineteen hundred years—the longed-for, the prayed-for, the sought-for, the most illustrious relic the world has ever known; and there, within touch of our hand, stood its rescuer, Peterson Pole, whom God preserve! It was an impressive moment.

To be exact, it was not a cup at all; it was not a vase; it was not a goblet. It was merely a saucer—a saucer of green glass enclosing a saucer of white silver. Both surfaces of the saucer were adorned with small flower figures in soft colors pierced with openwork, and through these piercings the imprisoned silver saucer could be seen. In size and shape and shallowness, this saucer was like any other saucer. It may have been a cup, or a beaker, or a grail, once, but if so time has shriveled it.

Mr. Wilberforce said that it was the true Holy Grail; that there was no room for the slightest doubt about it; that no vessel like it was now in existence anywhere; that its age could not be short of four thousand years; that its place of concealment, under four feet of solid earth, was another indication of its antiquity, since it takes many centuries to form four feet of solid earth. It was evident that Sir William Crookes, who as a scientist will accept no alleged revelation of science until it has been submitted to the most exacting and remorseless tests—and has stood the tests and stands absolutely proven—was quite satisfied with these juvenile guessings and empty reasonings, and fully believed in the genuineness of this Holy Grail, and did not even doubt the authenticity of that angel of indigestion that brought the news to the grain broker.

I am glad to have lived to see that half hour—that astonishing half hour. In its particular line it stands alone in my life's experiences; having no fellow, and nothing, indeed, that even remotely resembles it. I have long suspected that man's claim to be the reasoning animal was a doubtful one, but this episode has swept that doubtfulness away; I am quite sure now that often, very often, in matters concerning religion and politics a man's reasoning powers are not above the monkey's. Mrs. Myers has lived in an atmosphere of spiritualism for many years, and subscribes to that cult's claims; still the Holy Grail was too large a mouthful for her; she indicated this in a private remark to me.

If this had been an American episode, the newspapers would have rung with laughter from one end of the country to the other, whether the sponsor of the Grail was at the bottom of the Church or at its summit—but Mr. Wilberforce is a great *English* Church dignitary, the episode is English also, and that makes all the difference. We followed custom, and kept still. So did the English press.

# ON THE WHITE RACE

. . . I says, "Sandy, I notice that I hardly ever see a white angel; where I run across one white angel, I strike as many as a hundred million copper-colored ones—people that can't speak English. How is that?"

"Well, you will find it the same in any State or Territory of the American corner of heaven you choose to go to. I have shot along, a whole week on a stretch, and gone millions and millions of miles, through perfect swarms of angels, without ever seeing a single white one, or hearing a word I could understand. You see, America was occupied a billion years and more by Injuns and Aztecs, and that sort of folks, before a white man ever set foot in it. During the first three hundred years after Columbus's discovery, there wasn't ever more than one good lecture audience of white people, all put together, in America—I mean the whole thing, British Possessions and all. . . . Now I am going to be liberal about this thing, and consider that fifty million whites have died in America from the beginning up to today—make it sixty, if you want to; make it a hundred million—it's no difference about a few millions one way or t'other. Well, now, you can see, yourself, that when you come to spread a little dab of people like that over these hundreds of billions of miles of American territory here in heaven, it is like scattering a ten-cent box of homeopathic pills over the Great Sahara and expecting to find them again. You can't expect us to amount to anything in heaven, and we *don't*—"—MARK TWAIN, "Extract from Captain Stormfield's Visit to Heaven"

Much of Mark Twain on the damned race could also be called Mark Twain on the white race; on the Congo; on the "United States of Lyncherdom"; on the white treatment of Chinese and Filipinos. But such a classification would be false to his view of life. He was never deeply interested in skin color. What did interest him were the villainies which could be practiced only by people who had power. During his lifetime all—or almost all—such people were white.

The excerpts below are from *Following the Equator*, which contains some of Mark Twain's most terrible summaries of the behavior of white-skinned people to those of other shades. But he also observed, in his travels, some millions of dark skins of a kind he had never seen before—and cordially welcomed them into the idiotic race. For example, he reports, factually, the Hindu's belief that "if he should ever cross to the other side of the Ganges and get caught out and die there he would come to life again in the form of an ass," and adds:

> The Hindu has a childish and unreasoning aversion to being turned into an ass. It is hard to tell why. One could properly expect an ass to have an aversion to being turned into a Hindu. One could understand that he could lose dignity by it; also self-respect, and nine-tenths of his intelligence. But the Hindu changed into an ass wouldn't lose anything, unless you count his religion.

On the other hand, in the same book, is his recollection of hearing Ghandi discuss Hinduism, as a delegate to the Chicago Fair Congress of Religions, many years before:

> It was lucidly done, in masterly English, but in time it faded from me, and now I have nothing left of that episode but an impression; a dim idea of a religious belief clothed in subtle intellectual forms, lofty and clean, barren of fleshly grossnesses. . . .

This, of course, is the same Mark Twain who respected the great Christian teachings, but ridiculed so much that passed for Christianity. But in another way, Mark Twain's position on India is an inconsistency in the body of his work. For, in India, where dark-skinned people had held despotic power for centuries, he believed that the white conqueror performed valuable services for the majority of the conquered. Some fifty years later, versions of this view were also expressed by the Indian government—particularly in the years directly following independence. Indeed, Vera Micheles Dean has thus summarized the position of the Indian press, in those years: "India . . . after independence, freely acknowledged its indebtedness to Great Britain." [1]

There are blood-curdling descriptions, in *Following the Equator*, of some aspects of Indian life which a "handful of English officials" finally eliminated. But, above all, for Mark Twain, the white man was justified in India because he altered for the better some time-honored habits of the native princes, rajahs, and maharajahs.

There is, for example, his report on a ceremony in the Indian province of Jain, where delegates thanked their native prince for benefits conferred, and congratulated him on his knighthood, recently bestowed by the British government—as a reward for good behavior according to Mark Twain, and a part of shrewd government policy. For:

> It would seem that even the grandest Indian prince . . . will remit taxes liberally and spend money freely on the betterment of the condition of his subjects, if there is a knighthood to be gotten by it.

At any rate, the thank offering was long; the benefits, "factories, schools, hospitals, reforms." Mark Twain adds:

. . . a century and a half ago—[in] the days of freedom unhampered by English interference . . . an address of thanks could have been put into small space. It would have thanked the prince:
(1) For not slaughtering too many of his people upon mere caprice.
(2) For not stripping them bare by sudden and arbitrary tax levies, and bringing famine upon them. . . .

There is much more—and Mark Twain's conclusion that the empire was "the best service that was ever done to the Indians themselves, those wretched heirs of a hundred centuries of pitiless oppression and abuse."

That was his evaluation of one stage in the history of one nation. It was also an exception. For only in India did Mark Twain ever forgive forcible foreign interference in the affairs of another people. And, even in India, this description of a scene in a railroad station is more characteristic:

It was a very large station, yet when we arrived, it seemed as if the whole world was present—half of it inside, the other half outside, and both halves . . . trying simultaneously to pass each other, in opposing floods, in one narrow door. These opposing floods were patient, gentle, long-suffering natives, with whites scattered among them at rare intervals; and wherever a white man's native servant appeared, *that* native seemed to have put aside his natural gentleness for the time and invested himself with the white man's privilege of making a way for himself by promptly shoving all intervening black things out of it.

The excerpts below are on the white man in Australia, New Zealand, Africa, India, and the United States. But the white man in them is not Australian, Dutch, English, or American. He is an international horror. Many of the excerpts are Mark Twain's finest works; certainly he produced no greater polemic than "The White Man's Notion." But in another way he was greater—on this same subject of the white man—in *Huckleberry Finn.* For there the white man is a human being, and the only kind Clemens ever knew or claimed to know: his own countryman. As he pointed out, in "What Paul Bourget Thinks of Us," a writer may observe and report abroad, but he can only reproduce living reality from experience absorbed from birth.

Clemens was raised in Hannibal, Missouri, a slaveholding community; his father owned one slave. His friend Howells found him "the most desouthernized Southerner" he ever knew. But, in a sense, he was not desouthernized at all. None but a Southerner could have approached his understanding of Southerners, black and white. And none has: to the Northerner who wrote *Uncle Tom's Cabin,* neither slaveholder nor slave was human—one was a devil, the other a crude plaster saint.

But Mark Twain's view of human nature was spacious enough to include slaveholder and lynch mob; it even enabled him to imagine Huckleberry Finn, the Southern white teenager whose decency triumphed over the values of a whole civilization. The passage in which this occurs has long been regarded as the master-passage in a masterpiece. It is also about the white race.

The passage comes after Huck and his friend Jim, a gentle, middle-aged slave, have shared danger and trouble, fishing and fun, in their journey on a raft down the Mississippi; Huck is fleeing from his drunken father, and Jim to freedom. It begins when Huck finally realizes his wickedness in "stealing a poor old woman's Nigger that hadn't ever done me no harm. . . ."

"The more I studied about this the more my conscience went to grinding me, and the more wicked and low-down and ornery I got to feeling." He tries to excuse himself by saying, "I was brung up wicked and so I warn't so much to blame, but something inside of me kept saying 'There was the Sunday-school, you could 'a' gone to it; and if you'd 'a' done it they'd 'a' learnt you there that people that acts as I'd been acting about that nigger goes to everlasting fire.' "

Huck finally finds peace of mind—"I felt good and all washed clean of sin for the first time I had ever felt so in my life"—by scrawling a "paper" to the widow telling where her slave is. He revels in his clear conscience and shudders at "how near I come to being lost and going to hell" until:

. . . [I] got to thinking over our trip down the river; and I see Jim before me all the time: in the day and in the night-time, sometimes moonlight, sometimes storms, and we a-floating along, talking and singing and laughing. . . . I couldn't seem to strike no places to harden me against him, but only the other kind. I'd see him standing my watch on top of his'n, 'stead of calling me, so I could go on sleeping; and see how glad he was when I come back out of the fog . . . and at last I struck the time I saved him by telling the men we had smallpox aboard, and he was so grateful, and said I was the best friend old Jim ever had in the world and the *only* one he's got now; and then I happened to look around and see that paper.

It was a close place. . . . I studied a minute, sort of holding my breath, and then says to myself:

"All right, then, I'll go to hell"—and tore it up.

It was awful thoughts and awful words but they was said. And I let them stay said; and never thought no more about reforming. I shoved the whole thing out of my head and said I would take up wickedness again, which was in my line, being brung up to it, and the other warn't. And for a starter I would go to work and steal Jim out of slavery again; and if I could think up anything worse, I would do that, too. . . .

*Following the Equator*—with its other notes on the white race—was written because, at 60, Mark Twain went bankrupt. He paid his debts by returning to the toils of the lecture platform—but this time he lectured his way around the globe. The return to his creditors was more than the law demanded: a hundred cents on the dollar. The return to the world was his account of his travels, *Following the Equator*, published in 1897.

## The White Man's Notion

The "theatre for the drama" in this selection is early days in Australia when the shepherds' huts and stockmen's camps were scattered in the wilds of the primitive Australian bush, in the midst of increasingly hostile tribes. Mark Twain's quotations are from *Sketches of Australian Life*, by Mrs. Campbell Praed, in which she describes her childhood in that early Queensland.

In English literature, the satire most like "The White Man's Notion" is Jonathan Swift's "A Modest Proposal for the Poor People of Ireland."

THAT IS the theatre for the drama. When you comprehend one or two other details, you will perceive how well suited for trouble it was, and how loudly it invited it. The cattlemen's stations were scattered over that profound wilderness miles and miles apart—at each station half a dozen persons. There was a plenty of cattle, the black natives were always ill-nourished and hungry. The land belonged to *them*. The whites had not bought it, and couldn't buy it; for the tribes had no chiefs, nobody in authority, nobody competent to sell and convey; and the tribes themselves had no comprehension of the idea of transferable ownership of land. The ousted owners were despised by the white interlopers, and this opinion was not hidden under a bushel. More promising materials for a tragedy could not have been collated. Let Mrs. Praed speak:

At Nie Nie station, one dark night, the unsuspecting hutkeeper, having, as he believed, secured himself against assault, was lying wrapped in his blankets sleeping profoundly. The Blacks crept stealthily down the chimney and battered in his skull while he slept.

One could guess the whole drama from that little text. The curtain was up. It would not fall until the mastership of one party or the other was determined—and permanently:

There was treachery on both sides. The Blacks killed the Whites when they found them defenseless, and the Whites slew the Blacks in a wholesale and promiscuous fashion which offended against my childish sense of justice. . . . They were regarded as little above the level of brutes, and in some cases *were destroyed like vermin*.

Here is an instance. A squatter, whose station was surrounded by Blacks, whom he suspected to be hostile and from whom he feared an attack, parleyed with them from his house-door. He told them it was Christmas time—a time at which all men, black or white, feasted; that there were flour, sugarplums, good things in plenty in the store, and that he would make for them such a pudding as they had never dreamed of—a great pudding of which all might eat and be filled. The Blacks listened and were lost. The pudding was made and distributed. Next morning there was howling in the camp, for it had been sweetened with sugar and arsenic!

The white man's spirit was right, but his method was wrong. His spirit was the spirit which the civilized white has always exhibited toward the savage, but the use of poison was a departure from custom. True, it was merely a technical departure, not a real one; still, it was a departure, and therefore a mistake, in my opinion. It was better, kinder, swifter, and much more humane than a number of the methods which have been sanctified by custom, but that does not justify its employment. That is, it does not wholly justify it. Its unusual nature makes it stand out and attract an amount of attention which it is not entitled to. It takes hold upon morbid imaginaions and they work it up into a sort of exhibition of cruelty, and this smirches the good name of our civilization, whereas one of the old harsher methods would have had no such effect because usage has made those methods familiar to us and innocent. In many countries we have chained the savage and starved him to death; and this we do not care for, because custom has inured us to it; yet a quick death by poison is loving-kindness to it. In many countries we have burned the savage at the stake; and this we do not care for, because custom has inured us to it; yet a quick death is loving-kindness to it. In more than one country we have hunted the savage and his little children and their mother with dogs and guns through the woods and swamps for an afternoon's sport, and filled the region with happy laughter over their sprawling and stumbling flight, and their wild supplications for mercy; but this method we do not mind, because custom has inured us to it; yet a quick death by poison is loving-kindness to it. In many countries we have taken the savage's land from him, and made him our slave, and lashed him every day, and broken his pride, and made death his only friend, and overworked him till he dropped in his tracks; and this we do not care for, because custom has inured us to it; yet a quick death by poison is loving-kindness to it. In the Matabeleland today—why, there we are confining ourselves to sanctified custom, we Rhodes-Beit[2] millionaires in South Africa and Dukes in London; and nobody cares, because we are used to the old holy customs, and all we ask is that no notice-inviting new ones shall be intruded upon the attention of our comfortable consciences. Mrs. Praed says of the poisoner, "That squatter deserves to have his name handed down to the contempt of posterity."

I am sorry to hear her say that. I myself blame him for one thing, and severely, but I stop there. I blame him for the indiscretion of introducing a novelty which was calculated to attract attention to our civilization. There was no occasion to do that. It was his duty, and it is every loyal man's duty, to protect that heritage in every way he can; and the best way to do that is to attract attention elsewhere. The squatter's judgment was bad—that is plain; but his heart was right. He is almost the only pioneering representative of civilization in history who has risen above the prejudices of his caste and his heredity and tried to introduce the element of mercy into the superior race's dealings with the savage. His name is lost, and it is a pity; for it deserves to be handed down to posterity with homage and reverence.

This paragraph is from a London journal:

To learn what France is doing to spread the blessings of civilization in her distant dependencies we may turn with advantage to New Caledonia. With a view to attracting free settlers to that penal colony, M. Feillet, the Governor, forcibly expropriated the Kanaka cultivators from the best of their plantations, with a derisory compensation, in spite of the protests of the Council General of the island. Such immigrants as could be induced to cross the seas thus found themselves in possession of thousands of coffee, cocoa, banana, and bread-fruit trees, the raising of which had cost the wretched natives years of toil, whilst the latter had a few five-franc pieces to spend in the liquor stores of Noumea.

You observe the combination? It is robbery, humiliation, and slow, slow murder, through poverty and the white man's whisky. The savage's gentle friend, the savage's noble friend, the only magnanimous and unselfish friend the savage has ever had, was not there with the merciful swift release of poisoned pudding.

There are many humorous things in the world, among them the white man's notion that he is less savage than the other savages.

# Slave Catching from the Slave's Point of View

The Kanakas were Polynesian natives of the South Sea Islands. They were imported to work the sugar plantations in French New Caledonia, as well as Queensland, Australia.

CAPTAIN WAWN is crystal-clear on one point. He does not approve of missionaries. They obstruct his business. They make "recruiting," as he calls it ("slave-catching," as *they* call it in their frank way) a trouble when it ought to be just a picnic and a pleasure excursion. The missionaries have their opinion about the manner in which the labor traffic is conducted, and about the recruiter's evasion of the law of the traffic, and about the traffic itself: and it is distinctly un-complimentary to the traffic and to everything connected with it, including the law for its regulation. Captain Wawn's book is of very recent date; I have by me a pamphlet of still later date—hot from the press, in fact—by Rev. Wm. Gray, a missionary; and the book and the pamphlet taken together make exceedingly interesting reading, to my mind.

Interesting, and easy to understand—except in one detail, which

I will mention presently. It is easy to understand why the Queensland sugar-planter should want the Kanaka recruit: he is cheap. Very cheap in fact. These are the figures paid by the planter—£20 to the recruiter for getting the Kanaka—or "catching" him, as the missionary phrase goes; £3 to the Queensland government for "superintending" the importation; £5 deposited with the government for the Kanaka's passage home when his three years are up, in case he shall live that long; about £25 to the Kanaka himself for three years' wages and clothing; total payment for the use of a man three years, £53; or, including diet, £60. Altogether, a hundred dollars a year. One can understand why the recruiter is fond of the business; the recruit costs him a few cheap presents (given to the recruit's relatives, not to the recruit himself), and the recruit is worth £20 to the recruiter when delivered in Queensland. All this is clear enough; but the thing that is not clear is, what there is about it all to persuade the recruit. He is young and brisk; life at home in his beautiful island is one lazy, long holiday to him; or if he wants to work he can turn out a couple of bags of copra per week and sell it for four or five shillings a bag. In Queensland he must get up at dawn and work from eight to twelve hours a day in the cane-fields—in a much hotter climate than he is used to—and get less than four shillings a week for it.

I cannot understand his willingness to go to Queensland. It is a deep puzzle to me. Here is the explanation from the planter's point of view; at least I gather from the missionary's pamphlet that it is the planter's:

When he comes from his home he is a savage, pure and simple. He feels no shame at his nakedness and want of adornment. When he returns home he does so well-dressed, sporting a Waterbury watch, collars, cuffs, boots, and jewelry. He takes with him one or more boxes* well-filled with clothing, a musical instrument or two, and perfumery and other articles of luxury he has learned to appreciate.

For just one moment we have a seeming flash of comprehension of the Kanaka's reason for exiling himself: he goes away to acquire *civilization*. Yes, he was naked and not ashamed, now he is clothed and knows how to be ashamed; he was unenlightened, now he has a Waterbury watch; he was unrefined, now he has jewelry, and some-

* "Box" is English for trunk. (M.T.)

thing to make him smell good; he was a nobody, a provincial, now he has been to far countries and can show off.

It all looks plausible—for a moment. Then the missionary takes hold of this explanation and pulls it to pieces, and dances on it, and damages it beyond recognition.

Admitting that the foregoing description is the average one, the average sequel is this: The cuffs and collars, if used at all, are carried off by youngsters, who fasten them around the leg, just below the knee, as ornaments. The Waterbury, broken and dirty finds it way to the trader, who gives a trifle for it; or the inside is taken out, the wheels strung on a thread and hung around the neck. Knives, axes, calico, and handkerchiefs are divided among friends, and there is hardly one of these apiece. The boxes, the keys often lost on the road home, can be bought for 2s.6d. They are to be seen rotting outside in almost any shore village on Tanna. (I speak of what I have seen.) A returned Kanaka has been furiously angry with me because I would not buy his trousers, which he declared were just my fit. He sold them afterward to one of my Aniwan teachers for 9d. worth of tobacco—a pair of trousers that probably cost him 8s. or 10s. in Queensland. A coat or shirt is handy for cold weather. The white handkerchiefs, the "senet" (perfumery), the umbrella, and perhaps the hat, are kept. The boots have to take their chance, if they do not happen to fit the copra trader. "Senet" on the hair, streaks of paint on the face, a dirty white handkerchief round the neck, strips of turtle shell in the ears, a belt, a shealth and knife, and an umbrella constitute the rig of the returned Kanaka at home the day after landing.

A hat, an umbrella, a belt, a neckerchief. Otherwise stark naked. All in a day the hard-earned "civilization" has melted away to this. And even these perishable things must presently go. Indeed, there is but a single detail of his civilization that can be depended on to stay by him: according to the missionary, he has learned to swear. This is art, and art is long, as the poet says.

In all countries the laws throw light upon the past. The Queensland law for the regulation of the labor traffic is a confession. It is a confession . . . that sometimes a young fool of a recruit gets his senses back, after being persuaded to sign away his liberty for three years, and dearly wants to get out of the engagement and stay at home with his own people; and that threats, intimidation, and force are used to keep him on board the recruiting ship, and to hold him to his contract. Regulation thirty-one forbids these coercions. The

law requires that he shall be allowed to go free; and another clause
of it requires the recruiter to set him ashore—per boat, because of
the prevalence of sharks. Testimony from Rev. Mr. Gray:

. . . A captain many years in the traffic explained to me how a
penitent could be taken. "When a boy jumps overboard we just take
a boat and pull ahead of him, then lie between him and the shore. If
he has not tired himself swimming, and passes the boat, keep on heading him in this way. The dodge rarely fails. The boy generally tires of
swimming, gets into the boat on his own accord, and goes quietly on
board.

Yes, exhaustion is likely to make a boy quiet. If the distressed
boy had been the speaker's son, and the captors savages, the
speaker would have been surprised to see how differently the thing
looked from the new point of view; however, it is not our custom
to put ourselves in the other person's place.

## Clothes

Mark Twain's special white suits—for all seasons—were once a
trademark. He said that he wore them whenever his family let him;
in fact, he wore them whenever he felt he was among friends. This
was almost always in the United States. And according to George Ade
in *The Century* shortly after Mark Twain's death:

Being prejudiced in his favor, we knew that if he chose to wear his
hair in a mop and adopt white clothing . . . no one would dare to suggest that he was affecting the picturesque . . . Having earned 100 per
cent of our homage, he didn't have to strain for new effects.

The reason for the suits, according to Mark Twain's apology to
the London Savage Club on his last visit to England:

Now I think I ought to apologize for my clothes. . . .
If I had been an ancient Briton, I would not have contented myself
with blue paint, but I would have bankrupted the rainbow. I so enjoy
gay clothes in which women clothe themselves that it always grieves me
when I go to the opera and see that, while women look like a flower-bed,
the men are a few gray stumps among them in their black evening dress.
. . . When I find myself in assemblies like this, with everybody in black
clothes, I know I possess something that is superior to everybody else's.

Clothes are never clean. You don't know whether they are clean or not because you can't see. . . . I am proud to say that I can wear a white suit of clothes without a blemish for three days. . . . I do not want to boast. I only want to make you understand that you are not clean.

But it was not quite like that. The excerpt below on the sights of Ceylon reveals the depth of feeling behind Mark Twain's often expressed wish that he dared to dress like either a flunkey or an emperor.

THE DRIVE through the town and out to the Gallè Face by the seashore, what a dream it was of tropical splendors of bloom and blossom, and Oriental conflagrations of costume! The walking groups of men, women, boys, girls, babies—each individual was a flame, each group a house afire for color. And such stunning colors, such intensely vivid colors, such rich and exquisite minglings and fusings of rainbows and lightnings! And all harmonious, all in perfect taste; never a discordant note; never a color on any person swearing at another color on him or failing to harmonize faultlessly with the colors of any group the wearer might join. The stuffs were silk—thin, soft, delicate, clinging; and, as a rule, each piece a solid color: a splendid green, a splendid blue, a splendid yellow, a splendid purple, a splendid ruby, deep and rich with smoldering fires—they swept continuously by in crowds and legions and multitudes, glowing, flashing, burning, radiant; and every five seconds came a burst of blinding red that made a body catch his breath, and filled his heart with joy. And then, the unimaginable grace of those costumes! Sometimes a woman's whole dress was but a scarf wound about her person and her head, sometimes a man's was but a turban and a careless rag or two—in both cases generous areas of polished dark skin showing—but always the arrangement compelled the homage of the eye and made the heart sing for gladness.

I can see it to this day, that radiant panorama, that wilderness of rich color, that incomparable dissolving view of harmonious tints, and lithe half-covered forms, and beautiful brown faces, and gracious and graceful gestures and attitudes and movements, free, unstudied, barren of stiffness and restraint, and—

Just then, into this dream of fairyland and paradise a grating dissonance was injected. Out of a missionary school came marching, two and two, sixteen prim and pious little Christian black girls, Europeanly clothed—dressed, to the last detail, as they would have been dressed on a summer Sunday in an English or American village. Those clothes—oh, they were unspeakably ugly! Ugly, barbarous, destitute of taste, destitute of grace, repulsive as a shroud. I looked at my womenfolk's clothes—just full-grown duplicates of the outrages disguising those poor little abused creatures—and was ashamed to be seen in the street with them. Then I looked at my own clothes, and was ashamed to be seen in the street with myself.

However, we must put up with our clothes as they are—they have their reason for existing. They are on us to expose us—to advertise what we wear them to conceal. They are a sign; a sign of insincerity; a sign of suppressed vanity; a pretense that we despise gorgeous colors and the graces of harmony and form; and we put them on to propagate that lie and back it up. But we do not deceive our neighbor; and when we step into Ceylon we realize that we have not even deceived ourselves.


## War Monuments


Patriotism, for Clemens, was usually a complicated subject, and he wrote thousands of words on the difference between true patriotism and false. In "As Regards Patriotism" there is "second-hand" patriotism, which is lip service to whatever seems most popular. In *A Connecticut Yankee in King Arthur's Court* there is "animal" patriotism, which is not devotion to one's country but to its rulers, office holders, or institutions. But in this selection, patriotism is simple: "Patriotism is patriotism. . . . Even though it be . . . a thousand times a political mistake . . . it is . . . always honorable."

One explanation of this apparent inconsistency lies in a conversation recorded by Winston Churchill. The year was 1900; Mark Twain was sixty-five; Mr. Churchill was twenty-six and fresh from fighting in Africa against the Boer, in the home of the Boer, to teach the Boer what the English regarded as better ways. For young Mr. Churchill, this was patriotism. For Mark Twain, England was wrong. The men argued the war. According to Churchill:

After some interchanges, I found myself beaten back to the citadel "My country right or wrong." "Ah," said the old gentleman, "when the poor country is fighting for its life, I agree. But this was not your case!" [3]

It was the case with the Maori natives of New Zealand, whose patriotism Clemens is discussing here, and who had fought in defense of their lands and homes against the English settlers.

DECEMBER 8. A couple of curious war monuments here at Wanganui. One is in honor of white men "who fell in defense of law and order against fanaticism and barbarism." Fanaticism. We Americans are English in blood, English in speech, English in religion, English in essentials of our governmental system, English in the essentials of our civilization; and so, let us hope, for the honor of the blend, for the honor of the blood, for the honor of the race, that that word got there through lack of heedfulness, and will not be suffered to remain. If you carve it at Thermopylae, or where Winkelried [4] died, or upon Bunker Hill monument, and read it again—"who fell in defense of law and order against fanaticism"— you will perceive what the word means, and how mischosen it is. [5] Patriotism is patriotism. Calling it fanaticism cannot degrade it: nothing can degrade it. Even though it be a political mistake, and a thousand times a political mistake, that does not affect it; it is honorable—always honorable, always noble—and privileged to hold its head up and look the nations in the face. It is right to praise these brave white men who fell in the Maori war—they deserve it; but the presence of that word detracts from the dignity of their cause and their deeds, and makes them appear to have spilled their blood in a conflict with ignoble men, men not worthy of that costly sacrifice. But the men *were* worthy. It was no shame to fight them. They fought for their homes, they fought for their country; they bravely fought and bravely fell: and it would take nothing from the honor of the brave Englishmen who lie under the monument, but *add* to it, to say that they died in defense of English laws and English homes against men worthy of the sacrifice—the Maori patriots.

The other monument cannot be rectified. Except with dynamite.

It is a mistake all through, and a strangely thoughtless one. It is a monument erected by white men to Maoris who fell fighting with the whites and *against their own people,* in the Maori war. "Sacred to the memory of the brave men who fell on the 14th of May, 1864," etc. On one side are the names of about twenty Maoris. It is not a fancy of mine; the monument exists. I saw it. It is an object lesson to the rising generation. It invites to treachery, disloyalty, unpatriotism. Its lesson, in frank terms is, "Desert your flag, slay your people, burn their homes, shame your nationality—we honor such."

## Skin Deep

As has been noted, Mark Twain was not seriously interested in skin color. But he did have his esthetic preferences.

"The company present" were delegates from the Indian province of Jain, who had gathered to thank their prince for benefits conferred.

. . . THE COMPANY present made a fine show, an exhibition of human fireworks, so to speak, in the matters of costume and comminglings of brilliant color. . . .

I could have wished to start a rival exhibition there, of Christian hats and clothes. It would have been a hideous exhibition, a thoroughly devilish spectacle. Then there would have been the added disadvantage of the white complexion. It is not an unbearably unpleasant complexion when it keeps to itself, but when it comes into competition with masses of brown and black the fact is betrayed that it is endurable only because we are used to it. Nearly all black and brown skins are beautiful, but a beautiful white skin is rare. How rare, one may learn by walking down a street in Paris, New York, or London on a weekday—particulary an unfashionable street—and keeping count of the satisfactory complexions encountered in the course of a mile. Where dark complexions are massed, they make the whites look bleached out, unwholesome, and sometimes frankly ghastly. I could notice this as a boy, down South in the slavery days before the war. The splendid black satin skin of the South African Zulus of Durban seemed to me to come very close to perfection. I can see those Zulus yet—'ricsha athletes waiting in front of the hotel for custom; handsome and intensely black creatures, moderately clothed in loose summer stuffs whose snowy whiteness made the black all the blacker by contrast. Keeping that group in my mind, I can compare those complexions with the white ones which are streaming past this London window now:

A lady. Complexion, new parchment.

Another lady. Complexion, old parchment.

Another. Pink and white, very fine.

Man. Grayish skin, with purple areas.

Man. Unwholesome fish-belly skin.

Girl. Sallow face, sprinkled with freckles.

Old woman. Face whitey-gray.

Young butcher. Face a general red flush.

Jaundiced man—mustard yellow.

Elderly lady. Colorless skin, with two conspicuous moles.

Elderly man—a drinker. Boiled-cauliflower nose in a flabby face veined with purple crinklings.

Healthy young gentleman. Fine fresh complexion.

Sick young man. His face a ghastly white.

No end of people whose skins are dull and characterless modifications of the tint which we miscall white. Some of these faces are pimply; some exhibit other signs of diseased blood; some show scars of a tint out of harmony with the surrounding shades of color. The white man's complexion makes no concealments. It can't. It seems to have been designed as a catch-all for everything that can damage it. Ladies have to paint it, and powder it, and cosmetic it, and diet it with arsenic, and enamel it, and be always enticing it, and persuading it, and pestering it, and fussing at it, to make it beautiful; and they do not succeed. But these efforts show what they think of the natural complexion, as distributed. As distributed it needs these helps. The complexion which they try to counterfeit is one which nature restricts to the few—to the very few. To ninety-nine persons she gives a bad complexion, to the hundredth a good one. The hundredth can keep it—how long? Ten years, perhaps.

The advantage is with the Zulu, I think. He starts with a beautiful complexion, and it will last him through. And as for the Indian brown—firm, smooth, blemishless, pleasant and restful to the eye, afraid of no color, harmonizing with all colors and adding a grace to them all—I think there is no sort of chance for the average white complexion against that rich and perfect tint.

## Woman's Place

We easily perceive that the peoples furthest from civilization are the ones where equality between man and woman are the furthest apart—and consider this one of the signs of savagery. But we are so stupid that we can't see that we thus plainly admit that no civilization can be perfect until exact equality between man and woman is included.—*Mark Twain's Notebook,* 1895

Mark Twain was frequently described in his own day as "chivalrous" —and with reason. For, paradoxically, *A Connecticut Yankee* was written, and knightly values ridiculed, by an artist whose own attitude toward the weak and defenceless, and toward women, was often close to Don Quixote's. Perhaps this was part of the emotional soil out of which Clemens developed from the typical nineteenth-century male, who announced, in 1867, in the *Alta California,* that the prospect of women's suffrage made it "time for all good men to tremble for their country."

At any rate, thirty-four years later, in his Votes for Women speech, he could tell students of the Hebrew Technical School for Girls:

I have always believed, long before my mother died, that, with her gray hairs and admirable intellect, perhaps she knew as much as I did. Perhaps she knew as much about voting as I.

For twenty-five years, he said then, he had been a woman's rights man. And it was so. Twenty-five years before, he had delivered a paper to the Hartford Monday Evening Club and included these remarks:

All that we require of a voter is that he shall be forked, wear pantaloons instead of petticoats, and bear a more or less humorous resemblance to the reported image of God. . . . We brag of our universal, unrestricted suffrage; but we are shams after all, for we restrict when we come to the women.

But there seems to be some confusion in the selection below. For the treatment of women described belongs to one part of the Western world, and that old favorite of the Protestant hymnals—"From

Greenland's Icy Mountains," which Mark Twain described as "that most self-complaisant of all poems"—belongs to another. Perhaps, from India, all white civilizations seemed one—or perhaps he had his own reasons for writing this way. He liked to deliver his lectures to his countrymen whenever possible—and sometimes strained to do so. He can be caught at this trick in "War Monuments" where, as he excoriated the English monuments, he chose to declare that Americans were also Englishmen in a way.

At any rate, these passages were inspired by a drive through "the villages, the countless villages, the myriad villages" of India—on the way to Darjeeling, in the Himalayas.

. . . THERE IS a continuously repeated and replenished multitude of naked men in view on both sides and ahead. We fly through it mile after mile, but still it is always there, on both sides and ahead —brown-bodied, naked men and boys, plowing in the fields. But *not a woman.* In these two hours I have not seen a woman or a girl working in the fields.

> From Greenland's icy mountains,
>   From India's coral strand,
> Where Afric's sunny fountains
>   Roll down their golden sand;
> From many an ancient river,
>   From many a palmy plain,
> They call us to deliver
>   Their land from error's chain.

Those are beautiful verses, and they have remained in my memory all my life. But if the closing lines are true, let us hope that when we come to answer the call and deliver the land from its errors, we shall secrete from it some of our high-civilization ways, and at the same time borrow some of its pagan ways to enrich our high system with. We have a right to do this. If we lift those people up, we have a right to lift ourselves up nine or ten grades or so, at their expense. A few years ago I spent several weeks at Tölz, in Bavaria. It is a Roman Catholic region, and not even Benares[6] is more deeply or pervasively or intelligently devout. In my diary of those days I find this:

We took a long drive yesterday around the lovely country roads. But it was a drive whose pleasure was damaged in a couple of ways:

by the dreadful shrines and by the shameful spectacle of gray and venerable old grandmothers toiling in the fields. The shrines were frequent along the roads—figures of the Saviour nailed to the cross and streaming with blood from the wounds of the nails and thorns.

When missionaries go from here do they find fault with the pagan idols? I saw many women, seventy and even eighty years old, mowing and binding in the fields, and pitchforking the loads into the wagons.

I was in Austria later, and in Munich. In Munich I saw gray old women pushing trucks up hill and down, long distances, trucks laden with barrels of beer, incredible loads. In my Austrian diary I find this:

In the fields I often see a woman and a cow harnessed to the plow, and a man driving.

In the public street of Marienbad today, I saw an old, bent, gray-headed woman *in harness with a dog,* drawing a laden sled over bare dirt roads and bare pavements; and at his ease walked the driver, smoking his pipe, a hale fellow not thirty years old.

Five or six years ago I bought an open boat, made a kind of a canvas wagon-roof over the stern of it to shelter me from sun and rain; hired a courier and a boatman, and made a twelve-day floating voyage down the Rhone from Lake Bourget to Marseilles. In my diary of that trip I find this entry. I was far down the Rhone then:

Passing St. Étienne, 2.15 P.M.
. . . We reached a not very promising looking village about four o'clock, and I concluded to tie up for the day; . . . The tavern was on the river bank, as is the custom. It was dull there, and melancholy—nothing to do but look out of the window into the drenching rain and shiver; . . .

With the exception of a very occasional wooden-shod peasant, nobody was abroad in this bitter weather—I mean nobody of our sex. But all weathers are alike to the women in these continental countries. To them and the other animals, life is serious; nothing interrupts their slavery. Three of them were washing clothes in the river under the window when I arrived, and they continued at it as long as there was light to work by. One was apparently thirty; another—the mother!—about fifty; the third—grandmother!—so old and worn and gray she could have passed for eighty; I took her to be that old. They had no water proofs nor rubbers, of course; over their shoulders they wore gunny sacks—simply conductors for rivers of water; some of the volume reached the ground; the rest soaked in on the way.

At last, a vigorous fellow of thirty-five arrived, dry and comfortable, smoking his pipe under his big umbrella in an open donkey-cart—husband, son, and grandson of those women! He stood up in the cart, sheltering himself, and began to superintend, issuing his orders in a masterly tone of command, and showing temper when they were not obeyed swiftly enough. Without complaint or murmur the drowned women patiently carried out the orders, lifting the immense baskets of soggy, wrung-out clothing into the cart and stowing them to the man's satisfaction. There were six of the great baskets, and a man of mere ordinary strength could not have lifted any one of them. The cart being full now, the Frenchman descended, still sheltered by his umbrella, entered the tavern, and the women went drooping homeward, trudging in the wake of the cart, and soon were blended with the deluge and lost to sight.

When I went down into the public room, the Frenchman had his bottle of wine and plate of food on a bare table black with grease, and was "chomping" like a horse. He had the little religious paper which is in everybody's hands on the Rhone borders, and was enlightening himself with the histories of French saints who used to flee to the desert in the Middle Ages to escape the contamination of woman. For two hundred years France has been sending missionaries to other savage lands. To spare to the needy from poverty like hers is fine and true generosity.

But to get back to India—where, as my favorite poem says:

> Every prospect pleases,
> And only man is vile.

It is because Bavaria and Austria and France have not introduced their civilization to him yet. But Bavaria and Austria and France are on their way. They are coming. They will rescue him; they will refine the vileness out of him.

## Insult, Humiliation, and Forced Labor

Here Mark Twain is describing nineteenth-century Rhodesia. A comparable racial situation exists today only in the Union of South Africa.

Rhodesia was named for Cecil Rhodes, whose British South Africa Company once owned most of it; in fact, thanks to South African diamond mines, Rhodes was probably once the richest man in the world; certainly he was one of the most admired, hated, and powerful. The Jameson Raid was an attempt, in 1895, by his privately financed army, to "rescue" British settlers from the Boers, and, more than any other single event, brought on the Boer War.

From Mark Twain's account of Rhodes in his *Notebook:*

That he sh[oul]d have been hanged 30 yrs. ago is in my opinion an over-severe judgment; but if you make it twenty-nine & a half, I am with you.*

From *Following the Equator:*

What is the secret of his formidable supremacy? One says it is his prodigious wealth—a wealth whose drippings in salaries and in other ways support multitudes and make them his interested and loyal vassals; another says it is his personal magnetism and his persuasive tongue, and that these hypnotize and make happy slaves of all that drift within the circle of their influence; another says it is his majestic ideas, his vast schemes for the territorial aggrandizement of England, his patriotic and unselfish ambition to spread his beneficent protection and her just rule over the pagan wastes of Africa and make luminous the African darkness with the glory of her name; and another says he wants the earth, and wants it for his own, and that the belief that he will get it and let his friends in on the ground floor is *the* secret that rivets so many eyes upon him and keeps him in the zenith. . . .

I admire him, I frankly confess it; and when his time comes I shall buy a piece of the rope for a keepsake.

Mark Twain was mistaken. Rhodes died full of honors, and left most of his six million pound estate to public service. In this country he is chiefly known, not for Rhodesia, but for the Rhodes Scholarships, established in his will, which enable students from the United States, Germany, and parts of the British Commonwealth, to study in England.

UNDER DATE of another South African town I find [a] note which is creditable to the Boers:

Dr. X told me that in the Kafir war fifteen hundred Kafirs[7] took refuge in a great cave in the mountains about ninety miles north of Johannesburg, and the Boers blocked up the entrance and smoked them to death. Dr. X has been in there and seen the great array of bleached skeletons—one a woman with the skeleton of a child hugged to her breast.

* Philip S. Foner, *Mark Twain: Social Critic,* p. 257, © 1958, by International Publishers Co., Inc., printed with permission of The Mark Twain Company.

The great bulk of the savages must go. The white man wants their lands, and all must go excepting such percentage of them as he will need to do his work for him upon terms to be determined by himself. Since history has removed the element of guesswork from this matter and made it certainty, the humanest way of diminishing the black population should be adopted, not the old cruel ways of the past. Mr. Rhodes and his gangs have been following the old ways. They are chartered to rob and slay, and they lawfully do it, but not in a compassionate and Christian spirit. They rob the Mashonas and the Matabeles of a portion of their territories in the hallowed old style of "purchase" for a song, and then they force a quarrel and take the rest by the strong hand. They rob the natives of their cattle under the pretext that all the cattle in the country belonged to the king whom they have tricked and assassinated. They issue "regulations" requiring the incensed and harassed natives to work for the white settlers, and neglect their own affairs to do it. This is slavery, and is several times worse than was the American slavery which used to pain England so much; for when this Rhodesian slave is sick, superannuated, or otherwise disabled, he must support himself or starve—his master is under no obligation to support him.

The reduction of the population by Rhodesian methods to the desired limit is a return to the old-time slow-misery and lingering-death system of a discredited time and a crude "civilization." We humanely reduce an overplus of dogs by swift chloroform; the Boer humanely reduced an overplus of blacks by swift suffocation; the nameless but right-hearted Australian pioneer humanely reduced his overplus of aboriginal neighbors by a sweetened swift death concealed in a poisoned pudding. All these are admirable, and worthy of praise; you and I would rather suffer either of these deaths thirty times over in thirty successive days than linger out one of the Rhodesian twenty-year deaths, with its daily burden of insult, humiliation, and forced labor for a man whose entire race the victim hates. Rhodesia is a happy name for that land of piracy and pillage, and puts the right stain upon it.

## From Bombay to Missouri

OUR ROOMS were high up, on the front. A white man—he was a burly German[8]—went up with us, and brought three natives along to see to arranging things. About fourteen others followed in procession, with the hand baggage; each carried an article—and only one; a bag, in some cases, in other cases less. One strong native carried my overcoat, another a parasol, another a box of cigars, another a novel, and the last man in the procession had no load but a fan. It was all done with earnestness and sincerity, there was not a smile in the procession from the head of it to the tail of it. Each man waited patiently, tranquilly, in no sort of hurry, till one of us found time to give him a copper, then he bent his head reverently, touched his forehead with his fingers, and went his way. They seemed a soft and gentle race, and there was something both winning and touching about their demeanor.

There was a vast glazed door which opened upon the balcony. It needed closing, or cleaning, or something, and a native got down on his knees and went to work at it. He seemed to be doing it well enough, but perhaps he wasn't, for the burly German put on a look that betrayed dissatisfaction, then without *explaining* what was wrong, gave the native a brisk cuff on the jaw and *then* told him where the defect was. It seemed such a shame to do that before us all. The native took it with meekness, saying nothing, and not showing in his face or manner any resentment. I had not seen the like of this for fifty years. It carried me back to my boyhood, and flashed upon me the forgotten fact that this was the *usual* way of explaining one's desires to a slave. I was able to remember that the method seemed right and natural to me in those days, I being born to it and unaware that elsewhere there were other methods; but I was also able to remember that those unresented cuffings made me sorry for the victim and ashamed for the punisher. My father was a refined and kindly gentleman, very grave, rather austere, of rigid probity, a sternly just and upright man, albeit he attended no church and never spoke of religious matters, and had no part nor lot in the pious joys of his Presbyterian family, nor ever seemed to suffer from this deprivation. He laid his hand upon me in punishment only twice in his life, and then not heavily; once for telling him a lie—which surprised me, and showed me how unsuspicious he was, for that was not my maiden effort. He punished me those two times only, and never any other member of the family at all; yet every now and then he cuffed our harmless slave-boy, Lewis, for trifling little blunders and awkwardnesses. My father had passed his life among the slaves from his cradle up, and his cuffings proceeded from the custom of the time, not from his nature. When I was ten years old I saw a man fling a lump of iron ore at a slave-man in anger, for merely doing something awkwardly—as if that were a crime. It bounded from the man's skull, and the man fell and never spoke again. He was dead in an hour. I knew the man had a right to kill his slave if he wanted to, and yet it seemed a pitiful thing and somehow wrong, though why wrong I was not deep enough to explain if I had been asked to do it. Nobody in the village approved of that murder, but of course no one said much about it.

It is curious—the space-annihilating power of thought. For just one second, all that goes to make the *me* in me was in a Missourian village, on the other side of the globe, vividly seeing again these forgotten pictures of fifty years ago, and wholly unconscious of all things but just those; and in the next second I was back in Bombay, and that kneeling native's smitten cheek was not done tingling yet!

# Editor's Notes

# Editor's Notes

## Introduction

1.  When one examines Mark Twain's work . . . what does one find? One finds two juicy books about boys' life, the better of which, the immortal "Huckleberry Finn," is weakened by a tawdry and preposterous conclusion. . . . one finds the first few chapters of the book about "Life on the Mississippi," and beyond these items a succession of essays, stories, travel books, most of them of third or fourth rank, saved from immediate oblivion by the aroma of the author's personality.—Lewis Mumford, *Saturday Review of Literature*, May 6, 1933.

2.  Charles Neider, "Introduction," *The Autobiography of Mark Twain* (New York, Harper and Brothers, 1959), pp. xv, xviii.

3.  *Mark Twain and the Russians* (New York, Hill and Wang, 1960), pp. 17, 26–28.

4.  M. Mendelson, "Mark Twain Accuses," *Soviet Literature,* July, 1948.

5.  Theodore de Laguna, "Mark Twain as a Prospective Classic," *The Overland Monthly,* April, 1898.

6.  One of Mark Twain's rare references to South America is in a letter to Sylvester Baxter, written in the fall of 1889, when the Brazilian monarchy fell. It is exuberant—"Another throne has gone down and I swim in oceans of satisfaction"—and refers to "our great brethern the disenslaved Brazilians" and "our majestic twin down yonder."

7.  Van Wyck Brooks, *The Ordeal of Mark Twain* (New York, Meridian Books, 1955), p. 225.

8.  *Mark Twain in Eruption,* Bernard DeVoto, ed. (New York, Harper and Brothers, 1940). Mark Twain's remark is in his own prefatory note and Mr. DeVoto's interpretation of it is in his Introduction.

9.  And not only in his published work. He once told Howells that when Mrs. Clemens' illness confined her to her room she consoled herself with the thought that now she need not hear

quite so much about the "damned human race."—Albert
Bigelow Paine, *Mark Twain, a Biography* (New York, Harper
and Brothers, 1912), Vol. III, p. 1153.

10. Charles Compton, *Who Reads What?* (New York, The H. W.
Wilson Company, 1934), based on a survey conducted in five
geographically scattered public libraries.

### On the Damned Race

1. Albert Bigelow Paine, *Mark Twain, a Biography* (New York,
Harper and Brothers, 1912), Vol. III, p. 1129.

2. Richard Croker, Tammany boss of New York. When an ex-
ceptionally corrupt Tammany man was defeated that year,
after further attention from Mark Twain, a New York daily
newspaper burst into song:

> Who killed Croker?
> I, said Mark Twain.
> I killed the Croker,
> I, the Jolly Joker.

3. Colonial Secretary for Great Britain during the Boer War.

4. American troops were as well behaved in China as they were
brutal in the Philippines.

5. From Hong Kong, where he was in exile.

6. The cruelties and exactions of the friars were an important
cause of the revolt. Popular fury against them was deeper than
against Spain. "Long live Spain! Down with the friars!" was
an early Filipino slogan.

7. British Chief of Staff during the Boer War.

8. Three months later Congress passed the Platt Amendment,
which provided that the United States might intervene in
Cuban affairs almost at her own discretion. The amendment,
long resented in Cuba, was abrogated in 1934.

9. The facts of the Dreyfus case, which made world headlines for
more than ten years and which Mark Twain mentions so
frequently:

In 1894, French Captain Alfred Dreyfus was sentenced to
Devil's Island for treason. Two years later, Colonel Georges
Picquart, chief of French intelligence, discovered evidence
that the documents containing military secrets, supposedly

written by Dreyfus to the German military attaché, Major
von Schwartzkoppen, had been forged, in Dreyfus' handwriting, by French Major Ferdinand Esterhazy. Picquart was
silenced by the authorities; Dreyfus was a Jew and anti-
Semitism then permeated the French army. But the next year,
Dreyfus' brother independently made the same discovery and
the scandal rocked France. In 1898 the French novelist,
Émile Zola, was sentenced to jail for writing *J'accuse,* a
defence of Dreyfus, still on Devil's Island. In the same year
the suicide of Major Henry, who had manufactured evidence
against Dreyfus, forced a reopening of the case. The army
again found Dreyfus guilty, but reduced his sentence, and
French President Émile Loubet pardoned him. Agitation for
his exoneration continued, and in 1906 the supreme court of
appeals found him innocent, and he was reinstated in the
army as a major. In World War I, Dreyfus became a general,
and in 1930, his innocence was conclusively established by
the publication of Schwartzkoppen's papers.

10. "Truth, crushed to earth, shall rise again;
       The eternal years of God are hers;
    But error, wounded, writhes in pain,
       And dies among his worshippers."
                    —WILLIAM CULLEN BRYANT, "The Battle-Field"

11. The quotation appears this way, in *Mark Twain in Eruption:*
    "Carlyle said 'a lie cannot live.' It shows that he did not know
    how to tell them."

12. From an 1887 letter to Howells (*Mark Twain-Howells Letters,*
    Vol. II, p. 595):

    When I finished Carlyle's French Revolution in 1871, I was a
    Girondin; every time I have read it since, I have read it differently
    —being influenced & changed, little by little, by life & environment
    (& Taine, & St. Simon): & now I lay the book down once more, &
    recognize that I am a Sansculotte!—And not a pale, characterless
    Sansculotte, but a Marat. Carlyle teaches no such gospel: so the
    change is in *me*—in my vision of the evidences.

    The book was beside Mark Twain's bed when he died.

13. Arthur L. Vogelback, "The Literary Reputation of Mark
    Twain in America, 1869–1885." Unpublished Ph.D. thesis,
    University of Chicago, 1939.

14. During the Boer and Philippine Wars.
15. Ludwig Semmelweis, now more widely known as a medical martyr.
16. The passage from which, supposedly, President Franklin Roosevelt borrowed "new deal" is this one from *A Connecticut Yankee in King Arthur's Court:*

> And now here I was, in a country where a right to say how the country should be governed was restricted to six persons in each thousand of its population. For the nine hundred and ninety-four to express dissatisfaction . . . would have made the whole six shudder as one man. . . . It seemed to me that what the nine hundred and ninety-four dupes needed was a new deal.

### On the United States

1. Van Wyck Brooks, *The Ordeal of Mark Twain* (New York, Meridian Books, 1955), p. 235.
2. From *The Innocents Abroad:*

> Think of our Whitcombs and our Ainsworths and our Williamses writing themselves down in dilapidated French in a foreign hotel-register! We laugh at Englishmen, when we are at home, for sticking so sturdily to their national ways and customs, but we look back upon it from abroad very forgivingly. It is not pleasant to see an American thrusting his nationality forward *obtrusively* in a foreign land, but oh, it is pitiable to see him making of himself a thing that is neither male nor female, neither fish, flesh, nor fowl —a poor, miserable, hermaphrodite Frenchman!

3. According to Charles Compton's survey of five geographically scattered public libraries, *The Gilded Age* was, in 1934, the least read of Mark Twain's work.
4. Granville Hicks, *The Great Tradition* (New York, The Macmillan Company, 1935), pp. 44–45.
5. Dissenting opinion came chiefly from Mark Twain specialists; most distinguished of these, between 1920 and 1950, was Bernard DeVoto. But in the same period there appeared defences and appreciations of Mark Twain from De Lancey Ferguson, Frederick Lorch, Minnie M. Brashear, Walter Taylor, and other scholars.
6. Hicks, *op. cit.,* pp. 43, 46.
7. Constance Rourke, *American Humor: A Study of the National Character* (New York, Harcourt, Brace & Co., 1931), p. 211.

8. Roger Butterfield, *The American Past* (New York, Simon and Schuster, 1947), p. 205.

9. D. W. Brogan, "The Dilemma of the American Rich," *American Themes* (London, Hamish Hamilton, 1948), p. 41.

10. According to General Aguinaldo, he was given the "water cure" twice; according to General Funston, he talked voluntarily.

11. "They [the Maccabebes] had always been mercenaries; after fighting . . . for Spain they had switched allegiance to the United States. Indistinguishable in appearance and language from other Filipino Malays, they possessed such notorious proclivities for the rape, torture and robbery of their countrymen that the Americans had always had their hands full trying to restrain them."—Leon Wolff, *Little Brown Brother* (New York, Doubleday & Company, Inc., 1961), p. 341.

12. As brigadier general in the Volunteers, Funston had no permanent rank. He was made brigadier general in the regular army, and given the Congressional Medal of Honor.

13. President McKinley, who had been assassinated five months before by Leon Czolgosz.

14. According to Funston's report, he was so weak that, even after Aguinaldo's food, he could travel only by lying "flat on the ground every few hundred yards."—Wolff, *op. cit.,* p. 343.

15. "The Americans . . . became specialists in the 'water cure,' usually administered to elicit information. A blend (in the words of an observer) of Castilian cruelty and American ingenuity, it consisted of forcing four or five gallons of water down the throat of the captive, whose 'body becomes an object frightful to contemplate,' and then squeezing it out by kneeling on his stomach. The process was repeated until the *amigo* talked or died."—*Ibid.,* p. 253.

16. These orders, issued by General Jacob Smith, were carried out by Major L. W. Waller of the Marines. Eventually both men were court-martialed and retired from the service.

17. In the Boer War.

18. Headlines in the New York *Tribune* that day:

CRUELTY NOT TO BE TOLERATED

THE PRESIDENT ORDERS AN INVESTIGATION OF CHARGES

AGAINST OFFICERS IN THE PHILIPPINES

PUNISHMENT FOR ALL FOUND GUILTY OF BRUTALITY

The story: Major General Adna Chaffee, commanding in the Philippines, was ordered to investigate charges against General Jacob Smith, and against three officers charged, before the Senate Committee on the Philippines, with administering the "water cure" to the President of Igbarras. Courts-martial were to follow if investigation warranted.

19. Whether or not Mark Twain believed that rape was the "usual crime," most white Americans had no doubt, despite contemporary investigations into reasons. On May 9, 1901, the *Independent,* a popular New York weekly, published the reasons for lynching which had been supplied by communities in which they had occurred. Under "racial prejudice" are lumped such reasons as "mistaken identity, insult, bad reputation, unpopularity, violating a contract, giving evidence, frightening a child by shooting a rabbit." The figures:

| YEAR | TOTAL LYNCHINGS | FOR RAPE | FOR MURDER | RACIAL PREJUDICE |
|------|-----------------|----------|------------|------------------|
| 1896 | 86 | 31 | 24 | 31 |
| 1897 | 123 | 22 | 55 | 46 |
| 1898 | 102 | 16 | 47 | 39 |
| 1899 | 90 | 11 | 23 | 56 |
| 1900 | 103 | 16 | 30 | 57 |

20. The Chicago *Tribune*'s figures do not agree with the *Independent*'s. Other contemporary figures differ, but not widely.

21. Lieutenant Richmond Pearson Hobson attempted to block the mouth of Santiago Harbor, during the Spanish-American War, by sinking the collier *Merrimac* there. It was a dangerous job, but according to Admiral French Ensor Chadwick almost the whole fleet volunteered. The ship was sunk too far within the harbor to block the entrance.

22. In the years 1937 to 1946, inclusive, 273 lynchings were prevented by vigorous action of law enforcement agencies, according to the Department of Justice; in the same period, 43 were not prevented.

23. Chauncey Depew, then Senator from New York, had been Mark Twain's friend for more than thirty years. Thomas C. Platt was the other Senator from New York.

24. William Dean Howells, "Mark Twain: An Inquiry," *My Mark Twain* (New York, Harper and Brothers, 1910), p. 167.
25. Charles Neider, "Introduction," *The Autobiography of Mark Twain* (New York, Harper and Brothers, 1959), p. xi.
26. The Moros were not savages, but Mohammedans.
27. Mark Twain was in a benign mood. His ridicule of Theodore Roosevelt elsewhere in the Autobiography is merciless.
28. Mark Twain's publisher, and publisher of the *North American Review*.
29. General Leonard Wood was Governor General of the Philippines from 1920 to 1927. His attempts to exercise strict military control at this time created resentment there, and were sharply criticized by an American investigating comission.

## On Spain

1. Carl Russell Fish, *The Path of Empire* (New Haven, Yale University Press, 1921), p. 124.
2. Austrian Archduke Maximilian became Emperor of Mexico in 1864, thanks to French troops sent by Napoleon III at the request of the Mexican conservatives.
3. This was after Columbus' third voyage, on which he had discovered the South American mainland.
4. General Alva is still hated in the Netherlands, where he ruled for Spain from 1567 to 1573; in 1580 he conquered Portugal for Spain and permitted a massacre of the citizens of Lisbon.

## On France

1. Thérèse Bentzon, "Les Humoristes Americains: Mark Twain," *Revue des Deux-Mondes,* July 15, 1875.
2. Régis Michaud, "L'Envers d'un Humoriste—Mark Twain," *Revue du Mois,* April 10, 1910.
3. When asked by reporters why Americans should contribute to Maxim Gorky's fund raising campaign for the 1905 Russian revolution, Mark Twain replied:

"Because we were quite willing to accept France's assistance when we were in the throes of our own revolution. . . . It is our turn now to pay that debt of gratitude by helping another oppressed people in its struggle for liberty. And we must either do it or confess that our gratitude to France was only eloquent words with no sincerity back of them."—*The New York Times*, April 15, 1906.

4. One non-lady told him: "I wish I could marry a man who would be struck dead on his way back from church!" Bourget uses her to illustrate his theory that American women don't understand love.

5. Called the Mania Years, in England, because of the frenzied speculation in railroad stocks (1845–48); George Hudson was the Railroad King.

6. The Bubble was the Mississippi Company, established by John Law (1717–1720) for commercial exploitation of the Mississippi Valley and other French colonies. It produced an orgy of speculation in France; when The Bubble burst—mainly for lack of real assets in the colonies—Law fled the country.

7. A novel of peasant life by Émile Zola. The method is naturalistic and it is sometimes difficult to distinguish the characters from animals. Bourget's reply was that Mark Twain's taste had led him to the manure bed in the garden of French literature.

### On Italy

1. As published in *Mark Twain's Travels with Mr. Brown*, Franklin Walker and G. Ezra Dane, ed. (New York, Alfred A. Knopf, Inc., 1940).

### On the Jews

1. Philip Foner, *Mark Twain: Social Critic* (New York, International Publishers, 1958), p. 235.

2. "In my schoolboy days I had no aversion to slavery. I was not aware that there was anything wrong with it. No one arraigned it in my hearing; the local papers said nothing against it; the local pulpit taught us that God approved it. . . ."—*Mark Twain's Autobiography*, Albert Bigelow Paine, ed. (New York and London, Harper and Brothers, 1924), Vol. I, p. 101.

3. Edgar H. Hemminghaus, *Mark Twain in Germany* (Columbia University Germanic Studies; New York, Columbia University Press, 1939), p. 144.

4. As published in *Mark Twain in Eruption,* Bernard DeVoto, ed. (New York and London, Harper and Brothers, 1940).

5. This is part of the selection from Genesis 47 which Mark Twain quotes in his Autobiography to illustrate his point. It was published in *Mark Twain in Eruption*. The italics are his.

And there was no bread in all the land; for the famine was very sore, so that the land of Egypt and all the land of Canaan fainted by reason of the famine.

And Joseph gathered up *all* of the money that was found in the land of Egypt, and in the land of Canaan, for the corn which they bought; and Joseph brought the money into Pharaoh's house.

And when money failed in the land of Egypt, and in the land of Canaan, *all* the Egyptians came unto Joseph and said, Give us bread: for why should we die in thy presence? for the money faileth.

And Joseph said, Give your cattle; and I will give you for your cattle, if money fail.

And they brought their cattle unto Joseph; and Joseph gave them bread in exchange for horses, and for the flocks, and for the cattle of the herds, and for the asses; and he fed them with bread *for all their cattle for that year.*

When that year was ended, they came unto him the second year, and said unto him, We will not hide it from my lord, how that our money is spent; my lord also hath our herds of cattle; there is *not aught left* in the sight of my lord, but *our bodies,* and *our lands*:

Wherefore shall we die before thine eyes, both we and our land? buy *us* and *our land* for bread, and we and our land will be servants unto Pharaoh: and give us seed that we may live, and not die, that the land be not desolate.

And Joseph *bought* all the land of Egypt for Pharaoh; for the Egyptians *sold* every man his field, because the famine prevailed over them: so *the land became Pharaoh's.*

6. As published in *Mark Twain in Eruption*.

7. The union of 1867 between Austria and Hungary which established the dual monarchy.

8. The French.

## On the Belgian Congo

1. Roger Casement's revelations on the Congo had once a fame of their own. But Casement achieved more lasting fame in 1916, when he was hanged as a traitor by the British for

seeking aid from the Germans for the Irish rebellion. The Irish regard him as a martyred patriot.

## On Russia

1. The statement brought a letter from Charles Francis Adams, who wrote: "It attracted my attention because it so exactly expressed the views I have myself all along entertained."
2. "Plehve, Vyacheslav Konstantinovich, 1846–1904, Russian statesman . . . he consistently pursued an ultra-reactionary policy. He subjected minorities to forced Russification, secretly organized Jewish pogroms, and helped precipitate the Russo-Japanese War, hoping it would divert public opinion from internal conditions and increase Russian prestige. He was killed by a revolutionist's bomb."—*The Columbia Encyclopedia,* 1950.

## On England

1. Rumors that Mark Twain received his first critical appreciation in England are not borne out by the facts. These may be found in two unpublished works: *Mark Twain's Innocents Abroad: Its Origin, Composition, Popularity,* by Leon Dickinson, Ph.D. thesis, University of Chicago, 1945; and *Mark Twain in England; A Study of the English Criticism of and Attitudes Towards Mark Twain: 1867–1940,* by Robert Rodney, Ph.D. thesis, University of Wisconsin, 1946. Dr. Rodney's thesis also contains definitive research on the effect of *A Connecticut Yankee* on Mark Twain's English sales.
2. Van Wyck Brooks, *The Ordeal of Mark Twain* (New York, Meridian Books, 1955), p. 224.
3. *Ibid.,* p. 142.
4. Albert Bigelow Paine, *Mark Twain, a Biography* (New York, Harper and Brothers, 1912), Vol. I, p. 465.
5. Brooks, *op. cit.,* pp. 227–28.
6. "Rank in the army is still restricted to the nobility—by a thing which is stronger than law—the power of ancient habit and superstition. Let a commoner become an officer—he will be

snubbed by all his brethern, ostracized, driven out."—*Mark Twain's Notebook,* 1888.

7. By Sydney Brooks, the English correspondent whose accounts of the visit appeared in various American and English periodicals. According to Brooks, Englishmen everywhere hoped that "some order or decoration might be found that the King could give and Mark Twain accept with reciprocal pleasure." Nothing came of this plan.

8. Paine, *op. cit.,* Vol. III, p. 1382.

9. The Anglican Church, which replaced the Roman Catholic Church in the sixteenth century, continued to collect the tithes—from dissenters and Catholics as well as Anglicans—until 1868.

10. This is one way—Mark Twain's—of describing the career of Nell Gwynn, mistress of Charles II. From his *Notebook,* 1888: "To this day Englishmen revere the memory of Nell Gwynn, and speak of her with a smack of unconscious envy."

11. This judgment never interfered with Mark Twain's pleasure in Goethe's *Faust,* parts of which he translated into free verse.

12. Ralph Ashcroft was Mark Twain's secretary on his last visit to England.

### On the White Race

1. Vera Micheles Dean, *Builders of Emerging Nations* (New York, Holt, Rinehart and Winston, 1961), p. 68.

2. Alfred Beit and Cecil Rhodes were South African diamond kings.

3. Winston Churchill, *A Roving Commission, My Early Life* (New York, Charles Scribner's Sons, 1939), p. 360.

4. A semi-legendary fourteenth-century Swiss patriot.

5. From *Mark Twain's Notebook,* 1895: "Try to imagine the humorless depth of stupidity of the idiot who composed that inscription—and the dullness of the people who don't see the satire."

6. The religious center of India.

7. The Kaffirs are Bantu-speaking natives of what is now the Union of South Africa.

8. The hotel manager, according to Mark Twain's account of the same incident in his *Notebook.*